Cat in a White Tie and Tails

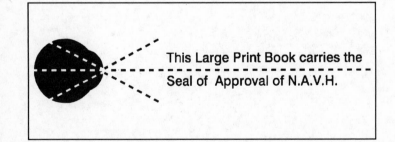

This Large Print Book carries the
Seal of Approval of N.A.V.H.

A MIDNIGHT LOUIE MYSTERY

CAT IN A WHITE
TIE AND TAILS

CAROLE NELSON DOUGLAS

THORNDIKE PRESS
A part of Gale, Cengage Learning

GALE
CENGAGE Learning®

Detroit • New York • San Francisco • New Haven, Conn • Waterville, Maine • London

LIBRARY OF CONGRESS CATALOGING-IN-PUBLICATION DATA

Douglas, Carole Nelson.
  Cat in a white tie and tails : a Midnight Louie mystery / by Carole Nelson Douglas.
    pages ; cm. — (Thorndike Press large print mystery)
    ISBN-13: 978-1-4104-5246-7 (hardcover)
    ISBN-10: 1-4104-5246-8 (hardcover)
  1. Midnight Louie (Fictitious character)—Fiction. 2. Barr, Temple (Fictitious character)—Fiction. 3. Women private investigators—Fiction. 4. Women cat owners—Fiction. 5. Cats—Fiction. 6. Large type books. I. Title.
PS3554.O8237C276995 2013
813'.54—dc23   2012038181

Published in 2013 by arrangement with Tom Doherty Associates, LLC

For Midnight Louie Jr. and Xanadu,
simply the best ever

CONTENTS

PREVIOUSLY IN MIDNIGHT LOUIE'S LIVES AND TIMES . . .

Las Vegas is my beat.

I love this rambling, gambling entertainment capital with a supersized dose of lights, action, and camera — security or otherwise.

The lights . . . the security and tourist cameras . . . and the action remain as bright and frenetic as always. Our landmark hotel-casinos and allied institutions are still puttin' on the glitz.

Me, although a Las Vegas institution, I have always kept a low profile.

You do not hear about me on the nightly news. That is how I like it. That is the way any primo PI would like it. The name is Louie, Midnight Louie. I am a noir kind of guy, inside and out. I like my nightlife shaken, not stirred.

Being short, dark, and handsome . . . really short . . . gets me overlooked and underestimated, which is what the savvy operative wants anyway. I am your perfect undercover guy. I also like to hunker down under the covers with my little doll. So would some other guys, but they do not have my lush hirsute advantages.

Miss Temple Barr and I make perfect roomies. She tolerates my wandering ways. I look after her without getting in her way. Call me Muscle in Midnight Black. We share a well-honed sense of justice and long, sharp fingernails, and have cracked some cases too tough for the local fuzz. She is, after all, a freelance public relations specialist, and Las Vegas is full of public and private relations of all stripes and legalities.

I must admit that our most recent crime-busting adventure took us a step beyond the beyond to a conspiracy of magicians and a collision with the mean streets of international terrorism and counterterrorism that left us both breathless.

Let me just say that everything it seemed you could bet on is now up for grabs and my Miss Temple may be in the lose–lose situation of her life and times.

Here is the current status of where we are all at:

None can deny that the Las Vegas crime scene is big time, and I have been treading these mean neon streets for twenty-three books now. I am an "alpha cat." Since I debuted in *Catnap* and *Pussyfoot,* I commenced to a title sequence that is as sweet and simple as *B* to *Z*.

My alphabet begins with the *B* in *Cat on a Blue Monday*. After that, the title's color word is in alphabetical order up to the, *ahem,* current volume, *Cat in a White Tie and Tails.* (Oh, yeah? I would like to see what three gorillas are going to stuff me into any such monkey suit. Watch this space.)

Since Las Vegas is littered with guidebooks as well as bodies, I will provide a rundown of the local landmarks on my particular map of the world. A cast of characters, so to speak:

To wit, my lovely roommate and high-heel devotee, Miss Nancy Drew on killer spikes, freelance PR ace Miss Temple Barr, who had reunited with her elusive love . . .

. . . the once and future missing-in-action magician Mr. Max Kinsella, who has good reason for invisibility. After his cousin Sean died in an Irish Republican Army bomb attack during a post–high school jaunt to Ireland, Mr. Max joined the man who became his mentor, Garry Randolph, aka Gandolph the Great, in undercover counterterrorism work.

The elusive Mr. Max has also been sought — on suspicion of murder — by another dame, Las Vegas homicide detective Lieutenant C. R. Molina, single mother of teenage Mariah. . . .

Mama Molina is also the good friend of Miss Temple's freshly minted fiancé, Mr. Matt Devine, aka Mr. Midnight, a radio talk show shrink on the "Midnight Hour" and former Roman Catholic priest who came to Vegas to track down his abusive stepfather and ended up becoming a syndicated radio celebrity.

Speaking of unhappy pasts, Miss Lieutenant Carmen Regina Molina is not thrilled that her former flame, Mr. Rafi Nadir, working in Las Vegas after blowing his career at the LAPD, and for years the unsuspecting father of Mariah, now knows what is what and who is whose. . . .

Meanwhile, Mr. Matt drew a stalker, the local lass that Max and his cousin Sean boyishly competed for in that long-ago Ireland . . .

. . . one Miss Kathleen O'Connor, deservedly christened Kitty the Cutter by Miss Temple. Finding Mr. Max as impossible to trace as Lieutenant Molina did, Kitty the C settled for harassing with tooth and claw the nearest innocent bystander, Mr. Matt Devine. . . .

Now that Miss Kathleen O'Connor's sad and later sadistic history indicates she might not be dead and buried like all rotten elements, things are shaking up again for we who reside at a vintage round apartment building called the Circle Ritz. Ex-resident Mr. Max Kinsella

14

is no longer MIA, although I saw him hit the wall of the Neon Nightmare club with lethal impact while in the guise of a bungee-jumping magician, the Phantom Mage.

That Mr. Max's miraculous resurrection coincides with my ever-lovin' roommate going over to the Light Side in her romantic life (our handsome blond upstairs neighbor, Mr. Matt Devine) only adds to the angst and confusion.

However, things are seldom what they seem, and almost never that in Las Vegas. A magician may have as many lives as a cat, in my humble estimation, and events now bear me out.

Meanwhile, any surprising developments do not surprise me. Everything is always up for grabs in Las Vegas 24/7: guilt, innocence, money, power, love, loss, death, and significant others.

All this human sex and violence make me glad that I have a simpler social life, such as just trying to get along with my unacknowledged daughter . . .

. . . Miss Midnight Louise, who insinuated herself into my cases until I was forced to set up shop with her as Midnight Investigations, Inc. . . .

. . . and needing to unearth more about the Synth, a cabal of magicians that may be responsible for a lot of murderous cold cases in town, and are now the objects of growing international interest, but as MIA as Mr. Max has been lately.

So, there you have it, the usual human stew — folks good, bad, and hardly indifferent — totally mixed up and at odds with one another and within themselves. Obviously, it is left to me to solve all their mysteries and nail some crooks along the way.

Like Las Vegas, the City That Never Sleeps, Midnight Louie, private eye, also has a sobriquet: the Kitty That Never Sleeps.

With this crew, who could?

CHAPTER 1
UNDERWATER

She was in the water, drowning.

Her hands pressed against her constricted chest, thumped it as if she could force the liquid from her lungs. *She couldn't . . . breathe. Move.*

She'd fallen from the top deck of a ship, a huge ship like the *Titanic.* Another ship was heading toward her, not like the *Titanic,* more like the *Black Pearl* pirate ship.

She knew she was dreaming then, knew she had to struggle to wake up because a nightmare had her by the throat. She knew someone was by her side to do it, if she could only move her paralyzed lips or body before the dark water sucked her under.

She could see the oncoming ship's billowing black sails scudding like storm clouds above her. It was as colorful and clear as a movie scene. She should remember this and write it down. . . .

Oh, God! The ship's bowsprit was a solid

metal lance twenty feet long, and the ship was wallowing deep in the waves to strike her right in the heart. The figurehead poised below that lethal weapon . . . was no naked mermaid.

It was a blindfolded and blinded man with blood trickling from his eyes, his battered body bound to the ship's bow, his mouth distorted around a dirty rag of a gag that bottled up his silent scream.

He was a dead man sinking.

And she knew just who he was and how long he'd been dead.

"Temple. Temple." Someone was shaking her awake. Her hero.

She looked into Matt's dark eyes blinking in the bedside table light. As she blinked herself, he crushed her into his arms. *Hmm.* Strong arms, warm bare chest . . . Her heart was considering a different reason to race.

"You're here, Temple. You're with me. You're safe."

"Yeah. Yeah! Oh, my God, it was an awful dream."

"About what?"

"Oh, high seas, and falling into the ocean to drown, and a ghastly, ghostly pirate ship and a handsome buccaneer to rescue me." She felt like Dorothy Gale explaining a Darkside Oz.

Matt laughed, relieved to hear her making sense. "You've never had a nightmare with me here. They common?"

"No, Matt." She sighed.

"We're going up in an 'airship' of sorts tomorrow morning. Maybe you're nervous about the flight." When she hesitated, he added, "About meeting my family?"

"Or maybe it's Chinese takeout for dinner?"

He laughed again and rolled her over atop him as he turned out the light. "Fiancées the world over go out of town to meet the future in-laws every hour. Granted, my family's a bit messier than most, but they don't bite."

She nodded and murmured as he rubbed her back and let him think what he wanted, needed to.

When she shut her eyes she could still see the grotesque dead man racing toward her. She'd never seen him dead until now, just knew about it. Knew his name. He'd roughed her up once. Clifford Effinger. Sleazeball, petty crook, family abuser, deadbeat, Matt's detested stepfather, and victim of an unnamed killer or killers, slain just the way she'd dreamed him, on the Oasis Hotel's famous sinking sailing ship attraction months earlier. This could not be a good omen.

CHAPTER 2
LET THE MIND GAMES BEGIN

A man without a memory's greatest enemy wasn't vulnerability. It was boredom.

That's what Max Kinsella was discovering. Here he sat in a parked car in Las Vegas, unemployed magician and ex-counterterrorist, staking out the Circle Ritz condo and apartment building.

After spending several days driving on the left side of the road, he had more memories of doing it in Ireland and Northern Ireland than in the U.S. So a car with the driver seated on the left side felt "wrong."

His recent visual memories still featured his slain mentor sitting in the place Max occupied now, as if Max were occupying the lap of a ghost.

Pathetic. Almost as pathetic was spying on a couple he didn't remember and hadn't "known" in his current state of amnesia until last week. He watched them walk out the Circle Ritz's rear door, luggaged up for a trip out of town. And he wondered like crazy where and why.

Blond Matt Devine wore his usual impeccable yet casual beiges. Temple Barr was dressed to impress in a shiny red pencil-skirted suit that looked like leather. Her dark strawberry blond hair glowed redder in the naked sunlight. A leopard-pattern tote bag and matching high heels spiced up the look.

A white-haired older woman in a hot pink muumuu and orange flip-flops shepherded them into boarding order as a Yellow Cab pulled up.

Used to the soothing grey greens of the Irish countryside, Max's eyes almost winced shut at all the bright colors glaring in the sunlight. Despite his ultra-dark sunglasses, it was like watching a Technicolor silent film. Matt Devine gestured to instruct the cabdriver on the proper order in loading the three bags. Temple hefted her bulky tote to the floor of the SUV's second passenger row behind the driver, and then hugged the landlady, Electra Lark.

How odd to observe people he had known and who knew him as if they were panto-miming strangers.

Temple turned to see how the luggage-stowing was going, waiting for an assist up the SUV's first big step. At her height in those heels and that tight skirt, she needed it. At around a hundred pounds, she would get it.

Not a casual girl, in any respect. Max could give her a lift in a second, even with his recovering broken legs, and spin her around. For an instant, his mind flashed inside the building to an earlier time. He saw himself doing just that, and Temple laughing.

His hands tightened on the Volkswagen's steering wheel. When Matt Devine came to the vehicle's side to do the escort honors, Max looked away, up the lone palm tree trunk toward the Circle Ritz's triangular corner balconies. One of those had been his — theirs — once.

A suspicious stirring among the tall oleander bushes edging the parking lot caught his eye. The cause of the suspect motion was a pair of stray cats, one black, one striped.

Neither was Temple's oddly inseparable guard cat, Midnight Louie. Ah. The oversize carrier was for one oversize black cat.

Max shook his head as the rear of the yellow taxi disappeared from view.

He badly needed to find a hobby.

He'd started the car, when something

hurtled atop the hood and pressed against the windshield, making him duck below the dashboard.

A cautious peek revealed no Molotov cocktail, but . . . Louie? What the — ? The resident black cat hadn't gone a-traveling with the happy couple?

Then he saw that the feline eyes glaring into his, utterly unafraid, weren't green, but intensely gold.

This cat was smaller and fluffier than Midnight Louie, but Temple had proved that size and delicacy were no issue, not even when recently tangling with a serial killer.

The cat's gaze was so hypnotically "trying to tell him something," Max settled back behind the steering wheel and began to open the driver's door to shoo it away.

And started again at a figure bending down to the window. Opening it admitted a wave of Las Vegas heat.

"Max Kinsella," Electra Lark said. "Stop lurking out here in the bushes and come in for a glass of iced tea, or stronger. I haven't seen you in far too long and I'm betting a quick tour of the premises might do your meandering memory some good."

"I was just —"

"Watching over us, like that colony of stray

24

cats that moved on but still visits. It's always good to remember where you came from. Isn't she a beauty?" Electra straightened to eye his new hood ornament. "I believe that's Miss Midnight Louise, the 'house' cat at the Crystal Phoenix Hotel. Not a stray. She'll find where she wants to go."

Electra turned and headed toward the building's rear glass door, her flip-flops slapping the hot asphalt like clapping hands. Max eased his frame out of the Beetle's surprisingly roomy driver's compartment. He eyed the black-marble-clad round building not unlike a bunker, except for the architectural frills.

Electra's hot pink–clad form — and there was plenty of it — was in perfect 1950s sync with the age of her building. Rock 'n' roll, Cadillacs, and skinny black ties.

She was right. It was good to remember where you'd come from. And he'd just now recalled the place had an attached Lovers' Knot Wedding Chapel where Electra officiated as justice of the peace.

Despite the view of the departing couple heading for places unknown, Max was not in a mood to dwell on forthcoming weddings.

CHAPTER 3
LAS VEGAS LEAVINGS

No one can say Midnight Louise was not there to see the Old Man off.

"Off" is right. He is again subjecting his keen hearing to heights of thirty thousand feet, plus. I suppose it soothes the male ego to board some shiny silver missile-shaped object that punches through clouds at five hundred miles an hour.

But clouds are merely cotton candy, and earth-bound troubles do not go away just because you do.

I was pleased to see that Mr. Max Kinsella also found it wise to oversee the ill-conceived jaunt to Chicago. That man has instincts that would do a puma proud.

Of course, they are a bit tarnished now. It is a sad day when my unexpected pounce would cause him to duck, but I made very sure that none of my exquisitely filed nails would scratch his vehicle's finish.

The velvet glove. That is my byword. Of

course, one must maintain a set of stainless steel stilettos underneath it. My kind often plays five-card stud, so to speak, rotating "hands," like changing out sets of brass knuckles in a fight.

Right now I play the faithful companion, running to brush past Mr. Max's pant legs into the Circle Ritz. I have always believed he is the one most likely to succeed at solving the schemes and scams that have woven webs around the Circle Ritz residents. Besides, a top 'tec can always use a savvy partner, whether he knows it or not.

"This cat," Miss Electra Lark notes, "looks like Midnight Louie's smaller, fluffier younger sister."

She could have added "smarter" too, but I am not one to carp, unlike the resident cat in question, though I emit a gentle mew of reproval.

"You seem to have a lot of black cats around the building," Mr. Max says.

Miss Electra notes his thick dark hair and winks. "Some of us are partial to black cats of all species."

After that they ignore me, so I am able to take the grand tour of my sire's famous home turf. I can see why it is dear to both humans and felines. Since the outer design is round, each unit has an interior private hallway with a front door and a doorbell.

I love doorbells, which are missing from all 1,200 doors at the Crystal Phoenix. I love using them for leaping practice so I can operate elevator floor panels. When the CEO of Midnight Investigations, Inc., assigned me to stake out Mr. Max's house for so many nights, I practiced ringing the neighbor's doorbells for exercise.

How amusing it was when they answered and thought no one was there, even though I kept myself in plain sight.

For Mr. Max this tour is a memory exercise. Miss Electra shows him into a couple of empty units and then we take the elevator down again. I am so tempted to show off my elevator button-punching skills, but realize it is best to keep my full powers concealed.

She does take him past the main floor wedding chapel, silent and dim at the moment, yet eerie, because she has peopled the pews with soft sculpture figures. I leap up to drape the lap of Elvis Presley's glitzy white pleather jumpsuit.

Umm, warm and highly worthy of paw-pummeling.

"Off of the King," Miss Electra orders. "It is the queen cats may look at."

I always appear to obey in public, so I trail my human escorts back to the charming circular entry hall with its single hanging chandelier.

In moments, Mr. Max and I are jerked from elegant interior to glaring sunlight on parking lot asphalt that duplicates what paves about half of American dirt.

Here I am at a crossroads. I can continue to shadow Mr. Max's butter-soft black leather loafers or I can go about my own business, which is always, of course, since I am a sleuth, someone else's.

So do I catch a lift in the silly clown car Mr. Max uses to keep a low profile now? That is a smart move undercover-wise but not what you would call a sweet ride. It does not soothe the savage soul when I know the old man has been hitching rides in limos lately. He is getting soft and could use a showing up, and I am the gal to do it.

Time to investigate on my own.

With that in mind I do a uey and head for the street, perking my ears for the unmistakable shake, rattle, and roar of a UPS truck. They are the unofficial public transportation for the more adventurous of my kind.

They make a lot of stops, their doors are always open, the drivers are always filling out papers and thus able to be slipped past, and they are loaded with nice bulky items to hide behind.

Of course, the drivers' routes are limited and the savvy hitchhiker must know when to forsake one chauffeur for another working nearer her goal.

In less than three "transfers," I am on the Las Vegas Strip, a mere mile or so from my destination. Yet one mile of hoofing it in the hot sun, to a four-footed individual with a three-inch stride like me, is like going for a six-mile hike were I a two-footed person with a fifteen-inch stride.

I am also not about to lose time zigzag-stitching my way through air-conditioned hotels. Taking a rest in the shade of a Strip-side bush at the Paris Hotel, I plot the next leg of my journey. I rarely show myself on the Strip. It causes unwanted comment and I also am in danger of being captured and possibly killed for my "own good." It is, as the cliché makes clear, a jungle out here.

Like my old man says, "Kits, do not try solo roaming if you live safe at home and consider a stroll to the litter box a taxing trek. We at Midnight Investigations, Inc., are Vegas veterans and professionals at eluding traffic and tourists and sunstroke."

Right now I am goggle-eyed at passing the parade of portable three-card monte games of chance; mimes; rap artists and tap, break, and ballet dancers; street musicians and magicians; men on stilts; women on Roller-blades and cops on patrol.

You would think the acts from Circus Circus Hotel and Casino up the Strip had gone on strike and taken their skills to the street. I must keep my tender toes dodging the emphatic stomps of tap shoes and toe shoes and clown shoes and sports shoes.

An endless drone of song and spiel drifts down to my level. My ears are unfortunately geared to pick up every sound, not drown them out. What is going on here? Then I realize this streetside show is not a special event, but a new curse brought on by today's Las Vegas, which suffers the lowest house values and highest job losses in the nation.

These bustling and hustling theatrical folk are all fancy panhandlers. Begging is against the law on most city streets, so they "perform" for their supper while the beat cops in their beige Bermuda shorts try to please the big venues and avoid irritating the tourists by moving the impromptu show folks along.

I have been known to cadge a meal, or three, a day. Then I won my slot as the Crystal Phoenix house detective, not to mention the services of the hotel's devoted Asian chef, who has an award-winning hand with what is called the "fruits of the sea" on the best menus in town.

This keeps me far away from the giant fish tank in the lobby of the Mirage, and most of those fish are really too big to consider prey instead of predator. The Mirage is not about to spotlight sardines and anchovies, except on menus or at sushi bars. However, when you are talking about the latest 3-D movie spectacular, that is where you will find me rapt and gazing at the big screen.

For now, though, I stare at the endless passing parade of street performers, which stops frequently to bilk the tourists of a buck or two. This is a job even my senior partner's Miss Temple could not manage. The hotels wish these colorful pests to be gone so all the dollars will flow into their own expensively housed coffers. Yet, to be seen hustling away folks likely hurt by the international wave of economic woes . . . is bad for business. So, for once, the powers-that-be in Las Vegas face a lose — lose situation, when it is always win — win in their casinos.

However, I am on a mission to foil a possibly international gang of robbers, killers, and bad actors far beyond what these sidewalk performers can manage. How will I make my smooth and swift way through such a milling crowd without losing toes to the crush?

Then I notice a new sight on ye olde Boulevard. Human heads skating along a full foot above the rest. The motion is too steady, and too slow, to come from any sort of skateboard.

I use my claws to ratchet up the nearest palm tree trunk, a tough, rough climb.

At that height, I spot a group of people who are rolling along together on a bicycle built for one, meaning it is *not* a bicycle. They are instead sailing forward while standing still on two fat wheels at either side of their lazy feet. Their hands curl pawlike around a very short handlebar.

The sight is enough to make a cat laugh. They all look so straight and solemn that boulevard strollers stop and turn, and make way for them. That is what I need! A royal escort service.

I immediately recognize a fad at work, the so-called Segway. Sadly, the rolling platform is only big enough for two admittedly flat feet. Once again we four-foots have been blatantly discriminated against.

While I fret at the injustice of it all, the leader of the Segway easy riders announces passing landmarks on the tour.

My goal is only three massive properties farther along the Strip. I twitch my whiskers in indecision, rejecting hitching a ride on the wheels' skimpy metal fenders that offer no purchase for claws.

I am lithe and supple compared to my

middle-aging deadbeat dad, but even a slip of a thing like me recognizes when there is no room at the inn.

The wheeled group sweeps on by, my opportunity gliding away with them.

Then I see what brings up the end of the Segway parade . . . a three-wheeled version for oldsters, wisely including a metal basket attached to the rear. With a leap and a bound I am in the last basket passing. I cannot claim this is a discreet or comfy mode of travel, but it is easy on the footpads.

My driver is a white-tufted snowbird in Bermuda shorts the better to showcase stilt-thin yet hairy legs. *Ugh.* Not an enticing sight, all that naked pink skin turning lobster red between the occasional whiskerette.

Speaking of whiskers, I cannot keep my long and delicate vibrissae from tickling the codger in the calves.

That sounds like a new nursery rhyme, "The codger in the calves."

This sight must have struck the milling pedestrians as amusing as well. Perhaps my hitching a ride has entertained the masses too. They begin twittering and pointing. When I say "twittering," I mean it in the old-fashioned sense, but the raised cell phone cameras mean they are also "tweeting" photos of my impressive forward motion, as they say in covering football games on TV.

I am thankful my old man uses antique investigation methods that will keep him from swiping, and then "swiping" Miss Temple's cell phone. It is possible I may end up on YouTube, the first in the family to go viral.

That would really frost the old dude's white whiskers. He is the sort who aims at being the only viral feline entity in Las Vegas.

Meanwhile, my Ride of Fame continues. My unintended chauffeur beams and doffs his plaid fishing cap with one hand, taking a bow. He simultaneously rubs his tickled calves on the basket grid while I offer pointed warnings by boxing his ankles with my famous Front Four defense, to continue the football analogy.

Whole lines of people on foot are stopping to stare and laugh. Dollar bills are showering over me and into my basket. I am about to turn to take a bow when my oblivious chauffeur, his head so turned by the attention, loses all concentration. His three-wheeled chariot runs straight into a palm tree trunk.

Whomp.

I had not anticipated such an abrupt stop and could clearly claim whiplash, but that would be fraud. In one fluid motion I do a triple back-twist out of the basket onto the sidewalk, landing on my tippy toes, to much applause and further media commemoration. This will outdo my unadmitted sire's recent local TV news caper finding the bodiless, booted feet in the dried-up bed portion of Lake Mead.

Several walkers rush to push the old fellow back onto the sidewalk and applaud as, like the Mississippi, he just keeps rolling along.

They then start looking around for me. Not a chance. Unlike Daddy dearest, I know when to duck the spotlight. My loyal audience assumes the worst, that I have fled to nurse my injuries. Cries of "poor kitty" grow faint in my wake as I work my way through the low landscaping under the Boulevard palms.

"Poor kitty" is right where she wants to be. I have it made in the shade once I thread through the leafy underbrush, past a lot of milling and sniffy sneakers and into the dim, ice-palace air-conditioning of my destination.

Gangsters is a boutique hotel. "Boutique" is one of those fancy French words my senior, very senior, partner likes to toss off in front of certain purebred females he is always striving, in vain, to impress. It means "small and expensive."

In Las Vegas, it means short-storied and off-Strip. Still, a very snappy neon sign of a fedora and a gun barrel set the theme atop the nine stories.

I am not expensive, but I am small, and

black like my old man, so moving around Vegas in the dark and indoors, which is almost always dark, is no trick. I head inside for the signature "fine dining experience" on the premises, which is not the kicky vintage carousel bar on the lower level, but a new top-of-the-tower eatery called Godfather's.

Yes, this is an ultra-macho venue. You will find no restaurant named Godmother's here. In fact, I think us Vegas girls of various species should get together and back a female-friendly hotel-casino called Chicklets. I nominate our friend Van von Rhine, lady Exec of the Crystal Phoenix Hotel, as chairman of the board.

Anyway, you work with the hand you are dealt, and my particular ace in the hole at the moment is one large black cat-dude more interested in expanding his waistline than building his sphere of influence. He makes the senior partner of Midnight Investigations, Inc., look junior.

First I have to weave through a lot of waxed legs and spit-shined evening loafers to the rotating restaurant ring with the window views of neon and natural sunsets. It might be impressive to tourists, but I usually have a floorside view.

I meander unseen among the seated lower limbs. How can fashionable femmes walk on these curved, rocking chair platforms and stiletto heels that make Miss Temple Barr's shoe fetish look like a low-end lace-up sneaker sort of love?

The super-stiletto-shod stars can barely totter to David Letterman's sofa to make knee-crossing a revelatory art on the scale of the now-common "wardrobe malfunction." But here their footwear fans are now, courting bunions and surgery en masse.

All I will consent to nowadays is a discreet pedicure on an upholstered piece of over-stuffed hotel furniture. I feel the Crystal Phoenix owes me that much for my services as unofficial house detective. I assiduously avoid leather as a nail-filing system, understanding that such furniture there is often high-design Italian and that my appropriating it as a scratching post would be courting extreme annoyance from the ruling Fontana family dynasty.

Meanwhile, here at the lower end of the franchise, Gangsters, I nimbly either avoid or blend in with the black-trouser-clad male and female waitstaff as I wend from table to table.

By the way, the word "waitstaff" is another favorite annoyance of mine. In the fever to eliminate the sexist terms "waiters" and "waitresses," human society has come up with another nonsense word on the scale of "brillig." Even Alice in Wonderland would be loath to "eat" and "drink" the many interesting concoctions of her expedition if they were presented by people called "waitstaff." That always reminds me of a wizard standing by with a big stick.

Even as I muse, I blunder into sudden impact with a large furry lump like a muff dropped at a lady's feet.

"Get your own table brushings," a voice grumbles.

"You *are* the table brushing I am seeking." I have finally tracked down my clan's patriarch, Three O'Clock Louie.

"This is an order of New York steak I am staking out," he says. "It is due hot and sizzling any minute now. Scram."

"Too much marbleized fat for the senior citizen. Overrated. You will be wanting a well-done butterflied filet with truffle oil."

"Yeah? Where is this mythical beast?"

"Already delivered and ripe for distraction and delectation at a table near the elevator."

The way to a male's brain is through his stomach. In three minutes I have a slightly seared but rare-on-the-inside Godfather's investor away from the dining arena and poised on the brink of the way down.

"Louise," he acknowledges me, boxing steak trimmings and shrimp crumbles from his midnight-black whiskers. "If you require my professional services, you should ask ahead of time, with a nice note."

"I require your backup. If you respond 'nicely,' I will put in a good word for you with Ma Barker."

"I need no favors from my street-gang-running ex," he answers. "Also, I am very picky about where and with whom I exert myself these days. Borrow one of Ma Barker's young toughs for backup."

"No time. I need a coconspirator fast to track a possible killer."

"Really? Crime most. . . . er, criminal. Junior, you know, fancies himself as the expert at that."

"Junior is off the map. I need a wise, sage partner I can rely on."

"And where will you be doing this 'relying on?' "

"At the Neon Nightmare."

"That is six blocks off the Strip and twenty down the Boulevard."

"Trust me, Granddaddy. You are not GoDaddy. We are not off to shoot elephants, but on a mission to preserve the wildlife in Vegas, as in four-footed. You can do the walk."

"You really need backup?"

"I do."

"And I will do for that?"

"You will."

"You are not wishing Junior was here?"

"Absolutely not."

"And we are after killers of the human sort?"

"Sneaky, treacherous killers of the human sort."

"Give me five!"

I hit him with my best shot, a five-finger exercise, feline style, but with the razor tips only out a centimeter.

"*Ouch!* That is my girl."

CHAPTER 4
LOUIE ON THE FLY

Leaving Las Vegas could be a hassle, but Temple hadn't done it since visiting her aunt Kit Carlson in Manhattan for Christmas. A lot could change in five months, she mused while temporarily stalled in the McCarran Airport security line.

Temple had been the missing Max Kinsella's girl back then and Kit had not yet met and married the eldest of the many eligible Fontana brothers, Vegas's last surviving pack of gangsters, designer gangsters on the Gucci loafer hoof.

As Temple daydreamed, Matt Devine, a superior fiancé, although newly minted, used his superior height to peer ahead. Almost any adult's height was superior to Temple's, but Matt was a shade under six feet.

"We've lucked out for a Saturday," he said. "I've seen lines four people wide snaking all the way over the bridge areas to the initial security checkpoints."

Temple's answer was a groan. Her carry-on was almost half her five-foot-zero size. Its chic leopard-skin-print exterior harbored twenty pounds of purse pussycat, Midnight Louie by name and furry anchor by weight and composition.

She'd insisted on toting the twenty-pound cat in his fancy new five-pound state-of-the art carrier. "Or what good are workout sessions at the gym?" she answered Matt when he attempted, repeatedly, to tote the load that was Louie.

And Temple had insisted Louie accompany them to see how he liked Chicago. Also, the Palmer House Hilton accepted pets under seventy-five pounds, so Louie was a lightweight when it came to hotel privileges.

"I can carry that." Matt again reached to claim the carrier's wide shoulder strap like the gentleman he was.

Temple shrugged his hand away. "You've got three bags to wrangle, and don't forget we have to strip to go through the security point."

"I do this routine three times a month. I'm not about to forget doing the gray rubber-tub tango."

"I bet doffing wearing apparel for the

security check is a real showstopper now that you've been on *Dancing With the Celebs*."

"It was your idea for me to do that downright risky show, remember?"

"And look what it got you? A knife attack followed by a fast-track samba toward your own network TV talk show."

"We'll see what happens in Chicago." Matt frowned at the large leopard-skin-print bag Temple wouldn't surrender. "What about Louie going through security?" he asked. "Did you look into that?"

"Time crunch," Temple said. "I know he can go through, I just don't know how."

A discontented yowl emerged from the bag.

They were shuffling through in a tight zigzag pattern of lanes that put every ear in its neighbor's projection range.

"Is that a cat in there?" A woman several spaces ahead of them was momentarily their closest neighbor.

She peered through the mesh with interest. With her steel gray cap of hair and many frown lines, she looked more like your terrorizing high school physical education instructor than the average passenger.

Temple fanned a protective hand over the bag, her left hand, thus flashing her ruby-

and-diamond engagement ring. Their interrogator raised an unplucked eyebrow at the
bling.

"Cats are allowed on planes if ticketed,"
Temple said.

"Well, you *are* in luck. I'm an off-duty pre-
board screening officer. I deal with pets all
the time. Usually the pet is removed from
the carrier, and then the passenger carries
the pet through the walkthrough metal detector."

The bag erupted with urgent movement.
Apparently Midnight Louie objected to
metal detectors.

The woman wasn't fazed. "Cat, huh? They
tend to be the bad boys of airport security
personnel. If you have any concerns about
your cat getting squirmy, just tell the person
at the front position that you'd prefer to go
into the private search room and take your
cat out there because he may try to escape.
My, that would be no exaggeration. Just
how big is your cat? It looks like he's fighting a wolverine in there."

It *felt* that way too. Matt was ready once
again to relieve her of Louie's carrier and
the woman's frown made a very rumpled
rug out of her forehead. Would Louie's
natural boyish energies make him a purrson
of interest to security personnel?

Their instant advisor's frown relaxed.

"Sometimes they fail to tell trainees this, but we do this all the time. Put your other bags through on the conveyor belt. Another screener will take your carrier with your cat inside, meeting you after you walk through the metal detector. Once you and your bags have cleared, you'll go into the private search room with your pet in the carrier. There you can safely take out the cat, and the carrier will be hand-searched."

Temple wasn't sure that Louie would put up with any hand-searching, even if it was only of his carrier. Now *she* frowned.

"The last thing we screeners want is a loose cat in the airport," the expert noted, "so the private search room is always available for pets, and also for passengers, for that matter. Good luck!"

Movement in the line whisked their advisor away.

Matt looked relieved. "Good to have a plan. *I'll* pass the carrier over to the screener, though. I think that operation requires some height and upper body strength. You'll only have to play the 'little woman' for a couple minutes, promise."

"I guess it's good that Louie knows he can count on you in a crunch as well as me." Temple conceded.

Midnight Louie's lonesome wail was either agreement or dismay, but only he would ever know for sure. Travelers behind their party were already buzzing and sighing about a forthcoming slowdown due to animal transport.

Now Temple knew how people traveling with kids felt.

Thirty-eight thousand feet in the air and six hours later, Louie dozed as Temple gazed out the semi-smeared airplane window, knocking off photo shots faster than a gangster mowing down rivals.

"I can't believe it," she told Matt when she leaned back to take a break. "This city is monstrous. It's the Nessie of Lake Michigan. Manhattan is just a garter snake in comparison. I can't believe how massive the buildings look."

"That's because you've never flown over Chicago before," Matt said.

"True. And this is only my second time in first class," she added in a lower tone, not wanting the presumed elite all around them to take her for a hick.

Matt thought for an instant, then gave a tight nod without comment.

Darn, Temple thought, *he's figured out my "first time" in first class was when Max and I left Minneapolis for Las Vegas.* That was *not* a good place to leave your current fiancé, picturing another guy in his place, in this case an actual airplane seat.

Being a practiced publicist by trade, Temple immediately switched into distraction mode, peering at the leopard-skin-print bag jammed under the seat ahead. This was one occasion when being five-feet-zero tall paid off. The capacious bag wasn't crowding her foot room at all.

"I bet I'm the only person in first class with a purse-pooch bag." Temple whispered to Matt, "And look. Isn't that a network news correspondent two seats ahead across the aisle?"

A cabin attendant cruised by checking seat belts. "Nice to see you again, Mr. Devine," she murmured at Matt.

Luckily, today's "stewardesses" weren't the man-pleasing bombshells of yesteryear, at least from Temple's point of view. This pleasant, almost plump woman was old enough to be Matt's mother, but that didn't stop her from sopping up his blond good looks. Temple eyed her as she moved away.

"That's right," she told Matt in another whisper, "you're a regular on this flight route from all of your *Amanda Show* appearances. Why would the producers fly you in on a family visit?"

"My booking agent — you remember my mentioning Tony Valentine? — explained it to me way back when. As long as I'm a current 'on-air personality,' even off and on, there's no such thing as my flying to Chicago *without* it being 'business.' That's why we're being put up at the Palmer House Hilton. As long as I'm a candidate for a new talk show, I'll be treated like a prince."

"I can do 'princess,' but maybe our getting married will hurt your career?"

"Temple, please. If my 'career' hurts any personal plans, I'm outta there."

"You're certainly cucumber-slice cool about your future stardom."

"Yeah. I don't need it."

"Keep up that attitude. It'll drive the producers crazy to procure you."

Matt made a face. "Doesn't this hoopla put you off?"

"I'm a PR person, Matt. Hoopla is my middle name." Actually, Ursula was. Temple hoped that it wasn't required for a marriage license, because she simply would have to beg off matrimony. *No one* could ever know her initials were TUB. What had her mother been thinking?

As the plane's interior operational whine shifted tones to begin its descent into

O'Hare, Temple bent down to make sure the under-seat bag was secure. When she straightened up, Matt was regarding her, his warm brown eyes sharp with sudden insight.

"That's right," he said. "I never knew Max Kinsella when he was still performing as the Goliath Hotel's house magician. You're *used* to being linked with a 'star.' "

"A PR person always makes the client a star. I'm used to being an essential 'nobody.' No ego involved, believe me."

Matt leaned close. "I'd be happy to be an essential nobody with you anytime." He pulled her close in the privacy of the high leather seat backs and engine drone. "Temple, traveling is brutally impersonal these days, but this trip is vital to me, not just because of the family thing. *We* need some time alone together. *We* need to become a team again. I'm afraid our own lives are getting lost in all these people and tangles from our past."

"Us? You think we're getting lost? I had to . . . do what I did —"

He fanned his fingers over her mouth. "*Shhh.* No rehashing. I spent too much time waiting and waiting and burning for you. If my 'career arc' threatens our relationship, I'll go back to being a volunteer hotline counselor in two seconds. I don't need anything but you."

"Matt, don't worry. . . ." His intensity surprised her. Touched her. Excited her. "It's just you and me against the world, and you are my world."

The roving cabin attendant paused to check on them. Temple looked up, smiled, and linked arms with Matt until she moved on. "And no stewardess is gonna ogle my guy. This is cozy, but not cozy enough for me right now." She kissed his neck and whispered, "I'm glad we made this trip together."

He smiled and relaxed back into his seat. "Meet my crazy family and then tell me you're glad."

"Mine's more competitive and crushing than crazy. It'll be good to start the 'meet the parents' thing in Chicago and work our way north to Minneapolis."

As a baby bawled relentlessly far back in the plane, a long, low yowl revved up at Temple's feet. Maybe there was another guy in her life competing for her attention, after all. She leaned forward, whispering vehemently.

"Pipe down. Your acid tones are going to strip the finish off your carrier and my matching leopard-pattern peep-toe pumps. You're getting total star treatment, including that cushy plush carrier interior. We can breeze out of here as soon as we land and you soon will have this 'toddling town' at your feet. The worst is over."

And indeed, the worst was over for Midnight Louie, if not Temple.

She believed in doing it yourself when it came to responsibilities and proving that a woman — a short, petite woman — could do anything all by herself. She had wrestled a lot of heavy display panels and moved a ton of folding chairs when it came to convention and special event emergencies.

Louie, however, was quite an armful on those long airport treks from terminal to baggage claim. So while she consented to let Matt haul her big bag off the luggage carousel, she was thrilled to look around at the crowd for the deplaning celebrities common to Vegas's McCarran. Other than *them*, of course. She spotted a Man in Black from cap to toes holding up a white card reading DEVINE.

"We have a car!" she told Matt. He looked up from attaching the carry-on to their behemoth bag in common and caught the dark-suited man's scanning glance with one of those raised-finger waiter salutes.

"And you have groupies," Temple noted, impressed.

Matt's usual genial expression screwed a couple turns tighter.

A gawking clot of people had spotted the name on the upraised card. They had clustered behind the driver to regard Matt with a blend of grins and raw curiosity.

"Welcome to Chicago," the driver said, approaching and appropriating the luggage.

"I'll keep this," Temple said, turning away as he reached for her shoulder strap.

Matt had kept "his" carry-on bag, which contained mostly what Temple would carry in her tote bag were Louie not hitching a ride on her shoulder.

Louie's claws were already doing the Swim inside the carrier but she was determined to manage the burden. Besides, she'd used tote bags in her working life before big clunky status purses were cool. Her life and interests were too diverse to be contained in the app-packed shell of a smartphone.

Nothing barred their way. Apparently the fans were content to look and eavesdrop.

Temple's precarious peep-toe heels sounded as steady as a heartbeat on the stone floor as she and Matt trotted after their urban native guide, nodding cordially but briefly to their staring audience.

"Who's she?" A young female voice wafted into their wake.

"Personal assistant," her gal pal stated, disdainful of her uninformed and, in this case, unimaginative companion.

"Personal assistant," Temple hissed to Matt between clicks of her shoes. "Apparently your fans are too nearsighted to spot my engagement ring. Your engagement ring." Temple frowned. "What's the correct expression?"

"Ours," he said. "It's not much farther. Just through the doors to the pickup lanes."

"Great." Temple tamped down the urge to pant. Louie wasn't getting any lighter.

Then the weight lifted off her shoulder all at once.

She turned to Matt. "I told you I can handle —"

He'd dropped his carry-on by her feet. "Watch that," he ordered.

Instead, she watched him race past the now-stalled driver, who looked as confused as she did.

Watch that. No "please"? Already they were acting like an old married couple. . . .

Oh.

"Watch that!" Temple ordered the driver, scooting after Matt and the disappearing leopard-print carrier.

The carrier strap was now hooked over the shoulder of the person carrying it —

the . . . the . . . petnapper — dressed all in black, a bulky figure in a trench coat. It was already halfway through one of the automatically opening glass doors.

Just then Matt caught up and grabbed Louie's carrier strap, slewing the thief around to face into the terminal's interior. The kidnapper slipped the shoulder strap and bolted for the glass doors again, then onto the sidewalk outside, charging into the flow of travelers, lost behind the confusing reflections of the glass walls.

Exiting passengers dragging bags jostled past Matt, forcing a retreat. He rejoined Temple and the driver, who were guarding the other bags. Fortunately, the one Matt carried still contained Midnight Louie.

A rat-a-tat of running footsteps from an oblique angle showed a woman in uniform bearing down on the one motionless vignette in the swirl of oblivious, expressionless people coming and going. That tableau would be the obediently stopped driver, their luggage, and Matt holding the carrier while Temple crooned at the unseen contents.

"Sir. Ma'am." The security cop was slightly breathless. "What's in that bag? Anything valuable?"

"Just a former À La Cat spokescat,"

Temple said.

"Just a *cat?*" was the next question.

"Midnight Louie is not 'just a cat,' " Temple said. "He's a particularly clever cat. He has been seen on major electronic media. He is well known in Las Vegas. He is —"

"Heavy," Matt said.

"Yes, he is a very substantial cat," Temple agreed. "A cat of substance in a trivial world."

The officer frowned. "But he's not, like, valuable?"

"To me, us, he is priceless."

"My point, ma'am, is that given the private car waiting and the flashy bag and the way you hung on to it, the thief probably thought you were carrying valuable jewelry. *Some* celebrities will insist on carrying valuables and arrange for a private security check, then trot the jewelry out of the airport afterwards in their designer bags. Opportunistic thieves will try to hoist it. I've called in the incident and the security staff stationed along all the exit doors are on the lookout for that black trench coat. Meanwhile, I'll escort your party to the car."

She eyed Temple. "I might advise carrying a less high-profile bag in future, ma'am."

She turned to Matt. "That was a lucky

save, sir, but the thief could have been armed. I don't advise personal intervention in incidents like this. Let's move on before another opportunist preys on you."

Temple looked around hard as they did just what the guard suggested.

She hoped none of Matt's fans had seen all the trouble, not to mention risk, his "personal assistant" and her purse pussycat had gotten him into.

But, an upside! At least the thief had the good taste not to mistake her for a personal assistant. Her modestly priced vintage fashion sense had totally remade her into Someone Worth Ripping Off.

CHAPTER 5
SECOND CITY KITTY

Well, I made it here, but I am not sure I would want to make it anywhere other than Vegas after that clumsy snatch attempt in the Chicago airport.

What can you expect of a city where the airport is named after a wildlife creature whose vaunted speed cannot obscure that it is prey?

"O'Hare." O lunch.

Of course I do not need to play the predator game anymore since I have reformed and converted to canned food and tracking human subjects, namely moved up to crooks.

Meanwhile, I am reclining on a cushy silk shantung fabric on a down-feathered sofa in the living room of a fancy hotel suite.

My Miss Temple and Mr. Matt are discussing our busy social schedule in between waxing anxious over my close call as a kidnap victim.

"That security guard was right," Mr. Matt is

saying. "This jet-set treatment is making me . . . and now us . . . into targets. If this is a taste of what's coming if I accept a talk show role, I will call it all off right now."

He stands poised at one of the four telephones in the suite, which includes one I most appreciate: the one in the large marble-paved bathroom, because of the litter box installed there. I also like to be accessible at all times.

I am very much aware that the network vice presidents are eager to show Mr. Matt that they can offer him plenty of deal sweeteners and they realize that my druthers are an important element in his personal life, along with my Miss Temple. One never knows when À La Cat may call. Reviving my commercial career as a spokescat would extend Mr. Matt's "platform."

"No, Matt." Miss Temple is wisely talking him out of dumping the career opportunity, but his regard for my safety speaks well of him. "Do not do anything rash. It is my fault for buying Louie a high-end, high-profile carrier."

What? I should be carted into the heart of the world-famous Chicago Loop in a burlap bag? Besides, I had the situation well in hand. Actually, well in fang. I had already worked a front canine (the tooth variety) into the handy hole at the top of the zipper pull-tag. I have unzipped myself from feeble human attempts to confine my breed in cheesy carriers so often in my career that I am the Houdini of my kind. That napper would have soon found himself holding the empty bag . . . and me affixed to his face with all sixteen shivs operating in plastic surgeon mode.

And, baby, as gravity pulled my solid twenty pounds down, I would make quite a lasting impression on the crook's epidermis.

"Maybe you should have left Louie at home," Mr. Matt suggests. "Vegas is pretty sleepy once off the Strip, but Chicago is a massive urban jungle where unaccompanied domestic pets have to scavenge."

"Of course I am not letting Louie loose on the town," she answers. "It would not be ready to cope with him. And now that we have had this close call at the airport, I am keeping tabs on him twenty-four seven."

This does not sound promising, but we are thirty-seven stories up and I have no immediate plans to leave my Miss Temple's side. From what I have overheard, Mr. Matt's circle of Polish relatives are old-fashioned and extremely religious.

Normally I understand the shock and awe that keeps one of any religion treading lightly when it comes to a godhead. If you have seen a statue of Bast, worshipped the world over for around five thousand years by those of the feline persuasion, you have seen a stern and demanding deity frozen in time and eternity, possessor of untold lives.

We nine-lifers of today are pipsqueaks.

However, I cannot understand supposedly modern folks who would frown on my Miss Temple as a suitable partner for any dude. Mr. Matt withdrew from the priesthood with all the right papers signed and sealed, from what I have heard. It might be iffier because he was the offspring of an unsanctioned match. His mama was one of these unwed individuals you read about, especially in Hollywood.

So is mine and no one would dare hold that fact up to my old lady, Ma Barker, leader of the pack. Unwed mothers, and fathers, go back into the nth generation all the way to Bast, a female deity. I can assure you that the ring in her one ear is not a wedding band.

I must admit that I will approach Mr. Matt's Chicago clan with my ears down and shivs sharpened. Any attempt to make my Miss Temple feel bad will be swiftly punished.

So, no. I am not leaving her side, as much as she thinks that she is not leaving mine. We have shared a bed for a long time and I dare anyone who would call ours an unsanctioned relationship to stand up on their hind feet and fight.

So there.

CHAPTER 6
FAST FOOD 4 THOUGHT

Max Kinsella brought home many memorabilia from his tour of the Circle Ritz, a full slide show in his mind. The first was a recaptured memory of the building's quaint wood-paneled elevator cars, small enough to be an elegant coffin.

Okay.

Click to an image less morose.

He envisioned the triangular patios at the "corners" of the four outermost units on each of the five floors. Electra had not let him tour any occupied premises, of course, especially not Temple and Matt's, which were above each other, his on top.

Okay.

Click the laboriously operated memory to something less . . . personal.

Electra did guide him to the attached wedding chapel with its soft sculpture figures in the pews. Nope. Still personal.

The circling narrow halls that led to short

cul-de-sacs with "front doors" for each unit seemed the safest territory. He remembered them well now, as well as the insecure French doors leading to the balcony patios, which he had used many times.

The only things he'd brought back to this safeguarded low-profile home, formerly the property of his slain longtime mentor, were more vague ghosts.

He was sitting in this chair with healing legs because someone in Vegas had wanted to kill him, as did a bunch of ex-IRA terrorists in Ireland who had plenty of U.S. contacts, including hitmen. Or women.

And now the one person — the only person — who best knew his past and present and his inner and outer demons had skedaddled off for a glamour tour of Chicago with the man who'd replaced him in her life and was also on the cusp of a network television career.

Onetime poor-as-a-church-mouse ex-priest Matt Devine had the job, the money, the girl, and everything. Max wasn't broke, but a sense of mission and love trump mere occupation every time.

Then the phone rang.

It wasn't the portable in Garry Randolph's dim living room, where a slightly sensationalized ancient archeology educational program on the big-screen HDTV was running silent and deep. Max had muted the sound, and the presentation was scholarly in the extreme.

Max cursed under his breath as his still-sore hips rolled slightly while he pried the smartphone from his back pocket. His contact list showed a creepy faceless profile, but he had no personalized photo contacts listed on his new phone except for a way-too-perky pic of Temple Barr, but he recognized the incoming number.

"Yes?"

"Home alone by the telephone?" The mocking voice was sour and low.

"If I deny that?"

"Look out your window when you click back the protective window blind."

He hadn't enabled all the security systems and his recovering broken legs could make him lazy and dependent on remote devices. He did *not* want to appear dependent with this caller. It wasn't easy, but he could rise and check for himself. He pulled back the heavy drapes when he got there.

"I don't see the wheels. You must have parked discreetly in front of a neighbor's yard. You driving a Crown Vic, Lieutenant? Or the faithful old family Volvo?"

"The impetuous *new* family Prius," Molina said. "Come out of your lonely lair and I'll take you to dinner."

"A Prius? Impetuous? Hardly. Daughter Mariah, the soon-to-be student driver, must be pretty slammed about that."

"A Mini Cooper was not in my game plan."

"And you wouldn't be fitting my bum legs into that model tonight anyway."

"I was tempted, but of course I thought of that fact and resisted. Get out here, Kinsella. I have more work for you. It'll be good for you to exercise your broken parts anyway."

"The legs are doing better."

"I meant those *Wizard of Oz* valuables, like brain and heart."

Ouch.

If he must be carted around in a family Prius, Max had at least hoped to be conveyed someplace quiet with exquisite food.

Alas, Molina's mood at the moment for eateries was fat-filled and franchised. This off-Strip joint had high-impact family noise, an overbearing odor of french fries, and grease-spotted wood-grain melamine tables in cramped booths.

"I figured," she said, watching him maneuver his long legs sideways into the seat, "this would save you a long walk through a major Strip venue, and I'm not paying valet parking as well as the tab."

"Saving for college, probably," he muttered. Max picked up the large, unbearably reflective menu in its coat of clear laminate.

"Exactly," Molina said. "And you cost more than a kid-sitter."

"When does a kid get to stay home alone these days?"

"I don't know about these days," she said, "but for this parent it's when *my* kid doesn't pull dumb stunts."

Molina set about studying the menu, a given in a place like this devoted to quick frying and slow service. They'd probably bread the shrimp in the shrimp cocktail appetizer.

Max eyed the busy restaurant crammed with kids and the smell of food so fast, it had chicken wings on it. He shuddered at the incivility, then looked around and blinked. There was method in Molina's madness. He was much safer here from unknown or undeclared enemies, which he'd apparently had a lifelong habit of acquiring, than in an upscale supper club. And anyone trying to eavesdrop or bug someone in this place would probably scream with frustration . . . and never be heard.

Still, he'd eaten well even on the run for his life in leg casts and without ID in Switzerland, with no aid but filched credit cards used only once and destroyed afterwards . . . unless the holder was a soulless corporate swine. Max smiled. Molina would have hated his survival tactics, including dragging along the sophisticated French-German shrink who might be his hostage, or hunter. Revienne had no reason to complain after the bling fling he gave her in Zurich as a parting gift.

Molina's voice halted the trip down recent-memory lane. "Dreaming the tap water in your giant plastic glass is a single-malt whiskey in . . . where? Paris? London?" she asked, all too accurately.

"More like sipping Hitchcock-blonde champagne in Zurich," he said, thinking next of his horizontal fling in the Swiss city.

"So Temple Barr winging off as arm candy with a guy headed to a dream job in Chicago is no loss to you."

"Why should it be? I don't remember my past life and loves, or enemies."

"Lucky you," Molina muttered. She rested her head on one hand as she scanned the entrées, giving him sum-up time.

Fingernails: unpolished and clipped short, but filed smooth. Unlined olive skin except for vertical tracks between her black eyebrows, which were sweeping, strong, and unplucked. The frown lines flirted with forty, a prime age for a woman. An angle of serviceable bob the color of espresso brushed her knuckles. She pushed it behind one ear. No earrings, no rings.

She tapped the menu's hard glossy edge on the tabletop before laying it down, for good. "You ready to order?"

A veteran waitress with a patina of perky overlaying tired eyes — and probably feet — had appeared like a magician's assistant beside the booth. The Mystifying Max had always worked solo. He made up for lost time by skipping his eyes past entrées like meatloaf and pot roast . . . and sides of baked potatoes that would be small and tough-skinned . . . and desserts like banana pudding and chocolate cake. He surrendered.

"Cajun-style blackened steak; baked potato with bacon, sour cream, and chives; the house salad to start." He skipped the vegetable sides, which would be watery with all the color leached out. No sense in ordering meat rare or medium here. Everything was cooked to death.

Molina jumped on the chuck wagon. "The grilled fish, salad, Italian dressing on the side, and the, ah, baked beans and green beans."

Max rolled his eyes as the waitress left. "My treat next time. I just risked death six thousand miles away. I'm not going to be killed by cuisine in my home city."

"What makes you think there will be a next time?"

"You said you have work for me. I don't see you as a penny-ante copper. Given the fine line of legality you've been walking to protect your personal issues for far too long, you're going to need a heap of help."

"Hired help."

"Yes, ma'am. I was going to add 'even from a memoryless cripple.' "

She snorted as their small salad bowls arrived with saltines on the side, tabletop. "Playing the self-pity card, eh? Spare me. Why take my offer? You don't need the money."

"I need the exercise. Both the mental and the physical."

She nodded. "That I buy."

"So what's next? Now that the Barbie Doll Killer and your unprofessional hiring practices have been exposed . . ."

"I suppose Miss Barr has been sharing my

longtime low opinion of you —"

"And it is based solely on bias and my sleight-of-hand reputation. I'm flattered."

"It was based on the fact that your act at the Goliath Hotel ended the same night a body was found in the surveillance passages over the casino area, and you disappeared that same night."

"It *was* a magic act."

"You bailed and left your loyal live-in squeeze to face the questions."

"Doesn't sound like me. I did hear recently you harassed my . . . then-fiancée for information she didn't have about my whereabouts. For months."

"Just doing my job. I don't like material witnesses disappearing after a murder. They could be perps."

"You don't know for sure I witnessed anything. *I* don't even know that now."

"Innocence by absentmindedness. Not a plea you can cop." She sighed. "Later events have convinced me you were more likely a target than a criminal."

"You mean that Garry Randolph's death at the hands of ex-IRA factions in Belfast last week convinced you that *real* bogeymen were after me in Las Vegas almost two years ago."

"Don't sound so bitter. Trust me, that's

70

no way to live."

Max raised his eyebrows. "Trust, huh? So what's happened to Dirty Larry Podesta, or whatever his surname really is."

"Out of town, out of law enforcement, out of my hair."

"I'll give you credit. You played him as much as he might ever have played you."

"Never, Kinsella. He never played me."

"Is that a challenge, Lieutenant?"

Their wilted salads had been sampled and then set aside for a round of crisp dialogue. Now they had to shut up and lean back and away from each other as entrées descended on their place settings, a plastic mat surrounded by the Chinese New Year symbols and a color-crayon-ready blank-white center.

"Trust? Try it," she said. "Meanwhile, your first assignment, should you choose to accept it, is looking into that Goliath murder you skipped out on."

Max gazed at his plate, a piece of meat more charred than blackened and a small baked potato in its brittle brown jacket. His ancestors had starved by the thousands for the want of these commonplace root vegetables. Even his happy-to-be-back-in-the-USA appetite for kitschy food had picked up its paper napkin and gone.

"I don't remember a thing about that place, that time, those people." Max began picking at his meal. "I walk into the Goliath Hotel now and someone, a lot of staff probably, will recognize me and I won't have a clue."

She smiled, having eviscerated the fish into flaky bites of white non-taste. "Too proud to be ignorant, are we? That's the beauty of it. Poking around the Goliath will prod your memory. It will take a smooth, prevaricating SOB to hide your disabilities. You can thank me when you make your first report."

"But —"

"Yes, you have accurately recalled the disadvantages of your situation. Your ever-helpful ex-redhead-in-residence is not in town right now. You can't rely on her extra-sharp memory. She's quite the little snoop and puzzle-solver. You'll be on your own. Might be interesting."

"Funny. Nobody mentioned you were a sadist."

"If you made it across Western Europe dodging assassins, I think you can navigate the Goliath Hotel. Consider it a challenge grant."

"The pay is lousy."

"And so is the food. Welcome to a menu

of plain, old-fashioned law enforcement, Mr. Kinsella."

He chewed on her assignment and the rest of the dinner, including the plain, old-fashioned tapioca pudding she insisted on ordering for him, saying it might spark memories of his childhood — she was indeed a sadist.

She also gave a dry, even skimpy, summation of the Goliath murder case files, which were basically the method of murder — knifed above a casino table, interesting — name of victim, and time of death and discovery.

This was a cold case and most likely a criminal hit, not a juicy crime of personal motive. It was the deep-freeze of cold cases and the most personally challenging crime she could ask him to investigate.

Game on.

CHAPTER 7
SUITE DEAL

Temple had finished her tour of the suite, cooing over all the posh designer touches.

She returned to Matt in the living room, where he'd slipped off his shoes and was checking out the six-foot HDTV offerings. Just like a guy.

Normally Temple never let bare foot touch hotel carpeting, but this stuff was so soft and expensive, it felt like walking through velvety grass on a golf course only billionaires played.

Louie reclined near Matt in his "King of Sheba" position, glossy black front paws straight out like the Sphinx's, head high, ears forward, and tail arranged into a graceful *S* behind him.

In this very pose he had made his rival TV commercial cat, the unlamented Maurice, look like yellow tabby hash at a greasy spoon diner.

"The producers called," Matt said over

his shoulder, clicking past the Home Shopping Network and QVC while Temple quashed a knee-jerk reaction to cry, *Wait. Accessory Alert!*

"Dinner Sunday okay?" he asked.

"That's family dinner day."

"The family get-together will be over by six P.M. Every Sunday dinner is Thanksgiving-size in my family. Given the beer, they'll be ready for naps. And the producers dine downtown, close by. That'll work."

"Do I have to meet the family all in a bunch?"

Matt shrugged, still channel surfing. "Not my choice, but we're the guests." He paused the screen to turn to her. "I tried to get Mom to meet us first, but Saturday nights are busy at the restaurant and I guess she couldn't get off."

"That big tourist draw must have *two* hostesses." Temple sniffed avoidance and Matt nodded agreement, about to say more. Although what can you say about a family so uneager to meet someone who is marrying into it?

"She's —," Matt began, sounding apologetic all over again.

The room phone rang, echoed by all the other phones dotting the suite. It made the

75

place sound like an office . . . or a command post.

Matt leaned over to the sofa table to take the call, then stood and turned to face Temple so she'd get the drift.

"Yes?" he said. And then, "Sure, Mom. Yes, the flight was fine. Except for an incident at the airport. Someone tried to snag Temple's carrier with her cat in it." Matt laughed. "He's a pretty big cat to snatch without pulling a muscle, so we got him right back."

"Tell them they thought my cat carrier held the crown jewels," Temple said.

Matt did, and added, "No, no diamonds. Only on her finger."

He listened, then smiled. "Sure. We'd love to have dinner at your apartment." His eyes questioned Temple, who nodded extreme agreement. "We'll cab it. And I guess we can bring the 'famous' cat."

Temple looked at Louie, who was lounging on the sofa like a sultan, one leg now draped over the pillow edge. Despite the playboy pose, he was a rough-and-tumble street cat adept at opening the French doors in her Vegas condominium. One shuddered to think what he might try at thirty-some stories if he decided he didn't like being left home alone in a hotel suite.

"That's good, excellent," Matt told Temple after he'd turned off the portable phone. "Looks like Mom got her courage up despite the situation that's got the whole family in an uproar."

"Will she discuss it in front of me?"

"Remains to be seen."

"And you said she shares an apartment with your young cousin Krys?"

"Yeah. Krystyna, all *y*'s, is doing performance art in her spare time. I can imagine. . . . She hates the Polish spelling of her name. Too Old World. She is a radical chick, a rebel as much as you can be one in my family. Mom was . . . pretty shut down for a lot of years. Moving in with Krys got her out of her shell, enough to meet this guy who wants to marry her."

"That was at the restaurant where she hostesses?"

"Right. It's a classy but down-home place. Polandia. Ethnic food."

"I can't believe he's the brother of your real father."

Matt nodded, with resignation. "Chicago is a huge city, but sometimes coincidence beats the odds."

"Maybe it's not just coincidence. Are you seeing your dad this trip?"

"Lunch Monday. He wants to meet you."

"You didn't tell me any of these plans beyond the Sunday dinner."

"And you didn't ask, wise woman that you are." Matt came around the couch to fold her into his arms. "I didn't know how it was going to work out. I'll probably be playing therapist all four days. You're just the gorgeous, charming distraction I need to keep me sane, and keep my crazy family on their company toes so a total meltdown doesn't occur."

"Funny, I'm just in this trip for the sex."

"And you'll get it," he promised, moving his lips to her ear. "After you see the way my family has messed up, you'll know we can't help but get everything right."

The moment was interrupted by a harsh, sawing sound. *Oh-oh.* Louie had abandoned his catbird seat on the couch. It sounded like he was making retching noises behind it. By the time Temple got there to tend him, he'd turned away and was vigorously scraping his nails all the way down to the tough jute backing of the costly carpet.

Obviously, Louie was sharpening his utensils in preparation for Sunday dinner, which was held, as it always was in the Midwest, in the middle of the day, after church.

The only more intimidating scene for their

first social appearance as an engaged couple Temple could imagine was at the Barr family home in Minneapolis.

CHAPTER 8
DOVES VS. PIGEONS

To enter the Goliath Hotel, one had to walk or drive under the three-stories-high statue of a straddling man, the said Goliath, although his kilt looked more like a sumo wrestler's diaper.

"Older" in Vegas meant cornier. Passing through the showy mirrored copper entrance onto a carpet bearing woven-in camel figures, Max wended around a twelve-foot-wide meandering lobby waterway called "the Love Moat," where tourists lounged in automated red-velvet-lined gondolas.

Finally he made it through the noisy, crowded casino to where red velvet ropes blocked off an attraction that went "dark" during the daytime.

Max stood staring at a placard mounted behind glass at the Goliath Hotel Sultan's Palace Theatre.

SOPHISTA, MISTRESS OF MAGIC OF THE 21ST CENTURY.

It didn't surprise him that he'd been replaced. . . . His run had ended almost two years ago.

It didn't surprise him that he'd been replaced by a woman. The magic field had been a male domain for too long.

What shocked him was that he'd been replaced by an utterly new name in the magic-show firmament.

Not that anybody would recognize him now.

He'd worn his usual self-effacing casual black but had sacrificed his thick black locks to a messy postmodern crew cut. Now he looked like any gel-laden spiky-topped hipster out there, vaguely gangsta but also slickly Hollywood. Pretty soon he'd be growing a soul patch . . . and goatee. Zeus forbid!

Given the new hollows on his already angular face, the look was hip and sinister enough to blend in like a lot of other Vegas wise-guys on the make.

"Hot, ain't she?"

Max corrected his line of vision from the magic show headline to the magician's Victoria's Secret pumped-up bustline. "But can she make rabbits leap out of hats?" he asked.

"Man, *I* would leap out of hats for that babe." The guy was a Chris Rock wannabe, too genial to be quite as hard-edged as he hoped for. He glanced up at Max. "You a fan of magicians, or those major perky rabbits?"

"I'm a fan of illusion."

"Wow, dude, you should have seen the magician they used to have here. The guy walked on air in a snowfall of pigeons."

"Doves."

"Oh, yeah, doves. Wonder what happened to him? Wonder what happened to all that bird shit?"

Max laughed. "No wonder he walked on air."

"Right. Right!" The guy shot his trigger finger at him. "Good one."

After the man moved on, Max remained staring at the glossy babe who'd replaced him without seeing anything but the makeup and costume. They might remember his act, but not his working name, or him. Good to know the new look was working.

He turned to wander back through the casino area listening to the chortles and screams and clucks of the push-button slot machines that silently swallowed five-, ten-, and twenty-dollar bills. "One-armed bandits" was a vintage expression now. Only the diehard slot addicts could find a machine with a physical lever to pull.

And if they did, the hotel would know. Sensors populated casinos like popcorn multiplied in movie theater aisles and seats. They resided on every slot machine, every ATM, every computerized door lock system. Computersville. Max refrained from gazing above the gambling tables and apparatuses. A casino this size might install three thousand eye-in-the-sky cameras but had only fifty monitors watched by six or so people. Casino surveillance was geared to archives, not live issues.

That meant a dead man among the camera-servicing pathways might lie undiscovered there for a while, given all the remote recording methods nowadays. Max needed to get up in the ceiling service areas to explore.

Some casinos also had catwalks in the ceiling above the casino floor, catwalks that allowed surveillance personnel to look directly down, through one-way glass, on the activities at the tables and/or slot machines. On him.

Luckily, casinos still lavished mirror on many surfaces. Max studied the camera placements in eye-level reflections.

All the casinos also relied on the old mechanical "eye in the sky," hyped up for the new century. Max checked his watch, knowing a PTZ, the devilishly versatile Pan Tilt Zoom security camera, could read the time and count the hairs on his wrist. The catch was, what was happening above the PTZ went unrecorded, and undetected . . . unless a tattletale body crashed through the fancy ceiling tiles.

Not his, he devotedly hoped.

CHAPTER 9
TUNNEL VISION

Max had finally found a service entrance and was elbow-crawling through the ceiling access tunnels above the Goliath casino area. The aging hotel's multimillion-dollar face-lifts over the years had left much of the interior infrastructure in place.

Sure, the cameras and remote-viewing equipment were state of the art. Yet the light maintenance modern cameras required meant that outmoded and bypassed air-conditioning ductwork that was as forgotten, narrow, and tortuous as secret passages in the Great Pyramid at Giza could be used. At least access to the murder scene hadn't altered since then.

Ga-cheez. Max sneezed at the dust. He was proceeding not by memory, but by what he could find about the hotel's layout on the Internet. What a pathetic amateur memory loss had made of him.

After scouting the building's well-disguised functional areas, he'd found the battered gray-painted metal door that led to this area. Service stairwells sported so many of these doors that the thrum of recognition in his mind at seeing it could have been déjà vu instead of resurrecting memory.

All he knew from Temple Barr, his lost love, and Molina, his unremembered enemy, was that a body had been found in the above-casino area of the Goliath. Molina, at least, had given him the vic's name. Max lifted an elbow to claw farther forward and banged his funny bone on a metal strut.

Not funny, he thought with gritted teeth, biting back monumental curses. The drilling pain made him wonder why torture by funny bone had never been popular. What had Temple said? The man had been stabbed. That method of murder made sense in these cramped labyrinths, but one sure couldn't lift an arm far to get in a decent killing blow.

According to *Review-Journal* archives the victim, Anthony Hedberg, had been the Goliath's assistant security chief. Had Tony happened on a crime in the making, say abetting big-time cheating on the gaming tables below, or blackmailing the cheaters, or even a heist? Or was Hedberg a good guy gone bad? Was he setting the stage for any or all of the above?

Like many multiple-choice questions, those speculations weren't solid enough to bet on.

Moving along mentally and physically in the dark, Max crawled right off the edge of a drop. Adrenaline peaked as he fell.

His latex-gloved fingers clawed upward to grab for struts, but his body swagged into a shallow depression, not a void. He tried to avoid scrabbling for stability and sounding like squirrels in the attic. The casino floor below chimed with choruses of cheery computerized sound from the slot machines, but the general racket would be more muted if he happened to be above a blackjack or craps table.

Exploring the miniature sinkhole, he concluded it was the equivalent of a duck blind in the sky. Back out a couple of bolts and you could shift the camera to look down on a Twenty-one table next to the cash-out area. A crook or a cop in this overlooking cradle could go country or pop: exploit the position for cheating at cards or know when the loaded cash cart was leaving for the vault.

So why kill the guy in the sweet spot? Maybe someone was trying a takeover bid. Or . . . Hedberg had spotted signs of a heist and was hoping to play the hero and expose the scheme at the last minute.

It had been his last minute, all right.

Max used his tiny high-intensity flashlight to inspect the overlooking post. Somebody with a sizable investment of time and stealth had prepared it. The area either suffered from black mold or the fingerprint dust from the police investigation two years ago remained undisturbed.

Max used the peephole station to jack-knife his long legs around so he could retrace his path face-first. The classic "stiff upper lip," gained by biting his lower lip with his upper teeth, kept the painful process quiet.

An echoing scuffle above the venting shadowed his withdrawal. It could be the hotel had installed a more modern catwalk above the old camera access route, with one-way glass to survey the casino.

Or . . . it could be his incursion had loosed a hound. The answer would soon be obvious as he approached the light leaking through the venting grille at the beginning of the air-duct tunnel, and now the end, for his retreat.

CHAPTER 10
FAMILY . . . MATTERS

Facing the blankness of the apartment door, Matt had no illusions about this apparently impulsive Saturday-night dinner for four. He was bringing Temple into something far trickier than your average possibly awkward family get-together.

He shifted the strap of Midnight Louie's carrier on his shoulder, marveling at her fortitude in carting around the hefty tomcat.

"What are you smiling about?" she asked, glancing nervously at the blank apartment door in front of them.

"Your secret strength."

"Right, midget Supergirl. Calves of steel on spikes of iron." She hefted one foot cradled in those shoes that were only thin leather straps on a platform high heel of pewter-colored metal.

She'd changed from hotel-room sweats back into the red leather suit that even Matt could tell meant business.

"You look very Waterplace Tower," he told her, "but I'm guessing you'll need those roach-stompers here in Chicago." He wasn't totally kidding as he knocked on wood for luck, and the usual reason. Admittance.

The door opened instantly to his rapping. Matt's younger cousin, Krystyna, filled the space like the real Supergirl. Her naturally blond hair was chopped into intersecting sprayed angles of magenta and black, the black matching her exotic eye makeup. Matt could hardly take in what she wore at one glance, except it was black and white and Lady Gaga.

"You must be Temple," Krys said, looking down on her older, smaller rival.

"Right." Temple was unintimidated by the Amazonian Alternative Lifestyle model looming in front of her. "I have an alter ego that would *lurve* your look, sister. Krys with a *Y,* is it, or are you going by a performance name now? Chris Angel is taken."

Krys blinked. She hadn't expected the conventionally but modishly dressed fiancée to understand her visual statement.

Matt escorted Temple inside while the doorwoman remained gawking. It had been evident on his last trip to Chicago. His fifteen-years-younger cousin was still "crushing" on him, as Temple's teen persona, Zoe Chloe Ozone, would put it. If it came to a smackdown between the two, Matt's money was on Temple and her secret weapon, Zoe Chloe. Plus, Temple had faced down a serial killer in her latest avocational stab at playing private detective.

His mom was hovering in the archway to the next room, letting her taller, broader niece and roommate be the front woman.

Matt hated to see his mother retreating again in that effacing way, as she had during his latest visit only a couple weeks ago. She was the real reason he'd come back. Mira had been blossoming lately, but had suddenly shut down. Matt reached to draw her forward even as he pulled Temple to his side.

"Mom, meet Temple. Temple meet Mira."

"Now I see where Matt gets his telegenic looks." Temple extended her right, ring-bare hand. Mira took it with a shy smile as the contact became more of a clasp than a shake.

Matt felt so much pride in his mother. She was wearing the blue topaz earrings and Virgin Mary–blue silk blouse he'd bought her that matched her eyes. The few silver filaments in her softly styled blond hair made her seem to glow, like the actresses who had glitter strands woven into their hair. His mom had earned every silver thread. She'd borne him at eighteen, but still looked more like an older sister of forty.

"You're beautiful," Temple blurted, despite her tactful nature.

"Not me," Mira answered. "I'm supposed to say that to you and it's true."

Krys edged beside Matt as his mother escorted Temple from the archway of the small foyer into the modest apartment's living room. Matt lingered to let them get acquainted.

"Going for miniatures in your old age, huh, Cuz?" Krys murmured under her breath.

"Don't do that cynical routine, Krys. Own what you are; Temple does. I remember you had a bleak time in junior high when the other kids called you 'Mrs. Ed.' "

It was hard to see highly rouged cheeks flush but Matt detected a sideways shamed glance.

"You're a shrink, sort of," Krys said. "What's with the girlfriend's overcompensating heavy-metal heels?"

"*You* noticed them, didn't you? Consider it akin to a gang insignia."

"You warned her about *me*?" Krys sounded cheerier. "You don't need a body-guard."

She pushed closer as Matt swung Louie's carrier around from behind his hip. Krys was staring into a dark feline face with slitted eyes and flattened ears that looked mighty like a black panther.

"Time to let the 'famous cat' out on his razor-bearing paws." Matt lowered the leopard-skin bag to the entry hall's ceramic tiles and unzipped the front flap.

Midnight Louie strutted right out. No peeking and peering and pussyfooting by lingering inside.

Krys jumped back. "Is that just a domestic cat? I mean, it's not one of those Bengal crosses with a big cat?"

Louie was so pumped by her reaction, he immediately twined around the sinister leather ankle cuffs of her footwear and rubbed his big black nose on them in turn. Matt kept quiet, only a wry smile showing his amusement. Cats love to sniff and bite leather, and Krys's rock-band look was providing enough of it to upholster a couch.

"Man," she complained, mincing backwards, "that big ole boy acts like he's ready to eat me alive."

"He won't hurt you . . . if you're not a crook or a murderer. Temple has a knack for running across crime in her profession and this guy is her guard dog in disguise."

"I believe it." Krys smiled at him, flirting again. "Much as I like having you . . . to myself, we should join the others."

Matt put a hand on her chain-draped forearm, some kind of uber-bracelet for the would-be motorcycle set, to hold Krys back a moment for a whispered update. "Why is Mom still acting so unnerved?"

"You'd be unnerved if you'd developed a romantic relationship with the brother of the man who knocked you up thirty-five years ago, a man she'd thought was dead in a foreign war all these years, thanks to his snobby, interfering lying family."

Midnight Louie's royal tour had made it into the living room and they could hear the two women bonding in rapture over the big rascal.

"That's awkward," Matt told Krys, "but it's happened before, especially on soap operas. Believe me, my birth father is no threat to her current relationship, even if it's with his brother."

"Why?"

"He's married and Catholic. He might as well be dead."

"That's cold," she whispered.

"That's a fact," Matt said. "Jonathan Winslow might be in an unhappy marriage, as I suspect. Maybe he might contemplate divorce, but he could never remarry in the Church, and Mom would never marry outside the Church. She even married that abusive rat, Cliff Effinger, in an eternally binding Church ceremony, private as it was."

"It still blows my mind she'd do that, marry someone so . . . icky."

"He probably snowed her. She wasn't reared to rebel or to be at all independent, like your Internet generation, who escaped the guilt and shame rap. They've lost all soul. Look at Internet bullying."

"Hey, I'm in my first year of college now and doing okay. Our high school class didn't go that far."

"They didn't yet have the option of being anonymous but ubiquitous." Matt shook his head. "Mom was desperate to get the label 'bastard' off me. She thought no one in her circle would marry her . . . after me. She was so pretty . . . and so low on self-esteem. Effinger just waltzed into a paid-for two-flat and an easy life living off and cowing her." He realized his hands had become fists. "You don't want to go there, Krys. I've done the time and it's not worth stirring up. I just hope she hasn't regressed to deny herself happiness again. This . . . insanely inconvenient brother, he's not dumping her?"

"Your uncle Philip, you mean." Krys produced a wicked smile. "No way. The guy's been frantic, calling the apartment continuously. She won't speak or meet with him alone; she won't listen to me. I had to talk myself indigo blue just to get her to meet alone with you and the Red Menace and that damn cat. She wanted to interact with your significant others in the crowded safety of the family free-for-all tomorrow."

"*You* accomplished tonight?" Matt was so pleased, he hugged her.

"I had ulterior motives," Kris said way too slowly, not pushing off. "I guess you're 'Catholic and almost married and as good as dead' too, Cuz."

Matt welcomed that diagnosis with a grin. "Get on with your own thing, Krys. Don't get hung up on the past, like Mom."

Temple had been making cheerful chitchat, watching Louie explore the room so he didn't do anything untoward with the rug, smiling and nodding at Matt's mother while straining her ears to overhear the whispered dialogue in the entry hall. That twentyish mired-in-teen-adoration sex bomb of a cousin had it bad for Matt.

Temple was expert at listening to two conversations at once, including one of her own, and breathed audible relief at the "married and Catholic and as good as dead" exchange. *Right on, Toot-tootsie-good-bye, Krys. You are out of luck with Matt. And if you don't back down, I'll download Zoe Chloe Ozone to give you a run for what you think is your honey.*

"What did your family say when you left Minneapolis for Las Vegas?" Matt's mom was asking.

"Pretty much what you did, Mira, when Matt left Chicago." Temple had graduated fast to first names. She knew Mira had picked the last name Devine for Matt out of some subconscious bin so his young life wasn't tarred with Effinger's last name, or her family's. He'd had a ready-made stage name, Devine, thanks to Mira's girlish fantasies. Once she and Matt were married she would be Temple Barr Devine, not Effinger and not Zabinski. TBD. Cool.

"I'm the only girl," Temple explained to keep the conversation going while she was still eavesdropping, "and the youngest child, with four older brothers. My parents worried about their little girl in big, bad Sin City, but I've done fine. I have my own PR business, a great place to live, and now a

97

fabulous fiancé."

"And this cat here earns his own way?"

"Sometimes," Temple said cautiously.

"He was in TV commercials."

"Oh, that. Yes."

"So you have *two* media men around the place?"

Startled, Temple said, "Yes." Then she realized what Mira was getting at. She wasn't used to strict religious concerns shading every word and act. "Matt's apartment is a floor above my condo in the Circle Ritz apartment building. Louie's my resident male. So far."

"Dear, I wouldn't be shocked to know you were living together."

"Great. But we're not. Quite."

"You'll have to watch it around my family tomorrow, but not me." Mira lowered her eyes. "It's easier to advise a younger generation than to make my own stand for independence from family."

"Hey. You're living here with a member of the younger generation. Mondo hip, mama." *Eeek!* Zoe Chloe had surfaced. Must be nerves.

Mira laughed. "You're so clever and funny. Matt told me you were."

"What else did he tell you?" She really, really wanted to know.

Mira looked past Temple, her smile staying too long, until it looked glazed and forced.

Temple's confidence crashed. She'd hoped she was making a connection with Matt's mother, but the woman was clearly putting on her emotions like a mask.

"Come in, sit down, you two," Mira invited Matt and his cousin with as much summoned warmth as if she'd been playing the hostess in a restaurant by rote. "Or . . . wait. Krys, can you get some glasses and that bottle of sherry from Christmas? We should toast the engaged couple."

Matt sat on an upholstered chair as Krys stood still, her expression a blend of distaste . . . and reluctance to leave the room for even a moment. The girl's territorial fixation on Matt would have amused Temple if she hadn't been involved.

Then Krys whirled and left, her short-short skirt hem flouncing. Bursts of hurrying steps and banging cupboards in the kitchen revealed Krys's rebellious mood, while Mira smiled apologetically at their guests.

Krys was back, openly annoyed. "I can't find that sherry bottle. *Any* sherry bottle. Any *frickin'* dessert wine bottle."

"Oh." Mira puzzled for a moment.

"Maybe we took that bottle to family dinner two weeks ago."

"I don't remember that, Mira."

"I'm sure that's what happened to it." Mira's appealing glance flicked from Matt to Temple. "Things have been so . . . busy. Krys, would you mind running to Woz´niak's and getting another bottle?"

"Uh, Mira." Krys pulled a cell phone from the tiny steel-spiked bag on her low-slung black leather belt, worn over that white tutu of a short skirt. "They close in less than half an hour."

"Then you'll have to hurry, won't you?"

"Uh, sure." Krys backed out of the room, and turned fast. Temple heard the scrape of car keys against a metal surface, likely a dish, then the apartment door opening and closing.

Mira sat back and closed her eyes just as Matt sat forward, his dark brown ones focused on her. "A Woz´niak's run will take Krys at least half an hour, Mom. Where's the wine bottle, really?"

Her blue eyes opened, looking haunted. "Empty. In my bottom dresser drawer."

Struck again by the dramatic difference in mother and son's eye color, Temple wondered what Matt's father would look like as she met his shocked gaze. She knew what he was thinking: Had his mom become a secret drinker?

Mira continued speaking, but her eyes didn't focus on them, only elsewhere in the room as if her own inner turmoil were lurking somewhere in the domestic landscape and she hoped to keep it at bay.

"Matt, I don't want your lovely fiancée dragged headfirst into family business, but I don't think I can stand the pretense anymore."

"You've been under a lot of strain lately." Matt was trying to remain neutral and supportive.

She laughed bitterly. "That's nothing new for me, Matt. My whole life's been 'a lot of strain.' "

"True." He took her hands. "And I haven't been here for you lately, but that can change right now. I can be here to see you through."

"You can't help."

"Sure I can. It's my job."

"Not this." She put white, cold fingers to her visibly flushed cheeks and shut her eyes.

Matt exchanged another glance with Temple. "Is it the . . . wretched coincidence?" he asked his mother.

"Of my possibly having your father for a brother-in-law? Your uncle-in-law? Things that cuckoo have happened in the Bible. No, that was just icing on the arsenic cake," his mother said.

"What is it that you think I can't help you with?" Matt tightened his grip. "I know you want to download the problem to someone who can help. That's great. You've started to . . ."

"Confess?" She laughed again. "No. I know you're not taking confessions anymore."

"Then why bring up something you won't let me help with?" Matt checked his costly watch from the producers. "Krys will be back and our privacy will be nil."

She took a deep breath and fixed her gaze for the first time. On Temple. "Actually, from what you've said, I'm thinking *she* can help."

"Temple?" Matt sounded unflatteringly astounded, realized that, and started to backpedal. "Temple would be happy to help but you don't even know her yet."

"You said she was so smart and clever, had even beaten the police to the solution of crime only recently."

Temple beamed as Midnight Louie came to sit at her feet and soak up the praise. "So you need a gumshoe?" she asked.

Gumshoes were the silent gum rubber-soled "tennis" shoes of their day. All eyes fixed on Temple's highly elevating but decidedly impractical and clattering gladiator sandals.

Apparently embarrassed, Louie hiked a rear leg over one shoulder like a shotgun and began grooming the hairs between his back legs. Talk about being embarrassing, Temple thought, in the bare-butt sense of the word.

Mira was too upset to take in the byplay. "I just don't want you fretting, Matt." She withdrew her hands and fisted them at her sides on the sofa. "I've been getting these messages."

"Messages?" Temple and Matt had questioned the word at the same time. It was so . . . old-fashioned. Did she mean e-mails? Phone calls?

"Notes." The word spat out of Mira's mouth like a dead fly found in her coffee, along with a shudder of sheer revulsion.

"In the mail?" Matt asked.

"No. In person. Wherever I happen to be."

Temple sat forward, her sudden move almost overturning the delicately balanced cat at her ankles. "Notes. Not mash notes?"

Mira shrugged. "They could be taken for that, showing up under my reservation book at the restaurant, under my napkin during dinners out. In my umbrella when it rains.

In my purse."

"Good God!" Matt's expletive didn't merit notice from his mother, much less a reproof. "You're being stalked. Why haven't you informed the police? Why are you making such a secret of it? Is it because of your new . . . romance? Is some disgruntled ex-girlfriend shadowing you? Is that really why you ended the relationship?"

"Yes, Matt. Stalked. No, I don't think it has to do with Philip." She put her hand to Matt's face. "Oh, dear one. I really didn't want to trouble you with it, not after the childhood I gave you."

"The childhood you gave me was fine," Matt said firmly, taking her hands again.

She avoided his gaze and looked at Temple. "I'm so sorry. I didn't mean to ruin your trip to Chicago."

"Ruin it? No way. Your son proved himself an ace skip tracer in Vegas and my nose may be as short as I am, but it's long on sniffing out liars, cheaters, and crooks. You have to in the PR game."

"Speaking of liars, cheaters, and crooks, Mom," Matt said. "What about the empty bottle in the bottom of your drawer? You're not a newly converted dipsomaniac?"

"Just the occasional drink before or after dinner. Truly, Matt."

Temple glanced at him, seeing the tension softening in his face and shoulders.

"That's a relief," Matt said, adopting radio shrink mode and a low, nonjudgmental tone. "Then what just happened here?"

The answer arrived in a rush of confessional frankness, just like on the air. "I poured the wine down the sink and hid the bottle so Krys would leave."

Matt registered her answer and then grinned. "Pretty sly move for a parochial school girl."

"Thank you," she said. "I just couldn't go through another Charade Sunday at Uncle Stach's house. They already think I'm half-crazy for calling off the engagement with Philip. They don't know who his brother is and I'm not going to tell him." She paused. "Are you seeing . . . him? This trip?"

"Yes, Mom. Temple's coming too."

Mira winced. "That's fine. You should have a relationship with your father. My . . . going forward with my unfortunate . . . encounter with his brother would have been so awkward anyway."

"Doesn't mean we let somebody scare you out of it." Matt was firm. "What does this anonymous coward seem to want, anyway?"

Mira bit her lip, hard. "That's why I tried not to mention this. He wants something he

105

thinks Cliff Effinger left behind."

"My lousy stepfather?" Matt asked. "Where are these notes?"

"In . . ." Mira looked apologetic. "In my dresser drawer."

"With the emptied bottle." Matt shook his head. "Temple's scarf drawer is another forbidden zone of explosive secrets. Let's see these threats."

When they stood in front of the drawer, it looked so innocuous. Just a small bottom drawer.

"What a wonderful dresser," Temple couldn't help but exclaim. "It's a reproduction of those 1930s-style ones." She ran her hands over the round frame holding the mirror.

"I got it years ago," Mira said, "at a St. Vincent de Paul's shop. It was cheap."

"I've always thought," Temple said, "of these big round mirrors as the moon, setting behind the two pillars of drawers on either side."

"Goodness." Mira examined the piece with new eyes. "You're right, but it'll always be the harbor of old poison to me now."

Matt had squatted to pull out the narrow bottom drawer. A battered manila folder was curved to fit into the space. He pulled it out. A sheaf of stiff, folded white typing paper lay inside. The front one opened like a book, showing signs of yellow glue around newspaper headline-size letters.

"We probably shouldn't handle them," Temple cautioned, leaning over to look. "The fewer fingerprints for the police, the better."

"No police." Mira hung over Matt and the drawer too, wringing her hands.

"YOU GOT CLIFFIE'S CRAP WE WANT IT LADY," Matt read the crazy-quilt printed letters. "It's simple," he added. "If you have anything of Effinger's, give it to them. Only we need to think up a way so you don't come in contact with these freakos."

"That's just it," she answered. "I haven't known what to do, or how. It's like that man is haunting me. I just can't get him out of my life, even after death —"

Her head whipped toward the bedroom door.

Someone was fumbling at the front door. Matt had stood and unconsciously turned toward the noise. Now he turned into a pillar of salt.

Temple was riveted too.

Cliff Effinger.

"He's dead," Matt mumbled, gazing toward the doorway as if he expected his stepfather's ghost to stumble in and he needed to do something about it.

"I know. You told me." Mira's voice was weary again. "And I may have made a big mistake all over again —"

"So here you all are. Wine steward's here," Krys caroled from the doorframe, hoisting a brown paper bag. "Mission accomplished. Just made the closing time. Who wants to pop the cork and celebrate?"

CHAPTER 11
COLLARED

Max was still elbowing along the dark air-conditioning vent, preparing to make a last right turn before the final twenty-five-foot crawl.

His knee joints felt swollen and numb. Every foot forward seemed like a yard.

A businesslike clang echoed from the tunnel's unseen end.

That wasn't a distant burp down the long-distance line of new venting that had replaced this disused old route. It wasn't an echo from some workman's hammer bounced the length of the Goliath's hidden guts. Too close. *No.* It was the rasp of the metal vent cover he'd temporarily replaced to hide his incursion. The grille was being wrested away again, and too easily, thanks to his incursion.

He shouldered ahead, faster but still as stealthy as he could manage. Finally his head and shoulders thrust into the freer air flow of the last passage. The cold blood in his inactive legs had spread to his chest.

The faint work-light glow from the mechanical closet should be welcoming him back to the home stretch.

Instead the way ahead was impenetrable black.

Another body was blocking the light.

No such luck it was another dead body in the same ductwork at a different time, as awkward . . . and sinister as that would be.

A whisper, a soft shift of cloth, promised another intruder had followed Max into the dark ductwork alley.

Memory blast.

His mind flashed back in time to a short blind struggle in the dark at the tunnel's other end. He'd locked down the windpipe of the man he discovered hiding there long enough to eel his way back out. Maybe long enough that a second visitor who had seen Max's expedition start and end had then followed in his elbow-crawls and killed the disabled Hedberg.

Someone certainly had seen, or suspected, Max's current presence. That made his decision to go unarmed iffy even if it confirmed his suspicions. Upper body strength had always been the best weapon in his onstage career and offstage espionage assignments. Now it would have to pull his weakened legs along while handling his unseen enemy and whatever weapon the guy was sure to be carrying.

Max hoped that this wasn't the same assassin as two years before, and that, if so, he hadn't upgraded to carrying a gun. Either way, knife or gun, the bad guy had to be using a shoulder holster to keep his hands free for crawling. And the "breast pocket" drawing action necessary to pull it in these close quarters would alert Max before the weapon was out of its sheath.

Max coiled himself into as much of a crouch as the space would allow and kept still. The pressure on his braced toes and stretched hamstrings was a torture Saddam Hussein's insane son would have been proud to invent.

But Max had to . . . wait. To not move, shift, or alleviate his pain even by a centimeter. The dark behind him was his shield and trap. That and his magician's patience to wait, wait, wait for the final triumphant "reveal." The more cramped the space, the more impossible the position, the better payoff, in illusion and in reality.

The dark tunnel ahead heaved into slithering sound and motion, heading right for him. Max unsprung his torso and leg muscles in a massive motion of relief that propelled him into the unseen obstacle, his right hand clutching the other man's right wrist as it bent to draw the anticipated weapon.

Max twisted until the snap of bone and the guy's bitten-back moan. He pressed the whole arm up and back. If he could drive the butt of whatever weapon was in that hand into the man's own left temple, hard and sharp, it would be a knockout punch.

Panting openly now, Max banged the unconscious man's hand to the venting floor as his grip relaxed. His rejecting gesture skidded the confiscated commando knife toward the visible exit grille. Then he wrapped his fists into the man's denim jacket — the stalker hadn't expected to have to follow Max into a small space — and heaved the inert body halfway behind him, using his chest and shoulder muscles, and crawled on past.

As he dug his elbows against the aluminum surface to crawl toward the light, he saw the grille shudder, then vanish. A hand reached up through the opening to retrieve the knife with its six-inch blade.

Max swallowed his frustration. Great. He wasn't getting out of here without jumping off into the light at the end of the tunnel, onto his barely healed leg bones, within easy reach of a new enemy forewarned and fore-armed.

CHAPTER 12
PRAWN PATROL

"So this is where my no-goodnik son likes to hang out," Three O'Clock mused, still licking steak 'n' shrimp atoms off his black whiskers as we gaze at the Neon Nightmare club, a shiny black pyramid off the Strip.

"This is where some suspicious characters of interest hang out, Grandpops."

"It is true, Louise?" Three O'Clock Louie demands. "You are my boy's daughter?"

"Not in his address book," I point out.

"I will mention that in my opinion you have the good looks to be a member of the family."

"Cut the gallantry. I am running Midnight Investigations, Inc., in the absence of the senior partner and I do not see the name 'Midnight' in your curriculum vitae. There will be no nepotism on my watch. You do a decent job, and I will put in a good word for you with Ma Barker."

"That is all very well, but I have a sweet spot at Gangsters with the Glory Hole Gang guys.

I am still the inspiration for their restaurant, even if my name is off the place. Why should I wear my footpads out trekking halfway across the Strip to be ordered around by a wet-behind-the-ears, fresh-from-mama's-washing kit?"

"Because I will pin your ears to your tailbone just to see how it looks on you."

"Oh." He backs off with a playful swagger, shifting from hind foot to hind foot. "I suppose that this, ah, Midnight Investigations, Inc., outfit you mention could use a temp head detective now that the main man is out of town."

"Sorry. That position is filled. *I* am the 'temp head detective,' and all I need is some warm bodies to tail the subjects in case they split up, which is likely. As long as you can walk and report in, you are hired. A couple of street dudes from Ma Barker's gang are en route."

"This private detective game sure requires using up a lot of footpad leather."

"That is why we hitch a ride when possible."

"The last time sonny boy did that with me, I was almost flattened in traffic, right in front of the golden lion at the MGM Grand. I do not like to look like a doofus in front of a major feline Vegas icon, especially a dead doofus."

"You referring to the statue, or you? One thing I can guarantee: You will *be* a dead doofus unless you quit complaining."

The old guy rocks back on his ample haunches, which allows the streetlights to reflect from the short white hairs on his nose and chin. His previous spot had come with being his own little icon at Three O'Clock's Restaurant, all the lobster droppings he could eat, and full social security being mascot for the aging Glory Hole Gang turned hash-slingers.

"I forget," I tell him, "you were living the leisurely lakeside life at Temple Bar on Lake Mead."

"Yes, indeed. I had retired off a salmon trawler in the Pacific Northwest to Arizona, as many well-heeled seniors do nowadays. I am not much for heels, but I am for tiring."

He sits to pluck a few stray hairs from between his toes, looking nonchalant. Where have I seen this air of male self-satisfaction before?

"That Temple Bar turf is barely in Arizona," I point out, "and seniors are scrambling like the rest of us to avoid severe lifestyle cuts these days. The pattern is to work beyond the age of retirement." I drum my forefront nails on the parking lot asphalt. "I can have you and Blacula tail one suspect together. There are only three. Pitch and I can take the remaining two."

116

"But these folks slink in and out, maybe even in disguise, Louise. How can we cut them out from that crowd that keeps coming and going?"

"That is why we were given superior night vision, Grandpops. And Blacula's hearing is sharper than a bat's. Where do you think he got the name? Midnight Investigations, Inc., is tops on night surveillance. Here are Ma Barker's footpads now."

I am happy to see the pair wears ninja black from ear-tip to toe-hair. We do the usual close encounter four-step as the newcomers edge around to eye me and Three O'Clock while we exchange the ritual sniffs, struts, and down-low growls.

The building's pyramid-shaped black-glass exterior shimmers with the reflections of nearby neon, making it hard to observe anything other than the lighted entranceway.

After having led Miss Temple to the secret rooms of the occultists who call themselves "the Synth," we spotted some main members in consultation: Czarina Catharina, the medium . . . retired mind-reader Hal Herald . . . and the slinky something or other dame who seemed quite familiar with Mr. Max as both the Phantom Mage and in his real incarnation. There is always a slinky something or other dame. Then shockeroo. Another party broke in on the proceedings via another route. From our hidden niche we witnessed the Synth trio being confronted by armed and dangerous taskmasters in the long black cloaks and full head masks of the . . . well, Darth Vader variety.

This was a cheesy disguise, but executed with state-of-the-art built-in altered voice technology. In other words, kind of like my old man — quintessential Vegas.

In daylight I had reconnoitered every inch of the pyramid's exterior "footprint," as they say in technological circles. I found a suspiciously smooth seam at the far parking lot corner. I had been spotted, but mistaken for a lower life-form looking for a private deposition station.

Here is where I commit and array my agents. We have visuals on only one half of the peaked edifice with the four-square base.

Then we hunker down. Few know the patience of my kind when we hunt prey. We can crouch, still as stone, on any turf from a smoking hot piece of Vegas concrete to an iceberg, motionless for hours, awaiting the slightest twitch of vermin in the neighborhood.

"Bugs, snakes, and lizards will not do," I tell my crew. "We are not after fast food tonight. I do not want to see one whisker twitch no matter what does the shimmy-shimmy past. You move only when I tell you, and then you track the prey to the final destination and watch until dawn."

They take my edict so to heart, their heads do not even nod.

I crouch last, putting myself into the silent state of self-hypnosis where I am a rock until called upon to move. Not even a solacing purr can ease our battle-tensed muscles. We practice the art evolved by our kind thousands of years ago, when it was be still or be killed. Be silent or be prey.

Only now, the paw is on the other foot. I could get used to this, especially on my own, with my inner nerves twitching but my outer aspect poised for the kill.

I am not aware of the passage of time. I do not carry a cell phone or wear a wristwatch. I only feel the hot night air weighing on my black velvet catsuit. *Ha!* My nails curl and loosen, curl and loosen, aching for purchase on something soft and evil.

A splinter of long bluish light flashes at the seam in the black glass exterior. A tall figure blocks it, then vanishes with it. My keen vision sees the plantings at the pyramid's base waver. I twitch my right ear in Pitch's direction. The statue that is he shifts and disappears.

I wait.

Oh, how human and clumsy! The light bulges this time, clearly silhouetting a figure with a melon-sized head and balloon-sculpture's body, tied off in puffy limbs indicating arms and trousers. Harem pants, actually.

My left ear signal bestirs Blacula to rise slightly and spur a snoozing Three O'Clock to life as they move to shadow the exiting medium.

I have saved the best for last. The secret doorway profiles for an instant the slick dame and last of the lot.

Mr. Max is my special pet. It may not make sense to any who did not come up in a multi-generational relentlessly carnivore clan, but woe to any who would trifle with the ex-squeeze of my supposed father's current human. Any disturbance on Mr. Max's domestic scene will be swiftly punished.

So I slide like an oil slick over the asphalt to a parked black Camaro that burps open at the snap of the sorceress's fingers on her key ring. It takes a moment for her to turn and spin her major spike heels into the car's front seat. I am used to such footwear-caused delays and do a Midnight Louie twist into the narrow space behind the driver's seat.

Three Synth members; four Midnight Investigations, Inc., operatives on their trail. Where will our assignments lead us and what will we learn there?

CHAPTER 13
SURPRISE PARTY

Naked was the best disguise, they said, but surprise was the better half of naked.

Max rolled out of the tunnel into the mechanical closet headfirst, his supple spine pulling his legs after him so he hit the floor on a roll he could push out of sideways and at the same time lift his hands in a defensive position.

The man waiting to ambush him had grabbed the unfastened grille and held it up like a shield, the other guy's lost knife in his right hand.

Max struggled upright against a wall of wooden shelving, his eyes getting used to the light that showed his opponent wore a security guard's uniform, complete with gun holster.

Max ducked, knowing he was busted.

The knife slashed toward him in an expert spinning arc that buried the blade point in an upright pine board near his carotid artery.

"Better your fingerprints are the last ones on that than mine," the guy said just as Max saw past the uniform to the man wearing it.

"Impressive aim. What brought you here?" Max asked, grabbing a dirty rag from the shelf to pry the knife loose and then wrap its slightly bloody blade.

"Tailing you."

"In your work clothes?"

"Guards are all over the Strip. Nobody notices them here, like mail carriers in residential areas. Is the guy in the tunnel dead?"

"I hope not."

"You need to ID him?"

Max shook his head, clearing his muzzy brain. "It was a tight place to tango. He wore cat burglar garb like me, and carried no ID. Nothing more than a pencil flashlight and a —"

"Assassin's knife."

"Tight quarters, tough weapon. It's a good thing you kept your feet on the ground and stayed out of that dead end up there. We good to go, Nadir?"

"Absolutely."

"Then you'll tell me whether you're playing spy . . . or babysitter, both of which I consider killing offenses."

"Go ahead," Rafi Nadir said with a sweeping gesture and a sardonic look. "I got your back."

"You know," Max said after they'd driven separately and discreetly to Gandolph's house in an established neighborhood of Las Vegas and gone to ground inside. "I don't know why I've got an ex-cop playing guard dog."

He handed Nadir a Baccarat crystal glass with three fingers of Jameson Irish Whiskey in it.

"You keep a good bar and pour generously?" Rafi quipped.

Max sat down opposite him in the living room, reflecting he'd had no memories of just hanging loose in the house, or entertaining anyone, not even a woman, having no friends but the post-Gandolph Garry Randolph. The way Garry had reinvented his given name into a clever version for a magician beginning a career in the late sixties still made him smile.

Nadir took a big gulp of citrine-colored whiskey and let it simmer as it trickled down his throat.

"And," Max said, holding off on enjoying his own hospitality, "I understand we have an . . . irritation in common in the formidable person of Lieutenant Molina. Now that Garry is dead, though, your job of supervising matters involving him and me here in Vegas is over."

"No, it isn't."

"I don't need a nanny. I don't like witnesses."

"Okay. I won't follow you anymore, but Randolph not only got me a decent security job at the Oasis, he also paid me a bundle, up front, to look into a bunch of other things."

"What bunch of other things?"

"The death of his retired assistant, Gloria Fuentes, for one. Then there was a professor killed at the university here, at some magic display on campus. I don't know what else. I don't carry my notebook with me. Besides, he pulled me off everything to watch your back at the Neon Nightmare when you did that Batman routine."

"The Phantom Mage." Max chuckled, to Rafi Nadir's visible amazement. "I've been brought up to date on that. What a corny name and act."

Nadir drank again, then said, "Easy for you to laugh it off. I'm the one who saw you fall and declared you dead so Randolph could highjack a hired private ambulance to get you out of there fast. Frankly, I still don't know why you *weren't* dead."

"I learned in my act how to fall and hit as if I was drunk, completely limp. So *that's* how Garry got me out of there so fast. He must have commandeered a private ambulance off the street."

"Yeah. I was undercover, working 'security' there. Even I didn't know what was what when the EMTs carted you away. I was starting to feel sorry for Temple Barr, she's such an okay gal. Then my cell phone rang and I heard Garry giving me my 'story' while that ambulance siren was still screaming in the background. He musta got you out of the country stat. What was he? CIA?"

"Confounding International Agent, yes." Max smiled again.

"He must have been ready for anything. Damn, he was good. I wish I'd known him longer."

Max bestirred his cranky frame to lean forward and click glass rims with Rafi. "To Garry Randolph, my friend and yours."

The expensive crystal rang, an exquisite death knell. Max was sure Garry would have approved the impulse, the toast, and the ingredients, including him and Rafi, resurrected victim and unseen guardian angel.

Enough Irish mist and sentiment. Max sat

back. "I have a posthumous assignment from Garry too. He wanted to figure out who's been dogging my existence here in Vegas."

"Yeah. I know you're working with Molina on something."

"*For* Molina, which means I'm working for myself first and foremost." The two men exchanged a tight smile. "So you've kept that close an eye on me."

"Not you, repo-memory man. Molina. That's all I'm after, shared child custody. And I can prove cause to get it if she doesn't give me some rope soon."

"From the perspective of one with impaired memory, she strikes me as the devoted mother type, and her rendezvousing occasionally with me is not exactly juicy, career-breaking news. Hell, I could be dating her."

"But you're not," Rafi said. "And she's still vulnerable if she's using you like she did Dirty Larry to cover up her illegal B-and-E at this very house and do some personal Peeping Tom work."

"Have you tried negotiating with her on the child custody?"

Nadir took another healthy slug and let it burn down fast. "A little. She knows what I want, says she's not 'ready.' Mariah, my kid, is thirteen. I don't have months, even weeks and days, to lose."

"Yeah, she'll be a rebellious teen with no time for parents in the wink of Pussycat Doll eye."

"Don't remind me." Nadir lowered his drink to the table and his head to bury his hands in his thick dark hair.

"Push it, then."

"You've seen Molina more recently than I have. She seem any mellower now that the Barbie Doll Killer case is solved and she isn't playing cat and mouse with that undercover narc?"

"Nope." Max stretched out his legs. "I don't remember her from before my near-death experience, but I can tell you that woman is not going to soften one tiny bit . . . unless you push it."

"She must be still bending the rules if she's hiring you for something. And now there's another guy found conked out in the Goliath mechanical systems."

"He made it out. Don't let the blood fool you. I cut off his air temporarily and used a sharp head blow. A quick out cold, but not forever. And don't think you can turn my exploits on Molina's behalf into blackmail. What'll impress a fiercely protective, seriously paranoid single mother like her will be how upstanding you are. And you are now, aren't you?"

Nadir rubbed his furrowed temples but still didn't raise his head. "I guess so. Your friend Garry got me a chance at the Oasis. I'm in line for the security chief job, but I'm not the dead cop hero Carmen made out I was to the kid."

"Carmen. I bet C. R. Molina despises that girly name."

"She always did."

"Whoa." Max poured a bit more whiskey into Nadir's glass. "Wait a minute. I was wrong. You *can* blackmail her. Don't you get it? *You* don't have to live up to *her lie,* but *she* has to live down *lying* to the kid." Rafi nodded, seeing the light. "That's something kids don't understand and forgive. She needs you to cooperate and help her explain away that unforgivable breach of trust. No wonder she's been such a mama grizzly. Hell, if that were a qualification, she could run for president on that platform. If I were you, I'd make nice and then nail her."

"Are you suggesting I *date* her?"

"No, of course not. I'm *telling* you to. And getting her into bed would seal the deal." Max laughed at the sight of Nadir's struck-dumb expression. "You've said you get along with the kid —"

129

"Mariah."

"— with Mariah already, since she and the always entertaining Miss Barr were competing in that teen talent reality show."

"Yeah. It cuts like a knife to hear Mariah wants that media-perfect ex-priest to take her to the junior high Daughter–Dad dance. What's he got that I haven't got, besides looks and money?"

"I could say the same thing, since he cut me out with Temple."

"You've got looks and money," Rafi growled.

"Had," Max said. "Had it all, and a live Garry Randolph."

Rafi slanted a suspicious glance his way. "Kinsella, are you getting drunk?"

"Maybe so." Max eyed the low level of Irish whiskey in his glittering glass and fixed that. "Not to go all metrosexual on you, but you're a buff, decent-looking guy. You turned your life around. You really care about being in that young girl's life. I say, use it. You and Molina had something going once."

"You *must* be drunk." Rafi sat staring into his glass, then grabbed the Jameson for a refill.

Yeah, Max thought. First had come the recent rerun of the Goliath episode he still

130

didn't remember. Now Rafi's account of his almost-fatal Neon Nightmare plunge was bringing back haunting glimpses. Both incidents merited a good dose of anesthetic.

And . . . where would Max with a Memory be now, instead of drinking with Rafi Nadir? Maybe at the Circle Ritz, sleeping with Temple Barr. The idea seemed ridiculous at first, but she sure had known how to reintroduce a morose amnesiac to his own life.

"Come home, Max."

Her parting words, sounding shell-shocked but game, would never leave his re-booted memory going forward. She had guts and grace, that little woman. And if Vegas still didn't feel like "home," nowhere did. Maybe the Circle Ritz could have. Maybe being with her again would bring everything flooding back. . . .

Max ended the maybes. That was the liquor nattering on.

He didn't need to star in a romantic melodrama. He needed to find out who was out to kill him, and why so many innocents were being drawn into that murderous end-game.

For now, if he could sic Rafi on Molina, distract her from the remaining unsolved criminal matters that she obsessed about, he'd have a much clearer field of operations for his own investigations.

Once he was totally sober again, that is.

CHAPTER 14
GOSSIP GUYS: DOING ONE'S NAILS

Well, trim my toe hairs with a hedge shears!

Or just step on a crack and break my mother's back, why not? She will make you pay, believe it. One does not mess with Ma Barker, and you do not tug on Superman's cloak or Midnight Louie's tail.

Here I have been trekked to Chitown in a designer carrier that gets me taken for a purse pooch and kidnapped, but I am still about to perish of boredom. Then I keep my ears perked and a nice, plump juicy family scandal plus a deranged stalker case gets tossed into my furry lap like a grenade.

Some would scramble to dodge falling family standards and potential bodies. Not Midnight Louie. I will be on the lookout for any malfeasance, not to mention bad actors.

Speaking of bad actors, my Miss Temple and Mr. Matt and Miss Matt Mama all do a lousy job of concealing the verbal bombshell Miss Mira has just let loose regarding her late demented hubby.

Cliff Effinger was the worst lowlife to hit Vegas and did not do a decent thing in his life, except draw Mr. Matt to my hometown to track him down.

I know the whole sordid story. It is as common in my world as in soap operas. In other words, it actually happens in real life but sounds too bad to be true. Seems Mr. Matt is the "product of sin." Yeah, we hip cats on the street do not get those ugly labels. We are all just called superfluous.

He was actually the product of this sloppy *Romeo and Juliet* scenario humans like to sniffle over when they are not busy casting stones. My kind has often been the object of such schizo reactions too. As I understand it, She Who Is to Become Matt's Naïve Young Mother is visiting St. Stanislaus Catholic Church near Christmastime to light a candle to the Virgin Mary. Watch out for that Virgin Mary! She is just a statue and may sometimes be asleep at the switch, as the Great Goddess Bast has been known to do for a century or two through her many millennia of worship.

Anyway, this young soldier going off to whatever war is the flavor of the moment is there to light a candle for his safe return, and *zowie, powie.* Human hormones strike, aka love at first sight. Believe me, I sympathize with the biological imperative. I have been blindsided by its pull a few dozen times myself.

It is the same old story as in my world. He is off about his business protecting territory for the feline race and she is left with a six-pack of kits . . . or just one if the leavee happens to be human.

You can imagine the wailing and gnashing of teeth in the church choirs come the ensuing months. Jeez, you would think they could leave a lone cub in peace to be born, but Mr. Matt comes into this world everything a human kit should not be. Father unknown, mother shamed, and a family secret forever.

Follows the dumb, desperate marriage to whatever lowlife will take a fallen woman to wife. Enter the lazy, worthless, haranguing Cliff Effinger. At least Miss Matt Mama gives poor Mr. Matt a false surname, her one act of defiance, changing that into something new, not the old Polish "maiden" name, not Effinger's, but something unique and Devine. Mr. Matt grows up with such lousy father figures except for the parish priest that he becomes one. Maybe his interior kit thinks he can redeem his mother's "mistake."

Me, I find life tough enough as a former homeless street dude. I cannot see adding on all this additional angst, but humans have over the centuries invented whole systems designed to make most things miserable.

Mr. Matt is a good priest; he has to be a perfect "father," after all, but he finally wakes up and smells the candles and realizes he cannot make up for anyone else's past. So he gets himself cashiered out as a civilian, but tells no one he wants to track down the Evil Effinger, who has long since left his mother for the dubious attractions of the criminal life in Las Vegas.

It could be Mr. Matt is primed to leave a lot of Mr. Cliff Effinger's skin on the asphalt. Whatever, he has an epiphany and puts the brakes on his revenge, but some other dudes take out the miserable cur. Murder, they wrote. The rest is a long slow dance to reconnect with his mother and encourage her to bury the past and grow strong in the new soil that has accrued over it during all these years.

Which is working great until Mr. Matt once again uses his tracking skills to find out his real father is not dead on foreign soil, as his mother was told by the guy's family lawyers long ago, but alive and well and rich and unhappily married in his old hometown, Chicago.

I guess this is a "what if Romeo and Juliet had lived" story, and it looks like acts four and five are still coming. With my Miss Temple in the midst of all this, I cannot let her do it alone, but perhaps I must let her do a teeny tiny bit of it solo.

Although the family dinner tomorrow is sure to be a slaughter of more than the main course — I am violently against any but vegetarian fare for humans, given they have the unfair double advantage of opposable thumbs and automatic weapons — I decide that while our current crew is out for Sunday dinner I will find reason to hang out at Mr. Matt Mother's homestead and see if I can catch whoever is spiking the place with billets-doux of a threatening nature.

CHAPTER 15
PRODIGAL CAT

"This city is way too tall," Temple observed as Matt drove their rented Camry sedan to the apartment late Sunday morning to pick up his mother and Krys. "And this car is way too conservative for people in their early thirties like us."

"You're not even thirty-one yet."

"I will be in a couple of months. I'm told that's the beginning of the end."

"That birthday was more like the end of the misguided beginning for me," Matt mused, referring to when he'd left his vocation. "And the older Chicago neighborhoods and suburbs are hardly high-rise." He eyed Temple uneasily. "I have to warn you. Carl Sandberg the poet was right: Chicago was always a brawling, sprawling city. The immigrant ethnics fiercely battled each other. No Irish priest would serve a Polish or German community church. There's still surviving prejudice."

"Good thing I'm a mutt," Temple said. "Anybody who calls me Irish because of my red hair will have to have his or her mitts up."

From the backseat, Louie seconded her assertion with a long, low growl.

"I just don't know how Louie would adjust to being an indoor cat," Temple said. "The sheer size of this city is stunning. Manhattan feels intimate in comparison, and Minneapolis is a shrimp. Now I see Vegas is really just a small town with a Disney World downtown blossoming atop the stem of a rhinestone Las Vegas Strip. The rest of it is low-rise and residential and alley cat friendly."

"Not by law." Matt's eyebrows had lifted over the top rims of his sunglasses as he made his point.

"Louie writes his own laws," she reminded him.

"Las Vegas is no longer in the lawless West, Temple. You know he should be confined to quarters at all times."

She sighed. "He'd break out. I don't worry about him there. Too much. Here, I would."

"This would be a definite reverse in life-style. I like the idea of having our nights together. Maybe you and Louie could get a Zoe Chloe Ozone and cat act going in some medium."

Another low growl from the backseat punctuated that comment.

"Sweet idea, but not likely," Temple said. "I'm glad your mother phoned this morning. She sounded more upbeat."

"Confession is good for the soul."

"Who invented that quote?"

"You don't 'invent' quotes, Temple, and you know it. *I* know you love a mystery, but Mom clearly wants us to set aside the ugly stalking situation for the moment, partly because the family sand trap is even more delicate to navigate. We can't do anything serious about it on Sunday anyway. Let's just try to get along."

"And worry about things tomorrow. Okay. New conversation. I'm glad I'll be arriving at your uncle's house with your mother and cousin. I won't stand out as an outlander too much."

Matt's laugh rang off the moonroof's tinted glass. "Oh, you will, don't worry. Low-profile and quiet don't work in my family anyway."

The Camry turned into the dark of the apartment building's underground garage. Street parking spots were precious in Chicago neighborhoods. Matt glided the car into a "visitor" slot and collected Louie in his leopard-print carrier.

"He could lose a little weight." Matt hooked the broad strap over one shoulder as he stood and locked the car.

This time Louie didn't even bother commenting.

"Uncle Stach is such a hoot! He still won't drink any German beer." Krys shook her particolor, multilength-cut head. "Party" was Krys's main mode. Zoe Chloe could take styling lessons from that girl.

Matt's mother had unearthed a family album for Temple to scan, with appropriate commentary from Krys, Matt, and Mira herself.

Temple's job right now was to share the long couch with the two women and look and listen as they flipped pages through Mira's album — "There's Matt at seven, in his white First Communion suit," Mama said proudly.

"Even then he looked divine," Krys kidded.

Temple thought he looked solemn and adorable, like a miniature really young Brad Pitt.

Krys was holding up her cell phone to run a more contemporary strip of shots. "This was Matt's third-to-last trip back." She thumbed the tiny button through photos she'd taken of them together by holding the phone camera at arm's length. "Matt had been AWOL for a long time before then."

Temple could believe that. The men looked boisterous, the women were always shown slaving happily in the kitchen, and the wall art was all religious. The entire scene would be a silent rebuke for anyone who'd left the priesthood. To the older generation, his act would be like leaving the U.S. Army to enlist in Al Qaeda. Unthinkable.

Krys, however, had no such scruples. She'd obviously ached to get her hot little hormone-charged teen hands on Matt and now was flashing this fact in Temple's face.

As the only girl in her family of five kids, Temple didn't get excited about female competition. There was at least one part of the Catholic religion she found sympatico and that was the concept of free will. If Matt found another woman (even if she was just an immature, overgrown girl like Krys) more interesting and attractive than he found Temple, he was welcome to walk.

Well, maybe Temple had just a tiny competition bone in her compact body. She did find Krys immature and note that her parade of photos was making Matt squirm in that well-concealed way he had of doing.

"Thank you so much," Temple told Mira. "It's so thoughtful of you to preview such a large, extended family to the new kid on the block." Followed by a flick of the eyes to Krys. "Even though I work in a 'people' profession, it's always nice to know the lay of the land." Another swift glance at Krys and her string of "she smiled, he smiled" photos. What else could the poor guy do?

Matt was trying not to smile now and his dear mother remained oblivious.

Temple already felt her native, ex-reporter indignation rising in Mira's behalf. It must have been a nightmare for the sensitive girl she'd been to "disgrace" her own family. She'd obviously not been given Instruction One about protecting herself from an early age, the way girls today were.

If the despicable Cliff Effinger was haunting her even from the grave — the watery Las Vegas grave, in fact — it had to stop here and now *and* in Vegas. She and Matt had stayed up half of last night in their posh suite shish-kebabing their brains for all they could remember about Effinger and how he might possibly have had something anyone would want, besides his cold dead slimy body in the deep, dark ground.

"Time to get on the road," Matt said now,

standing up. "Are we ready?"

Temple was reminded of *The Magnificent Seven* mounting up for an assault on the bandits terrifying the Mexican villagers.

"Ready," she said. "Maybe Krys would like to carry Louie. It's good exercise for the biceps and pecs. And you have all us ladies to shepherd to the car."

But when Krys hefted the carrier, she stuttered backwards in surprise, having over-compensated. "Either your cat has lost a lot of weight, or it's empty. What is he? The Cheshire cat, all teeth and no body?"

Temple hastened over to shake the bag. Empty. "*Hmm.* The zipper's open. Louie will do that," she told the two hovering females. "He, uh, makes his druthers known."

"And he has a way with zippers?" Krys asked, skeptical.

Matt answered for Temple. "He's the Houdini of the cat world. Nothing can cage him if he doesn't want to be confined."

"He's loose in here?" Mira asked, looking around in alarm.

A good question. The apartment was only on the sixth floor, but Temple wanted to check all the windows. Every one was locked. They surveyed each room, hunting high and low and finding no trace of hide or black hair nor dashing white whisker.

144

"Will we ever find him?" Mira fretted.

"Not until he wants to be found," Temple said. "He can pull this vanishing act in my tiny two-bedroom condo in Las Vegas."

Privately, Temple was glad to have Louie confined to quarters by his own choice than pulling a stunt like this in a whole strange house, which was exactly where they were headed. Maybe this was a protest move on Louie's part. Everything in Chicago would be strange or even risky to out-of-towners like Louie and her.

"This trip has been a huge break in Louie's routine." Temple told the puzzled non-cat associates, "I'm sure he's hiding away somewhere to soothe his frazzled nerves."

"So he's high-stung?" Krys sounded disdainful.

"Willful," Temple answered. "Like all cats, he often knows better than we feeble humans do." She exchanged a glance with Matt.

They both knew that Louie was opting out of the highly charged family reunion coming up. Too bad they weren't cats and easy to hide.

CHAPTER 16
SEARCH AND UNEXPECTED SEIZURE

Alone at last.

My ears had been burning up a bonfire overhearing all the speculation about my druthers and whereabouts.

I had done the Houdini trick of hiding in plain sight. Well, for one of my species.

I had been lounging in a hammock . . . the canvas sling at the bottom of the kitchen laundry bag, inhaling the comforting, homelike scents of antiperspirant, cosmetics, and shampoo. After all, my current roommate enjoys being a girl.

How wonderful to have all the social murmurs and palavers reduced to the hum of the refrigerator. Actually, refrigerators mimic major digestive upsets nowadays, have you noticed that? They do so many tricks with ice and water and defrosting and burping like Tupperware that one is tempted to throw Pepto-Bismol at their stainless steel faces. That would be like topping the Taj Mahal with strawberry sauce.

Anyway, I am in official search and seizure mode, accompanied by a canny glaze of lying-in-wait.

No one here had noticed that I noticed that Miss Matt Mama had kept the noxious threatening notes in a folder in her bottom dresser drawer, so as to keep Miss Krys's nosy nose out of them.

Drawers might be an obstacle for one of my limited digital dexterity, but my primal brain knows how they work, so off to work I go.

First I flip onto my back. Then I drag my muscular torso beneath the drawer under siege by planting all sixteen of my built-in pitons in the feeble wallboard people use as mass-produced furniture these days.

No way would I have been able to perform this feat on, say, Sam Spade's desk. Those days produced men and file cabinets of steel and noggins and drawers of walnut, as in "hard walnut to crack."

Now, my motions as I shimmy under the drawer bottom might be adult-rated but we are all friends here. Once in position, I start driving my leg pitons into the wall-to-wall carpet, pushing with my mitts. The resulting push-pull action inches the drawer forward. In a thrice — well, after several full body rolls — I can wriggle out from under the dresser, snag a few shivs inside the drawer's now-ajar gap and wrestle the insert out.

Okay. It takes me about five times longer than some light-fingered career criminal to open a drawer, but they have the weight and opposable thumb advantage.

Once in, working out the papers in question is kit's play, nothing any curious puppy could not accomplish with three brain cells. Leaving them unchewed, priceless.

I use my main four-finger shiv to spread the missives out like a hand of playing cards.

I have been known to decipher printed matter, but human handwriting is a tougher problem. I recognize the messages are formed of that old crime story staple, individual letters in different type fonts cut out from that disappearing artifact of contemporary life, the daily newspaper.

I may not be able to read the tortured text, but my eyes and nose tell me two suspicious facts: I do not pick up the odor of ink on pulpwood paper, a scent I have been known to shower with my ill will on the few occasions I have been incarcerated. Newsprint is a favorite litter box filler for the group homes that shelter many of my kind at a time.

There is no such fulsome scent on these missives, only the faintest whisper of toner power, which means they were computer generated. Now, what kind of degenerate stalker is computer literate?

I recognize key words from my long list of oldie movies viewed on cable TV when my Miss Temple is out gallivanting, or at home gallivanting in a manner that ejects me from my own bed.

You will recognize such cherished turns of phrase as: "We know you know." "We mean business." "Or else." "Comply or die." And I read the same ugly words I saw in tiny print in a tiny news story on Miss Temple's coffee table copy of the *Las Vegas Review-Journal:* Clifford Effinger. Along with the also corny phrase of "mysteriously found dead."

A fancy computer font combined with corny vintage clichés? Who do these bozos think they are intimidating? Obviously, they think they are scaring Miss Matt Mama and Mr. Matt, by means of the ghost of *her* crummy husband and *his* stupid-mean stepfather.

At this moment of deep cogitation, which must be accompanied by a trancelike state often mistaken for a nap, I hear a door creak in the living room.

Doors do not creak except in scary movies, folks.

Has someone in the Sunday dinner party forgotten a crucial something . . . such as breath mints or Tums or gas pills? From what

I have been hearing about the joys of Polish cooking and beer drinking I am sure that they would be the least required.

So I scramble to push the threatening missives into a pile, prong them back into the drawer, and reverse my physical exertions of the past ten minutes in two, trying not to make any noise. I will not bore you with the details except to say I am fairly twisted into a knot when I leave the dresser closed and shimmy under the bed.

Footsteps — large careless stepping-on-tail footsteps — clomp onto the bedroom carpeting.

"I heard something in here," a deep male voice says.

"Yeah," mocks another. "The wimpy curtain hitting the window glass in the draft of the ceiling fan. We saw them drive out of here in the rented sedan, all four, all dressed up like for a funeral. They ain't coming back soon."

Spare me the crude contractions. This is not an episode of *Jersey Shore.*

I gaze out on mud-edged work boots.

"Good," says Mr. Hearing Things. "I will leave a note under the old lady's pillow. That ought to put a wasp in her —"

No lady will be the object of crude language when Midnight Louie is around. I strike like a snake, a shiv finding the sweet spot between the ankle-boot top and the wrinkled jeans bottom as the creep bends to place his latest poison pen note under Miss Mira's pillow.

"Ow!" he yells, straightening up in a hurry.

"What is the matter now?"

"A wasp stung me."

"Get real."

"No. Look. My leg is all red in this spot. It is bleeding."

"I am not looking at your bleeding ankles. Maybe you got an allergy. Leave the note and I will do something nasty with a butcher knife and whatever is in the meat drawer in the kitchen on the way out."

"It is not just the two chicks now. They have visitors."

"So. We back off because of 'visitors'? We been hired —"

I wince again. As grammar goes so arrives the coarseness of modern life.

"— to terrify and that is what we do best. That dude is the woman's son. I bet if we got a hold of him we could get her to come across."

"I would rather kidnap the little redheaded chick. Less trouble and more fun."

Their footsteps thud out the door and into the living room, then soon stomp onto the kitchen tiles like jackhammers.

I rocket out after them, intending to do massively more epidermal damage with my own butcher knives. Well, X-acto knives on steroids.

I run right into the open maw . . . of the leopard-print carrier, which a rude boot kicks shut on me before I can turn around in the canvas tunnel.

"I told you I heard something in the bedroom," says one. A boot kicks in at me. "Wasp. I was right. Kiss your kisser good-bye, puddytat."

Light returns to the tunnel as the boot draws back for a kick. I gather into a crouch. Luckily, Miss Temple has chosen a commodious carrier, I am planning to land atop the boot, sink in my staples, and ride it out of captivity. Of course, I may be flung spine-first into a wall, but I also plan to use the Mr. Max Kinsella survival strategy and go as limp as a kitten before I hit.

I admit I am being a trifle optimistic about my survival chances here.

"Hold it," the other guy says, kicking my assailant's boot aside. He bends to zip the lip of the carrier shut.

"This plays right into our hands. Talk about smaller and less trouble. We have got our hostage. You know how regular people go all puddly about animals in jeopardy. Just let me write a note and stick it into the maple countertop with a butcher knife and we are outta here."

Mr. Kickapoo is not convinced. "Should there not be blood on the knife? There is on my ankle."

"Will you forget about your friggin' ankle?"

"Or we could hack off the tip of his tail."

"You want to put your hands into that wasps' nest? You could contract blood poisoning. I am not going to drop you off at the ER. Too risky. You will end up in the same landfill I will leave the cat in. I will bury the little devil and you so deep, it will make the Jimmy Hoffa disappearance in Detroit look obvious."

Landfill. Great! I have found some very tasty snacks around landfills. Plus there are trash trucks coming and going constantly on which to hitch a ride back to town. One man's doom is another cat's opportunity.

Am I glad to have distracted this two-man destruction crew into leaving my nearest and dearest alone.

First the news shows reported that "troubles" in Ireland still showed signs of life — and death — thanks to surviving veterans of the years of civil strife.

The lighted screen served almost as an LED crystal ball for Max, opening up the world of Garry's own investigations and questions.

Now it seemed the IRA links in Las Vegas were alive and well also.

Max hunkered down again over Gandolph's laptop at the kitchen table, a glass of Jameson at his right hand. Thanks to Lieutenant Molina's thorough search of the cupboards recently, he now knew where the hard stuff was kept.

He sat back. Molina. He was ideally placed regarding her. Rafi Nadir, her ex, was loyal to Garry and now to Max by proxy. The homicide officer wanted to keep Max busy solving the mysteries of his own life and times for some reason.

Suited him. While burning personal issues distracted Molina and Rafi, he was in emotional limbo and better able to concentrate on why he'd been marked for death here and in Northern Ireland.

Max took a slug of whiskey. It would be tricky, but he needed to get closer to Temple Barr. She was a walking memory bank of his past as well as all these pesky Las Vegas crimes that had haunted Garry and maybe caused his death on foreign soil, putting him into an unmarked grave, maybe.

Max's fist hit the table, sloshing whiskey too close to the computer and its precious information.

Temple Barr. She was young, she was lovely, she was engaged. Only a jerk would deliberately get between her and her righteous fiancé, the honest ex-priest turned media hottie. And could he still pull that off, in his diminished condition?

Max smiled ruefully. Probably *only* in his diminished condition. Temple was too softhearted for her own good. And gutsy. *"Come home, Max."*

Damn. He'd needed that from her then. Now he needed to know what Miss Temple knew; she'd probably tell him gladly if he asked. He had no time to waste. He was too obviously back in town and sure to draw the wrong sort of attention. If only he could crack Garry's computer password. There must be more on it than the Ireland tourist information he was pulling up.

He sipped and thought. Rafi remained his best bet now. That professor's death on the UNLA campus was also the best trail to follow when Max wasn't shadowing himself for Molina. The newspaper archives were skimpy. RESPECTED PROF FOUND DEAD. MAGIC WAS HIS MINOR.

Max had located an old calendar entry on Garry's computer about a magic-show poster exhibition at that same time. *Garry, Garry, Garry.* He'd kept Max alive. Max had to honor his memory and answer all the questions Gandolph the Great had been pursuing.

Max brought up the UNLA site on Garry's computer. Las Vegas aerial views were "weary, stale, flat," as Shakespeare's Hamlet had described his life before it all blew up and went to hell.

But not "unprofitable."

The landlocked campus was a compressed intellectual island in a sea of commercial "strip" developments and sprawling residential desert areas. Like moats of hot metal, traffic hemmed in the campus most of the year. It had no place to expand, yet needed to establish a strong physical presence.

That was exactly how Max felt at the moment, hemmed in by his loss of memory and self, "tasked" as the bureaucrats put it, to change his world and help the people in it, including himself.

An on-campus visit might be most enlightening.

CHAPTER 18
TRAPPED, STACKED, AND ZAPPED

I am not surprised. My nappers repair to a deserted building probably on the south side of Chicago cheek by jowl and growl with Bad, Bad Leroy Brown of song fame. They dump my carrier on a hard concrete floor dulled by forty years of dust, dirt, and random elimination.

They leave me in the carrier, deprived of food, water, and facilities.

They have no idea that I can unzip my prison with the flick of one fang. They have no idea that I am a self-directed "plant," not the green growing sort, but a live listening device.

"I still say we should have snatched the little redhead," the one I will call Lefty says.

"Nah," says Shifty. "This is better. The little redhead will get real hysterical about the pussycat being grabbed. You saw her in the airport."

"If we'da got the cat in the airport, we'da have the goods by now. Whoever thought

Cliffie Effinger had anything anyone with big-time cred would want?

"You remember that little piece of plumbing poison?"

"From back in the street gang day, almost forty years ago at St. Matthias."

I hear packing crates being shoved around, beer can tops being popped, and, ugh, cheap cigars being lit.

"Hand me some of that sausage. Ole Effinger sure landed in a soft spot. The wife do not look so bad even now."

"She was younger then."

"So were we then."

And *I* was not even *here* then, so get on with it, fellas. Although it is interesting to realize that Mr. Matt's given name — which is Matthias, not Matthew — has a long Chi-Town history.

"What are we doin'," Lefty says, burping, "holding alley cats hostage?"

"The Vegas contacts are under a lot of pressure on this. Money's money. And I hear ole effing Effinger knew the key to where a lot of it is just lying there waiting to be claimed. Nothing on the Vegas end is coming up likely, not even that big underground safe that was found a few days ago. But a few months ago rotten little Cliffie made a trip back to Chicago just before the honchos nabbed him for a little waterboarding interrogation."

Lefty shudders. "I would have screamed like a girdle."

" 'Girl.' Screamed like a *girl*."

"They do not scream as good as they used to."

"That is because they are 'liberated.' Anyway, Effie gave them nothin' and then had the bad taste to croak. After-hours at a major Strip attraction, no less. The thinking in Vegas is he left the key to the stash up here with the ex-wife. Well, not ex-wife. Widow. Some folks still do not believe in divorce."

"Chicago is a very backward place, compared to Vegas."

"Right. The thinking in Vegas is Cliff's priest stepson going there to look him up gave the rat religion and he went to Chicago to leave the wife he left a pot of gold. Or the secret to finding it."

"Who went to Chicago? Cliff or the priest stepson?"

"It is the *ex*-priest stepson."

"The blond guy with the redhead?"

"Right."

"He did not dress much like a priest."

"None of them do these days. It is a marketing thing. Jeesh."

"I do not know if I want to mess with priests. They can call down all sorts of trouble on you.

I have never had one tackle me so hard like he did in the airport over this sissy cat carrier."

"*Ex*-priest, otherwise he would not be traveling with the redhead. Forget him. We have the carrier. We have the pussycat in it. We have the hostage. The thinking in Vegas now is we can shake up Cliff's Chicago connections, and get what he hid up here."

"Who is doing all this thinking in Vegas?" Lefty asks.

"The answer to that is above our pay grade."

"We have a pay grade?"

"No! It is just an expression. Now forget about who is behind this. Knowing that will get you a ride on a sinking ship. Do you want some easy dough?" Shifty eyes my carrier. "Who is gonna stop us now. Animal control?"

The mutual yuks echo off the concrete ceiling twenty feet above.

Lefty nods, finally appeased. "The Congressional crooks in Washington are eating into my Medicare coverage. I have a lot of work-related injuries. They are killing the middling class. Let us do it."

"So," says Shifty, "I will leave a message on the phone. Gawd, these little lit-up buttons do not always depress. It is depressin'." His dexterity on a smartphone keypad is like watching King Kong tap dancing on a piano keyboard.

"You do not have the victim's number on speed dial?" Lefty asks.

"These busted fingers cannot punch in all those little keys." Shifty (who cannot shift, it seems) grunts. "*Hmm.* No answer. They are still out. Good. I will leave a message to make them squirm."

He takes a deep breath, then coughs. Cigars will do that to you.

"Listen, folks. We got your damn cat. We do not like your damn cat. We will call every hour to see if you got what you know we want. We will chop off an inch of your damn cat's tail each time we call if you do not come across with the, uh, stuff we want. You know what we mean. Then we will start on the legs. So, uh, cough it up, and we will have an exchange where you can leave . . . er, what we want and collect what is left of your cat."

There is silence as Lefty shuts off the cell phone.

"That was not very professional," Shifty rebukes him.

"Whadda mean, 'professional'? We do not even know what the Vegas bunch wants. They have left us in the dark looking stupid."

I could point out that is not very hard, but hold my tongue in case they get an itch to chop it off in sections.

"And I do not know about all that cat-chopping you have committed us to. They have nasty, infected claws, you know. We could get rabies."

"I was just saying that. You gotta threaten the hostage, and not with something namby-pamby. You gonna eat the whole sausage roll?"

CHAPTER 19
TAIL END

Riding back from Sunday dinner in the Camry's backseat, Temple felt both well fed and well feted.

Apparently, she was too darn cute to be considered the femme fatale who stole Father Matt. She passed the religion test when she sweetly told Uncle Stach that she was considering three wedding ceremonies, his, hers, and theirs and that St. Stanislaus Cathedral near downtown was her first choice. The Old World architecture was breathtaking, glowing golden paintings and arches and vivid stained glass.

Matt had taken Temple, Mira, and Krys there for Mass that morning. Temple had attended Mass with him at Our Lady of Guadalupe in Las Vegas, but she'd been impressed to realize that a formal church wedding would bring Matt full circle in both his faith and his future.

Also, walking down that long impressive

aisle as a bride would be so British royalty. Her parents were extremely open-minded about sex and religion except for the first one when it pertained to their baby daughter. So the open-minded Unitarians would sop up the traditions and her mother would sop up her hankie because every mother of an only daughter really wants her daughter to have a white-gown pomp-and-ceremony wedding day.

A freeway had cut close to the cathedral, leveling the old Polish neighborhood. A statue of the New World's Our Lady of Guadalupe in her vivid blue cloak gleamed amid all the gold-flecked Old World icons of Madonna and Child. This must have been where Matt's parents had met, Temple thought, eyeing the tiers of flickering votive candles, although no one was talking about that.

So Temple wasn't surprised when they drove out into the suburbs to Uncle Stach and Aunt Wanda's house, which was filled with Zabinskis large and small. Nothing marred the Thanksgiving-festive dinner, starting with *barszcz,* beet soup. The whole family enjoyed spelling out their consonant-heavy words for Temple's benefit, and Krys was particularly articulate on intoning the full form of her name, *K-r-y-s-t-y-n-a.*

Matt leaned near to tell Temple that Krys had used to "hate" her Old World name spelling.

Every kind and color of kielbasa were available, sausages colored from beige to yam golden to oxblood red brown. Given the large contingent of cousins both older and younger than Matt, there were various meats from breaded pork to Americanized turkey with giblets and gravy, boiled potatoes and noodles and lots of cream and poppy seed pastries for dessert, along with wine.

The long after-dinner recovery time showcased Krys's slow burn at Temple's easy adoption by her demanding family. She flirted furiously with Matt's younger male cousins, of which he had enough to make up a new Fontana brothers gang. She drank way too much beer. And she declined driving home with them at 6 P.M., saying she was having too good a time. She would be along later. Maybe.

"Krys," Mira had rebuked her. Matt just smiled and escorted Mira and Temple out the front door.

"She's a big girl," Matt told his mother on the way to the car.

"I never knew she was so silly."

"She's what . . . just past twenty, Mom? A

good age to still be silly. Anyway, I thought the afternoon went well. Not the usual awkwardness about my decision."

"Or me," Mira agreed.

"We're a triple threat," Temple said, linking arms between them and thinking how odd it was that people would let their nearest and dearest become outcasts, to any degree.

Then she thought how Max's parents and aunt and uncle couldn't handle his survival when his cousin Sean had been killed, driving Max away into the itinerant life of a magician-cum-counterterrorist at an age when he should have been entering college.

Her own family had never "approved of" her move to Vegas with Max. Or of Max.

As Matt installed his mother in the front seat, Temple claimed the back, then sat in the middle and leaned forward to chat with them both, relieved to have passed the not-Polish, not-Catholic test. Mira was as happy and relaxed as Temple had yet seen her. Maybe it was the two glasses of dinner wine.

Krys and her glowering postadolescent pout had bonded them. All three were over and done with familial disapproval.

They were still laughing and joking about the *golonka,* pork knuckles, Uncle Stach had teased Temple about refusing to eat when they entered the apartment.

"Sit on the sofa," Mira said. "I have some Madeira Krys didn't know about, given to me by the restaurant long ago. I would like to make a private toast to the engaged couple."

Matt pulled Temple down beside him on the sofa for a not-so-quick kiss while his mother bustled away. He mouthed at Temple, "*Mo-ther?* A third glass of wine in one day? *Ma-deir-a* in her cupboard?" he whispered.

Mira returned, three tiny cut-crystal stemmed glasses fanned expertly in one hand and the labeled bottle in the other. Breathlessly, she put the pieces on the coffee table and poured the rich amber liqueur, making the glass bowls into cut-topaz jewels.

Matt kept his arm around Temple's shoulders as Mira raised her glass. Temple's toes curled in her shoes. Being "family" so fast felt amazing. She missed her own. *Next.*

"To my wonderful son and the perfect partner he has found for his new life. *Na zdrowie.*"

Temple eyed Matt, who toasted her. "To your health."

"*Na zdrowie,*" Temple repeated with a lift of her glass, echoing the accent.

"Perfect," Mira said, beaming. "Like a

Polish girl."

She rose to return the bottle to the kitchen. Matt's mother apparently went light on alcohol, probably because of Effinger, Temple supposed.

Mira had stopped in midpace.

Matt noticed and looked beyond her. The wall phone in the kitchen was blinking red. "You have a message, Mom. It's okay. Take it. Temple and I will just make out on the couch."

"Matt." Mira turned on him in admonition, but she was blushing. "I won't take it now and desert my guests."

Matt frowned. "Krys was pretty pi . . . perturbed. Better check."

Still Mira hesitated.

Temple rolled her eyes at Matt. This might be the rebuffed swain calling. Mira didn't want them to hear.

"Just check it, Mom," he said. "We'll go into the dining room and page through the family album again, now that Temple has met so many of us."

They did as he suggested, keeping their voices hushed.

"She's in a horrible position, Matt," Temple whispered. "The soap operas are all going off the air, but your mother, after trying to live as low-profile a life as possible

169

for years, is cast by fate in a doozy, caught between two brothers." Her eye fixed on a tall young guy early in the album. "Is that Uncle Stach? Life certainly was broadening for him."

"All that beer and sausage. Strange, I don't care for the ethnic menu."

"You didn't grow up on it."

"No," he said, turning serious. "I never developed a taste for Polish conviviality." He and his mom had always been on the fringe, awkward reminders of the family's inability to deal with real life.

A cry from the kitchen followed by something hitting the floor made them jump up in tandem, the album slapping shut on Uncle Stach and Aunt Wanda and their brood.

It took only steps to reach Mira. She was standing stricken beside the telephone, the receiver dangling on its curlicued cord at her feet.

Matt swooped on it and straightened, putting the receiver to his ear, then skewing it sideways so Temple could stand on her toes to hear the last bit of the message. A brusque cold male voice was saying . . .

"— chop off his tail inch by inch."

CHAPTER 20
LEFTY BEHIND

Ah, Sweet Home à la Obama.

I am still in Chicago. I am still in stir.

Beer tops pop again. Cigars reek. I peer squinty-eyed out the black mesh at the end of my carrier. The cigar smoke is rising up from the beer cans upon which the stogies are perched while my captors chow down.

I must say that Chicago sausage is some of the most highly spiced and aromatic I have ever sniffed, no doubt because so many Poles, Germans, Czechs, and other Eastern European folks settled here.

"What was that?" Shifty stirs and lowers a foot from the crate to the filthy floor. "Is that damn cat growling?"

"Let it growl. We can always cut off its tongue."

Actually, it is my ungovernable stomach growling and if the boys get in a position to do my innards violence, it will already all be over for Midnight Louie.

I have had enough of this nonsense.

I know what I came to find out. Effinger died in Vegas with a certain valuable something or piece of knowledge in his possession and a year later it is still missing, yet so desired that the Vegas outfit, whoever they are, are digging into his past to locate its hiding place.

Luckily, these boys have very little muscle tone and dumped my carrier with the zippered opening facing away from their cozy little campground. My paws punch the side where the zipper closes, forcing it open an inch or two. Then I lift my whiskered lips in "silent snarl" position and tilt my head so my right fang is bared and ready for action.

It takes a few "casts," as in fishing, but I am a master koisnagger. I finally push the fang tip through that nice little hole on every zipper tag. No doubt it is for the ladies to put a gizmo through if they are seeking to do or undo a back zipper solo. Handy dudes are not always handy, you know.

Now I jerk my head up in stages, easing the zipper open bit by bit. Yes, it is tedious work, but the cause of freedom can never be taken for granted.

As my nose lifts higher and higher, the odors of sausage and cigar smoke engage in an almost unendurable duel in my olfactory senses. I crave the one and abhor the other and must also resist a strange urge to sneeze. . . .

The carrier end finally falls away like a . . . sausage casing. After a last glance at my captors snoozing off after their stomach-stuffing feats, I spurt into the cavernous space filled with abandoned hulks of factory equipment casting massive shadows.

Your ordinary hostage might be intimidated by the iron bars on the high windows and the small broken-down entrance on the far side of my captors.

However, I have allies — or shills, if you will — everywhere, especially in down-and-dirty presumably empty places and locales.

I climb a shaky tower of empty crates until a bit of daylight shows through the broken chicken-wire backed glass. Once elevated, I hiss softly through the bars an irresistible code word.

Sssausssage. Fresssh Polissssh ssssauss-sage, kielbasa alive, alive-o.

How sweet it is to have a native secret language. I do not wait for my troops to arrive, but scamper back down to the concrete floor, the crates now crashing and scattering from my uncontrolled weight and pace.

The clatter brings Shifty and Lefty awake. They blink and look up, perhaps searching for Santa. I rocket right toward and under Shifty's propped-up legs, slashing as I go.

"*Arghhh!*" As he falls over sideways he reaches for a stabilizing crate, but they are all shaky. I see the comet of a falling lit cigar. "My eye!" he shouts. "It is burning. I am blinded."

Lefty swipes an arc of cheap beer at his pal's face, leaving Shifty's head dripping, one eye closed and the other blinking out beer.

Meanwhile I jump onto a crate and get a sausage round down and rolling toward the entry point just as a flood of cats comes bounding through.

"Rats!" Shifty cries, turning around to see with his one eye. "We are being attacked by rats."

Shifty has pulled the pocketknife from his pants.

"That is all you have for a shiv?" Lefty demands. "It is not big enough to chop off a rat's tail and now they are all coming for us."

I turn and make for the piled crates rimming the space, racing up them in plain sight. If you have both eyes.

"That cursed cat," Lefty yells. "Get him!"

"Why bother?" Shifty yells back, quite rationally. Now that they have phoned in their threat, my well-being is moot.

"He has stolen our sausages."

Enraged, Lefty charges toward the decrepit

crating even as I dig in my taloned hind claws to dislodge a particularly large one with a great white shark's jaw-worth of exposed four-inch sixteen-penny nails, all rusted and corroded and sharp as a giant serpent's business fang.

I kick it right into the oncoming would-be chopper.

He trips on a shattered piece of crating, lifts his arms to protect himself from the handy cat's version of a spiked Iron Maiden torture device closing on him, screams and flails into embracing the inevitable, and falls over forward right on it.

Meanwhile, Shifty, stumbling madly to escape the "rats," has knocked himself into a crate, spilling open beer cans and the second cigar, so his pant legs are now catching fire and his upper torso is beer-soaked.

I turn. The chaos is complete. I eye the one untouched item, an island of calm integrity, sadly. My Miss Temple was so proud of her leopard-pattern carrier. Now it is mere salvage.

The locals surround me.

"You are the dude who cried 'sausage'? What do you want for them?"

"They are all yours, boys and girls. All I need is to be pointed toward a ride to the near northwest side."

"You are not from around here. Which ward is your turf?"

I doubt these homeless street types have ever shared a sofa with a human, much less a Las Vegas condo. And I do know Chicago is divided into political "wards."

"My line stems from Ma Barker of the Vegas turf."

Sagacious whiskery nods all round.

"Yeah, but where do you reside here?" a lean and hungry yellow-stripe Tom asks.

"The Palmer House Hilton Hotel."

Tommy shoots off his mouth. "You are not a Gold Coast Michigan Avenue swell, fella."

I nod at the abandoned carrier. "Eye my personal transport and weep. Never mind the ride advice. I will catch my own."

I stalk out onto the street, looking for the golden glint from a pimpmobile, preferably an Eldorado. That will get me to the nearest high-end lucrative corner for some set-upon hookers eager to help out a fellow street denizen, and then I can catch less glitzy transport. I tell you, lore has it half-right. A fur coat will always win over the ladies . . . especially if you are a dude in need wearing it.

Vegas teaches a cool cat more ways of the world than Chicago ever thought of.

CHAPTER 21
PAST TAX DUE

"Louie," Temple intoned mournfully.

And stared in a daze at the checkered tablecloth.

They'd all sunk onto the kitchen table chairs as Matt had replayed the message, twice, stopping before the tail part. No one needed to hear that again.

"The airport," Temple said. "I wasn't mistaken for a rich witch. It wasn't an attempted jewel robbery. They were after Louie as a hostage. It's all my fault. I didn't think beyond what the security guard thought."

"Who did?" Matt's warm hands squeezed her cold fists. "How would these creeps even know Midnight Louie was along?"

"It's my fault," Mira said firmly. "It's just that I was . . . am . . . so easily bulled when it comes to Clifford. I've wished so much for so long he had never existed, which is a sin, I know, Matt." Her anxious glance skittered off his concerned expression.

"It's human, Mom. I wished the same. I was even in a position to end his existence."

"Matt!"

"It's not what we think. It's what we do."

"Cliff said he'd found you," Mira answered, confused. "Snickered about it. That made me so angry."

"No. I tracked *him*. I found *him*. He was a petty criminal around Vegas. And when he died, it was a lot worse than anything I could have contemplated doing."

She put her hands to her ears. "I don't want to hear anything more about that miserable creature. I never wanted to see him again. And when he came here —"

"He came here?"

Temple was starting to think beyond the blame game, but she didn't dare interject anything into the mother — son dialogue.

"Months ago." Mira pushed her hands into her freshly done hair, ruining it. "He wanted to know where I'd stored things from the two-flat when I'd sold it and moved out. There was one of those fireproof file boxes. I'd looked through, and it was mostly tax forms. He did all that, probably lied, probably got tax refunds I didn't know about. I always let him have the money because he'd leave for a while then, and leave us alone."

Temple closed her eyes and wished she could close her ears. It ached to hear so much ingrained misery. She could only imagine how Matt felt to revisit his mother's awful marriage through adult eyes. No wonder he'd gone into the priesthood straight from high school. He would probably have murdered Effinger otherwise.

"Mom, what about the file safe?"

"The tax returns? I was afraid the IRS . . . I kept it. It's stored in the basement."

"So Effinger took it a few months ago?"

"No. He just wanted to make sure I had it. He said not to touch it." She winced bitterly. "I didn't want to. He said to keep it . . . warm . . . for him," she spat out. "I had a big knife in the kitchen block."

Temple's eyes went to the countertop, as did Matt. Sure enough, a knife block.

"I thought . . . ," Mira said. "But I didn't want him to have the satisfaction of knowing he'd driven me to do wrong. Now do you see, Matt, why I can't marry anyone? I thought I could, but I have too much to hide, too much to hate about myself."

During the extended pause, Temple saw Matt taking a long look at his mother. "Yeah. You're right. You can't love anyone if you hate yourself. You can't forgive anyone if you don't forgive yourself."

Tough love.

"Anyone?" Her voice trembled.

"Anyone." He was adamant.

Mira swallowed, digesting the back draft of her emotional meltdown, finally listening. "That can't come overnight."

"No. But it can start right here, right now. It has to, Mom. We can't go on otherwise."

She sighed, her shoulders straightening. "If someone wants what's in that file safe, I can give it up."

"First," Matt said, "we'll look at what's in it. Temple and I."

Mira's look of panicked appeal at Temple made it hard to insist she really had to see the contents. But it was her cat, her case. She did.

"Possibly fraudulent tax returns might seem scary," Temple said. "So is what those thugs called to say about my cat. If someone wants what Cliff Effinger had, considering he was probably killed by the mob, we'll all be a lot better off knowing where and what it is."

CHAPTER 22
WE CALL THE WIND MARIAH

Rafi Nadir's palms were sweating.

He'd been street-tested in East L.A. and Watts. He could handle facing down a gun barrel. He'd been among a detail that had subdued some King Kong on angel dust without going all Rodney King on the guy. He'd patted down a transsexual hooker who was armed, drunk, disorderly, and threatening to cut off all working parts in the vicinity, his, hers, and theirs.

But he'd never had to call Carmen Molina and ask if she'd allow him to take her and their daughter out to eat. Maybe Kinsella was right. He should start solo with Molina and work into "them." He couldn't decide which tactic would make his ex-significant other more suspicious.

He finally touched the Contact bar on his cell phone, bracing his feet on the hassock in his apartment and preparing to sound confident and relaxed.

"Yes?"

Jeez, she sounded irritated already, and he was sure his home number wasn't on her cell phone.

"It's Rafi." At least he had a distinctive name. There'd be no confusion. Not that she'd had many men but cops calling her at home, or calling on her, just that Columbo clone, Detective Alch.

"I can see that," she said.

So she did have his number. In the right way. Before he could segue into a casual approach, she continued.

"I'm glad you called."

What?

"Do you know what your encouraging Mariah's *American Idol* ambitions has done now?"

"I know kids need encouragement and ambitions, but I didn't okay her running off to chase them."

"Oh, Mariah hasn't run off."

Good. Mariah "running away" from home to enter another reality-TV teen talent show had led to exposing Matt Devine and Temple Barr to a deranged killer.

"Or rather," Molina went on, "she's run off only at the mouth. She used her friend's karaoke machine to record a song she wrote and mount it on YouTube."

182

"YouTube? Really? What's the song called?"

Pause. "Bleu Doll-ya."

"Isn't that the name of the place you used to sing sometimes?"

"I still could."

"The YouTube site isn't coming up on my iPhone. Just the local nightclub."

"Mariah's version is spelled *B-l-e-u D-o-l-l-y-a.*"

"Bleu as in the cheese?"

"As in the French."

"I knew that, Carmen. It's French cheese. Yeah. Here it is."

"Cheese as in cheesy," Molina grumbled.

"Let's see. Production values are nil . . . tween friend's bedroom. Standard laptop camera and mic, but the song is kinda catchy."

"Like the measles."

"We need to discuss this new wrinkle in person. Maybe we can grab a bite." He got inspired. "At the Blue Dahlia, say."

"That's more than 'grabbing a bite.' "

"So who says you don't deserve a quiet dinner out? And I hear the band is good. Where's Mariah now?"

"Grounded."

"You have a handy watchdog for her, right? Being you're on call."

"A couple live in the neighborhood. I could check. I'm not sure I'm —"

"Ready to go out on short notice? You never wore much makeup. Didn't need it."

"Not ready to see you in a social setting."

"Oh, come on. I helped out on that last case, didn't I? And we have a big something in common to discuss."

"Apparently *you're* primed to do the town since you got that Oasis assistant security chief job."

The comment was out of left field and a bit catty for Molina, but Rafi shrugged it off. "I'll be by in half an hour, okay?"

Another pause. "Angela is off today. I saw her working in her yard when I got home."

"Done deal." His thumb ended the call before she could change her mind.

He ran the YouTube song again with the sound higher. The kid had perfect pitch and decent pipes, and she was smart enough not to cover copyrighted songs. Lyrics and melody were not there. She needed to study her mother's songbook, get some classic underpinnings.

He remained slouching on his secondhand couch, thinking.

Molina was already regretting her decision. She was glad Mariah was staying in her

184

room while her mother was bumbling around her own bedroom, hunting up non-work clothes that looked good enough for more than kicking around on errands.

She ended up recycling Dirty Larry odds and ends, like the dressy top she wore to Mariah's performance at the *Teen Queen* reality TV show and the side-studded jeggings and . . . she paused in casing her selection of low-heeled boots, loafers, and moccasins on the floor of her closet. There were those kitten-heeled electric-blue pumps Temple Barr had nagged her into getting, on sale, when they were shopping for undercover clothes for Zoe Chloe Ozone and Mariah for that same show.

She got on her knees to pat down the dark at the back of her closet until she dragged them out. She'd never worn them, needing to minimize her five-foot-eleven height. Tonight . . . let Rafi stretch his spine a little, kinda like on the medieval rack. She was not kowtowing to male insecurity with him.

"You look nice," Angela said when she arrived to house-sit and Molina opened the door, sounding too surprised and then looking dismayed.

The twenty-something cop needed to master noncommittal demeanor. And not insulting her superiors. Not *too* nice, Molina hoped. So clever of Rafi to invite her to the Blue Dahlia, her sometimes singing venue. She had an image to uphold with the management there even when she wasn't appearing as the chanteuse "Carmen."

Mariah had finally learned about her mother's hidden hobby and occasional gigs there. That didn't help matters either. Molina had plenty more reason to carp at Rafi.

She slipped out of the house before his car arrived to avoid inconvenient introductions, and slid into the front passenger seat as soon as it did.

"I need to make an early evening of it," she warned.

His cursory glance was as noncommittal as Angela's wasn't. "You've worked there; we should get fast service."

"I'm not sure what you want."

"Neither am I, besides the obvious."

She didn't want to put Mariah's name on the table until they were seated at a dinner table masquerading as a bargaining table. Meanwhile, she should keep things pleasant.

"How's the Oasis job going?"

"Good. The head security guy is leaving and I'm up for the slot."

"Already? That's a suit-coat job." She eyed

his black denim jeans and the Bob Seger screaming eagle graphic T-shirt worn under a black linen blazer.

"Yeah, like a detective," he agreed.

"How'd you get the major hotel-casino gig, anyway?"

"A well-connected friend gave me a rave review."

"A friend? Here in Vegas?"

"Not anymore."

She saw his jaw tighten. Had to be a bruising backstory there. Rafi knew how not to give away emotions, but that had failed him for just a moment. Interesting.

They kept silent the rest of the way. Not delving into cherished old misunderstandings made conversation harder. Recriminations come easy, Molina mused, regretting she'd imploded when she discovered Mariah's YouTube adventure.

She exited the car as soon as it was in Park and headed for the club's entrance. Rafi and the jingle of his car keys being pocketed caught up with her just outside.

"Classy joint," he commented.

"A contradiction in terms." She stopped to take in the blue-and-magenta blossom of neon sign shining down on them and smiled. "But I'd forgotten. It is indeed a classy place."

Rafi had reservations. Nancy, the sixtyish hostess, showed them to a fringe table with a good view of the band.

"I've never actually dined here," Molina said after recovering from the shock of Rafi offhandedly holding her chair out. He was on seriously good behavior and by the time they were both seated it seemed natural.

"Then you can't recommend anything on the menu." He was studying it, not her.

"Nope." She nodded and smiled at Rick, Dave, and Morris making cool jazz very hot on the small, one-step-up stage. "Eat at your own risk." She skimmed the menu, recalling eyeing a very different bill of fare with Max Kinsella the other day. She reconsidered Rafi. Another dark-haired guy, swarthier though. She'd always been attracted to blonds, like Matt Devine, when she admitted to such impulses.

"We go dutch," she said at the same time Rafi said, "I'll get the check."

The hovering waiter retreated discreetly.

"Let me play the guy, Carmen," Rafi said.

She felt her cheeks flush, then reached for her water glass and toasted him. "You definitely are entitled." Shock was a good negotiation tactic. "I was panicked and paranoid all those years ago and didn't give you a fair trial. You know cops. We think we've seen it all, solved it all. That can foster jumping to wrong conclusions."

"Yeah. Me too." He nodded to the waiter, who swept back toward the table with genial efficiency.

"A white wine spritzer," Molina said.

"A spritzer?" Rafi gave her a look. "Kahlúa on ice." As the guy exited, he leaned in and asked, "Watered down wine? Isn't that . . . girly for you? Don't you trust yourself? Or me?"

"Actually, I upgraded. I'm usually a beer drinker."

"Really. That's changed. A lot's changed."

She let that one lie.

Rafi had taken out his smartphone and was fiddling with it. She heard the tinny buzz of a musical ring tone. Or something. *Oh, no!* Mariah's silly YouTube upload. She recognized the voice. Rafi turned the phone's bright, sharp image surface for her to view.

"Yes, I know my kid has made a fool of herself for all to see. . . ."

Oh. This wasn't Mariah. This was an older girl with a not-too-bad contralto, like Lady Gaga before everyone went gaga. Molina was forced to sit on her expletives while the waiter delivered their drinks with a pleased flourish, hers pallid, his coffee dark.

She leaned across the table, hearing the accusing hiss in her voice only after she'd whispered, "That's *me*!" She straightened up and swigged from her wineglass like a sailor. "Where'd you get that film?"

He smiled nostalgically at the sharp image on his smartphone. "I had old camcorder footage of when you and I were working on your act in L.A. I played around with some home computer sound and film programs and made it into an MP3 file."

"And empty what — ?"

"A music file. Mariah's got your voice."

"That's a dirty trick you played on me."

"Talent is not a 'dirty trick,' Carmen. It's a gift. People with talent need to use it, grow it."

"She'll be ridiculed online. 'The world is mean and man uncouth,' Rafi, even more than in our day. Sure, she can put herself out there, but everyone with a user pseudonym and password is a critic and an insensitive critic these days. She could get bullied at school. Look at that cheesy glitter eye makeup, the stuffed toys and vampire boys posters in the background of her friend's bedroom. She's Miss Hello Kitty in the headlights, damn it!"

"You're right." He sat back. "It's always a risk to be creative. Kids today can be Justin

190

Bieber or Amy Winehouse, hit or sad, sad miss. That's why you . . . we . . . need to manage this stage Mariah's going through. It might fade away like morning dew in someplace a lot wetter than here. Or she might have shot at a career."

"Is this why you asked me to dinner tonight? To lure me into your schemes, to get close to Mariah by turning her into a . . . an online *product*?"

"No. I wanted to convince you to let me into Mariah's life, not as her father, just to get to know her, to see that she knows and maybe likes or needs me. That YouTube piece showed me that Mariah does need me, as an advocate, as I was for you. That's right, Carmen Regina, I got you out of your buttoned-down older-bastard-sister, responsible-for-everything girl pursuing some of your dreams but quashing others, in your own stepfamily. You know you'd not be singing today if it hadn't been for me."

She sat still, fingers twined around the cool stem of her glass, slowing her breathing to a crawl. She'd always had killer breath control. "I'm not singing today."

"Not good, Carmen. You needed that outlet. It's been months."

She looked up, burning. How dare he check into her off-hours?

"I asked the management, yeah. 'When's that great torch singer performing again?' I asked. The answer? We. Don't. Know. You had a dream gig here. You could come in when you felt like it, when you had to burn off the pressure of being responsible for a kid and a house and every last civilian on the mean streets of Las Vegas. And you shut it off and shut it down. Why?"

"Work got intense."

"Your after-hours, under-the-table investigations got intense, you mean."

She held her tongue.

"You always were by the book, Carmen. We fought about that even in L.A. I'm no saint, never was, but I come here and find out you're playing two iffy guys against each other, having them investigate each other. And me. What's the matter? You don't trust men, right? Especially men you're attracted to."

She drew on her patented laser-paralyzing, icy-hot blue glare. Worked on the job. "You sure you want to rattle my cage this badly, Rafi? Isn't there a little something you want from me?"

"A little support and humanity would be nice. I'm sure Mariah would second me on that at the moment."

Her head snapped back, her rarely worn,

thin hoop earrings striking her neck. She'd trained herself to be impassive or aggressive, as called for by her job. That wasn't working here, with Rafi, and it was no longer working at home, with Mariah. Her fingers twined around the other hand, clenched in a fist. It was a prayerful gesture, she realized, maybe even pleading.

"Give me time."

"Thirteen years out of my daughter's life is way more than enough 'time.' I *will* post *your* 'debut' on YouTube if you don't ease up on Mariah."

"That's despicable."

"Maybe that's what you need to drive us both to where we need to be, Mariah and me."

"All right," she said, drawing a deep breath.

" 'All right,' what?"

Rafi's wary suspicion had insulted her at first, and then it had made her very, very sorry. For the first time she could take out and turn over and touch her regret for abandoning him on such an emotional impulse. Maybe the hormonal earthquakes of being unexpectedly pregnant had something . . . a lot . . . to do with it.

"It's not a bad idea," she said, stunned to hear herself sound so calm. "Instead of reading Mariah the riot act on her *American Idol* dreams, I'll let her pursue them. Within limits." Fierce again. "She . . . met you at the reality TV teen competition. I'll let you, will suggest, you'll work with her on her . . . aspirations. Within limits."

"Okay." He was smiling at her, she didn't understand why, after all the empty years, but it made him look handsome and even kind. "Can I ask — within limits — if you'll stand up and sing with the band tonight? Just a casual number. They've been glancing our way every sixty seconds. They miss you."

She gave them another regretful glance. So much had been expendable in her life.

"And Carmen," he said as she rose. "I'd suggest you start working up that oldie, 'Begin the Beguine.' That would get this place on the map."

"And me?"

"On YouTube for sure."

He laughed as she made a face and walked toward the guys in the band.

They were grinning like idiots and she had missed them and the music so much, she could scream. She guessed she'd sing instead.

CHAPTER 23
THE SECOND COMING

Planning a triumphal return is where I excel, particularly when it is my own.

I have no doubt that consternation must be running amok, particularly on my Miss Temple's part, when the residents and visitors to the apartment in Pulaski Park discover I am not merely hiding out in an insanely clever spot no human could discern with the naked eye or nose, but that I am totally gone . . . kit, caboodle, and carrier.

Knowing what dismay my kidnappers caused my nearest and dearest led me to annihilate them without mercy and to literally "nail" them. Street smarts now have led me into the proper neighborhood. Finding the exact address is no problem, since I am an . . . ahem . . . eidetic-savant.

Now, if Miss Midnight Louise were here, she would jump on that assertion, as well as my back. No, I did not mean "*idiot*-savant." That is a human stunted on all sorts of everyday knowledge but a genius in one particular area, usually music or mathematics. This eidetic-savant just never forgets a thing, especially my own scent and trail.

Anyone who knows me also knows that I do not much do mathematics past the number of fighting shivs on each foot. As for music, my nocturnal jazz riffs are as well known among the furred contingent of cultural cognoscenti as are the classic stylings of the singer known as Carmen at Vegas's Blue Dahlia nightclub. Let us just say that crime-solving and cater-wauling make good partners.

Meanwhile, I am marooned in Chicago, on the outside looking in.

My next trick is to enter this alien apartment building and get to the appropriate floor.

Were I in Las Vegas, I could accomplish my surprise return in a minute flat, since the round and layered Circle Ritz building is a piece of cake to scale and infiltrate. Here, not so much. I stroll around the brick exterior. The rear Dumpsters are not appetizing as a stepping-off place for a second-story assault. I have nothing against Dumpsters. They are to be admired for daily serving the homeless as well as the discriminating customer in search of a rare tidbit accidentally consigned to the scrap heap.

However, this is Chicago, folks. Here you

find a trend to corned beef and cabbage, baked beans and bacon, sausage and dumplings, and other odiferous, gassy foods.

I am maybe the returning prodigal son; however, I do not really want the fatted calf, but only 99 percent lean. I decide that the velvet glove rather than the hooded claw is needed for the last leg of my epic journey.

So I groom my always elegant formal black suit to satin perfection, tame my prone-to-be-bushy eyebrows and whiskers with a patina of saliva, and go to sit patiently by the front entrance. This place is not high-hat enough to have a doorman, so I am looking for a female of the species. They have an inborn soft spot for dudes of my sort.

Luckily, in Chicago, a lot of them live in apartments.

"Well, well. You are a sleek, handsome fellah."

When will men learn the lure of meticulous grooming? Too late. I am happy to fill the gap. Also, big tip here: The ladies adore soft furry ankle rubs. If you cannot afford to bestow faux fur-lined boots on your Chicago ladylove, grow a mustache and use fabric softener on it.

My figure-eight moves around this particular lady's calves escort her to the elevator doors, never impeding her footsteps.

"Did you get left out of your home somehow?

You are in far too fine condition to be a stray."

Yes, frequent fishing expeditions in the Crystal Phoenix koi pond, marathons down the Las Vegas Strip avoiding overbuilt guard dogs, bouts of rappelling down the handy palm tree at the Circle Ritz. All this is fine "conditioning."

I slip through the open elevator door with her. Her finger pauses over a floor button high above my head. "But where do you belong? I do not know every pet owner in the building."

Hmm. I will have to come up with a Stupid Pet Trick to communicate with a stranger. What would David Letterman do . . . or applaud? I turn around. Once. Twice. Then sit and cock my head like Fido.

"Two? Floor two?"

I circle again, twice more.

"Four."

Two more circles add up to . . .

"Six? Oh, pussycat, I must get off at five. I cannot send you up all alone in the elevator car. Who knows what might happen to you?"

Not boredom in just one floor.

I have imparted my message. I hold my place and sit tight. She will either send me on to floor six, or not.

Her forefinger hits a button and I wait to see what she has decided. Which floor she has selected is a mystery to me. If she insists on bringing me to her own place, I will do the gigolo bit, dine enthusiastically, pretend to be perfectly enamored, and sneak out first thing in the morning never to be seen again.

"Here we are. Floor six. I hope you were not simply annoyed by vermin when you kept turning around."

I step out without commenting on that slur and sniff along the hallway until I have reached the right door. How do I know it is the right door? I always leave a hint of mint on every exit wherever I am likely to be locked in. We of the superior breed may not be as finely tuned for following scent trails as the ordinary dog, say, but we are adept at leaving our extraordinarily individual colognes on sur-faces.

My new escort pauses to shake her head, then knock.

I wait. I know the small round fish-eye hole in the door will allow inspection of my compan-ion. She strikes me as the ideal pickup: a totally respectable lady of a certain age.

The door opens.

"Is this yours?" my companion asks.

It takes a moment for Miss Krys to interpret the woman's hand gesture and look down.

Her eyes and mouth both make cute *O*'s of surprise.

Her head turns over her shoulder as she

broadcasts to those within. "Call off the dogs and the police. That damn cat is back from the dead."

I am not displeased by my dramatic introduction, but I am sure that poor lady at the door has been badly shaken.

CHAPTER 24
A TALE UNTOLD

Temple had never before had a full-house audience for eating crow in her career as a public relations specialist.

She did now. Matt and his mother were seated at the small kitchen table, rapt with unspent tension. First the Effinger revelations, then this. Louie had lofted atop the kitchen counter to suddenly lick at a twitchy shoulder blade when he wasn't staring implacably at Temple.

His long tail dangled over the counter side, swinging back and forth, untouched by anything but his grooming tongue when he occasionally swung it up as if to reassure that it was all there, every last black hair.

Temple clutched the old-fashioned kitchen wall-phone receiver in both hands, back-pedaling while her audience eavesdropped on a desperate monologue.

"No, it was not a kidnapping. Well, technically, yes. I mean, no! No, it was not a 'catnapping.' The cat is back and is fine. A neighbor lady returned him. It was a prank call. Not mine to the police! The call to *us* about the cat being kidnapped was a prank call.

"Yes, 'malicious mischief' would describe the incident." Temple nodded and sent a relieved glance at her audience.

"Is the cat . . . licensed, by the way? Ah, not here. He's visiting from out of town. What kind of cat visits? He's, ah, he's worked as a commercial cat. TV commercials. Yes, you could say he is valuable and that is why I, we, were so concerned. Yes, I do understand that legally a pet is considered property and can only be worth a small amount of money. Oh. I might get something in civil court.

"But that's not necessary now, Officer. He's back and all right.

"No, sir, there's no way to identify *what* kids may have called. They were older kids. They sounded very serious. We're all mostly visitors here, and we're most impressed by the Chicago PD's sharp response to small cases as well as large ones. I'm sorry we've been a bother, but this *is* Chicago. I'm sure another call for a crime — or three — in progress has already come in that is right on the dispatched officer's way.

"Oh."

Temple eyed the others and nodded, gratefully, at the phone. "Thank you. No, he's not the yellow-striped one. No, not the fancy fluffy white one. Black hair, green eyes, as my first call mentioned."

Temple finally hung up and stared back at Louie. "We're off the hook with the cops, but how'd you escape the crooks?"

Louie wasn't talking. He jumped off the counter, flourishing his untampered-with tail behind him.

"Not a hair out of place," Matt commented. "*We* might succumb to mass apoplexy but Midnight Louie rocks on."

That made his mother laugh ruefully. "I hope his opinion of Chicago after this incident doesn't change your mind about considering moving back."

Temple rejoined them at the table, which was covered with old papers of no apparent value from the fireproof file box.

"Where's Krys been since Louie got back?" she asked.

"In her room." Mira watched Matt rise, retrieve the wine bottle Krys had gone out to buy the previous night, and take the dry glasses from the dish drainer. He handed them around, filled again.

Mira shrugged. "Krys is always on some

'device' or other, cruising the Internet, working on her Web site. She's a mature girl in some ways and in some ways —"

"Not," Temple said. She sipped from her wineglass. "I suppose we'll never know what happened to Louie, or his carrier."

"Adios, carrier," Matt said with a toasting gesture. "Small loss, unlike Louie. I wonder if it's a good idea to call the police off. Those phone threats meant business."

"It's especially disturbing that the creeps knew we and Louie were here," Temple agreed. "There must be something explosive in these papers."

"That would be silly." Mira flicked her nails at the yellowed array of paper. "Except for the first manila folder with official documents in it — Cliff's grade school report cards, high school graduation certificate, and driver's test results, things his late mother must have kept, poor woman — it's all tax returns, as I feared."

"What about the high school yearbook?" Temple flipped through the worn booklet, attracted to the vintage hair and clothes on the cover. Dorky. Compared to now, teens dressed like forty-year-olds.

Yellowed newspaper clippings thrust between the pages memorialized meaningless athletic games and the usual horrific teen-driver car crash that seemed to plague every graduating class, even today.

Matt pulled the book toward him. "Somebody who died, maybe? Could that have been significant to Effinger?" He pulled out a couple tattered pages covered with crude doodles and cartoons.

"That's nothing extreme," Temple noted. "Just the usual superhero comic sketches along with endless outlines of cars guys in my high school class drew. What did you draw?" she asked Matt.

"I don't know. Jet planes and angel wings."

"Escape," his mother said, pretty perceptively.

Mira was threatening to get teary, so Temple jumped in with a comment. "Technological and spiritual. That's our media guy, Mr. Midnight." She shuffled through the high school yearbook again. "These sketches aren't bad. Captain Marvel fighting off the octopus is pretty anatomically correct. I mean muscle-wise."

"Why would Captain Marvel fight off an octopus? That would be Aquaman."

Temple was amused to see Matt grabbing the page and turning it his way to study the raw pencil sketches. She exchanged a knowing "boys will be boys" look with Mira.

Matt was frowning even more once he had

the sketch right side up.

"This is . . . this is *traced.* It's a copy of that classical sculpture in the Vatican collection."

Mira was astounded to the point of laughter. "Clifford? Drawing a classical sculpture in high school? Matt, maybe he was just a regular boy once, but he got caught up in the gangs once he got out. He concentrated on dressing sharp and getting jobs he could hang out on street corners to do."

"You married him graduation summer," Matt reminded her, and himself. "Maybe you saw the boy who drew."

"I was one of 'those girls' who graduated with whispers, not hope and celebration. Clifford didn't seem so bad at first. No one else would have me."

Temple looked down, finding her fingers smoothing the slick cover of the old yearbook. The same whispers haunted her high school graduating class. *This girl. That condition.* And then she *vanished.* It never ended. Odd about the Vatican preserving all those old Greek and Roman statues, most naked and anatomically correct, and all revived in the age of Michelangelo. Comic book supermen were modeled on those muscular ancient gods and heroes. . . .

Temple grabbed the sketch Matt was

regarding with an expression half puzzled and half repulsed.

"I know what statue you're thinking of," she told him. "It was the man who angered the gods and they sent a sea serpent to kill him and his sons. It's an amazing evocation of sheer human struggle and agony . . . and it's also — wait for it — very similar to the man fighting a serpent constellation that was just in the news recently."

"Serpent. Constellation?" Mira was confused. "Isn't Constellation a jet plane name, like those you drew when you were a kid, Matt?"

"Not in this case," Temple said. "I mean the constellations of stars in the sky the ancient Greeks named, just as they sculpted the 'man versus sea monster' statue. Matt." She eyed him in triumph. "This is not the star map, but the full, founding image of the constellation called Ophiuchus."

"Oh-fee-you-cuss?" Mira was seriously confused. "Or 'Oh, fie! You cuss?'"

"The accent is on the 'you' part," Matt said. "And nobody cusses."

"It's ancient Greek," Temple explained.

"It certainly is to me." Mira's smile was bemused.

Temple spelled it out for her. "Just think of it rhyming with 'mucous.'"

"I'd rather not. You kids." Mira was chuckling now. "Krys, and now you two. I think the younger generations speak in code."

"This may have been used as a code by some very bad people," Temple said. "Ophiucus is the lost thirteenth sign of the zodiac that a secret society in Las Vegas called the Synth took for its signature. Matt's tracking Cliff Effinger to Vegas might have kicked off a sequence of crimes tied to the conspiracy of magicians and . . . other worse elements."

"The mob?" Mira asked.

"Those two catnappers sure were." Temple was also thinking of the international terrorists Max had been tangling with half his life.

"Whatever is going on," Matt said, "Effinger must have salted away something in these memorabilia that will shake Las Vegas to its criminal roots."

"Clifford was still using me," Mira said, furious and showing it. "That ends here and now."

Krys came charging in from the depths of the apartment . . . the two hundred private square feet of it otherwise known as her bedroom.

"*Squee!*" she shouted. "People! Where's that so not-Manx cat? I'm gonna make him a YouTube star."

"You don't like him," Temple pointed out. "Or me."

"That's before I saw the local TV news hot flash on the Internet. That is so cool what he did. A major piece of pussycat performance art. And the centerpiece is that totally shallow materialistic icon, the leopard-pattern purse-pet bag! All the scene lacks is a stiletto heel, so if you'll leave one behind, Tempie dear, I'll immortalize it in 3-D."

Temple rose, trying not to overturn her kitchen chair. "If I leave it behind, it'll be implanted in someone's shallow, competitive irreverent rear end."

"Tush," Krys said. "All's forgiven. You rock. You all have to come into my room and get a load of Five News footage."

Temple opened her laptop on the kitchen table. "Show us right here and now."

"O-kay." Krys commandeered Temple's seat and moved the laptop cursor to a browser, then a news page. Listed along the right side were the local items.

She clicked on one reading CHICAGO HOODS NAILED AND JAILED and clicked the video arrow to show a slow pan of a warehouse that looked as if a *Die Hard* movie had been filmed there just last week.

A voice-over told the tale.

"Police alerted to gang activity zeroed in on an abandoned warehouse on the south side today, finding two long-wanted criminals bagged and snagged in a trap of crating materials studded with rusted carpenter nails, apparent victims of assault via nail-gun, something new for the mayhem crowd.

"Benny 'the Viper' Bennedetto and Waldo 'the Weasel' Walker were found unconscious and suffering from numerous 'packaging' wounds in a scene of chaos. Abandoned in the middle of the mess was what police describe as a 'high-end cat carrier.' The conclusion? These would-be mobsters must have been trying to round up rats and got caught in their own trap. Call Paris Hilton's abused designer bag rehab center. The petty crooks come free for the taking."

The video's last image showed the incongruous leopard-pattern carrier sitting untouched in the middle of the scene perhaps stage-managed by Spielberg's Industrial Waste and Wreckage spin-off company instead of Industrial Light and Magic.

Temple ID'd the artifact in tones evoking a blend of bereaved mother and indignant shopper.

"*Oooh,* that's the cat carrier I got in the Treasure Island shopping mall. This accessory in the wilderness shot reminds me of my last. . . . actually, my *first* official case, which included Louie's discovery of the marooned Boots Benson concrete-encased cowboy boots found high and dry in the drought-revealed bed of Lake Mead."

"Imagine what your cat could find in a real lake," Krys said. "Lake Michigan is almost the size of West Virginia. There are whole big ships down there."

"Louie doesn't like water in larger than drinking bowl quantities," Temple said, quashing Krys's plug for her hometown. "And, apparently, he *really* doesn't like low-level mob functionaries."

Louie kept his druthers to himself, maintaining his lofty sagelike position on the kitchen counter. Only the very tip of his dangling tail switched back and forth like the tuft on a lion's terminal appendage, demonstrating that neither Viper nor Weasel had touched Hair One.

"Louie isn't much mourning the loss of his high-class carrier," Matt said.

"We'll never get it back. I've found the police to be very *high*-handed about stowing irrelevant evidence in their lockers," Temple said, musing on Molina's unwarranted custody of Max's promise ring, only recently returned. Maybe that was the only way Molina could get and keep one of her own.

Everyone's intent gaze awaited the source of her assertion about police behavior. Temple was not going to back up her comment in *this* crowd with *that* example.

"But I suppose," Temple went on quickly, "the police would not exactly welcome me calling again, anyway, asking for a personal favor. And I couldn't bring up the carrier without . . . letting the cat out of the bag that my cat really was kidnapped and at the center of that whole scene. It was a one-of-a-kind accessory, though."

"Krys," Matt said, "would you be a doll and pick up a new carrier for Louie? Temple and I have lunch and dinner dates tomorrow and fly out first thing Tuesday."

"Sure." Krys sounded stunningly unenthusiastic. "Why shouldn't I shop and schlep for the cat? I'm an artist. I have no money, but all the time in the world."

Matt's hand lighted on the briar rose tattoo on Krys's right wrist. "We'd really appreciate that, and it's in a good cause: to get the cat out of your hair and apartment."

That was the magic touch. She melted. "*He's* all right. Just the usual spotlight hog."

Temple did not miss noticing it was much easier for Krys to accept her cat than to accept her as Matt's fiancée.

Family matters! She and Matt were getting a double dose of it tomorrow and finishing up the day by dining with network executives.

All Temple wanted was to get her boys back from Chicago and on the trail of Cliff Effinger and a shopping list of other Las Vegas cold cases that would finally get those she loved out of clear and present danger, including Midnight Louie.

CHAPTER 25
ANGST À LA CARTE

Temple appreciated one advantage of living in a city like Las Vegas with its spine of world-class hotel-casinos and shopping and entertainment. She could walk into a five-star Chicago hotel for lunch with awkward relatives or relatives-to-be — or dinner with network execs — and feel not one whit intimidated.

Minneapolis–St. Paul had been the metropolitan oasis for all the Upper Midwest states of the Dakotas, Minnesota, Iowa, and Wisconsin, but Vegas mimicked the crème de la crème of the country and the world.

She hadn't realized that before and knew now that she owed that confidence to Vegas moguls Steve Wynn and company and . . . Max Kinsella.

Matt had always been a "people" person like her, and despite the evolution he'd worked through, his innate interest in other people and the common good would always allow him to mix equally well with the high and mighty and small and meek.

But personal business offered more emotional minefields than business-business, so Temple linked arms with Matt as they moved through the lavish Water Tower Place toward the elevators to the hotel high above Chicago's Miracle Mile.

"Do you look like your dad?" she asked.

"Not yet," he answered wryly. "We'll see what the male-pattern baldness odds are on that side of the gene pool if we ever glimpse his brother."

"They're . . . uneasy with each other?"

"Who knows? This is pioneering territory. I doubt either one of them can appreciate what my mother went through."

"You too." She shook his arm slightly.

"I'm the mediator here. My issues are off the table."

"Can you do that, Matt?"

"Supposed to be good at it." He smiled and folded her hand into his as they waited for the elevator. "Your presence will lower the territorial testosterone."

"I see. I'm a mother substitute here."

"Kinda." He grinned. "You're a very versatile woman. These midlife men will be on their best behavior in front of a hot young chick like you."

"You've planned all this out."

"Darn right. On the radio I have to improvise. It's made me adaptable under pressure. On TV or here, I'll need an underlying plan, to be more in control. The producers and I have talked about that. The audience needs to identify with both the host and guests."

" 'The producers and I,' " she whispered affectionately in the elevator as they streaked up at stomach-swooping speed. "I feel like I'm engaged to Prince William."

"Now, that's a male-pattern baldness family history I'd rather not have for all the jewels in the Tower of London. Also the paparazzi. Kate Middleton is a brave woman."

"Oh, you'll get the paparazzi, brother," Temple said.

By then the maître d' was showing them over a carpet where the soft hush of hundred-dollar bills falling had been replaced by the sweet chime of seventeen-hundred-dollar-an-ounce gold rings clinking against the finest French crystal.

A stocky blond man stood at Temple's arrival for Matt's introduction.

"Miss Temple Barr, this is Jonathan Winslow." Matt waited for them to shake hands.

Then the waiter pulled out Temple's chair and — as waiters everywhere did, from

pretentious low-end to plushest high-end —
pushed it in not quite far enough for a
woman as short as she. *Darn!* On this thick
carpet, trying to inch the seat forward would
be more awkward than a father and his
bastard son having lunch together, which,
double darn, was happening right under her
nose.

"Temple owns a PR business in Las Vegas,
including the Crystal Phoenix account,"
Matt told his father, "and her problem-
solving talents sometimes extend to murder."

His father's snow white eyebrows lifted
above the reading glasses he'd donned.
"Murder she wrote. How interesting as well
as attractive. I'm a garden-variety businessman, I'm afraid. No special talents except
managing the money other people made
before me."

"Sounds like a good trick these days,"
Temple said.

"I'm delighted to meet the lovely Miss
Barr. May I call you Temple?" he asked. "I
really like the name. I have a daughter
named Torrence."

"Of course. What does Matt call you?"
Temple asked.

The men's exchanged looks went from
surprised to rueful.

Matt answered, "We've managed to avoid addressing that issue so far. I'm Matt, of course, being younger."

"And I'm Jon," his father said. "I travel in circles where nothing is abbreviated, including names, and I'm damn weary of being Jonathan."

Temple decided "Jon" was a clever diplomatic way to find a "special" name for just Matt to use, skirting any adoption of a role — "Dad" — both would regret and couldn't use in front of others anyway.

"Jon without an *h*." She almost tasted the spelling. No unnecessary elements. "It suits you, Mr. Winslow."

"And you will now use it forthwith, Temple?"

"Of course, Jon. As a PR person I'm a great believer in the right name for the right occasion." Actually, her using the familiar form of address before Matt did would help ease him into the new relationship.

Meanwhile, their water glasses had been swiftly and silently filled by the technique of pouring from the ewer's side, not its spout. The spa water bottle remained on the table for refills.

Temple had worn her highest heels, the David Letterman female-star strutters that were pretty much as hobbling as bound feet . . . and still the linen napkin wanted to slide off her lap. The "lovely Miss Barr" could use bib clip.

"I think drinks are in order," Jon suggested when the waiter reappeared.

The drink menu was an abridged version of *War and Peace* between an obesely padded leather jacket.

Temple ordered an obscenely expensive glass of white wine whose vintage and vintner she didn't recognize. Jon ordered single-malt scotch, the kind Max favored. Matt surprised her by asking for a Bombay gin martini.

"Unfortunately," Temple said of her wine, "I'm the designated walker."

"Yes." Jon grinned. "What is with the women wearing all these extreme high heels? They can't be comfortable."

"Temple's always been a footwear connoisseur," Matt said. "Don't worry. She works at home in bare feet most of the time."

"In my case," Temple added, "I got the short stick in the genetics lottery. Also, the heels make excellent defensive weapons."

"It'd be better to run," Matt said.

The menus came next, just as padded as the liquor ones but larger. They all studied them as if needing to pass a test.

"You are my guests, of course," Jon said. "So how are you?" he asked Matt. "How's the trip business going?"

"You *are* the trip business."

"How's your mother?" Jon had turned businessman brusque.

"Well, but more than somewhat confused, as you can imagine."

"Same with my brother." The waiter came to take their orders and then they were left in blessed peace for a few moments. The level of attentive service at this restaurant assured a good many necessary "time-outs" in the conversation.

Temple suspected they all ordered just to get it over with. Salads were too messy for delicate, groundbreaking conversations, Temple knew from experience. Your mouth was always sprouting spinach leaves that wouldn't chew, or your fork was pursuing vagrant bleu cheese crumbles just as words were most urgently called for. The guys ordered steak entrées and she wild salmon.

"You should know," Jon told them while the tablecloth still hosted only drinks, the roll basket, and butter containers, "and this might be a bit shocking. I want to come out of the closet."

That shut their mouths.

"In terms of our" — he gestured back and

forth between himself and Matt — "relationship."

Matt, shocked, opened his mouth to speak.

"You're right, Matt. Secrets are corrosive. Besides." Jon looked sheepish. "My brother knows something is wrong. I can't keep him in the dark much longer."

"I don't even know your brother's name," Matt said. "Why should *he* be the deciding factor in anything that involves my mother, as well as you?"

"Because he loves Mira and wants to marry her."

"If he does, he'll let her come to terms with the problem on her own. She won't even talk to me about it."

"It's not a problem." Jon smiled the same heart-stopping way Matt did when he was pleased. "Knowing Philip, he'll win her over. Consider me the advance guard for a better future trip to Chicago," Jon told him. "You're not exactly nobody. The extended family only knows you're a 'distant relative,' but is wild to meet you," he added as ruefully as Matt spoke of his birth father's family. "Now that I've seen the lovely Miss Barr, that'll go double."

Matt just shook his head, trying to imagine — like Temple — who, when and where, would tell Mira the family that had banished mother and infant son thirty-five years ago was strong-arming their belated introduction into their bosom.

After a few sips all around, Jon broached what seemed an even more uneasy subject for him. "Since the . . . revelation, I've studied the family financial structure."

"I'm financially fine," Matt said. "I'd be financially fine if the best job I could find was at a fast-food place."

"I understand that. I admire where you are. I admire your independence. I'm not thinking according to need. I'm thinking according to . . . justice. Moral responsibility. My parents' family had an inflated notion of their position. They opposed my enlisting in the armed forces. They wiped my wishes and obligations and responsibilities away like bread crumbs off a table."

He gestured at the recently brushed white linen cloth.

"They sinned against me, and your mother, and you. You of all people should understand those terms."

"I do," Matt said. "I just don't want to apply them to anyone else."

" 'Vengeance is mine, sayeth the Lord,' " Temple put in helpfully.

Jon sat back and took a hit of scotch.

"That's what my family always feared."

"Someone alien having a claim on their money, right?" Temple said. "Especially someone their heirs might have liked or loved. 'Money is the root of all evil,' et cetera. Oh, heck, Mr. Jon Winslow. I've always been a working girl. All I need is a decent place to live where there's a really good selection of vintage and resale rags, an honest man to love and love me, and a job that challenges my brain. The rest is luck or compromise, and I don't believe in either."

Jon took a big belt of single malt, and closed his eyes momentarily. "Paying off your mother," he told Matt, "paying for a two-flat for her and you and nothing more, was written off as a 'bad investment.' If you can turn the other cheek on that, I can't. My parents were like a minor league version of the Kennedys under old Joe, the bootlegging womanizer. Men had to excel in power positions and the women didn't count except as props."

Matt sat silent. Temple saw the muscle flexing in his left jaw because she faced it and Jon didn't.

"I'm not guilty," Matt told his father, "of forgiveness and mercy toward your family any more than I'm guilty of rage and revenge. I'm just certain, lousy as my low-end so-called family situation was, I came out better than if I'd been condescended to and manipulated in the high-end success factory you were put through."

Temple clapped softly.

"Yeah," his father admitted, "I did it all by the family code after I got my 'going rogue' stage over. It's golden and shiny on the outside, but hollow on the inside. I think I always missed the genuineness of my youthful patriotic instincts. My most treasured moments are the ones least plotted."

"Not mine. What about your brother?" Matt asked. "Did he fit the family mold?"

"Just who is interviewing whom about who's fit to marry into whose family?"

Matt shrugged, but smiled at that bit of humility. "I couldn't defend my mother then. I can now. Or try at least."

"I wish I could say that for my kids. They've all done 'well,' but . . . anyway, Philip and his wife weren't able to have children. They put their spare time into charity work for kids. That seemed to bond them better than board dinners and corporate cocktail parties. It was an awful thing when Sarah died. Cancer. So . . . I'm shocked, but fine with what's happened. The only mystery is why Mira is so freaked about it. That was thirty-five years ago."

"Simple for guys," Matt said. "You had an incandescent one-night stand to idealize."

Jon's inbred control shattered. "How did you know it was 'incandescent'?"

"I'll never tell," Matt said, but Temple knew.

His mother had given him a new surname from a soaring Christmas carol, "O Holy Night," also called in the lyrics, "O Night Divine." She totally approved of Matt's not getting his father's ego or interest up by keeping this most personal of his mother's secrets.

"The woman had to bear the consequences, as it's so coyly put," Matt went on, "and you can never imagine how hellish that was." He took the gloves off. "You couldn't have used a condom?"

His father's ruddy middle-aged complexion reddened more. "Being prepared made the sin bigger."

"I bet you got over that in the military." It was Matt's first slightly bitter remark.

Temple hadn't thought of that, of Jonathan Winslow getting clued in to "protect himself" while Mira's "lost" innocence was paid for again and again through the years.

"It was my first time too," Jon muttered. "I was scared about what I'd done and where I was going . . . I had just turned eighteen and was trying to prove I wasn't the kid my family thought I was, but I still was. As soon as I got back, I started looking for her."

"She'd never be the same. She thought you were dead all those years. Then you were resurrected. She regrets every decision she made since that time. That's why she refused to meet with you when I tried to arrange it. You were still dead to her. Now, if she marries your brother, there'll be this bitter family secret with a walking, talking souvenir.

"Either of you told your brother?" Matt asked last.

"I don't think so."

"You don't *know* so?" Matt sounded incredulous.

"Mira refused to meet me, remember. I know the restaurant where she works, of course, Polandia, because that's where Philip met her. I don't dare show up there, but I made it my business to know where she lives, her phone number. She doesn't have e-mail."

Matt shared his father's disbelieving smile. "Without a kid at home she had no one to update her on new technology, including social networks. She's living with a much hipper niece these days, so I'm guessing the e-mail will come. In her own good time."

"Not Facebook," Temple put in. "Too dangerous given the situation. It's all about connections and Mira is still all about keeping connections apart."

Jon sipped his drink. "I'm a married man, whether I still want to be or not. I'm just a hangover from the past, but I don't see how frankness and 'being open' is going to resolve anything."

"Did I say it would?" Matt said. "I'm not a miracle worker."

"Trouble is," Jon continued, "any . . . unfortunate bit of personal history goes viral in this Internet age. If I held out hope that 'an honest mature discussion' could do anyone any good, I'd get it out on the table between the three of us. But it wouldn't stay discreet. You know that, Matt." Jon's forehead wrinkled. "This might blow up your career opportunity too."

"Just what Temple was saying. That doesn't worry me. Blowing up people's lives does."

Jon Winslow lifted his glass in Temple's direction. "Good thinking. You must be wondering what kind of families live in Chicago. Mira thinks her own relatives are demanding and judgmental and my relatives are egocentric and snobbish."

"That's okay," Temple said with a grin. "Matt and I are the opposite of all that . . . well, one at a time. I can't say that I don't get all crusading and judgmental sometimes, and that Matt doesn't expect everybody to be the best that they can be."

"Nobody's perfect," Matt said, "but gossip is the new hard news."

"I'm sure your mother would never want anybody — her, me, you, or the pixie PR woman here — to do anything to jeopardize your future. I'm sure everything she did in the god-awful situation I left her in was meant for your betterment."

"Yes," Matt agreed. "It was all meant for me."

Temple bit her lip. Parents' best intentions often go wrong. She was sure her parents didn't intend their protectiveness toward their only daughter and youngest child to be smothering. Or that Matt's mother's cruelly driven quest for respectability would put her *and* her son in a domestic abuse lockdown. Or that Max's parents and grieving aunt and uncle ever expected that having one dead and one surviving son would drive an unbridgeable wedge between everyone, forcing the victim, Max, out.

"My mother and I," Matt told his father,

"are facing some blowback from the past right now. There's no way she could possibly settle her present dilemma without that being confronted and put to rest. That's what Temple and I intend to do as soon as we can."

Jon looked back and forth between them. "You're that kind of a team already?"

They looked at each other and shrugged with a smile.

"I guess we are," Temple said.

"So that's the way things will have to stay for a while longer," Matt said. "In suspended animation."

"It's killing my brother." Jon frowned and then sighed. "He's coming to *me* for advice. If we all sat down and you refereed —"

"No. Not yet." Matt was firm. "You're a heck of a nice guy and so, I bet, is your brother, or my mother would never have fallen for the both of you. I'd be proud to have a new father *and* uncle, but my mother isn't ready for a 'one big happy.' And she's the one who's borne the burden of your mutual regard for her. "Don't you get it?" Matt asked his father. "Thirty-five years is a nanosecond when it comes to the human heartbeat."

Temple noticed that Jon had been looking more and more sheepish as Matt spoke, and now made his closing argument.

"Face it, Jon. She's scared to death she'll still feel something for you if you met again, under any circumstances. And I bet you are too."

"Do *you* believe she does?"

Matt turned to Temple. "What do you think now that you've met the birth parents?"

"I haven't met Philip," she said, "so this is a half-boiled opinion." Temple was not about to mention she was personally quite familiar with romantic tangles, popularly known as "triangles."

"Mira needs to see you again," she told Jon, "to see for herself that the past is buried, even if you aren't."

"Wise advice, Miss Barr," Matt told her, his penetrating eyes reading hers. "Would you like to appear on my talk show?"

"Of course." She smiled. "But I get a lifetime contract."

CHAPTER 26
LURKING LUSTY LADDIES

"I may be off-duty," Rafi told Max, "but this is my territory."

The Oasis was Las Vegas's answer to the Taj Mahal. In fact, the giant gazebo by the pool out back *was* a re-creation of the Taj Mahal.

The Oasis's fabled towers shimmered like glitter-dusted alabaster in the daylight, and a giant pair of exotically painted elephants stood at attention, glittering palanquins on their distant backs, flashing polyurethane tusks long enough, and strong enough, to seat the Mormon Tabernacle Choir for a photo opportunity. One foot and two faux ivory tusks each were eternally raised in welcome, along with their one-story-long trunks. Those hiked painted toenails, if animated, could have flattened a Humvee.

The human curbside greeters up front were costumed as Sabu, the elephant boy, with sun-burnished to gleaming cinnamon skin, wearing only brocade turbans and harem pants.

What snagged Max's attention though, were the almost seven-foot-tall giant-bellied harem eunuchs holding three-foot-long curved swords and guarding a horizontal freezer-size transparent Plexiglas treasure chest crammed with paper money. Turning his head, Max could inspect thousands of slices of the Great Inventor's face, aka Benjamin Franklin, gracing hundred-dollar bills.

"What's with the cash wishing well?" he asked Rafi.

"Mucho security headaches until Friday. It's a prize for the week's biggest slot machine winner. A million bucks."

"The sidewalk and undercarriage are wired, right?"

"Right. And don't ask too many questions or I'll think you're really here to knock it off. And I'd have to shoot you."

Inside, the visitor pushed through crowds milling in an exotic jungle landscape, complete with monkeys and birds, in which the ringing of slot machines chimed like dimly heard temple bells.

"Impressive," Max agreed as they passed the elephants. "I've always wanted to make an elephant disappear."

"Better you make *us* disappear." Rafi was

terse, and tense. "Remember. If you get into any fisticuffs in the hotel surveillance underbelly, it's my rear."

"There's only one anatomical site I'm interested in here, and it's a murder site, past tense."

"I was in on the capture of a murderer at the *Dancing With the Celebs* reality TV show here recently. That was in the theater area."

"Good for you." Max smiled. "Don't worry. I won't jinx your career in security. According to maddeningly vague references in Gandolph's home computer, there've been a string of unsolved deaths that have nagging connections to . . . me."

"Oh, great. And here I volunteered to be your backup buddy."

"It was a paid position."

"Originally. And now?"

"And now, if Gandolph's notes and my need to figure out who tried to kill me at the Neon Nightmare club helps solve this string of rather bizarre but possibly related deaths over the past two years, I can see you get cred with Molina for the breakthroughs. That'll melt the Iron Maiden of the Las Vegas Metropolitan Police Department's stony heart into raspberry slush, or at least into giving you visitation rights with your daughter."

"You underestimate the calcification of Carmen's mercy muscle, but I'm working on it," Rafi said with a grin. "If we go trolling around the Oasis together for too long, though, it'll look like I've got a new boyfriend."

" 'Prospective employee,' " Max said. "I just need to see the Oasis's revamped sexy pirate girl show and inspect the ship that comes round the bend to sink so spectacularly."

"Most tourist guys want to inspect the sexy pirate girls."

"I don't think *they* killed anybody, do you?"

"The tourist guys or the sexy pirate girls?"

"Either."

"It's a popular attraction, night and day. Who knows what evil lurks in randy tourists."

Rafi led the way out of the hotel and through the usual milling throngs. The pirate ship show was free, which accounted for the tourist hordes lining the sidewalk outside the hotel. A wooden walk-the-plank bridge connected to a hotel entrance over a broad moat of water.

The attraction had resembled a set for a pirate film long before Captain Jack Sparrow went viral, so Max knew what to expect. His six-foot-four height made it easier to see over the hundreds of heads, even with many arms extended straight up to record phone videos of the show.

"Do we start," Max asked, "by ogling the nearly naked girls in the crow's nest or the naked female figurehead on the sinking ship's prow?"

"We'll check out the enemy ship that comes around the bend in the landscaping just to sink later. This script is cheesy. 'Lusty Ladies and Laddies' at war. The special effects aren't."

Rafi, who'd obviously had a chance to watch the attraction on slimmer attendance days, or nights, pointed out the obvious. "This used to be a rousing, family-friendly all-out action battle between freebooting pirates and the pursuing government ships."

"I remember those days." Max surveyed the bikini-clad "sirens" clambering over the three-masted sailing ship that anchored the show. "Now it's become an arousing battle between the sexes. The only suspense factor is what will stay put longer, the pirate showgirls' mic packs or their same-sized bikini pieces."

"I sure wouldn't take my teen daughter here to see good role models."

"Parenthood makes new men of us all. These chorines have been trained into pretty solid athletes," Max said after observing the action. "Those swordfights and fiery dives from the top rigging are tough routines."

"Nothing new for you. Didn't you have the usual magician's assistants who could go topless for the late show?"

"No. I preferred to invent less blatant distractions for my audiences. I worked alone. More cerebral."

"Art imitates life, huh?"

Max grinned at Rafi's comeback, then craned his neck to see the show again. "I think the climax is coming for our hip-slinging crew of seductive beauties on the anchored ship set — I glimpse a ship of lusty male pirates sailing around the bend, to be sunk. Ahoy! The ship is called *The Bull.* Not too subtle."

Max peered through and over the packed tourist crowds. The boys' ship was basically a large 3-D stage set running on an underwater track. The prow's figurehead of a large-bosomed naked mermaid personified Las Vegas.

"Imagine," he told Rafi, "a man is bound like a mummy against that figurehead."

"White wrappings?"

Max nodded. "Probably. Molina would have access to the details and Grizzly Bahr at the morgue would have the bindings filed away."

"Man, that was harsh. The guy was probably conscious, but gagged. Blindfolded too?"

"Not by sadistic killers like this."

"So he saw the whole spectacle. While hundreds cheered the fighting and fireworks up top, making any cries for help, he slowly sank with the ship and drowned on cue. Cold."

"It *was* cold. Happened right at New Year's."

"Holy not-hot water! The temperature in the 'cove' gets down to around thirty-eight degrees in the winter. If the water didn't drown him, hypothermia would have killed him. What got him the royal sinking-barge treatment?"

"I don't know. The victim was the scumbag stepfather of my ex-girlfriend's new fiancé, who'd come to town to look the loser up."

"You mean Temple's significant other, Matt Devine. I've met the lovebirds. Man. Your life is even more messed up than mine."

"Thanks," Max said wryly. "It's good that

I excel at something besides amnesia."

In fact, he'd forgotten his more recent personal life, yet not Vegas landmarks like this.

His eyes narrowed at the scene now as perfect as a motion picture still, a snippet from *Mutiny on the Bounty,* say, with the first ship at anchor in harbor. The serene beauty mocked the grim reality that had brought him here.

"So," Rafi resumed, "we're ruling out Miss Temple's ex-priest fiancé as the killer? Big of you."

"Not really. Only mob muscle would be so vicious," Max said. "Or ethnic hatred. Obviously, this Effinger guy didn't give them information they wanted. Didn't have it, probably, unless he had more guts than the minor-league gofer he was."

"When did this happen?" Rafi asked.

"Before your time. What's the security around here?"

"Not much. This area has no overlooking views and is concealed by landscaping. The whole idea is the ship sailing around from behind here is a big surprise out front. Since no one has access except performers and maintenance staff, this is one of Vegas's few discreet locations."

Max nodded. His scan of the building and

overhanging palm trees found only camou-
flaged outdoor fixtures aimed at uplighting
the swoop of the hotel's central structure.

"Satisfied?" Rafi asked, checking his
watch.

Max nodded. "Like I said. A job for
mobsters or terrorists. Nobody much cared
about the guy, alive or dead, not even the
police. That's what bothers me. This was a
risky, elaborate style of execution and
technically tough to pull off, even if the
victim was a man who knew too much."

"But he was your rival's evil stepfather."

"You can't have a 'rival' if you're not
contending for anything."

"So *you* left the redhead, not vice versa."

"I'm assuming I let nature take its course.
It's impossible to sustain a relationship
when you're MIA off and on."

"For sure." Rafi thought for a few seconds.
"This crook was the only father Matt Devine knew. Garry Randolph, aka Gandolph,
was your father figure. Your real father must
have died."

"No," Max said. "I did."

"Another of your famous disappearing
acts?"

Max cocked a dark eyebrow "Sort of was,
only much longer ago. I walked after high
school."

"Really? You seem an educated guy."

"Roads scholar. Roads in the British Isles, and roads on what used to be called the Continent and is now the European Union. Garry Randolph was my tutor."

Rafi opened his mouth to ask another question, but Max cut him off. "Why the interest in my family history? Once I follow the trail Garry was on here to the end, our association is over."

"Fine." Rafi sounded angry. "I'm just trying to figure out how you get to be an okay father. I guess no one much has them anymore."

Max relaxed and chuckled to himself. "There are about as many deadbeat dads out there trying to elude their paternity as there are fighting for their custodial rights. You don't need a role model, you just have to decide if you achieve that best working with Molina, or against her. You're in a position to go either way."

"Which means I have two ways to lose, as much as win."

Max nodded. "Life" — he looked at the dead-in-the-water ship — "and death, are like that. Before any early-bird maintenance crew shows up we need to inspect that figurehead and keel until we know how, if not why, it was turned into a killing machine."

Rafi checked his watch with a sour expression. "I could lose my job if we're caught, and I don't want to dive overboard for a dip in cove. At least it's bathwater warm this time of year."

"If we raise any alarms, we can cast off and catch the ship when it's next at anchor, me hearty."

Chapter 27
Brothers, Where Art Thou?

The landmark lunch was over. Matt stepped behind Temple, reaching to pull her chair out when the waiter whisked it away much more authoritatively.

Suddenly standing, Temple jerked around to address the overly solicitous waiter.

He was a white-haired man with beetling black brows wearing a costly suit with a subtle four-figure sheen.

"I can't let you two leave Chicago," he said, "without laying my cards on the table."

"Philip," Jon said, standing in surprise himself. Obviously, he was the younger brother.

"I assume this young man is my nephew."

By then Matt had Temple's back and a protective left hand on her shoulder. He extended a right hand past her to the newcomer. "Matt Devine of Las Vegas. This is my fiancée, Temple Barr. I believe we know who you are."

The brothers glared at each other briefly across the table.

Then Philip smiled broadly at Temple and Matt. "I'd like to buy you all a drink in the bar. It's pretty deserted during the busy lunch hours and I'll make sure we get a quiet corner."

Somehow his light guiding touch on their shoulders had turned Matt and Temple, Philip easing them through the tables like the friendliest of hosts.

"This must be a whirlwind trip for you two," Philip said. "I know Matt has a date with syndicated radio five days a week. What about you, Miss Temple?"

"I'm self-employed, so I don't answer to anyone for my schedule but me."

"Smart woman."

"Don't kid yourself," Matt said. "She's a dynamo and will move the world to make her public relations clients happy."

"And you too, I bet."

The chitchat covered their relocation to the bar, where a waiting hostess escorted the party to a charming banquette with high, enclosing leather upholstery that ensured privacy. Philip, Temple saw, was a dynamo himself, but a charming one, far more outgoing than his brother. Then again, he hadn't had a secret love gnawing at him for more than thirty years.

The brothers bracketed them in the banquette, which was a teensy bit uncomfortable. Matt squeezed Temple's hand on the seat between them. She saw his eyes sizing up the fact that the brothers faced each other across the white linen, and a faint smile touched his lips.

Matt was a born negotiator, and he was really liking this turn of events.

Temple relaxed, swinging her heels against the banquette bottom. Her feet didn't reach the floor, as usual, but in this situation, nobody could see that. She slipped her hose-clad feet out of the heels. Hated pantyhose! However, important meal dates at fancy restaurants in a habitually colder climate like Chicago required sacrifice.

She could see Matt looked more like his father, but he thought more like his uncle.

When the waiter arrived, Philip cut to the chase, ordering Tia Marias and coffee for everyone, with a raise of his prominent eyebrows for any order modifications. All nodded cooperatively, and Matt's faint smile expanded.

"Sorry to bust in on you folks, and Jon. I figure you were discussing Mira, and that's one topic I can't leave to others, even if she can pretty much leave me hanging in limbo."

Matt leaned forward. "How did you figure out you two had my mother in common?"

Jon spoke first. "Philip isn't one to hold back. When he started seeing Mira, he brought a photo of them taken at the Polandia restaurant where they met to a family gathering. I recognized her from the time you tried to have us meet at a Chicago bar . . . Matt."

Temple saw Jon was still unsure how to relate to his long-lost son.

"So you told Philip?" Matt asked his dad.

"No. It looked like a friendly dinner, nothing more."

"But, Jon," Temple asked, "if you were keeping Philip in the dark, how did Mira discover you two were related?"

"Oh, boy." Philip leaned back as the coffee cups and tiny liqueur glasses were presented. After the clinking and stirring subsided, he said. "The children's charity fund we . . . I sponsor a big fund-raiser. Got five seconds on the local nightly news, Jon and I center-screen with Angelina Jolie. Everybody recognized us on the street after that."

Matt got the picture too. "So my mother did a meltdown and simply refused to see you anymore."

Philip nodded. His white hair was thick but receding, unlike Jon's blond thatch. Oddly, that gave Philip's face a thinner, more youthful look.

"Not right away," Philip said. "It's the darnedest thing. If I look back, I can see she became a bit more . . . guarded after that event. But she didn't cut me off at the knees and refuse to see me or take my calls until a few days after that. A delayed reaction, maybe. She'd had time to think about the ramifications, which are damn awkward, but that's no way to live when you've been around as long as we three. Not many second chances going to be dealt us at our age."

Matt exchanged a significant look with Temple. He leaned even farther forward. "What are your intentions toward my mother?'

"Why, to marry her, you impudent pup," Philip said with a laugh. "This is sounding like a Victorian novel."

"Then," Matt said, "I have no objection and it's basically only between you three. It's not that I don't understand 'modern' living-together arrangements, Philip, especially between older couples and maybe with big money in the family, but marriage means a lot to my mother. I think you two guys are uniquely liable to understand why, and why she deserves it. Period."

In the silence, the brothers looked down and nodded their heads.

"Good," Matt said. "There's no need for you to share what happened thirty-five years ago with any of your family members. Or," he told Jon, "to mess with family inheritances out of a sense of guilt. Money never makes things better, it just buys lawyers boats. Mira is a widow with a son from a previous marriage. I even have a different surname. Book closed. If Mom does marry Philip, she'll be well provided for without Jon having anything to do with it."

Jon's head was still lowered, but now he shook it. Not in disagreement, Temple saw, but with both gratitude and regret for Matt's generous dismissal of the past and all its pain.

"I'd be proud," Jon mumbled, "to introduce you as my son."

"But you don't need to," Matt said, "and I don't need that either. The best gift we could give my mother is a discreet, happy ending. Now," he added, "if the brothers Winslow will allow Temple and me to escape to have some time to anticipate another stressful dinner date with network executives, I'll leave you two with a three-step program.

"Jon and Philip. Talk it all out until you're sick of your own memories, grief, uncertainty, and guilt. Then, Philip, call my mother. Her withdrawal had thirty percent to do with the brothers thing and seventy percent with a 'hidden planet' in her life even I didn't know about. Let that go. Last, she needs to meet with Jon so all of you can be sure that her love for Philip is unshakable."

"Wait." Philip put a hand on Matt's forearm. "You say she loves me?"

"Yes, but we all need to make sure she can put that *Romeo and Juliet* thing behind her.

"Then . . . ," Matt said.

The brothers were sliding out of the banquette to make way for Matt and Temple to exit, a mutual expression of dumbfounded hope on their faces. *Now* they looked like brothers. Temple jammed her feet back in the high heels and prepared to scoot out.

"Then, what?" Jon asked.

"Someone call me in Vegas and let me know what happens. Nice to meet you. Thanks for lunch." Matt handed out two business cards and took Temple's elbow to

248

head for the exit.

She was still breathless as they waited for the elevator to the street level. "Wow. Mr. CEO of reconciliation," Temple said. "That was . . . like a takeover bid, Matt."

"I knew it would be all right the moment I saw Philip."

"He's a pretty likable guy."

"That's not it," Matt said. "He doesn't look anything like his brother."

Temple gazed at him blankly for a few moments.

"Oh. You mean your mother didn't fall for the family resemblance, but the real man."

Matt produced a Cheshire cat grin. "Smart girl. You *and* her."

"Our last night in utter Luxe coming up in about six hours," Temple announce lazily, staring up at the ceiling, which was bordered by white enameled decorative molding on a glossy white surface that discreetly reflected them in bed.

It was not so discreet that it didn't reveal He and She in the altogether with a tangled sheet in the general vicinity and a big black blot at the foot of the huge mattress.

"We look like Hollywood stars from the bedroom-glamour thirties on the Big White Set," Temple said, stretching luxuriously. "I feel so Jean Harlow. Bring on the satin sheets tonight! Do you think room service will accommodate us?"

"We just acted like that," Matt said, rolling over to replace the Big White Ceiling in her view. "We don't need satin sheets, and we're running way behind schedule."

Temple put her hands on his jaws and smiled into his eyes. "You were just so hot, the way you manhandled the situation with the older, richer, guiltier guys. Prince Valiant, only blond. Your mother could not have had a better champion and I could not have been prouder. I love you."

Well, that comment didn't exactly make up for any lost time on the getting-ready front, and Louie was forced to flee to the floor again.

"Dinner." Temple groaned as they were dressing and duding up for the dinner with the "network people" forty minutes later. "Can one actually tire of five-star food? I crave a simple Happy Meal."

Temple turned from the suite's full-length bedroom mirror. "Does this look sufficiently enough like what these guys' wives would wear?"

Matt peeked in, topless, from the bathroom clasping a buzzing electric razor. "I'm no expert, but that must be an exquisitely expensive suit."

He eyed the short pale gold silk dress under a bolero jacket with glitz-dusted cuffs.

Temple shimmied her shoulders twice and spun to show off the subtle glitter woven into the outfit's classic Coco Chanel lines. "I figured your possible future bosses would notice. St. John's knit."

"Yeah? I don't think any saint designed that. It's like you're wearing liquid Karo syrup on the way to a mud-wrestling match."

She laughed. "Glad you noticed. Sophisticated slink. Courtesy of the Grand Bahama Mama resale shop on Charleston in Vegas."

"I can buy you upscale business clothes."

"No way. Recycling is virtuously 'green.' The *Gilmore Girls* TV show mother/grandmother often wore St. John knits. All the male stars' rich-bitch mothers on TV sitcoms do. Must be because there are so many thirty-something male scriptwriters and so many unemployed skinny older actresses."

"Huh?" Matt shrugged too. "That's a secret code I'll never crack, but I did visit a very not-resale shop on Michigan Avenue on my last trip here."

He fished a small blue box from the side

pocket of his Pat Sajak–stylish suit.

"Tiffany?" Temple accepted it with raised eyebrows. Inside lay a delicate web of diamond-dewed rubies on blue velvet.

"Oh." She rushed to the mirror to insert the neck-brushing earrings. They must have cost a couple months of her salary from the Crystal Phoenix. "They match my engagement ring, but, Matt, I wear my hair longer now. That's why I only use little gold studs occasionally to keep the piercings open. No one will ever see them unless I put my hair up."

She fluffed her shoulder-brushing strawberry red curls to show him.

He came up behind her, nudged the obscuring hair out of the way, performed CPR on her earlobes and earrings. "I will. That's the way I want it. I might catch a glimpse now and then, but no one else will know."

"Oooh," she said, turning to face him. "That is super sexy."

"So you're not going to complain about the expense?"

"Not since it's so deliciously private. When you get to the matching navel ring, we'll see."

He did not object to the threat.

She put a hand on his shoulder. "Thank

you. I'll let you count the ways again later."

They paused to enjoy a mutual smile even though they needed to rush.

Temple could also count the ways this trip was so important for Matt, and the ways it had almost been jinxed. First, the ghastly Louie incident, then the unsettling revelations about his stepfather. Then meeting his mother's brotherly beau. Events seemed designed to distract Matt from his amazing career opportunity. Temple had no trouble in deciding her role. She was here to totally take his mind off the negative and accent the positive for the rest of the trip.

"You are so going commit even more mortal sin when we get back here tonight," she threatened with all her heart. That ought to take his mind off the negative. Meanwhile, she had to play the good little wife-to-be, but she had no issues with that. Temple understood perfectly that when it came to a media career, a significant other could be an asset but was usually viewed as a possible detriment.

The Michigan Avenue restaurant stunned diners with soaring ceilings and blue-velvet banquettes amid a stark black-and-white décor. Matt and Temple were ushered to a private dining area that nonetheless featured a curved banquette, and a private bar for standing drinks and introductions.

Their entrance caused a flattering break in the chitchat as all eyes turned their way.

No problem. Temple was here to slay network dragons for her man. Super PR Woman had brought a '40s envelope purse bristling with golden spangles. She could tuck it under one arm to keep both hands free for cocktail-holding and hand shaking.

Her literally killer French shoes slayed her aching arches — '70s Charles Jourdan heels hosted two sets of unseen but sincerely felt Dr. Scholle's cushioned inserts. A slight platform from the period put her on an easy interaction level with taller men and women, who were usually in the majority.

She mingled generously, sipped stingily, chatted. She wondered if she could get used to a life of this.

Scents of expensive perfumes and cologne vied with the costly waft of world-class whiskeys and gins.

The other guests were older but so well-kept, both men and women, that Temple expected to see a manicurist and airbrush makeup artist hovering on the fringes and available for touch-ups.

At last the man with the most distinguished wings of silver hair at his temples suggested they sit. Temple and Matt ended up shuffling on the sticky velvet banquette to the back seats of the huge horseshoe, ranks of three wives on Temple's side and three execs on his.

She felt a bit like an invitee to a feast hosted by Genghis Khan. They'd been "cut from the herd" and would each be given a good going-over by the jury of their own gender.

Matt leaned to whisper in her ear as they unfurled their origami napkins. "Courage."

"Love your dinner suit, Miss Barr," the glossily groomed woman on Temple's left leaned in to say. "Your fiancé is instant Ben and Jerry's Karamel Sutra on a stick."

Temple shot her an admonishing look.

"You'll have to get used to that reaction, dear. Media is brutal today. Crazed fans rule the air waves and the Internet."

Her apparent husband across the way leaned in. "Miss Barr has her own media appeal. Your Zoe Chloe Ozone profile and following numbers on Twitter were quite a pleasant surprise. Don't be so shocked. We're looking for multiple platforms today. Even multiple personalities. That you could invent such a zany Internet persona on a whim is quite intriguing."

"I was doing undercover investigative

work to protect a vulnerable teen on that reality TV show," Temple said, trying not to sound huffy.

"Better and better." The man eyed his wife. "Daughter of Dr. Phil. Daphne, please interrogate Miss Barr on her fascinating online sidelines. And ask her about the cat."

"The cat?" Daphne beamed. "I have a bichon frise I adore."

Temple couldn't resist saying, "Oh, I've been considering that haircut myself. Would you mind giving me the name of your stylist?"

Daphne bristled, then snapped, "Fifi's Fashionable Fursians." Her narrowed eyes studied Temple. "You were just kidding."

"Yes, but now I know the name of *the* primo pet groomer in Chicago. You know, I'm surprised that the reality TV craze hasn't gotten to animal companions and their service industry."

Daphne blinked her false eyelashes. "That's not a bad idea. Care to come up with a concept for my husband to kick around?"

Temple was thinking she'd probably discover she'd rather kick the network veeps around.

Did she have the makings of a docile corporate wife?

Probably not.

Could she rejoice in Matt's success and reinvent herself in some interesting and fulfilling way?

Definitely.

Could Midnight Louie handle a big rough-and-tumble city like Chicago?

No contest.

CHAPTER 28
THE POST-MIDNIGHT HOUR

"You're a regular human fly," Rafi Nadir said, hanging over the *Bull*'s rail to watch Max inch along the ship's sides to the prow.

The night was dark and the moon was yellow and it reflected — along with the Strip neon — in the otherwise dark and silent artificial cove.

Before they'd started the assault on the deserted ship mock-up, they'd come up with a good excuse for being here.

"If anybody challenges our presence," Rafi had told Max, "I can say you're a rigging expert checking out an equipment problem with the last show."

"I really *am* one of those." Max had grinned. "Darn. I could do a lot of grunt jobs in this town now that I have no career as a headlining magician."

"You've got the guts for high-wire work, I can swear to that. Your Neon Nightmare crash was . . . 'Cirque du Soleil: Suicide.' "

"It was attempted homicide," Max said, "and believe that I take that personally."

Now, it was attempted interference with a major Vegas hotel's prize attraction, and that would be taken personally by some very big powers, including law enforcement.

Max took a deep breath. He paused, having used his legs and feet — and toes — more than he had in months and feeling it. He'd commandeered some stage rigging to attach a rope to his waist, but doing a "Dracula climbing down the castle walls face first" act was no longer second nature.

Max would rather be compared to the master vampire than a human fly, but he had to roll with what meager audience he had these days.

"Thugs didn't do this," he said softly. His baritone voice carried well around water. "Muscle is required but doesn't make up for dexterity and skill. Could *you* lower a trussed body over the prow?"

Rafi shuffled to the ship's pointed front and leaned over the gilded gingerbread decoration applied to the exterior.

"Yeah, but it would hang straight down. Unless you got the guy rocking back and forth like a pendulum, it'd be hard to snug him up against the naked lady."

"That's what they did, then." Max's

questing hand had found enough niches in the elaborate façade to work himself under the figurehead, face-to-face with . . . considerable frontage.

"Look," Rafi said. His voice sounded way too close.

Max looked up to see Rafi perching on the mermaid's head with its carved ripples of flowing hair. Rafi was dangling a prop trunk dripping faux jewels from the deck by a rope. It spun and swung, threatening to swing right into Max's head.

"Three guys," Rafi went on, whispering. "One on each side of the prow with ropes, one above to lower the corpse-to-be. Yeah? Right?"

Max grunted an affirmative. Working under a slanted surface, no matter how strong or fit you were, was the hardest position to maintain possible. He grabbed the swaying trunk by the rope around its middle and threaded another dangling piece of performance rigging through the gap his grip had made. The bulky object stopping swinging and started spinning left and right.

Assuming Effinger had still been alive at this point, the method of impending death was beginning to look like medieval torture. Who'd taken a low-level creep like Effinger's life in such a ritual, wrenching way? Why?

"I'm hearing something." Rafi's voice was a warning rasp. "I've got to —"

Max heard scrapes on the deck boards above as Rafi's words cut off.

Great. Here he was, dangling almost upside down, linked like a spider to a thread of web, a rope, trying to figure out what was happening far above his miniature world.

Only one thing to do: cut loose from the safe harbor that had been so deadly for Effinger and swing out like a footloose, freebooting pirate.

Max used his legs to rappel off the mermaid's, *hmm* lips and hips, and around the ersatz ship's side. Amazingly, the stunt worked.

No time to rest on his laurels, or legs. Rafi could be in trouble.

He scrambled hand-over-hand up the rope.

For a dead stage set, the *Bull*'s deck was suddenly swarming with unlicensed boarders. Max used the rigging rope he still clutched to barrel into the three figures surrounding Rafi, scattering them like bowling pins. Only now they were separated, so while Rafi pummeled one, the other two were coming at him.

His momentum swung him high out of reach. As he plunged into the inevitable low of his returning arc, he had no choice but to use his legs as battering rams, one to each oncoming chest.

Impact. Shock and awe and . . . pain. His whole frame shuddered. Max gritted his teeth. He'd urged Nadir into this and he'd get him out of it. No more bodies left behind.

He dragged a foot on the decking, a bit too late. He was headed into another wild, uncontrolled arc over the dark water.

Then he looked down. One of his attackers had hit the waterline with a splash and came surging up to the surface, almost walking on water. Maybe a great white shark had grabbed a bite from below.

The man's scream turned into high-pitched stutters. Max watched his body stiffen and sink with an audible sizzle.

Max's set his teeth and sucked breath between them in a matching hiss of air. *What the hell is going on?* He was out there on a rope, and now a prayer, swinging over open water. Water that had been *electrified.* His heartbeat drummed in his ear as he tried think over the thud.

Someone must have overridden the

ground fault interrupter for the whole damn water attraction. Raw electrical current was flowing. The cove was a giant bathtub into which someone had thrown a hair dryer.

That had happened in dozens of low-end crime films. The unsuspecting victim lowers her/himself into the drawn bath and . . . the quick toss of a hair dryer or electric razor, into the water. Zapped.

Max's madly pedaling legs swung him back over decking. The ship, built of wood as in days of old and molded plastic pieces as in the stage sets of today, couldn't conduct electricity. *Yo, ho, ho,* and an oaken cask of rum. He dropped onto the deck, rolling to take the brunt of the landing, his legs scrambling for purchase on the rubberized no-slip surfaces installed for the dangerous stunts.

Rafi grabbed his arm and pulled him upright.

The last deserting "rat" was scrabbling over the ship's side to the shore. Max could swear a small agile dark form was hot on his heels, but Midnight Louie was safely away in Chicago. Rafi grabbed his arm, distracting Max before he could be sure he'd seen anything odd.

They looked back toward the dark water on the same impulse. A sacklike form floated there. Max grabbed a prop belaying pin and threw it into the water. No reaction. It merely sank.

As he and Rafi followed the vanished thug into the tangled landscaping, alarmed voices and running footsteps were fast approaching the ship.

A high-powered flashlight beam swept Rafi. He beat Max to the draw with an expletive.

"I'm made," he said. "The water's dead now, but so is that guy. Get away!"

"No —"

"Go! I can explain myself being here better than I can me *and* you. If you ever needed a disappearing act more, it's now."

Max remained frozen and indecisive, out of flashlight range. The beam had steadied and fixed on Rafi. The moment felt like deserting Garry again.

"Get away!" Rafi's low-toned snarl finally pushed Max to the bordering elephant ear plants. Their four-foot leaves could hide a Brink's armored truck, or a rhinoceros. Pick your poison. Not ivy, he hoped. He ducked and dodged into the rubbery, flagellating dark, moving fast so no sign of shivering foliage would reveal his getaway path.

Max heard the shouts calming into talk, and then barked orders. He kept working around the hotel building's thick greenery until he heard nothing but his own rustles and heartbeat. He emerged in the rear parking lot, looking for a low black roof amid the pumped-up SUVs and pickups.

The Volkswagen was near the second row of parking lights, halfway between two lurid pools of greenish illumination, just the way he liked his rides placed, on the down low.

Max got in, started the engine, and sat awhile before putting it in gear.

Someone had tried to kill him. Again.

This was getting monotonous.

CHAPTER 29
BYE-BYE WINDY KITTY

At last.

We are back in the hot, dry, lizard-loving arms of McCarran Airport. No more O'Hare, or undignified inspections.

So there I am, no longer wearing leopard pattern, but wrapped up in a black-and-white and flamingo pink carrier customized by Miss Krys Zabinski for maximum embarrassment.

Personal expression is valued these days, and she does plenty of it. In fact, I am planning my own page on Facebook and expect to "tweet" my close encounters with various tweety birds early in my career, including those from that pink plastic flamingo case in my past.

But.

I do not need to be passing through major airports looking like a sissy on steroids. In fact, I am longing for the sudden-death high of a good kidnapping, though I can assure you that no thug worth his brass knuckles would lay so much as a pinkie finger on my current carrier.

"Oh, that old-style newspaper theme on your pet carrier is so fun," strange ladies coo at me. When I say "strange," I mean we are not formally introduced, not that they are loopy, although they very well may be.

"I bet the 'Extra, Extra' headline on the front means your cat is extra loving. Give us a smooch, big boy."

"It's actually for being 'Extra' heavy," my Miss Temple (sellout!) says sweetly.

"Oh, you poor thing. You need a Chihuahua. They are light and sooo cute."

My Miss Temple needs a Chihuahua like Ma Barker needs a Yorkie canapé.

Mr. Matt, meanwhile, handles all the luggage while looking like a brute for "letting" her cart massive me around.

I tell you, this celebrityhood is a bum rap. Everyone is so ready to be judgmental. Like I am a burden and Miss Temple is a silly lightweight and Mr. Matt is a spoiled media darling.

When it comes to spoiled media darlings around here, that will be me, the once and future king of cat food spokespersonery.

All in all, though, I am pleased with our jaunt to Chicago.

My media value was enhanced by a couple

dramatic kidnappings.

I was able to get in a high-power workout while on vacation and meet a new lot of street buddies and future sources, should I elect to move my base of operations to the Windy City. Perhaps I could relocate the junior partner north instead. Miss Midnight Louise might establish an outpost for Midnight Investigations, Inc. I have not done too badly here on an extended weekend visit.

I helped uncover dastardly lingering plots from years ago that are still alive and ticking, or kicking.

Also, I have learned valuable lessons on making it through security.

Now that we are home I will get back to pursuing evil weevils like the Viper and the Weasel all the live-long day. And night.

Evil Weevils is what I privately call the bad guys and girls, both of which I am hoping to foil and eradicate like bugs on the beautiful neon desert lily that is my native town of Las Vegas.

Now that I have taken down a couple of Chicago hoods I am ready for a no-holds-barred campaign against these Synth characters who have been messing up my compadres' lives since day one.

Life would be dull without vile forces to battle, be they fleas or felons, however.

CHAPTER 30
SURPRISE PARK

Cop cars often met at the far end of fast-food joint parking lots, pulling up to each other with the noses pointed opposite ways so the cops could speak through the driver's side windows.

That was impractical in Las Vegas, given the usual heat and the vehicle's air-conditioning blowing in the wind and burning expensive gas.

So Max left his Volkswagen well hidden behind a tall stand of pampas grass and hiked into the picnic area of Sunrise Park.

He passed Molina's new Prius, a classic silver color ideal for the Vegas climate, unlike the heat-absorbing and apropos black of his Beetle. Still, it was low and easy to hide, especially at night.

Unlike Sunset Park, tucked under McCarran Airport on the south side of the city, Sunrise Park was smaller, less well kept, and tucked under Nellis Air Force Base on the city's north side.

It was twelve miles north of McCarran and eight miles from the Strip. Meeting here was as far off the hustle, bustle, and recognition factor of the Strip as you could get and still be convenient.

In the early morning, both tennis courts were occupied, although the surfaces looked rugged.

Molina was sitting on a picnic table in one of her signature khaki summer pantsuits, her buckskin loafer-clad feet planted on the built-in seat.

Max broke into a lope to get there.

"No need to rush. You're right on time," she said, checking the serviceable watch on her wrist. Everything she wore was serviceable. On the job, for sure, and often off it.

The suit jacket pockets would contain a cell phone, but an overworked homicide lieutenant wanted faster access and the precision of the second hand.

Someone really needed to take this woman to the Bellagio shops and outfit her.

Max slowed, surprised he had to catch his breath a bit.

"Moving better, but still not in prime shape," she noted, watching the lime green tennis balls lob back and forth over the nets through her drugstore sunglasses.

"It'll take time." Max planted a leg on the seat and pushed up to sit on the table, not too close, glad the leg accepted the pressure without buckling, although a quiver of pain ran up the thigh.

"What's to report?" she asked.

"The Goliath murder is not a cold case."

"Because?"

"Because someone is watching the old security camera access shafts."

"You know this because?"

"I had to punch him out to escape once I'd reached the observation nest over the casino table where the DB was found a couple years ago."

"DB. Dead body. Very *CSI* TV. You could have phoned that information in."

"Yes, but I can't plea-bargain long distance."

"What did you do now?"

He laughed. "You sound like my mother."

"You have one?"

"Had."

"Sorry."

"That's past tense in the distance sense, not the death sense. As far as I know," he added.

She frowned at the implication. Max realized he'd never heard a whisper about Molina's family of origin. It was just mother and daughter, maybe too much so.

"How do you know *anything* about your family history, Mr. Amnesia Man?" she asked.

"Garry and I discussed it on our . . . European idyll." The last two words came out far more acidic than he'd intended, like a tart lemon-rind twist in a glass of gin. It *had* been a fabulous road trip, except for the unearthed tragedy, pain and death, his own and others'.

"You were with Randolph from — ?"

"Zurich to Dublin to Belfast."

"Four days?"

"About that. I wasn't counting."

Her eyes left the lame tennis match to acknowledge his proximity for the first time. "Then you have more good times to remember than bad."

Her moment of empathy was surprising. He'd often had to push past empathy to survive, as she must have often done too. With her, it was her job. With him, it had become his nature.

"Could you say the same about Rafi?" he asked. "More good memories than bad?"

She hissed something he couldn't hear, even interpret or imagine, and jumped down to the ground to confront him. With her height, they were face-to-face and she was furious. He'd trespassed on her personal issues.

"Come on," Max said. "He can't have been as bad an ex as, say, the late and very unlamented Cliff Effinger."

"Matt Devine's ex-stepfather. That skunk! What was his mother thinking? I'd really like to meet her."

"You can't. Temple is up in Chicago right now doing that."

That stunned her. "So that relationship is long-term serious?"

"Looks like it. Any reason you'd think it wasn't?"

"You coming back."

"Hardly. That's a blank slate, anything that was is wiped clean. And I don't believe Temple's my type. My infatuation must have been an aberration."

"If Matt Devine were here, he'd flatten you for saying that about his fiancée and I've half a mind to do it myself."

"Temple is savvy, smart, and charming, but I'm no threat to any couple at the moment. I still need to get my feet on the ground."

"Yet you somehow linked up with Rafi Nadir?"

"Maybe you sicced him on me in your time-tested method of hiring unwanted men to trail wanted men."

She ignored the gibe. "The only couple I'm interested in now is you and Rafi. Give."

"I checked out the observation vents over the Goliath casino and found the area is still 'live.' Something was and still could be planned there."

"Where did Nadir come in on that?"

"He, ah, had followed me. So I had unexpected backup."

"He helped you out?"

"Yeah. I told you, he's a good man. Maybe not for your purposes, but —"

"That's enough. I can buy that both you ex-heroes got caught up in my widespread net for the Barbie Doll Killer. Why you're going steady now, I can't figure."

"I wanted to examine the pirate attraction where Cliff Effinger had died at the Oasis, and convinced Nadir to take me there after hours."

"Oh, yeah, the new Hardy Boys. How'd you convince Rafi to risk his precious job?"

"Believe it not, I'm very convincing."

"Who's sorry now?"

"I am. Much more was going on than either of us would have believed. When the attraction was closed for the night I was able to board the sinking ship set and determine that the bizarre act of binding Effinger to the figurehead was meant to torture, not kill."

"Cliff Effinger was worth torturing?"

"If he knew something he wasn't ever going to give up. Maybe it was a Something worth a lot of money."

"So the ghost of Effinger appeared on deck and gave you postmortem evidence on what happened to him."

"No, but the whole thing went down —"

"The ship?"

"The expedition. It went down the same as at the Goliath. Somebody was either waiting or had followed us. More than one someone. Only neither Rafi nor I was tossed overboard into the temporarily electrified pirate's cove waters. An attacker was."

Molina's gently mocking demeanor had dropped like a mask. "Electrified water. That could kill innocent tourists when the attraction is open. Someone died on scene?" She was punching out her cell phone like Mike Tyson. "Nothing at the Oasis on the roster last night. Just a drunk and disorderly report on an unidentified man at the ship attraction site."

"I assumed the flashlight brigade that interrupted us was hotel security and they would immediately notify the authorities about the dead man floating. Maybe the

275

men out there weren't with the hotel. That night attack is sounding sinisterer and sinisterer."

"So this whole phantom encounter resulted in the death of one anonymous man who's vanished, and you two get off with a vague drunk and disorderly report not even attached to an ID'd suspect."

"They had Rafi in their lights and were carrying firearms. Maybe they threatened him with exposure to shut him up."

"So you left him there?"

"He'd told me to run for cover in the jungle-like foliage around that area before that."

"And you always do what you're told? Where is he now?"

"I don't know. He's not answering his cell phone."

"And you're not out looking for him?"

"You rang, and I came running. I was heading back to the Oasis to make sure he didn't lose his job, dammit. You and I got the poor sod into this."

"Not me. So what do you think Effinger got *himself* into?"

"It has to be mob activity."

"Haven't you heard? They went corporate long ago."

" 'Corporate' doesn't mean clean. Far

from it. Just as 'peace' isn't a synonym for the end of violence."

"You seem to attract violence wherever you go."

"Maybe *I* know something I shouldn't."

"That's a bad place to be with a temporal lobe on leave."

"I know it. Doesn't mean my memory doesn't work going forward."

"Mob." She consulted her own perfectly functioning memory. "They're pretty on the down low these days."

"This Effinger death was overkill. And he was meant to be found to scare someone else, some mob or gang or other outfit."

Molina nodded. "You could be right. That might explain . . . you wouldn't remember —"

"What?"

"Just remember that you need my input. There was a false alarm about Effinger's death earlier."

"Yes?"

"Man fell out of the Crystal Phoenix ceiling, dead."

"Another ceiling murder? Unsolved?"

She nodded. "He looked a bit like Effinger, but had no ID."

"Somebody mistook him for Effinger and offed him."

"Or . . ."

He got it. "Effinger wanted to be thought dead. He doesn't strike me as the killer sort. He *is* from Chicago, though, like Devine. The mob is plenty active there."

"Don't think too big," she cautioned him. "Think personal."

"Devine! Matt Devine was on his trail. He wanted *Matt Devine* to think he was dead." Max reconsidered. "No. Devine wasn't that big a threat."

"He was if his dogged search for Effinger was drawing attention, and drawing attention to Effinger. And don't underestimate Matt Devine. He's with your girl now, isn't he?"

"I'm not possessive by nature. I think. You're pushing the wrong buttons, Lieutenant."

"Maybe. Then there was that crazy incident involving your ex-girlfriend and her cat being kidnapped from a Shangri-La magic show and being spirited down the highway in a semi filled with magic-act paraphernalia and contraband drugs. I sensed your ghostly fingers at work in the scene of their escape when my people got there. Any memories of tearing the contents of that semi to pieces to find the pair before they suffocated?"

Magical boxes, big enough to conceal an artfully arranged human body, boxes with false bottoms and sides and mirrors. They crowded his memory, begging for recognition. *You used me in this illusion. No, Garry did. No, Temple Barr was your assistant and did the switch with you, and then you pulled her cat out of a hat.*

He blinked as the deceptive rummage sale images of the past faded away and smiled at Molina. "You are truly a tree of knowledge of good and evil. Or just evil."

She smiled. "Thanks. My job. Another little tidbit for you. About that old-time magician found dead in the underground safe that your ex-girlfriend tried to use as a promo opportunity."

"Cosimo Sparks," Max said. "I heard about him." Not only that, he'd dreamed about him, had known the man while still living, at the Neon Nightmare. He was a confirmed Synth member, but Molina would laugh that idea off.

"He was stabbed to death, but prodded viciously first."

"Another reluctant information-giver. Hasn't someone been arrested for that?"

"We had to let him go. A South American larger-than-life personality known as Santiago, just Santiago. Blood traces too insignificant for court. One always thinks of drugs. That would tie in to the Shangri-La kidnapping."

"What about that lady magician as a suspect?"

"Dead too."

"You have a . . . an outhouse-load of cold cases, Lieutenant."

"Why do you think I hire freelancers?"

"From what I can see, usually it's personal reasons."

"And what would those be in your case?"

"My Irish charm."

"I favor Latin charm."

"With those blue eyes? It's a fact that the Irish and the Spanish mix like whiskey and soda. Soledad O'Brian, the news reporter. I can't think of others. The memory, you know."

"What are you and your overblown Irish charm getting at, Kinsella?"

"Have you ever considered the . . . Irish mob?"

"You talking Boston?"

"I'm talking Northern Ireland."

She made a *tsk*ing sound. "I've heard that eternally from your ex. I don't doubt your counterterrorism work in the past, but that conflict is ninety-eight percent over and done with. Face it. You're not a downtrodden minority anymore. And your fixation on this topic is obsessive romanticism. The 'Troubles' are over. Those political crusades are over, and whatever will you do without them?"

Max stood, and stood at mock attention. "Work for you, Lieutenant, until you can see past your personal, private 'troubles' and discern the vast terrorist conspiracy surrounding us all."

CHAPTER 31
MISSING LINKS

Temple and Matt trudged toward the baggage claim area, thankful that Louie would have no more close encounters with airport security. These did not turn out well for the carrier-searches.

Temple was in that automatic nirvana of ending a short trip that had been packed with stress and uncertainty, so it was Matt who spotted the fly in the ointment.

"Unwelcome committee of one at three o'clock high," he warned under his breath.

Temple had seen enough WWII fighter-pilot movies to look to her right at midlevel.

Slouching against the giant rattlesnake sculpture among the famous assembly of desert critters on the terminal floor was . . . Max.

Fitting. He was long and lean and deadly when in counterterrorist mode. His black ensemble suggested that magician mode was also back and operational, and then some.

He straightened to snag Louie's gaudy new carrier from Temple without a by-your-leave or by-your-left-or-right and joined their pace without losing a beat. Neither did his opening patter.

"Welcome to Las Vegas. Lieutenant C. R. Molina is my new secret boss. In the wee hours of this morning someone tried to electrocute me at the Oasis Hotel's 'Lusty Ladies and Laddies' pirate adventure attraction. And Rafi Nadir could be under suspicion of murder, although any evidence would be only circumstantial. May I give you two — excuse me, three — a lift home?"

Matt took it much better than Temple did. "Are you driving anything with trunk space for luggage these days?"

"And a belted seat for Louie's carrier?" Temple asked.

"No, but I rented a minivan that fills the bill."

Temple couldn't keep from hooting. "You in a minivan. That'd be worth seeing."

"Then walk this way," Max said, stepping ahead and feigning an exaggerated limp, like the hunchback of Notre Dame. It was eerie how his height shrank.

Matt sighed and conversation ceased until

they got to the close-in parking lot and beside a blue, yes, minivan.

"How did you know where and when — ?" Temple asked Max, repossessing Louie's carrier.

"Font of all knowledge of things Circle Ritz."

"Electra." Matt paused in loading their luggage. "You're relying on gossipy senior citizens these days?"

"Any port in a storm, as we say at the Oasis. Well, perhaps not so much today."

"And what about Rafi? Murder?" Temple finished arranging Louie's carrier in the backseat although he was pummeling the canvas sides. He was keeping quiet, though. "Just a short ride home," she assured him, "and then you'll be free to be feline."

Through the black mesh portion she detected a wide, pinkmawed yawn, the cat equivalent of "yadda yadda yadda."

"Circumstantial evidence," Max said as he put the Odyssey into gear. Matt rode up front with him, Temple and Louie in the middle bank of seats. Max twisted his head to regard the couple in turn. "You two are dressed mighty like city slickers."

Like Louie, they kept mum.

"Oh, right. Chicago. I get forgetful." He lifted a finger off the steering wheel to ndicate Matt. "You do the Ann Landers bit on syndicated radio and also do some national TV."

"OOD," Temple caroled from the back-seat. "Out of date. 'Dear Abby' survived the advice column wars when the newspapers were sinking fast. And they were both from Chicago. Imagine, twin sisters who were newspaper column advice queens all their lives, and only one byline survives their deaths."

"Got it," Max said, "but I don't play Trivial Pursuit, so don't need that info. Don't think you can distract me with minor matters, Temple. I still want to know the dish on where you're coming from. In Chicago." His voice had grown speculative. "And why would you lug that overweight cat along?"

"Merely," Temple said, "to keep the great Mystifying Max guessing and his recovering memory agile."

Max declaimed, "They drew a circle that shut me out. I drew a circle that took them in."

" 'Heretic, rebel, a thing to flout,' " Matt quoted, eyeing Max. "That's the poem's second line. If the description fits . . ."

"Heretic, no. Rebel, yes. A thing to flout, ately that seems very appropriate."

Temple wasn't getting any of this except the rival guy vibe, so she leaned forward over the seat. "Back to Rafi Nadir. What did you mean by 'circumstantial' evidence in a murder?"

"The death occurred at the Oasis Hotel. That's Rafi's turf as assistant security chief."

"And you were there too?" Temple asked. "Why?"

"Doing what you do so well. Sticking our noses into other people's business. I should mention it was three A.M. and the attraction was shut down."

"So Rafi wasn't on duty," Temple guessed.

"Rafi wouldn't have been there if I hadn't drawn him into the web of Vegas cold cases I'm investigating on a wing-nut brain and a prayer. The dead man was an anonymous thug and if fighting him off is murder, I probably did the deed and Rafi was a deer caught in the headlights, prepped to take the fall."

"Why would Rafi Nadir even be there?" Temple wondered.

"He's a good guy."

Matt raised his eyebrows to look over his shoulder at Temple.

"And," Max added, "I'm trying to shut down any lingering poisons from my British Isles adventures way back when and recently. Namely Kathleen O'Connor and anyone responsible for the dead man in the Goliath Hotel surveillance system and a certain unwanted . . . relative of yours by marriage." He nodded to Matt. "The late Cliff Effinger."

In the silence, Max added a chilling coda. "Not what I wanted, to get snarled up in your tragic family history, but Kitty the Cutter certainly involved you in mine."

A silence inside the idling vehicle reflected everyone's mutual shock, Temple refected. Max couldn't know that the Chicago trip had stripped bare a link right back to Las Vegas and possible Synth activity. And Matt had to realize that Max couldn't resolve his long forced involvement with Irish terrorism and a true femme fatale stalker without treading on part of Matt's family history Matt wanted no one but Temple to know.

Holy Kowabunga. Temple had a vintage surfer T-shirt to wear around home that paid tribute to that catchword from Chief Thunderthud on the *Howdy Doody* kiddie TV show in the '50s. Like slang that kept on reinventing itself for future generations, Kathleen O'Connor and Cliff Effinger were old nightmares that kept recycling again and again, both supposedly dead and both surprisingly potent up to this very minute.

"Call me an obsessive compulsive amnesiac," said Max, "but I think this all adds up. Somehow."

"Who's called you an obsessive compulsive amnesiac?" Matt asked. "That sure sounds like a gripe."

"Nobody important. Just an amateur psychoanalyzer like you."

"If you mean I can analyze psychos —"

"You know," Temple said, "I don't think I'm comfortable riding here in the backseat like the distant top of a pyramid with you two guys in the front driver's seat."

Sometimes Temple didn't realize the full meaning of things she said until her own voice stopped. Not often. It was not a good habit for a successful PR woman and in the personal arena it was a sound example of clunky, size 5 wedgies firmly inserted in mouth.

Describing a functional triangle at this point was not productive. Something jammed her in the hip. Louie was rocking his carrier over onto its side and into her space.

Oh. Right. They were a dysfunctional quadrangle, not a triangle.

How comforting.

CHAPTER 32
BAD MEWS

Naturally, I have used my incisive incisors to spring the zipper on my new low-end carrier. The less time spent in Miss Krys's truly ucky idea of a cat carrier from hell, the better.

By the time Mr. Max drives his exceedingly boring rented minivan into the Circle Ritz parking lot, I am free, black, and pushing twenty-one pounds of muscular male physique out of the first opening vehicle door. (My layabout lifestyle in the Windy City has added a tad of avoirdupois around my middle, but that is a French condition and cannot help but be an attractive addition.)

I make a four-point landing on the still-warm asphalt of my native soil: the mean streets of the country's loudest and liveliest entertainment jungle, and inhale the hot, heavy air.

Aaah. Tar so melt-in-your-mouth sizzling, it could trap a brontosaurus; pad-searing sand; and egg-frying-hot concrete. I am back in civilization! Not for me dank, deserted warehouses down mean streets so dark, not a ray of ultraviolet neon can penetrate those Bast-less byways.

Not for me petty thugs who cannot even make an effective and grammatical threatening phone call.

Here in Vegas, style rules. And I am just strutting my stuff toward the parking lot fringes when I come up nose to nose with one of the city's least famous fixtures.

"Huh," I say. I do not want to admit that I have hit a wall of pretty impenetrable fur and chutzpah. I am the expert at that. "Louise!" I cry.

I was about to make a pilgrimage to the Crystal Phoenix, but she pops out of the large oleander bushes ringing the Circle Ritz parking lot as though to pounce upon me.

"Where have you been?" I inquire.

"If you wish to sit your unprotected rear down on the sizzling hot asphalt, I can remain in the shade and regale you with a long and winding journey through Vegas hot spots more noted for sin than fever."

Aaah. I have bounded onto the cooling dirt and sand surrounding the oleanders.

"How was Chicago?" she asks.

"All right. There is a lot less street-level action and entertainment value there. I could get all my exercise jumping up to hit elevator buttons in the high-twenties and up."

"Home is the hunter, home from the five-star hotels and the lure of hot studio lights," Miss Midnight Louise observes. "At least you managed to keep your two fragile human charges in one piece."

"Them? Fragile? Yeah, they were facing family matters more incestuous than Ma Barker's clan, aka clowder, but, Louise, you have no idea how imperiled I was in life and limb and carrier in Chicago."

"Where *is* that leopard-spot carrier fit for a reality TV Chihuahua, by the way?"

"I left it as a headstone for a couple of Chicago gangsters."

Miss Midnight Louise's airy whiskers lift above her censorious features. (This censorious features stuff means she has a scowl on her puss that would sour a Green Appletini. Not to mention a decent dude who has only been doing his guard duty out of town.)

"Were they dead or just happy to get you out of their nightmares?"

"Let us simply say that, thanks to me, they knocked themselves out to commit mayhem and got snagged by the cops."

"Meanwhile," she notes, "Mr. Max has been out on the town performing acts of derring-do that threaten to undo his precarious healing process. Can you say the same?"

"My acts of derring-do have threatened to undo other entities' healing processes. It is the Chicago Outfit, zero; and Midnight Louie, two."

I push closer, not to get cozy, mind you, but to exchange privileged information.

"I am happy to hear you have been sticking closer to Mr. Max than a coat of black graffiti spray paint while I have been transported across state lines to eavesdrop on some amateur episodes of *The Old and the Restless.* My Miss Temple and Mr. Matt are a done deal, whether you or I like it or not. What would occasion Mr. Max to greet the network-approved lovebirds on their return to the nest? He does not live here anymore."

"He is lucky to be alive and not-living somewhere six feet under after last night."

"Last night? There was some more hot homicidal action in town while I was gone? No!"

Miss Louise takes this moment to admonish a possibly verminous intruder on her back forty. Or she could be allergic to something, like me.

"Well?" I demand, gently tapping her shoulder.

She responds to my friendly overture by swatting my mitt to the pavement. "First tell me what went down in Chicago."

"The usual. We prepare to fly. I am the VIP of airport security in Miss Temple's admittedly sissy poodle portage bag."

" 'Por*tahge*'?"

"That is French for 'transportation,' " I respond airily, waving my posterior *plume de ma tante* for emphasis. It always distracts Miss Midnight Louise when I talk à la the Divine Yvette, my Persian *petite.*

"I am the object of a kidnapping attempt at the moment of our arrival in O'Hare," I say vehemently, nipping at the vermin that left her for higher-end pastures.

At this she hoots. Well, she rolls over on the ground exposing her soft underbelly with no fear, as if I were a bunny rabbit instead of Chicago muscle.

"They were obviously after your carrier," she manages to mew between rude snorts.

"Actually, that is too true," I admit. "Airport security suspected I was acting as a mule for smuggled celebrity fine jewelry. Unfortunately, the only fine jewelry my Miss Temple owns is the engagement ring on her finger and an MIA opal ring in her notorious scarf drawer. No, Louise," I add. "They were after me as a means to information hidden by Mr. Matt's louse of a late stepfather, Mr. Cliff Effinger, in goods held by his widow, Miss Matt Mama in Chicago."

By now she is again upright and skeptical. "So these Chicago hoods believed someone would give up valuable info to save your hide?"

"Not 'someone.' My Miss Temple."

"That I can believe. You have become a kept cat on her account, so I do not doubt some schmaltzy unnatural link holds you two together."

I am not about to defend my personal life to one who scorns the human–feline bond while maintaining quite a crush, if you ask me, on Mr. Max Kinsella.

Meanwhile, Miss Midnight Louise is chewing on my revelations, suiting word to act by gnawing on a loose nail sheath, reminding me of my brilliant ruse with the rusted carpenter nails and the crooks.

"I am afraid," she finally admits, lifting her head to spit out the sheath, "that Mr. Max has seen plain evidence this very weekend that Mr. Cliff Effinger's bizarre death by drowning on the old Oasis Hotel pirate ship attraction is not a closed case, but one of interest to various sinister elements around town. I followed him on two expeditions to the Oasis to check on the Effinger drowning site and the last one was nearly fatal to him, if not Mr. Rafi and me."

"Hmm," I say judiciously. Acting judicious

gives one time to think. "Are you saying that Midnight Investigations, Inc., might be forced to indulge in some wet work?"

"I am saying that our job wrangling the private and public part of our human associates' lives will have to get messy before we can be sure the right people come out of this mess alive."

CHAPTER 33
TEMPLE'S TABLE OF CRIME ELEMENTS

"Nice place," Max said, prowling around behind Matt's red suede sofa. "Should I recognize it?"

"Not at all," Temple said.

They'd "convened" at Matt's apartment. Her suggestion. It held no unsettling memories for Max to unpackage. Matt would be on his own territory. She was the most adaptable person present.

Max finally settled his long frame on one of the upholstered side chairs, leaving Temple and Matt the sofa.

"How'd you end up at the Oasis pirate ship attraction?" Matt asked.

"Gandolph —" Max paused to eye Matt. "You know better than I remember that he was my former stage partner in Europe and mentor at counterterrorism work for half my life. I suppose he was my spiritual father."

Max's blue eyes had become soft-focus as

he looked inward, a new habit for the Max Temple had known. "He's the only person I still feel . . . felt a real personal link with."

Temple couldn't stop her eyes from flashing to meet Matt's at the same moment. Max's insight and declaration, if accurate, cleared away a ton of emotional sand traps looming between Temple's former and current fiancées.

Max was still figuring out his reactions. "He'd been born Garry Randolph. I keep calling him by his stage name as a magician and his civilian name interchangeably. Maybe it's because I've lost part of my mind." He made a humorous grimace. "Or maybe it's because I can't separate what he meant to me."

"He needs no further introduction here," Matt said. "I get spiritual fathers. I also get very unspiritual faux fathers, like Cliff Effinger. You know, if that Oasis drowning case ceases being 'cold,' this new death there could make *me* a suspect again in Effinger's death."

Max shook his head. "Don't worry. I've managed to bollix things up so much that right now Rafi Nadir is a likeliest suspect for the latest death at the Oasis. And Molina might be eager to buy that because it takes him out of the running for joint custody for her daughter. Fortunately, the probable victim vanished."

"Why is Rafi involved?" Temple asked. "You've said he was a good guy. So any personal bones Molina had to pick with him are not relevant?"

"I say that because Gandolph secretly hired Nadir as our Vegas backup. Even I didn't know about that. When I crashed, Rafi was onsite at the Neon Nightmare as a security man. He was really there to keep an eye on me. When I went down, he was in instant touch so Gandolph could have me spirited away by fake EMTs, which covered up the murder attempt and made my apparent death convincing."

"Gandolph has been way more central to all this than we suspected," Temple told Matt. "The Synth has been looking like some lame woo-woo group of delusional magicians pretending to be powerful occultists lately, but Gandolph's 'retirement' years were spent unmasking fraudulent mediums. Apparently, he still took the Synth seriously."

Max bestirred himself on the upholstered chair, a sign that his battered frame was revitalizing. "Parts of it. The Synth is not a united front."

"How do you know?" Temple asked.

"I have Gandolph's laptop computer from our last recent dash across the Continent and the British Isles. And now I have access to some ambiguous files on his home computer. He wasn't one to commit the obvious, or the devious, to any lasting form, but he had to pay Rafi and those records are intact."

"Why are you and Rafi the new Starsky and Hutch?" Temple wanted to know.

"I told you. I inherited Rafi Nadir from Gandolph. He owed Garry a lot, including the recommendation for the Oasis security position. That was a prime job for an ex-cop who'd flunked out after Las Vegas's current finest homicide lieutenant left him without notice when she got with child. Anybody know why she ran? Was he abusive?"

"Suspicious mind," Temple said promptly. "She believed Rafi had sabotaged her birth control to get her off a career track at LAPD. They were both 'minorities' at the time and competition for the few token slots was harsh."

"So they both ended up losing out in L.A." Max smiled at the irony.

Matt entered the exchange. "Classic case of 'a failure to communicate.' Forgive the cliché."

"So why were you and Rafi snooping around the Oasis pirate ship in the wee hours?" Temple asked Max. "That's the kind of stunt I'd pull."

"Molina is out of unofficial legmen," Max said. "She hired me to investigate the crime she fingered me for as likely suspect. She has a sense of irony, I'll say that for her."

"But that was the dead guy in the eye-in-the-sky service area above the Goliath casino area."

"Right. Rafi followed me there in his role of posthumous Max guardian on Garry's payroll, and I encountered a fly on the wall of the service ducts, armed and dangerous only to himself."

"So," Matt said, leaning forward, "you team up with Rafi and on your next stop at the Oasis, you both get waylaid and some anonymous attacker ends up drowned. Why were you nosing around the scene where *my* stepfather died months ago?"

Max produced a quizzical look. "And you swore you weren't the possessive sort."

"You don't know me well enough to know what 'sort' I am, Kinsella. So why?"

Max shrugged. "Gandolph had stored a lot of references to Las Vegas crimes in his computers. Don't forget that he faked his own death at the Halloween séance to bring back the ghost of Harry Houdini. You can get a lot done when people think you're dead."

Temple produced an unladylike snort. "So *that*'s your excuse for your AWOL episodes. What about this? Maybe *Effinger* isn't dead."

She'd been exaggerating to make a point, but both men stared at her, the shocking suggestion shaking their separate assumptions.

Matt spoke first. "Temple, we need to tell him about Chicago and Louie and Effinger and Ophiucus."

She kept silent. Did they really want to let Max in on all of Matt's family issues. Did she?

"Chicago my long-term memory has down cold," Max told them, sensing they needed reassurance. "Midnight Louie I've met and concede is a formidable cat. Garry's computer notes make Effinger's relationship and character clear as the battery acid he was spawned in. But . . . Ophiuchus? I probably knew what it was just a couple months ago, but it's not downloading from the backup drive. Is it an ancient Greek curse?"

"Not a bad guess." Matt smiled to recall his genteel mother's similar reaction to the word. "It means 'serpent-bearer.' "

"It's the 'lost' thirteenth sign of the zodiac," Temple added. "Astrologers are trying to resurrect it right now because they say the sky or whatever has shifted since the traditional signs of the zodiac were designated centuries ago and all the autumn babies are not the same scales, scorpions, and archers they thought they were."

"Whoa." Max put his hand to his forehead. "I don't remember much, but I can sense that science was never your strong suit, Temple."

"So maybe the sky didn't shift. Exactly," she said. "What is making *our* specific spot of earth move is that Ophiuchus is the chosen symbol for the cabal of disgruntled traditional magicians that have been operating in Vegas, and out of the Neon Nightmare nightclub for years.

"And," she added, "the Synth may have had ties to guns and money for the Irish Republican Army both before and since the peace was made. That's why you were there posing as the Phantom Mage, to investigate it."

"That I buy," Max said. "Gandolph briefed me on the Synth during our European travels and it's been in his computer for ages. He liked them as a serious set of miscreants, but they strike me as rather pathetically mumbo jumbo. Or as a tooth-less front group."

"Maybe," Temple said, "but at least two of the unsolved deaths floating around this town in recent years involved magic or magicians and a corpse displayed in the form of the major stars in Ophiucus, which form what a kindergarten child would draw as the shape of a house."

"The *houses* of the zodiac," Max said.

"Nobody's put it quite that way," Matt admitted. "Anything zodiac seems too out there to take seriously."

"Says you!" Temple was indignant. "I read mine in the newspaper every day and some-times it's eerily accurate."

Max smiled at her. Tolerantly. "Accidental affinities are the long-mined territory of mediums, mind-readers, and scam artists."

"Is it an accident," Temple asked, "that Midnight Louie was just catnapped in Chicago to force Matt's mother to turn over items left behind in a fireproof box by the late Effinger? An accident that the only pos-sible thing relevant we found is what may be a biker tattoo in the form of a drawing of Ophiucus?"

"Ophiucus?" Max was no longer compla-cent. "Connected to Effinger?"

"And then," Matt said, lighting fire, "there

were the 'she left' murders, one at the Blue Dahlia where Molina sings sometimes and one . . . Temple, you wrote all this down in a table, didn't you?"

She regarded Max with super-sleuth intensity. "Call me unscientific, will you? I've compiled all those eerie details into a Table of . . . Crime Elements, Ophiuchus and all."

"Then show me, by all means." He leaned back and spread his empty hands. "Dazzle me with your superior organizational logic."

Temple left the sofa to dredge her tote bag from behind it. It sported a leopard pattern bought to match the late, lamented Midnight Louie travel carrier.

First she flourished the drawing of Ophiuchus at Max. "Zodiac signs may be junk science and superstition, but this 'lost' one is leaving star tracks all over Las Vegas."

Max took the drawing to study. "It *would* make a terrific tattoo."

Temple shuddered delicately. "It's called the serpent-bearer, but the muscle man looks more like he's fighting for his life than giving the snake a lift."

"Effinger had some tattoos," Matt said, "crude homemade ones, so this design may only have been a tattoo dream for him."

"I'm not enamored of making skin into

maps," Temple said, pulling out her netbook.

Its hot pink cover clashed with the red sofa when she sat back down to bring up a file.

She handed the computer to Matt while Max sprang up to lean down over the sofa back between them to see. He was indeed moving like the Max of old.

They all stared at the screen.

"That is worthy of Dame Agatha Christie," Max said, giving a long, low whistle after studying it.

Temple shrugged modestly. "I *have* read a Poirot and Marple or two."

Max's forefinger speared the table. "I'm right there as a suspect for Murder Number One at the Goliath. And, Devine, you're down as a suspect for the murder of a call girl named Vassar at the same hotel. My, my. No wonder the closemouthed and manipulative Molina is on all of our cases." Max eyed Temple. "You're amazingly unbiased in your suspect list, but I don't see *you* on it anywhere."

"I'm innocent of everything," Temple said blithely. "This table lists suspects the police would find likely for taking the rap. I'm an objective reporter and recorder. I just find some of the suspects likely, period."

WHO	WHEN	WHERE	METHOD	ODDITIES	SUSP
dead man at Goliath	April	Goliath ceiling	knife		Max
dead man at Phoenix	Aug	Phoenix ceiling	knife	Effinger looka-like, his ID	unknow
Max's mentor, Gandolph	Halloween	séance	faked death	dressed as woman	assorte psychic
Cliff Effinger, Matt's stepfather	Jan. New Year	Oasis	drowning	ship's figure-head	Two mu men
Woman	Feb	Blue Dahlia	strangled	"She left" on Molina's car	nun kill
Cher Smith, stripper	Feb	strip club parking lot	strangled		Strippe Killer
Gloria Fuentes, Gandolph's assistant	Feb	Church parking lot	strangled	"She left" on body in morgue	Synth
Prof. Jeff Mangel	March	UNLV hall	knifed	ritual marks	Real Sy
Cloaked Con-juror's Khatlord assistant, Barry	April	New Mil-lennium ceiling	beating or fatal fall	masked like CC or TV show SF alien	Synth/C enemy
Vassar, call girl	?	Goliath	fatal fall	After seeing Matt	Kitty/Ma
Art Deckle/ Shangri-La	May	New Mil-lennium	Fatal fall	CC's partner	Synth
Cosimo Sparks, Synth	May	Phoenix Chunnel	stabbed	Wearing white tie and tails	Santiag

Her impish grin had both men backing away like nervous tomcats. Max left his casual post at the sofa back that had made them a threesome as Matt frowned at the image on the screen.

"You've added the Cosimo Sparks death," he noted.

"If the Synth is a paper tiger," Temple said, "why was Sparks killed and his scarlet-lined cloak left in the distinctive 'Ophiuchus house' shape?"

"Maybe to misdirect the blame." Max sat back in the upholstered chair and tented his hands to support his chin. "Most of the cast of characters on your chart, Temple, are mentioned in Gandolph's computer files. What stands out for me is the murdered professor, Jefferson Mangel That killing was off the Strip and there were no overt links to magic."

"There was one," Temple said.

"What?"

"You."

"How would Gandolph miss that?"

"Jeff Mangel was a professor of philosophy, but a magic fan. He was found dead, in that telling Ophiuchus-Synth position, among a classroom exhibition of magic show advertisement posters. People collect that kind of ephemera. And one of your

Mystifying Max posters was on display."

Max suddenly pounded his temples with his fists. "Damn this MIA memory of mine! I'm useless."

Temple's dismayed look consulted Matt.

"Not useless enough for someone's taste," Matt said with a bit of Max's own sardonic drawl. "There've been two attempts on your life in the time it took us to make a whirlwind trip to Chicago."

Max lifted his head, the fury dispersing as fast as it had come. "And on Midnight Louie's life. Apparently me and the cat have too many of those pesky lives for someone's security. You're right, Devine. The more I investigate, the more I'll flush out the rats. Rat bait is an honorable role."

"We *all* need to investigate." Temple said, "Why are these cold cases that involve one or more of us suddenly hot again? The trouble is, when you look at my, ahem, brilliant Table of Crime Elements, there are so darn many ways we could go and way too much ground to cover."

"Can you get the Fontana brothers as backup?" Matt asked Temple. "We don't seem to have a choice on staying out of what's going on, but Rafi's going to be plenty busy with Kinsella, or Carmen Molina."

"I don't want Nicky getting all über-protective about me," Temple said.

"Do all those big boys tell their little brother everything, even though he's the hotelier?" Matt prodded.

"Probably not."

Max held one hand fanned over his eyes and braced an elbow on a chair arm listening to them, as if the light were too bright.

Before Temple could make an alarmed murmur in his direction, he spoke. "The Fontana brothers. Is that a juggling act at the Sahara or something?"

She and Matt exchanged a totally blitzed look. Where to kick-start Max's memories when he had such serious blanks as already-demolished Strip hotels and Las Vegas legends like the Fontana brothers, high-profile owners of Gangsters custom limo service, not to mention the boutique hotel of the same name?

Temple should change topics to touch on Max's more immediate experiences. This would also be an apt time to admit her risky Neon Nightmare adventure and the showdown she'd stumbled onto in the Synth's secret clubrooms there.

"I can't say I'm much impressed by the local Synth crew as capable of murder," Temple said, "although its symbol flashes itself around murder scenes."

"Why not?" Max asked. "I've had 'flashes' of being at the Neon Nightmare in my Phantom Mage persona and they were certainly planning something. I'm recovering memories in a grid like a Mondrian painting, or pixels when a HDTV picture breaks up . . . islands of clear images in a sea of nothingness."

"Uh," Temple said, "before we leave the topic of my incisive mental powers, I have to mention that I've had a close encounter recently at the Neon Nightmare's secret Synth clubrooms."

"And you didn't mention it to me?" Matt was shocked.

Temple grimaced. Time to confess her sins to Matt. "When I went to Neon Nightmare — which every guy I know wants to lecture me for doing, including Nicky Fontana, my boss at the Crystal Phoenix, where I do PR —"

"I know this," Max said.

"Uh. Okay. It was a very tacky and woo-woo experience, lacking only Rod Serling as narrator intoning, 'Welcome to the *Twilight Zone.*' "

"Extreme stage effects," Max said, "often are used to divert an audience from what's really going on. Cirque du Soleil is masterul at that."

"Also the Mystifying Max," Temple said with a smile.

"So," Matt challenged. "You were an audience of one subjected to delusional magic tricks, Temple?"

"Maybe," she told Matt. "It involves ninja cats and double Darth Vaders."

"Oh." Matt sat back.

"Oh." Temple shrugged. "I *had* been exposed previously to inferior cocktails, would-be wild and sexy single guys, and the screamingly loud, shrill, and robotic noise that passes for dance music these days, not to mention circling neon laser lights that cast the spinning zodiac signs, including Ophiucus, on the black glass dance floor and walls."

"Takes me right back to my near-death experience," Max murmured.

"I figured out, though, that all those light-works hide entrances to the interior pyramid-shape of the nightclub. I found a narrow upward ramp that has spring-loaded doors into the walls."

"Temple!" Matt was horrified. "Why would you go there? That sounds like a drug trip."

"Just think of the doors on fancy home theater equipment storage units. They're always black lacquered and you just touch a corner and they spring open. That's how got into a maze of rooms behind the walls and the Synth clubrooms, which overlook the dance floor with a one-way wall of black glass."

"Sounds like a private high roller club," Max said, "at some of the upscale hotel casinos where a lot goes on that isn't legal So? If a group of fantasizing fakes want to pretend they're magicians with an agenda . . ."

"We know from the empty safe buil between the underground tunnels where the Crystal Phoenix and Gangsters hotels mee with one from the Neon Nightmare tha your old IRA enemies had been amassing money and guns in Vegas for a couple de cades."

"What kind of safe?" Max asked.

"A giant walk-in one. That's where Synth member Cosimo Sparks's body was found wearing white gloves, top hat, and tails. . . Well, the top hat didn't stay on when he was stabbed to death. A couple silver dol lars were found on the floor, along with a bearer bond for twenty thousand dollars a rat dug up from the adjacent hidden tunne to . . . the Neon Nightmare."

"Rightly named," Matt said. "You never

told me you'd broken into the Synth's lair at that nightclub."

"Well, that's because what I saw there wasn't exactly believable."

"In what way?" Max wanted to know.

"It wouldn't pass the C. R. Molina test."

"In what way?" *Matt* now wanted to know.

Temple kept jerking her head from one interrogator to another. "It does sound a bit too much Mad Tea Party."

Into the continued silence she had to commit truth. "The club room held a middle-aged woman who looked like a medium, or Gandolph in the guise of a female medium at that Halloween séance. The other woman looked like Morticia, the slinky Goth wife from *The Addams Family*. And there was a pretty ordinary guy there. They were upset about Cosimo Sparks's death, and then another spring-loaded door opened and these two . . . figures . . . showed up."

"Figures?" Matt questioned.

Temple decided then and there to leave out the pack of black cats that closed down the private party minutes later, but she was now committed to describing the figures.

"They were disguised. In black. Head to toe."

"Head to toe?" Max snorted. "Were they wearing blackface?"

313

"Gloves and long cloaks with hoods."

"Old magicians' tricks to blend in with the background," Max said. "Houdini used it."

"That's not all. Full head masks. I thought of them as the Darth Vaders."

"Now, that's an elaborate getup," Matt said. "Hokey, though. Are you sure that's what you saw, Temple?"

"It was dark, but I'd entered through a sheltered niche between bookcases and it was like being an audience at a peepshow." She took measure of the two men's dubious expressions. "Not that kind of peepshow. Let's just say it was a gathering of dramatic personalities. The Darth Vaders were clearly the stars. They had guns and they wanted money."

"Temple!" Matt was shocked. "You put yourself at risk in the middle of some kind of heist? People who rip off casinos go for the extreme disguises, don't they, Kinsella?"

Max looked quizzical. "You're relying on my memory? Fortunately, it's the personal history that's mostly gone missing. Yeah. Because of the intense visual security and scrutiny in casinos, people who knock over cash transfers at money cages wear masks at least. They're safe physically."

Temple wasn't so sure. "They always get

caught."

"But they are never interfered with as long as they're armed and dangerous and out on the casino floor among hundreds of clients and players," Max said. "Hotel security and police want zero collateral damage."

"So," Temple said, "you can get out with the money, but your chances of keeping it are —"

"Zero," Max said.

"What about the plans I overheard, for the Synth magicians to create a multi-Strip free-for-all distraction of illusions to cover a major heist?"

"Again," Max said. "Great idea. Would work for getting the money. As in every robbery from a modest ATM stick-up to a major planned assault on a Strip casino or Fort Knox, for that matter, the real trick is the disappearing act afterwards."

Temple nodded. "That's why the Glory Hole Gang hid out for decades when Jersey Joe Jackson absconded with the train robbery money."

"Jersey Joe," Matt reminded her, "got away with the money and cheating his buddies, but he had to hide the ill-gotten goods for so long, he died bankrupt and alone."

"So this IRA money raised over a couple decades could simply be left hidden forever?" Temple asked.

Max sighed. "The Synth members are pawns. From what you said, they were in it for the revenge and the prestige, in the sense of the payoff in a magical illusionary statement, when jaws drop. So how did you and they escape being mowed down by two Darth Vaders?"

"Jesus," Matt said prayerfully.

Temple shrugged. "I . . . just bowed out. They sorta noticed me finally —"

" 'Sorta'?" Matt sounded pre-cardiac.

"And I just said I was looking for a ladies' room and they were really hard to find here and I wouldn't be back. Stephanie Plum always gets out of pickles with girly candor."

"Stephanie who?" Matt demanded, exasperated.

"The book series," Temple said. "Chick lit mystery."

Max chuckled. "She must mean Nancy Drew rebooted. You do know who that was?"

Matt shook his head, mystified.

"How do *you* know about Nancy Drew?" Temple asked Max.

"I don't know." He blinked. "I had a younger girl cousin, I guess, in Wisconsin." His contribution ended in one of his memory-exploring silences.

"I know all about 'younger girl cousins,' " Temple said, eyeing Matt.

He opted for silence too.

It was all just too nicey-nicey, Temple thought. Everybody was so busy not stomping on everybody's else's toes — or previous and current relationships — that any honest analysis was impossible.

If they couldn't work together, they darn well might hang separately.

"You can see why I'd never mention this Neon Nightmare stuff to Molina," Temple said into the extending silences. "I'm even sorry I discussed it with you guys. We need to divvy up the cold cases and investigate on our own."

"How do we 'divvy up' this imposing table of multiple murders and possible perps?" Max asked.

"Mathmatically," Temple said, then quipped, "MaxiMattically."

Both guys shot more bolt upright at the idea being equated in her investigative formula. Good. Their competitive natures were kicking in after this very refined and very boring Likefest.

"And some say girls can't do left brain," Temple finished up.

She consulted her Table of Crime Elements like an efficiency expert, rubbing her hands together.

"Max. Your assignment. Assignments, plural."

He pulled his long, lounging frame to attention. Temple was happy to see his core muscles and core spirit were, uh, she couldn't think of a description that didn't involve "hardening" or "stiffening," so, like Scarlett O'Hara, she didn't think about it anymore.

"You understand magicians," she told Max, "whether you remember that or not, so your assignment will be the Cloaked Conjuror, the role model for the Darth Vaders, and the death of Professor Jefferson Mangel, a lover of magic and your magic act in particular. He was the first victim found dead in the Ophiuchus position and that's an off-Strip site on the university campus."

"What about the Goliath and Oasis murders I've already looked into?" Max wasn't so much objecting as reminding her he'd done the groundwork.

"You've proved assassins are still out to get you, so you need to keep a low off-Strip profile. One involves Cliff Effinger, so Matt can deal with the Oasis now on that."

Matt raised his eyebrows, pale as they were. "Uh, free will come into any of this assignment-making?"

"No." Temple raked her Table of Crime Elements with another rigorous glance. "You're already neck-deep in Cliff Effinger and his death, so you get the Phoenix ceiling death that looked to be Effinger but wasn't and the Goliath, courtesy of Max defaulting, but also the scene of the death of the call girl you encountered called Vassar."

"Wait a minute," Matt said. "You've got me or Kitty the Cutter listed as the possible instigator of that 'fatal fall.' Granted I feel horrible about Vassar's death and I did visit her at the Oasis, but I'm hardly a suspect on the Kathleen O'Connor level."

"Just being thorough," Temple sang out, aware that an unspoken rivalry was galvanizing the guys to feel possessive about their assignments, if not specifically about her.

Her best option as queen of the board and the Table of Crime Elements was to be bossy, move them to their best positions of personal safety, and herself take on the untidy murders that didn't seem directly linked to current kidnapping and death attempts.

"I'll look into Gloria Fuentes, if Max will e-mail me Gandolph's notes on her, and see if I can track down the Synth members who knew Cosimo Sparks. His death had to have rattled them."

"Hasn't that South American entrepreneur been arrested for that?" Matt asked.

"The evidence against him is circumstantial," Temple answered. "So far. And, of course, need it be said we'll all keep a leery eye out for any traces of Kathleen O'Connor?"

"What would be her motives," Matt asked, "after all these years?"

"Follow the money," Max said. "She raised money for the Cause and doesn't want it to line any private party's pocket now that the Irish Republican movement is dead."

"What about the news reports of resurfacing violence in Northern Ireland?" Matt asked.

Max waved a dismissive hand. "That's the corpse having postmortem involuntary muscle tics."

"You didn't have money for the IRA as an idealistic teenager," Matt pointed out.

"I had ideals. Look. What drove Kathleen, especially given her state of pariahdom from birth, was tricking or seducing people — men — into feeling the same self-loathing she herself did."

"Luring them into genuine states of sin?"

"You could — and would — put it that way, ex-Father Matt. She just wanted her victims to feel as low-down and guilty as she could. I don't think she toted up Sean and I competing for her affections as a duel of pride, lust, and betrayal. *We* didn't think that way. If either one of us had scored with a girl after our sheltered upbringing, we would have been shocked to our jockey shorts and more about bragging to our mates back home than running to confession. The better 'man' would win."

"And you were it, as usual," Matt said.

"No, I was the one who . . . fell in love with her," Max said in a tone of dumbstruck self-revelation, shocking Temple to her Daisy Fuentes undies, speaking of undergarment shock.

Matt looked pretty astounded too.

"Sorry." Max shook his head as if finding the "reset" for his memory. "Some of my bits of recovered memory hit like sledgehammer strokes. And it's all the distant, teen-drama ones, God help me. At that age, guys try to pretend they're heartless to other guys and sincere to girls in such alternating impulses, they get whiplash. My gut knows I loved my cousin like a brother. I guess I didn't have a brother. I don't remember. At that age, you don't have the maturity to admit family feeling, you're trying so hard to break away. So. I encountered first love and first loss in a stunning double-bill."

"Do you think," Temple asked, "Kathleen had real feelings for you too? That your fury at your cousin dying in that IRA pub bombing wiped out her chance of any further relationship with you, and that really put her over the edge?"

"I don't remember." Max shook his head. "I don't even remember the details of our assignation. I suppose that says something. Yes, I could think of nothing else but revenge on the IRA bombers, because I thought it was my fault I wasn't there to save Sean, or to lose my own life too."

"As much as it'd be fascinating to psychoanalyze Kathleen O'Connor in light of her roots," Matt said, "you run a close second, Kinsella."

"You're not exactly Mr. Average yourself."

Temple was not willing to probe into dueling guy adolescences. "So you're both saying to know our greatest enemy is to outwit her. Why did she become a slut — ?"

"That's harsh," Matt said.

"That's written in her history," Max said. "She was living up to what her mother was reviled for supposedly being, and she was herself labeled as from birth."

"Let me finish," Temple said. "Why did she whore for a noble cause? For religious and ethnic freedom, for equality and tolerance? Did she have a sinner-saint complex? Excuse me for asking. We UUs don't much go in for extreme moral judgments."

"UUs?" Max asked Matt.

Matt laughed. "You may have never known, or forgot. When pushed for her religious upbringing, Temple will be amusing and claim to be a 'fallen-away' UU. Universalist Unitarians reject age-old intolerances, like warring religious identities and condemning classes of sinners outright. No burning at the stake. With charity for all and malice toward none."

"It sounds a bit wishy-washy," Max said wickedly.

"You and I came up in moral boot camp," Matt agreed.

Max nodded at him. "Like Kathleen. No wonder she's targeted us both."

"No wonder we've both survived her." Matt waited for Max's reaction.

He grinned. "So far, my lad. So far."

Temple huffed out a loud, theatrical sigh. "I'm so happy seeing the two of you make common cause, but this woman is a walking war zone and you both bear her scars, visible or not. I may be ex-UU, but I'm not feeling at all tolerant about Kitty the Cutter. She's obviously been lurking on the fringes of lives, shifting personas, pulling strings on her patsy associates, taunting us with her mysterious 'gifts' and 'thefts.' Was she Shangri-La? How can she have apparently died twice and still be around to haunt us? What's the bottom line on her messing with us here in Las Vegas as if it's the last stand before the end of the world?"

Matt was the first to answer. "She may be unconsciously searching for someone incorruptible, but she isn't equipped to recognize such a person even if she found him. Or her. And doing that would so shake her negative world-view —"

"She'd implode," Max finished. "And the fallout would be lethal."

Temple tapped her Table of Crime Elements. "When I look at this, I'm struck by how many of these unsolved deaths involve falling. I'm a press release writer, not a logician, but it's got to mean something. Maybe it's an unconscious metaphor."

"Falling from grace," Matt intoned slowly. "Falling from a 'state of grace,' as the Church calls it. Kathleen's mother was a 'fallen' woman. She was expected to live down to that. So she did."

"Satan," Max said, "tried to tempt Jesus

to step from the top of the temple."

Matt spun the crime table to face him and scanned the rows. "That could mean Kathleen O'Connor is responsible for almost all these deaths."

"That would make her a serial killer." Max said. "And that may not be her only method. Someone tipped the warring IRA remnants off to Garry and my movements in Belfast."

Temple grabbed back her death list to study it again. "Then we'd better organize and 'out' her before she can do us all in."

CHAPTER 34
FUR FLIES

Miss Midnight Louise and I are enjoying an extended eavesdropping session beyond the flimsy French doors on the corner patio that borders both Mr. Matt's and Miss Temple's Circle Ritz digs, a floor apart.

"Well, this is awkward," I comment.

"Yes, human breeding behavior is prefaced by many long and tortuous episodes and deep and lasting emotions."

"I mean, Louise, that our human amateur sleuths are divvying up the list of murderous events and victims and locations into three separate investigations, and we are but two."

I think for a millisecond, and then continue. "Of course, I am up to performing the work of at least two, but I am not able to be in two places at the same time. Yet."

"*Pshaw,*" Louise spits, nailing me in the eye. "Who do you think has been Johnny-on-the-spot at Mr. Max's residence and elsewhere for all these suspicious comings and goings ever since the Neon Nightmare impact?"

"Unfortunately, the investigations from now on focus on multiple major Vegas sites, such as hotel-casinos, the Neon Nightmare night-club, and even the singular institution of learning in our midst, the University of Nevada at Las Vegas. Few know that Vegas is a center of learning as well as —"

"Lechery?" Miss Midnight Louise suggests archly. In other words, her whole back makes like a croquet hoop. She is such a felinazi.

I ignore what is patently a personal swipe, and she had the paw to do that with. Oops, now she has me ending my thoughts with prepositions. I am feeling very Mr. Maxlike as my little gray cells go MIA.

Quickly, I point out, "That adds up to at least three, if not seven scenes of the crime or crimes." I have always been better at math than the female of my species.

"Then," says Louise, "we must round up seven, or at least three of the Cat Pack to shadow our human friends."

"Now you make sense. I will take my Miss Temple. She is in need of objective yet stead-fast male support now that her two beaux are both back in town."

"Bow? She has two bows? You make her sound like a Yorkie fresh from the groomers."

"Obviously, as with the sad case of Miss

Kathleen O'Connor, you suffer from a stunted upbringing and have never had reason to learn that language so vital in show circles of our kind, French."

"Oh, can it, Pop. Preferably with three-day-old tuna fish in a garbage bag. The airs you put on sometimes smell as bad as a card-counting scam at a Laughlin casino. The last time I saw you cozying up to those pampered Persian sisters in thrall to Miss Savannah Ashleigh, they had been assaulted by an electric fur trimmer and looked more like weasels than supermodels."

"You should know that a deal may be in the works to revive my commercial career with the modishly restyled Divine Yvette and Sublime Solange."

"Hmph," Miss Louise sniffs. "I will believe that when I see it."

"Meanwhile, you can visit Ma Barker at the police substation near the Circle Ritz and see how many likely Cat Pack members she has in her clowder. She always cottons to you better than to me."

She does not waste time arguing with me, but turns tail and rockets away. I must admit that the kit has a gift for tailing, whether it is Mr. Max or giving me the brush-off.

Chapter 35
Double Down

Dark of night in Las Vegas, and Max was just where he wanted to be, making like Spider-Man in darkness high above the New Millennium Hotel's massive stage. He was back to his apparently favorite death-defying persona, undercover high-wire artist.

Every few seconds, a shifting stage effect or a neon-bright light from the performance below forced him to skid five feet down a four-story ladder or duck behind the bars of rolled-up scenery scrims.

How do you finagle a private audience with a man advertised as "the world's most mysterious and reclusive and richest magician"? Max had probably done just that in the recent past. Now . . . all the shortcuts in his brain were short-circuited. Any magic formulas he'd known had tangled on his tongue. He needed to contact his quarry in the split second between leaving the stage and stepping into the arms of his security forces waiting in the wings just beyond the audience's line of sight.

Operating under the radar and slipping past security had proved to be one skill still solidly in place. Just the act of scaling the complicated set pieces put his mind and limbs into motions that should shake loose the blocks of memory loss.

The noise bouncing off the hard concrete walls up here made his memory synapses jolt as the pulse-pounding music vibrated the metal framework he perched upon. Gigantic light sabers washed the four-story box's inner walls in rhythm with the approving roar of the crowd.

Max waited to pounce on his one perfect moment, linked to the height by a thick thread, his favored and always potentially fatal bungee cord. These tensile bundles of elastic nerves made Cirque de Soleil's many franchised arty acrobat shows — in Vegas and on the road — a billion-dollar business.

The stage floor below was broken into round elevator platforms that lifted magic effects to different levels, and then sank them below view for set changes. And through this magic mushroom stage-scape strode the king of the jungle, his dreadlock mane surrounding a tiger-striped face mask, with a muscular-shouldered leather cloak concealing six-inch platform boots off some seventies' rock album cover.

As applause thundered, Max timed the departing magician's stride length. He pushed off the high framework to land on point beside the moving man, unfastening the bungee cord at the same time his hand crushed the leather cloak shoulder and his mouth spoke against the cat-head's broad striped cheek, right on the hearing amplifying device.

"Me Tarzan." Max's low, gritty tone would thrum inside the hollow mask. "*You* in jeopardy."

"And you're a dead man," came the answering rasp. The Caped Conjuror had flicked off his voice amplifier as quickly as Max had appeared.

Now his huge gloved paw waved off three security guys a-leaping in front of sixty fans with backstage passes a-pushing. His arm clutched Max's shoulders in a bear hug, signaling friendship to his hair-trigger crew, and feeling like custody to Max.

You mess with a big cat, you might catch some claws.

The hold carried Max along at the center of the exiting cadre, leaving behind a crush of fans and the blinding blinks of cell phone cameras held on high.

Only yards away was the dressing room door made of heavy metal: big, blank, and bank-vault solid. Once it slammed shut on them, the two men were alone.

"Lucky I recognize your voice." CC slung his heavy cloak onto the shoulders of a super-tall mannequin standing in one corner. The base had been bolted to the floor to handle the weight CC carried two shows a day. "So you're back from the dead."

"What made you think I was dead?" Max asked, throwing himself into the cushy leather armchair CC had indicated with a wave of his doffed gauntlets. "That didn't get out."

"I have kept an eye on every magician's act in and out of this town, especially some new cat calling himself the 'Phantom Mage.' That costume and routine treaded awfully close to my franchise, pal."

CC stepped off his platforms while holding on to a bathtub bar screwed into the wall. "My security setup doesn't permit me having a dresser. Too easily bought off. Give me a hand?"

Max pushed himself upright.

"If you can give me some leg," he said wryly, absorbing the big guy's weight while CC stepped over the bulky platforms and dropped down into the upholstered chair at his dressing table. He was shorter than Max, but stockier.

"I would ask how you can walk on those things," Max added, eyeing the Klingon-style height-enhancers, "but I have several female friends and Lady Gaga ready to swear it's no problem."

"It's a problem," CC said. "This costume is a sweatbox, a molded plastic and felt and fabric prison."

Max nodded. "As for ripping you off in my Neon Nightmare persona, a mask and cape aren't copyrightable wardrobe items. Ask Zorro or Batman. And, as you discovered, those costume bits are the only way to disguise a face and build. What tipped you off to my pseudonymous act?"

"You were too good for the Neon Nightmare. You were having fun. I recognized the first impish cavorting of working masked. It feels like freedom."

"We've talked about this before," Max said. Suspecting.

"You're the only magician I'd speak to." The huge feline mask cocked like an inquisitive dog's. Max almost laughed at the effect. From skirmishes with Midnight Louie, he knew cats expressed their curiosity with laser eye intensity and pointed paw examinations, not cutely tilted puzzlement.

"I'd hoped that was the case," Max told him.

"Why wouldn't it be? Don't you remember?"

"Not . . . completely."

The Cloaked Conjuror sat up straighter, abandoning the exhausted post-show slouch that Max recognized so well, now that he thought about it.

"What are you saying?" CC scratched his huge big cat nose, apparently a stock gesture for uncertainty. Max found it both odd and sad that he'd adapted so thoroughly to wearing the mask.

"I had a 'brain crash.' " Max shrugged. "Memory loss was a side effect of the two broken legs that came from hitting the Neon Nightmare wall on the swing of a frayed bungee cord."

"Damn!" CC's striking bare fist, large folded fingers with hair-dusted knuckles, made the items on his makeup table, which weren't makeup, bounce. "Onstage assassination attempt. I figure I'm going to end that way. When you've made a career of unmasking other magicians' hallmark illusions, someone is going to get mad enough and is expert enough to do you in, no matter the guards. Look how close you came today. If you'd wanted to knife me instead of talk to me —"

"You'd be fine," Max said. "The cloak is fine-woven chain mail, and the equipment-loaded mask collar puts your neck off-limits. I *would* have had time to slip a stiletto down your gauntlet, though, and cut your wrist veins."

"Damn again! We've never thought of that in our security meetings."

"You'd probably recover and I'd be dead," Max said in consolation.

"Maybe not." CC sounded morose. "You survived that Neon Nightmare impact. Why are you my friend?"

"I need one. And I'm nobody's hired gun."

"I've always thought we had common ground, Kinsella, that you were in some way imprisoned by your career as much as I am. That you were as really and truly solo as I have to be, not able to trust anyone, or ever let down my guard."

"True enough," Max said.

"And yet I do with you." CC braced his armored right forearm on the dressing table, holding up a bare fist as an invitation to arm-wrestle.

Max hesitated, then braced and flexed his own right arm. His legs were iffy. His arm and upper body strength were the foundation of his career. He'd win in two seconds. Instead of grasping CC's fist for a contest, he gave it a bump, the current gesture of camaraderie.

The man's laughter sounded faint compared to his supplemented onstage voice. Max guessed he'd never see CC's face unless he was in a casket. And the Cloaked Conjuror would probably want even that closed.

"I never exposed your 'walking on air' illusion," CC said thoughtfully. "Of course it wasn't magic. It was timing and astounding physical discipline. Loved the doves, man. That was a message."

Flashback.

Strobe lights raking an empty stage faster than the blink of an eye. The audience hushing when the first dove flew to its invisible black perch against the stage's velvet-black backdrop. The next dove flickered onto a different level on the other side of the stage. Then the next landed elsewhere until all you could see were doves fluttering like snowflakes, dozens of them, archangels landing on a cloud, wings lifted, balancing. The audience was now mentally adding the words to the instrumental music playing softly behind the first dove and getting louder. Upbeat. It was the "Believe It or

Not" Mike Post theme from *The Greatest American Hero* TV show about an ordinary Joe becoming a superhero.

Only . . . blink again and there was the magician, standing upright on nothing, Max standing taller than a straight pin, wearing traditional magician's garb. Dark hair, dark formal garb with strobe flashes of white tie and flying black tails, holding a slim white-tipped black wand. Wearing a shiny black top hat.

CC chuckled. "You were something else. Hugh Jackman doing Tommy Tune doing Fred Astaire as even Fred Astaire had never imagined it. I could never do that Lightfoot Harry act."

And no matter where onstage Max had appeared, it was among a flutter of those constantly landing white doves. The strobe lights caught him flashing from one impeccably posed position to another, dancing in the dark, never captured striving or moving, walking on air, always the iconic image of the Magician. The Mystifying Max.

Flashback again:

"That effect," he heard himself saying authoritatively, "was the product of years, five bird handlers, a tech crew of seven and a wonderfully calming dove cote only three miles off-Strip, plus the inspection and fiat of animal welfare groups."

Max could shut his eyes and hear the doves' low warbling chorus. Lovely, gentle creatures. Reality pushed him out of the past when his recovering mind flashed a newspaper headline shot of DOVE HUNTING SEASON OPENS. Not on his turf.

So. Did the Synth have a Cloaked Conjuror–hunting season? They might well, Max believed. He'd found a possible target. Now he had to find the potential perpetrators and figure out what they planned and where and when.

"Speaking of 'messages,' " Max said, "that's why I'm here. You could be closer to ending the way that you fear. Someone cut the Phantom Mage's cord at Neon Nightmare."

"That's why the act went dark a couple months ago!" CC couldn't convey expressions, but Max could almost see a lightbulb winking on above his heavy-maned head. "And why you made the remark about your memory."

"Right. I could have been killed, and I'm putting the why and who and how together. My mask certainly didn't keep me safe. What about your mask, any known imitations out there?"

"I don't just have one mask, I have three.

338

One to wear, one in the shop, one at the cleaners. They've been marketed as Halloween masks, but I don't really have the kiddie audience."

"The full head?"

"No, just my adorable kisser."

"I'm thinking of full head masks, with voice-altering capabilities. That Darth Vader vibe."

CC leaned back, folding his arms over his impressive chest. Here, without his boot platforms and gauntlets, the character's roots in the entertainment wrestling game were more evident. "Nothing commercial. Some of my fans buy pricey kids' helmets like that, supposed to be Darth Vader or Septimus Prime from the *Transformers* franchise."

"Those would be shiny plastic, mechanical-looking masks, not animalistic strips in flocked stretch velvet dotted with tiny Austrian crystals like yours."

"No. The Vegas Strip glitz is subtle and costly. But my fans are cagy and devoted. Craft store adhesive felt and dollar-store glitter work wonders when my fans get a hold of them for a redo. But most of those costly toy helmets have voice mechanisms that are more an echo chamber effect than a real alteration. And you'd be surprised how many adults fit into them and get a kick out of playing a kick-ass character."

Flashback.

Swooping down fifty feet to hover above an awestruck crowd, cape billowing, face masked, while even the air vibrates with the heavy bass beat rocking the triangular-shaped inner space of Neon Nightmare, and neon lights of the zodiac wash every person there with pulsing colors.

"You're right. I enjoyed doing the Zorro bit at Neon Nightmare." Max smiled as he recalled the kick. "But it made me an easy target, as you are every night."

"I know it. And you just proved that again tonight. Is there a reason you're trying to make me insecure?"

"I'm trying to make you safer."

"Why?"

"I know what it's like. I made myself a target of professional killers at seventeen."

The Cloaked Conjuror whistled in surprise, a common reaction. The mask made the sound into an eerie high-pitched wheeze. "You were a pro at magic that early?"

"Magicians aren't usually a target. No, it was because of my naïve ideals."

"You at least had some. I always just wanted to be a magician, but I wasn't very good at it."

"So you became good at debunking it." Max smiled. He wondered how often the Cloaked Conjuror saw that ordinary expression off a stage. Perhaps he had call girls in. "Proves the axiom. 'Those who can do; those who can't . . . criticize."

"I thought the old saw went, 'Those who can't . . . teach.' "

"Not in this Internet age."

"Yeah, the threats on my life are up four hundred percent with my name out there for 'instant feedback' on hundreds of sites."

This time Max whistled, and it worked so well, the dressing room door banged open. Two musclemen bearing major small arms filled the doorway and scanned the room, weapons at the ready.

From the glowers they gave Max, his magical aerial entrance next to their boss rankled mightily. It must rankle even more that Max had turned out to be a bosom buddy, so to speak.

"That's okay," CC's weirdly emotionless voice said. "Old friend. Get a couple drinks in here."

CC rested his booted feet on an unoccupied chair drawn up to the dressing table. For him, this must be an unexpected but pleasant social occasion.

341

"Thanks for shaking up my guards, Kinsella. I owe you. In fact, I should put you on my payroll to test my security regularly."

"Don't need the money, but, sure, I can do that anytime you want a drinking partner." Max hoped CC's invisible grin match his own. Meanwhile, he was getting an outside-in look on his own life.

They remained silent until a New Millennium sexy robot girl waitress in silver body paint sashayed in with a tray, a bottle, and two crystal low-ball glasses. She deposited the burden on the dressing table as CC pulled a hundred-dollar bill out of his palm and let it waft down to the empty tray.

"Thank you, Tiger," she said with a very nonrobotic wiggle and a smile, and bustled out again.

"Irish whiskey all right?" CC asked, opening the bottle and pouring.

"Slainte," Max said, painfully aware of his last pub visits on Irish soil, of solid but not spectacular ale, of pursuit and death. "To your health."

With CC, that was always a sincere toast.

CC picked up a flexible aluminum straw and inserted it in the drink before he sipped whiskey through the mask's mouth slit.

"Is it worth it?" Max asked.

"I don't know. I thought so when I was

younger. I can retire. And may soon, in a flash of fire."

"Not literally, I hope."

"Not at the hands of enemies, I hope. No, I want to go the way you exited the Goliath Hotel gig. Finish the contract one night and be gone the next. People always wondering . . . where I went . . . who I was . . . how I'm spending all my money."

"And then you'll return as your own self to Vegas and play the high roller at all the casinos, still gaming the odds."

CC laughed, the only sound the mask made that seemed happy, as if it came from a mechanical Santa.

Flashback.

Max crawling through the Goliath air duct system, having spied an anomaly in the cameras above the gaming tables. Max and his double, old and new Max, crawling like an infant in a rut through the same hidden paths two years apart.

"I had to leave that way," he told CC, told himself. "I had assassins on my trail."

"Well? Am I different?"

"You aren't. We aren't."

CC thrust his expensive glass forward for a rough toast. Max made the gesture but avoided the close contact of breakable glass. He wondered if that described his life.

"If you want me to save you," he told CC, "you'll have to show your hand, and heart, if not your face."

CC lifted and wriggled his bare fingers. "Most people think I'm a gauntlet, not flesh. And heart, it's all in my work."

"One of your men died, during that science fiction convention held here at the New Millennium."

"TitaniCon," CC said promptly, not showing much heart.

"One of your assistants fell, or was beaten and fell, or was pushed from the upper reaches of the stage mechanisms. He was wearing a costume that mimicked yours, that also suggested a 'Khatlord' from an insanely popular science fiction TV show."

"Silliness." CC sucked hard on his straw of Irish whiskey before continuing. "Those costumed TV characters were supposedly from an alien race that was a cross between a *Star Trek* Klingon warrior and . . . me and my mask. The hotel PR department wanted to play up the similarities. I went along. It seemed harmless at first blush."

This time emotion had colored the mechanical voice. Bitterness.

"Barry died," Max said.

The Cloaked Conjuror didn't respond for a moment. "You know magic shows are based on doubles. Barry was my body double. The police never started a murder investigation. There wasn't any evidence. People in the circus, people on window-washing rigs, people in high-steel construction sometimes fall, and sometimes die."

"I'm the poster boy for that fact," Max said. "What about your late performing partner for the hotel's signature Russian artifact exhibition?"

The Cloaked Conjuror kept statue-still. It must be torturous to remain always behind the mask, behind the façade, literally caged by his costume, his larger-than-life persona.

"Perhaps people around me are fated to die," the mask intoned.

"Perhaps," Max said, leaning forward intently, "people associated with magic and who dabble in aerial illusions are fated to be killed in this town because something is killing them."

"Besides hubris, you mean?" The flat of CC's palm hit the dressing table. "Did you see Shangri-La perform?"

"On a couple of occasions."

Major flashback.

"And —"

Max found talking to CC, talking to a fellow magician, like Gandolph, produced ripples of recovered memory. This time he saw a flying woman falling from grace, from life to death.

He knew what to say. "She was . . . amazing in performance. She managed to combine the gravity-defying martial arts moves of the artiest recent Asian films with classical magic illusions."

"Yes." The CC's shoulders lifted with a sigh. "She was a tiny thing, but fierce, like that trick Siamese cat of hers that could balance on a wand, or so it seemed. Hyacinth and Shangri-La were much more interesting than rabbits and top hats. Everything in her act was a delicate Asian watercolor overlaid on a samurai sword. She died because of an attempt on my life."

She died attempting to take your life, Max's memory spoke up. *She had already taken Temple's ring during an onstage trick and then kidnapped Temple and Midnight Louie, the cat who was hardly a tiny thing, but fiercely devoted.*

Max's memories were becoming quite a chorus. He could hardly think past their jumbled, tumbling rush to escape the lockbox in his head. He could hardly talk for the oncoming noise.

"Why remind me of that awful loss?" CC's deepest inhuman voice asked, with justification.

"Because I don't think the deaths are done."

"Deaths are never done, you know that, Max. Part of magic is the constant reversal of death. The rabbit is gone, the rabbit is there. The girl in the box has been sawn in half, the girl in the box is whole. Shangri-La — or the Phantom Mage — is defying gravity. Shangri-La — or the Phantom Mage — falls to a harsh death. Only you didn't die and Shang actually did."

Max sat there stunned. "Only I didn't," he repeated.

But he'd been there at the New Millennium, had tried to save her. Was it actually Shangri-La who died while working with CC's aerial magic show above the Russian jewels exhibition?

Or a body double under that heavy Asian face paint that even the Cloaked Conjuror had probably never been permitted to see past?

Chapter 36
I'll Have a Double . . .
Agent

Max ordered a drink at the bar, cozied up to it, and proceeded to let himself mourn his lost profession of top-ranking Vegas magician.

It was unfortunate he'd had to look himself up on the Internet to get an overview of just how good he'd had it.

No doubt, he'd enjoyed a "brief, shining moment" that extended from his last road tour through settling down in Vegas for more than a year . . . until his counter-terrorism past caught up with him. Having his only friend, a retired Garry Randolph, and a smart, upbeat girlfriend at the Circle Ritz must have made Vegas seem like home, sweet home. At last.

Then he'd had to go undercover as a masked acrobat-magician at this hinky, kinky nightclub and mess up his legs, memory, and private life. If he ordered a drink for every attempt on his life, they'd be rolling him out of here on a cash cart.

So it wasn't hard to appear deeply morose. He just had to order another drink until someone significant recognized him. While he made himself into an apparently stewed sitting duck, he wondered what his self-appointed "savior," Temple Barr, would think to see him now. She'd either admire his chutzpah . . . or take him for a lousy lush.

He was on his third whiskey sour, when the words "Max Kinsella, I'll be damned" came confidentially close to his ear. Someone shouldered onto the momentarily vacant barstool next to him. This was a popular place.

The voice had been male and the face, when he looked up from his drink, was genially handsome but fading with age. The guy was dressed impeccably in a suit and tie, both a touch extreme in style. The duds reminded Max of an old-time Broadway promoter. Maybe it was the quintessential extrovert's plaid bow tie that did it.

"Hal Herald," the guy introduced himself. They had to huddle together to hear each other over the loud, pulsing music. "I wouldn't expect you to remember a low-ender like me, but what the hell happened to you after your big break headlining at the

Goliath?"

"I had a bad manager. Me."

"So . . . a comeback in the works? Not a lot of magician slots are out there, now that everything in Vegas and beyond is that damn Cirque de Soleil nonsense. Most tourists can't even pronounce the name, but they sure flock to their shows."

"Very confidentially," Max said, leaning a bit too close, speaking a bit too sloppily, "I am working on a comeback gig on the Strip. And now I just learned the damn Cloaked Conjuror will be adding the secret to my six-swords illusion in his act at the New Millennium."

"Nah? That bastard. He's left you alone so far. You must be furious."

"Furious enough to make that joker disappear for my new act's finale." Max signaled the bartender. "Something for my friend Hal."

"Another failed-magician parasite living on dissing the lifework of others." Hal pointed at Max's glass to banish the bartender as fast as possible. "And now the recession. There must be a couple hundred magic acts out of work in this town. I'm not talking your level, I'm talking small clubs and motels and even the kiddie party circuit."

"People don't want mystery in their lives anymore," Max said. "They want everything and everybody revealed. It's Gossip Nation."

"That's right." Hal grabbed the whiskey sour as soon as it landed. "I'll get the tab, don't worry. Magicians are an endangered species. We entertained. Hell, we made them *think*. People wanted to know, *How the heck did they do that?* That's healthy. That's an inquiring mind. Now the public only wants to know what celebrity is screwing whom. Don't get me going."

"Amen, brother."

"Listen." Hal gulped half his drink. "I'm meeting some folks, but I'd like to go into this more. Can you hang here for a few minutes?"

Max lifted his mostly full glass in answer. It had been window dressing anyway.

"I'll be back."

The minute Hal Herald vanished into the crowds on the dance floor, Max turned to the guys on either side of his and Hal's empty seat. He slapped a hundred-dollar bill in front of both men. "Hold my places for five minutes and you'll own these pretty pieces of paper permanently when I come back."

"That's an ex-shpensive leak, buddy," one

said in serious slur mode.

But when Max slid off his perch, both men were hooking an ankle on the footrests of the empty barstools. Besides, the unfinished drinks were a claim too.

Max threaded through the crowds like a whip snake, elbowing and shouldering a path with just enough force to make people shift without getting territorial.

The men's room was darker than an Egyptian tomb, all black reflective surfaces, even the urinals. He ducked into a cubicle, lucky the busy clientele had their backs to him and no mirrors on that wall.

Max cruised the Internet on his cell phone and had Hal Herald's Wikipedia bio in hand. Pushing Medicare. Had a pretty good engagement for a lot of years at the Frontier in the old days. One of his ex-wives had been a successful medium, got some cred from "finding" a dead body for the police, late did an act as Czarina Catherina. Wait! Had shared bills with Gandolph the Great and — bulletin Miss Temple Barr would die for — the recently late Cosimo Sparks.

Herald's busy biography until the late 1980s confirmed what he saw as "the death of magic." What else was obvious now, twenty-some years later, was the death of *magicians* and people associated with them.

Max returned to the "reserved" barstools in plenty of time to convey the two Ben Franklins to the bracketing drinkers, who grabbed them and probably exited to hit the casinos.

Only a couple minutes later, Hal Herald reappeared. He didn't claim his expensive barstool. "Say, we don't have to sit here with the going-deaf-slowly crowd. I happen to be one of the owners. We have a private suite upstairs. We make a point of keeping it on the QT. Game?"

About time. Max followed Herald up the same subtle staircase to the same pressure-operated door Temple Barr had described. Oddly, he remembered the next part from his recent dream of being closeted in secret rooms with the Synth. Probably that had been the Phantom Mage's dream, but that persona was truly dead and gone.

And he needed to convince the people here of that, because this would be Max Kinsella's big play. Only a real commitment would win him entrée to the circle of vengeful entertainers or clever criminals or just plain crazies who called themselves the Synth.

CHAPTER 37
THE SHADOW NOSE

My feet and heart are both primed to hop, skip, and jump over to the Oasis Hotel and Casino in the dark of my namesake hour.

Great Bast's Ghost! When is a dude to get some downtime on his own in this world? When I was not in the bosom of my Miss Temple and Mr. Matt and his family members during the weekend Chicago jaunt, I was in the clutches of the low-end mob boyos and TSA security checkers coming and going.

These are not happy travel memories and involve many personal indignities too indelicate to describe, including derogatory comments about my carriers, especially Miss Krys's homemade one, which occasioned open hoots of laughter. If I do return to Chicago, I will have to have a nose-to-nose with her.

Then, I come home on Tuesday and Miss Midnight Louise is always hovering somewhere, needing to unburden herself of endless "reports."

Now, at last, my role as CEO of Midnight Investigations, Inc., and my need for a roam of my own have met. Something fishy is going on at the Oasis, at least in the Lusty Ladies and Laddies ship attraction.

There are times when I wish to keep a low profile and enter a major casino by the well-hidden rear service areas. This is not one of them. Crowds are milling in and out of the Strip joints despite . . . or because . . . of the nearing wee morning hours.

Most Strip hotels gussy up their entry approaches with large iconic sculptures and lush landscaping, so I can tiptoe through the manicured jungles as unnoticed as dirt: rich, almost-black loam is imported for the exotic greenery. I can also slink around the massive statues, in this case one of the facing elephants who suffer from a severe condition common to Las Vegas, called "gigantism." These painted and overdressed pachyderms would be big even to the towering statue of Goliath down the Las Vegas Boulevard.

Getting through the casino's front door is not the slick process I can usually execute. A lot of people are standing statue-still around something right in front of the rows of brass-framed doors.

I am forced into an intricate and risky weaving maneuver to pass but not tickle a forest of bare and hairy ankles so I can survey the object of their interest.

Hmm. Louise did not mention the megabucks forced into an elephant-palanquin-size treasure chest sitting on the front door-step for all to see, and see through. The chest is clear plastic and rather ghostly. She is so fixated on Mr. Max Kinsella that she cannot see the moolah for the mush.

The ersatz sailing ship in the cove at the hotel's side may be the scene of Mr. Cliff Ef-finger's gruesome demise and now haunted by supervising thugs. And there may be an infestation of electric eels in the cove water. And it is somewhat interesting that Mr. Max was attacked there Monday night (yet again, yawn), but that is the price you pay for being nosy.

I say the big dough up for grabs Friday night is the far more likely target at the Oasis. And the dead-certain *likeliest* target to be found in the entire vast hotel-casino layout is the one I intend to track now, whose likeness is plas-tered above the doors nobody is watching now that so much fresh green money is on display.

Midnight Louie always has his eye on the prize, and in this instance it is not bankable.

An hour later, I am still searching. Vegas

casinos would deny the comparison, but they are laid out like an Ikea store combined with a maze the size of Massachusetts.

I would bet all the money in the out-front treasure chest that the clever Norse pattern the Ikea store on a route where you can walk and walk and never quite exit. That way you see all the wares and make impulse buys. Same thing in a casino.

Just as I am about to be terminally overcome from the floor level foot odor, I am making a three-foot dash to the next craps table when a white tornado comes churning in my direction.

Busted! I am caught out in the open, the object of every eye that is not pinned to a slot machine or a gaming table.

Luckily, that is very few people. Unluckily, my right ear is the target of a hot wet slap in the face.

"Louie, old pal," yaps the white dust mop of fur sporting hot pink satin bows about the ears, "whatcha doing here at the Oasis, huh, huh?"

Before I can answer this silly creature, a dog that weighs less than half what I do, speaks for himself.

"I have been riding at human shoulder-height for hours, sucking in secondhand smoke. I envy you having a job where you work best at foot-odor level."

The little guy has a point. There are no health warning labels on Odor-Eaters. Some might sniff at this dainty excuse for a canine as a "ladies' lap dog" but Nose E. has one of the most dangerous assignments around Las Vegas: hanging around the big social events and casinos, using his small but potent sniffer to target illegal drugs and explosives. Usually he is carried around by a hot chick or a big beefy guy like Mr. T who can flatten anyone prone to snicker at a man with a purse pooch.

"So what is up here at the Oasis," I ask, "besides the million bucks awarded Friday to the gambler of the week?"

"That is chump change." Nose E. paws at the inner corner of one black button eye, and seeming to stroke the side of his valuable nose like giving the high sign. White breeds have a tendency to eye stains, not a problem for one born to be black and beautiful. "The management is concerned about explosive traces in the casino."

"This place could blow?" I cannot help sounding alarmed. "You are investigating the pirate ship attraction on the cove?"

"Not in the assignment. I am not as credible in the great outdoors as you are, Louie. No, my beat is the casino. I am picking up very faint traces, meriting only a muttered whimper, not a full-blown aria of alarm accompanied by a paw lift and head tilt, which signals imminent danger."

"*Manx!* Are you a prima donna or a narc?"

"A bit of both," Nose E. growls. "It is a very specialized position."

"Speaking of 'position,' why are you not — ?"

Before I can finish my query, our down-low floor-side confab is joined by a third . . . I guess I should say . . . twins.

They are a pair of female feet attired in towering platform spikes that would be a nine on the Lady Gaga Scale. My poor Miss Temple is only a six even at her most extreme. Some are not born for glitter rock 'n' roll.

Anyway, I have not seen the rest of this babe, but the ladder of leather strings from her toes to well above her ankles is severely challenging to my chaw-and-claw instincts. Ah, leather! So tangy, so pierceable, so . . . dead prey.

She is obviously Nose E.'s partner on this assignment and an updated clone of Miss Savannah Ashleigh, whose day has come and gone.

This new-model starlet bends down to regard Nose E. "Here you are! Cozying up to the house mascot. Naughty, naughty, boy! That is not your job. Oh. Speaking of jobs, if you had to have a bathroom break, you need only have done the blink-and-arf signal and I would have escorted you to the sward out beside the elephants."

Bathroom break? I mince backwards. Nose E.'s kind is known to lift, aim, and spray on carpeting like this, whereas my breed is civilized enough to dig our own latrines far from the madding crowd. "House mascot"? What does that mean? I am nobody's mascot.

She bends down again, no doubt attracted by my movement. "Oh, you lovely thing!"

A small improvement.

Her taloned hands feel my neck. Is this a Jacqueline the Ripper? I try to wriggle away but she is quite . . . firm.

"You are supposed to have a prize charm on your collar, but you seem to have slipped your collar, you naughty girl!"

What a dim bulb. This woman is twelve on the Savannah Ashleigh meter if she has mistaken Midnight Louie for a *girl.* And a common collar-wearer! Blasphemy, O Bast, hear me and be avenged.

I show my fangs.

"You must be tired," she coos. "Such a big yawny-wawny."

I . . . am . . . being . . . forced to discharge a hair ball onto the carpet like a misbehaving dog. Begone, foul temptress!

By now, thankfully, she has swooped up the

unfortunate Nose E. to silicone bosom height. "You naughty, naughty boy. It is off to work we go."

Nose E. is right. I have the better job.

The pair of stilettos stomps off, damaging the carpet with every steel-heeled step. I hear a hiss behind me and turn to find the object of my quest glaring from under the craps table. Her fabled golden orbs are in full phase, the pupils mere black dagger slits.

I swagger over as best I can while dodging shuffling tourist steps. In a moment we share our own island retreat in the chaos.

"Those purse pooches are taking over the neighborhood," the lithe and lovely Topaz says.

She is the short-hair sort, black-panther sleek, and her larger-than-life image lounges on all the hotel-casino signage. The Oasis is a trendy multicultural mélange of Indo-Asian with a touch of Mediterranean. Topaz is the best thing on the premises.

I dare to greet her with a Nose E. pass (sans slobber) at her Cleopatra-collared neck, dangling its precious topaz jewel. This is a custom necklace, no lowly collar from a pet store. Topaz roams free in the hotel-casino, different charms on her neck netting the customers a nice prize. Tonight she wears the grand prize. No wonder the poor girl is hiding out.

"Why are you here, Louie?"

"Need you ask?"

Her purr would soothe the deaf.

So I warn her. "I am worried about something bad going down at the Oasis. There was a murder once on one of the cove ships and an attack there just last weekend."

"I am not surprised," she tells me in an urgent hush, "since my job is literally to 'get around' and allow the maximum number of tourists to spot me and thus win the daily prizes. Our security chief is meeting with suspicious strangers in the hotel-casino's hidden service areas. . . ."

"As the murderer did when we solved my last case here during the reality TV dancing show . . ."

"Yes," she hisses, "but this is no cakewalk. Security preparations for the big Friday-night prize drawing outside are complex, but I fear they are not enough."

"So you suspect our inside man, Mr. Rafi Nadir?"

"No. However, I clearly see he suspects everybody else."

"Not good. What can one man do against a mob?"

"You have uttered the word I dare not say. I

am getting the distinct whiff of 'mobster.' "

"Someone needs to stop this."

"I am so glad to see you here, Louie." She does the velveteen brush all along my side. "This is my home. I am the logo mascot. A mere canine bit of comb-leavings cannot do the job. I need major muscle."

I am easy. "Do not worry, Topaz. I can provide that."

You and what army? I can hear Miss Midnight Louise jeering.

And then I feel Topaz's bristly pink tongue doing a swirl inside my ear and hear nothing else but purrs.

CHAPTER 38
GAME FOR ADVENTURE

Pretending to stumble through the familiar dark mazes inside the Neon Nightmare pyramid, Max at last followed Hal Herald through the concealed pressure-sensitive door into a firelit and incandescent-bulb glow.

Polite applause greeted him. There were only three people clapping, but they were all standing. One wore the frowsy flowing garb of a medium, like Electra Lark gone *Sunset Boulevard.* The other was dressed for excess as a Latina Cher, only half the diva's age. The third was bar-mate Hal, who had stopped and turned around to face him.

"Lovely, dear people," Max said with a bow. "Thank you. And *I* applaud your civilized retreat from the buffoonery that now commandeers the Strip."

He nodded at the two women in the room, addressing the elder first. "Czarina. Wonderful to meet you in person. And Ramona.

Always a pleasure."

"Wonderful to see you so well."

"Why shouldn't I be? I've been in retreat working on my new act for ages. Speaking of retreats, I missed this magnificent room. It's like something air-lifted from the Magic Castle in L.A."

That mention had been intended to land in their midst like a Molotov cocktail. Has-been magicians like this crew would not be invited to perform there, or even be members. Max remembered at that moment that he was one. No wonder his participation in the Synth would be a "catch" for their private club here.

"It's better than that pretentious place," Czarina said. "And we own this entire club, not just some fusty old mansion."

"The building and nightclub are spectacular. All they lack is a magic act."

Three glances exchanged fast as whip snaps. Max's apparent ignorance of the Phantom Mage's performance run had them guessing.

He let them toss that idea around in their devious heads and played the unsuspecting pledge at a fraternity house. "And look at this room. So cozy and yet so charged with secrets, I bet."

As in his dream, the room had not only

that Vegas rarity — a gas-log fireplace — and several expensive and comfy upholstered wing chairs, but also a mantel holding exotic objects Sherlock Holmes would have envied.

His brain was doing double-time, flashing visions of previous visits here through the masked eyes of the Phantom Mage. He strode to the fireplace to further confound them. They had to have suspected him of being the PM, given his long apparent absence from Vegas and reputation for aerial illusions.

His back to them, he studied the mantelpiece, his glance passing over a crystal skull and elaborately jeweled dagger to the wax embodiment of a severed human hand. As he reached to examine it, the fingers pulsed and the hand spider-walked toward the dagger.

"Marvelous," Max said, laughing even as he'd jumped back. "A prop from *The Beast with Five Fingers* or *The Hand* remake?" He seized the dagger before the mechanical hand reached it.

"And this?"

"From a production of the Scottish play where the actor starring as Macbeth died onstage," Czarina confirmed. "Several interested Hollywood types were in the audience."

"The curse strikes again." Theater superstition had it that saying the name of the Shakespearean play, *Macbeth,* led to death among its cast. Max palmed the dagger, produced it in his other hand, and tossed it in the air to land in the empty space produced by the wandering hand.

"You *have* been practicing," Ramona said.

"Cheap trick," Max said modestly. "I wasn't expecting to be anything more than drunk at this point of the evening."

"Sit," Czarina commanded.

So he did, crossing his long legs and settling into the wing chair as if the lord of the manor. Ramona, surname Zamora, had borne an arresting stage name at birth. She mirrored his posture in the matching chair opposite. She was right. They'd make an interesting stage pair. A pity she was a suspected murderess.

"Now," she said, "the great Max Kinsella knows why we once-established magicians are furious at being relegated to some Illusionists' Boneyard by Cirque-du-Everlasting-Soleil and robbed of our secrets by the Cloaked Conjuror."

Ramona's fury reminded Max of the Evil Queen from *Snow White.* That was fine. The short-circuiting wires in his memory tossed out the fact that, as a kid, he'd loved the Disney version for her wicked tricks, amazing image transformations, and sexy jealous rants. That lady had drama down cold.

"Now," Hal pointed out, "you're one of us disgruntled ripped-off performers, from what you said."

"Absolutely. I returned from more than a year away fine-tuning a new act, and, presto, one of my former construction assistants skedaddles to sell the mechanics of my signature illusion to the Cloaked Conjuror for a few paltry thousand. Or so the rat's former partner says."

"Oh, it's true." Czarina was huffy angry. "CC has millions to throw around, and your last act was legendary around here. You have a huge following on Twitter."

"I do?" Max was astonished. "Don't you have to ask for that?"

"Anybody who wants can 'follow' you," she said. "It helps," she added seductively, "if you follow back."

"That's just it." Max threw up graceful hands, his long fingers the envy of most of his peers for their dexterity. "I'm a magician, not a PR flack." He winced internally to think of Temple Barr hearing those words from his lips. "I just want to do my job in peace, without some parasitic imitator trying to 'expose' me when he's getting great notices and rich for doing it."

"Hear, hear." Hal pumped a fist into the air.

"Even worse," Czarina said, watching him with all the shrewdness in her soul, which was considerable, "we think we lost our house magician to an assassination."

"That's ghastly," Max said, "and worth prosecuting. Why haven't I seen any media on the case? I must have still been out of town when this happened."

"Out of town, where?" Czarina asked.

"Out of the country, actually."

"Oh, where? I swear I got a couple cryptic messages from you." Ramona lifted raven's-wing eyebrows.

"Did you? I didn't roam as far as anyone might think. North of the border."

"Oh, clever," Hal said. "Nobody looks for anyone up there in Canada but aging Vietnam War protesters. Good show."

Max detected the triumvirate exchanging flash glances again. His story was holding up because of its very humdrum nature. Why had he said Canada? It had felt so right and reasonable, and wasn't someplace spectacularly suspicious, not as if Max had claimed to be on the run on the Continent.

"You think someone is bumping off your

membership?" he asked. "Someone did die here."

"The Phantom Mage was a mere hireling," Czarina said, all heart. "Probably a Cirque reject. That flashy bungee cord swishing around did distract the drinking crowd, but his magic technique was nothing to get excited about."

"Some of us," Hal said, "thought he was a spy."

"Some of us," Ramona added, "thought he was *you*. But then he died, or was killed, and you weren't, unless you're now a vampire or a zombie."

"Excellent ideas for my new act, Ramona. 'The Mystifying Max: Back from the Dead.' "

"We don't *know* the Phantom Mage was killed," Hal said.

"Really?" Max felt his muscles tensing for a rapid getaway. Had they invited him up here for an interrogation and possible extermination?

"He could have gotten careless," Czarina admitted. "He seemed overconfident."

"And you never suspected it was me," Max chided with a smile, an overconfident smile.

The silence was uncomfortable. He'd confronted the weakness in his story head-on, like the Phantom Mage had faced his apparent death, but that crushing impact had been too convincing for any doubt, thanks to Rafi Nadir's falsely official presence and diagnosis.

Max nodded soberly. "Perhaps the revolving lights of the signs of the zodiac disoriented him. They sure distracted me from my troubles. Did you know you've repeated one?"

"Repeated?" Czarina asked.

"I was slow to be served and had nothing to do but watch the mirrored bar-top light show. That's the idea, I know, but I counted thirteen of those zodiac glyphs going around. It was like counting sheep, only the ram kept showing up, and the fish and the scorpion and the boa constrictor and the lion."

"You *were* sure in your cups, my friend," Hal said, chuckling, "if you were seeing snakes in the zodiac. What's your sign?"

"I never paid much attention to bar pickup lines."

Czarina snorted. "You wouldn't. You've never needed to do that. Born between the first day of spring and the anniversary of the Oklahoma federal building bombing and assault on the Waco cult, dates of new life and hope as well as political insanity, you are obviously Aries. That's a sign of power and fearless strength, a muscular body and mind. You seek thrills and challenge, but you can be deceptive. Am I right?"

"I hope so," Max said modestly. "At least I was born in the first half of April. All of those traits sounds useful for a magician. So the symbol of my zodiac sign is a —"

"Ram," Ramona said lustily.

"And the boa constrictor I glimpsed in passing?"

Hal was happy to instruct. "That is Ophiuchus, my Aries friend. The ancients identified it as a constellation. The 'ophidian' coils indicate the biological suborder Ophidia or Serpentes, from the Greek *ophis:* a snake. Some versions of the zodiac do show it, but it's always been the unlucky thirteen in a set of signs that fit the twelve months of the year. So, despite some tabloid buzz recently when an astronomer suggested it needed to be made room for, it's a lost sign that we have taken for our symbol of forgotten magic and magical powers."

"Cool." Max nodded. "An apt symbol. Best that it stay out of the common parlance. Besides, who'd want to murmur 'Ophiuchus' in someone's ear at a bar when they could whisper Aquarius or Virgo, and roar Leo or Taurus."

"See, my dear boy," Czarina said, "you know more of the zodiac than you thought."

And he also knew why the Synth had adopted a man-crushing snake as its poster glyph.

"So what form will your revenge take? Do you plan to disrupt the Cloaked Conjuror's performances at the New Millennium? I'm not saying kill the man, merely show him up."

"You're right," Hal said. "We are not about killing, but we *are* being killed. Just a couple weeks ago, Cosimo Sparks would have been here."

"Yes," Czarina said morosely, "wearing his white tie and tails, adding class to the assembly."

"You wore that in your Goliath act," Ramona said. "Ultra classy. I still think you needed a dancing-on-air partner."

Max nodded slowly. From what he remembered of her, she'd been an able illusionist.

Ramona blinked at him after giving him a good long stare, like a cat. "No longer determined to be a one-man band?" she asked.

He blinked back. "Maybe not. What do you expect to accomplish, then, besides sitting around this attractive hideaway mourning your losses?"

"We're a lot more organized than we look, young man," Czarina said.

"Just how many members do you have?"

Czarina laughed. "Don't make the mistake of taking our lot as the sum total. We're the leaders, but we have a lot of unemployed magicians and their assistants and technicians to call on when we make our big move."

"We're more than the Neon Nightmare owners and operators," Hal added. "We have a couple hundred investors and we can call on that many 'extras' if we need to. The idea was to get a nightclub going, introduce a magic act, then use the building as a daytime facility for small but magical birthday and retirement parties, special convention outings, weddings, small fund-raisers. Make money for all the 'little people' who got pushed out by the big shows, and now are blitzed by the recession."

"Meanwhile," Max said, "chasing some legendary pots of Vegas gold wouldn't hurt."

Hal leaned forward in his chair, intent, recruiting. "We have powerful sponsors. There are forces in Las Vegas who want to take a lot of money out of it because a lot of money is stashed here in hidden places."

"The mob? If you work for them, you'll

need to corrupt a forensic accountant," Max said. "The magic of numbers isn't my game."

"No, not the mob in that respect, although they'd love to take over our venture if they knew the details," Ramona said, leaning forward also, although her plunging neckline when she did it was a lot more convincing than Hal Herald and his plaid bow tie.

"The thing, Max . . . I may call you that?" Hal smiled as Max nodded, eager to hear more. "Is that certain illegal entities have always stashed money around Vegas. The trick is getting it out."

"As in all casino cash cart robberies," Max put in. "If you're armed and dangerous, they'll let you walk away with the loot, but they'll grab you and the take once you're away from innocent bystanders."

"No one is innocent in Las Vegas." Czarina's hard tone reminded Max of Ma Barker, the '30s female gangster.

"Cosimo Sparks." Max located the name tap-dancing in his mind and found the correct connection. "He was a friend of my mentor, Garry Randolph."

"The truly 'great' Gandolph the Great," Czarina agreed. "Have you never questioned his death at the Halloween séance?"

Max shook his head numbly, perfectly in

character, perfectly stricken. No one could ever know who Garry really was, how he'd really died in Belfast, far from Vegas and its smoke and mirrors that Garry had manipulated so expertly.

"You're saying we magicians have enemies who'd reduce our numbers one by one?" Max said. "And you're inviting me to join you? Dare I say, thanks?"

Ramona licked her lips, selling hard. "There's been a game of hide-the-prize going on. The prize could be worth a couple million. Yes, it's a duel as to how many of us are left before the others who want to use and destroy us win. If we can pull off one major illusion, a Synth victory that will be talked about for decades, we'll prove the value of traditional magic and make the people who killed Cosimo and maybe even Gandolph pay."

"And the Phantom Mage, whoever he was?" Max waited for a reaction.

"Him too," Hal said impatiently. "He was a patsy caught in the Great Game, like the Cloaked Conjuror's assistant."

"What?" Max said, recalling Temple's oh-so-handy Table of Crime Elements, created way back when as if a memory aid for his future befuddled self. CC had not suspected his assistant's death was murder despite the death threats. Neither had the police.

"Yeah." Hal nodded. "Barry's was a terrible death and a loss to the Synth."

"So the Cloaked Conjuror's assistant fell to his death, too." Max eyed the women. "Was he a plant for the Synth on CC's team?"

"No." Czarina was the usual dogmatically certain. "We were working on engineering a super mass illusion to highlight traditional magic, maybe even making one of the iconic hotels disappear, the ultimate in 'street magic.' You know, like they do National Dance Day, only it would be Major Magic Day. People all over the country could chime in by Internet or YouTube. Barry was interested. Like a lot of faceless people in the discipline, he had hopes of making a name for himself someday. Vegas would be the centerpiece."

"That's an A-one idea," Max said. "You could encourage school-children. . . ."

"Yeah, yeah, yeah," Hal said, echoing a Beatles song. "We had all sorts of civic plans. Then these outsiders found and talked up Cosimo."

"They'd never show their faces," Czarina mentioned bitterly, "but they pushed their way in, dealing with Cosimo mostly, but promising us revenge on the prepackaged magic world and touting 'a really big score' and 'hidden treasure.' I don't understand why he was buying their schemes."

"Now these tails are trying to wag the dog," Ramona said. "Cosimo was our point man. He got way too dazzled by some rumored jackpot these 'contacts' of his promised. Meanwhile, the Great Recession made the Neon Nightmare a very shaky venue, so we really did need mondo cash."

"I hate to hold up the stop sign for the greed train," Max said, "but from where and how Cosimo was killed, I think your anonymous new foxes in the henhouse have pretty much decimated any lost treasure that existed."

"That hidden underground safe was built to hold something," Czarina said. "We just don't know what. The secret tunnel itself dated to Jersey Joe Jackson's day in the '40s and '50s. The Crystal Phoenix is a remodel of Jackson's founding Joshua Tree hotel and the management even keeps his rooms in original condition, if unoccupied. Jackson was famous for stashing his loot underground."

Max did know what the safe likely held: bearer bonds totaling hundreds of thousands of dollars and actual old-time silver dollars, also high-value objects. Perhaps even heavy weapons, all stockpiled for the IRA, maybe by Kitty the Cutter, the IRA's chief fund-raiser in the Americas, who definitely had not signed a peace accord with anyone.

"So," he said, hoping for confirmation, "you're after Jersey Joe Jackson's rumored loot stashed in and around Vegas in the early days?"

"Maybe. Maybe something more." Czarina's lips pouted in pinned-shut position.

"She means," said Hal, "we don't talk unless we know you're willing to join us."

"Why should I commit to the Synth? I have a comeback attempt to lose."

"You could headline our big surprise splash on the Strip," Hal said. "You have a name still."

"Great. While I divert everyone's attention, you knock off a casino cash cart to fund your nightclub and the hunt for hidden money in and around Vegas. I get nailed as an accomplice."

"It'll look coincidental," Hal argued. "All our street people will back up your act."

"You expect me to come up with a major illusion in a day?"

"You're the Mystifying Max," Ramona announced. "You love a challenge."

He did. He also was getting a very wicked

idea. "From what I've heard since I've come back —"

"From Canada," Ramona interrupted.

"From Canada," he answered with a look as pointed as her dubious comment. "And from the Keystone Kops charade of the underground safe opening in the new Chunnel of Crime," he told them, "poor Cosimo Sparks had already played hound dog for these buttinskis, these people who muscled in on the Synth, but the cupboard was also already bare. That may be why Sparks was killed. They thought he'd moved the loot."

"Poor Cosimo." Czarina sighed. "Such a major loss. He was our leader."

Max could sympathize with their loss. Cosimo Sparks and Garry "Gandolph" Randolph shared a lot of life history. Both were traditional magicians in formal dress whose performing time had passed; both were cut down while struggling for a future goal they passionately believed in, although in vastly different areas.

"This Synth is quickly becoming a rather minor cabal, and now looking seriously unfunded," Max noted.

"Maybe the great Max Kinsella could help us with that." Ramona had slouched down in her cushy armchair, crossing her legs so the slit in her long gown displayed them in

David Letterman girl-guest perfection.

Max mirrored her slouch, but not the bared legs. "Maybe I can."

CHAPTER 39
COLD CASE CONTACT

Call her an old fogy, but media maven Temple Barr could not give up her daily newspaper as long as there was one to be had, even though she'd worked for a time as a TV reporter.

She'd really enjoyed seeing the Chicago papers recently. How thick the Sunday editions had been, promising hours of serial perusing while lounging and eating forbidden carbs and sipping high-calorie lattes. Web cruising was efficient, but it was like Web shopping; you got a cut-and-dried list. You couldn't meander and surprise your eyes with something, well, 3-D.

So she was returning her Chicago-stressed mind to all things Las Vegas, which was mostly show openings and bad economy news, when she ran across a familiar but obscure name in print.

WOMAN'S DEATH STILL A MYSTERY

Unfortunately, that was not a startling headline in any U.S. city, but the name in the article's first sentence was a shock.

"Gloria Fuentes," Temple exclaimed aloud, disturbing Midnight Louie at his tongue bath in a large square of sunlight on the parquet floor. He regarded her with the long measuring gaze of a cat minding his own business and wondering why she was not minding hers and refraining from disturbing his grooming session. Then the lazy gaze narrowed to green slits and he bounded over to sit doglike by her feet.

Surely Louie had no interest in the name, just her sudden animation.

Temple examined the below-the-fold snippet more carefully. Newspapers nowadays were like trendy tapa appetizers: a palate-teasing dozen or so small stories arranged on the front page to intrigue a range of readers . . . if anybody read cold type anymore besides Temple.

Her fingers were tense as she paged to the "jump" on page six. What jumped out at her first was a logo reading, CCF: VEGAS, THE COLD CASE FILES.

This was a running feature she hadn't noticed before, and a clever play on the venerable *CSI: Vegas* TV series.

"Louise Deitz." She muttered the reporter's byline to herself, giving Louie a glance in case he was interested in more than the rattling newsprint. His ears perked up over the still-slitty eyes. Perhaps he'd been reminded of the Crystal Phoenix cat named Midnight *Louise* after him.

Temple hoped being married would stop her habit of talking to Midnight Louie. Folks who lived alone tended to get into monologues with their pets. It did help her cogitation system to think aloud.

She scanned the short paragraphs that ended with a request for fresh information from anyone having it.

The facts were correct. "Yes, strangled in a church parking lot. Yes, professional magician's assistant." Gandolph didn't merit a mention as Gloria's former employer. Born in Chula Vista, California. Single and never married, an "attractive" forty-eight years old, with no known relationships outside her job. No known exes.

Temple digested some new information. A head shot accompanying the article reminded Temple of performer Chita Rivera. *Muy* attractive. And never married? A mystery. Temple remembered an even greater one about Gloria's death. The fact that the words "she left" had appeared on the body at the coroner's like a nightclub's light-sensitive tattoo.

She turned back to the front page to read the byline. "Louise Dietz. Not familiar, but she soon can be."

Temple lowered the newspaper to the coffee table top, thinking. Then she picked up her cell phone.

It rang before she could make a call. Matt on the line.

"Matt. I may have a lead on Gandolph's assistant."

"That's great. What I've got a lead on is that crazy situation up in Chicago. I'm going to have to fly up. So, sorry, no amateur detecting for the immediate future. I'll fly out after tonight's show, really early Friday morning, getting back just before Friday's midnight show. So you'll never miss me."

"Not possible. I always miss you. What's up?"

"Mom's agreed to see Philip finally, but only if I referee."

"Gosh, the airfare on a one-nighter will be —"

"Steep, but well worth it if I can break this impasse."

"I hate to think of you all alone up there with that barracuda cousin, Krys."

"I hate to leave you all alone down there with that walking sympathy-sponge, Max."

"Then I guess we'll just have to trust each other."

"Exactly what I'm going to tell those crazy middle-aged kids in Chicago."

" 'Love is all you need,' " she quoted the Beatles.

"You've got it, love."

"Mine, too. Good luck."

Temple sat for a few moments after the call ended, wondering if Matt could pull off a miracle reconciliation.

Meanwhile, she had a murder to look into.

CHAPTER 40
BRASSY AND BREEZY

So you think I would get an invite to accompany my Miss Temple to the local rag offices to interview the reporter known as Miss Louise Dietz? No such courtesy. And here I had acted as obnoxiously alert about the article as, say, your average hyperactive Chihuahua.

Yes, the words "Miss Louise" do provoke a visceral reaction in me. Unfortunately, I cannot stop my insensitive human associates from thinking it is "cute" to name another black stray cat they have come across after me, in the distaff version of the moniker of "Louie" revered in song and story.

How many famous Louies are there? Let me count the cherished examples.

There is the title song in my honor, "Louie Louie." It has 1,500 recorded versions, numero uno. Take that, Beatles. You are so "Yesterday."

Of course, every bartender in the world is

named "Louie," only he doesn't know it. Louie rules.

As for "Louise," there is only that one oldie song how "every little breeze seems to whisper Louise."

Right now I could use that breeze for a short-wave communication.

Who do you think uses my proven methods of breaking and entering through Miss Temple's patio French door, but the previously contemplated Miss Midnight Louise.

She seems seriously out of breath.

"So what have you gotten your exercise doing?" I inquire.

"Now that you are all alone and lounging around maybe you will listen to a report of import from me. I have activated the Cat Pack, and have heard from a night crew I put on duty. I borrowed a couple of Ma Barker's best to shadow the suspicious parties at the Neon Nightmare club. There are only three in residence now that Cosimo Sparks was killed in the underground Chunnel of Crime between Gangsters and the Crystal Phoenix Hotel. Did you know, Daddy-O, that the world-class magician David Copperfield had sought to establish a franchise of underground restaurants?"

"No! So the Fontana brothers' concept was not the first. What is with all these humans yearning to go underground before their time?"

She sits to twist and groom the tip of her long, fluffy train with long, lavish licks of her tongue, just to aggravate me. True, she could be one of those intellectual longhairs . . . or of rock band ilk. Maybe aristocratic blue-blood runs in her veins, but it is sure not from my side of any family tree, which scotches claims she might put forth for a personal relationship.

She desists bathing to lift her head and answer. "Perhaps it is a death wish," she muses, "but I think it is the human quest for quiet and privacy."

"Especially if they have something to conceal, like the mob would. Ma Barker hear of any mobs in Vegas besides hers?"

She shrugs as if having an itch right between her shoulder blades, that section so infuriating to reach.

"The mob always has a game or two going. The glamour and glory days celebrated by the Chunnel of Crime are over. Now it is hijacked meat trucks and gambling and girls."

I make a face. "I would rather go after the Synth."

"Well, I did, and I can tell you that led to a surprising conclusion."

"What do you mean?"

"You assigned me to keep an eye on them and I had a crew of three to follow the three surviving Neon Nightmare operators. We split like a banana's foster dessert to track those two women and a guy when they slipped out of a side door in the Pyramid of Pretense."

"And — ?"

"Me and Pitch solo, Three O'Clock and Blacula put the shadow on the trio."

"Three O'Clock? He could not tail his *own* shadow!"

"I did not need all wet-ears on this job. He did fine."

"So. What was the result?"

"We split up, we crawled on our bellies like snakes to trail these secretive humans all over Vegas, and we were there when each of the three landed for what remained of the night. You are right, O Ancient Sage. There is some master plan these Synth people are putting into motion."

"And you know this because . . . ?"

"They all," she says sourly, "and we all ended up at the same destination."

I control myself and do not anticipate her answer. Las Vegas has just too many sites that are ripe for crime and chaos.

"And — ?"

"It appears they are going to knock off the Oasis Hotel."

I play flabbergasted. Not only is the Oasis an old established venue, far from the nouveau flash of the Aria and Palazzo, but few see it as a prize target, although a heist at any Vegas hotel-casino will be rich takings . . . for the scant half hour the crooks have to enjoy lifting the loot before the combined fist of the casino security and police surveillance comes down on them as hard as the Cloaked Conjuror's gauntlet.

I can believe the mob having such designs, but . . .

"This is crazy," I tell Louise. "Why does a cheesy group of magicians think they can keep the heist cash? One of their own is dead, struck down in his white tie and tails in an empty underground safe, and their mysterious masked backers are about to cut the connection with bullets. Obviously, I must hie myself back to the Oasis and investigate for myself."

"I will show you the site of the recent attack on Mr. Max aboard the ship."

"I have already done my derring-do on that location, Louise, for an earlier case. You must keep an eye on the Goliath, because I would not put it beyond the Synth to try to make Mr. Max the fall guy on any schemes they have going."

Of course, I do not mention that the house mascot at the Oasis is the lovely and lithe Topaz, she of the black velvet gloves and golden eyes. She has already clued me in that the mob is a clear and present danger, not a bunch of rogue magicians. Some might point out that Midnight Louise herself benefits from that sublime coloring, but since she claims to be kin, she is off my wish list for good.

Her loss.

CHAPTER 41
SOB SISTERS

Newsrooms nowadays were quiet and orderly compared to when they filmed *All the President's Men* about the Watergate political scandal. Temple sat in the one chair pulled up beside Louise Dietz's tiny cubicle and scanned the newsroom's mixture of empty and occupied matching cubicles. No-drama Cinerama. Columnists and feature reporters worked from home nowadays.

Louise Dietz was a poised forty-something blond woman secure enough to let a few silver hairs show through.

"So you're the PR rep for the Crystal Phoenix Hotel, but you have a tip on the latest CCF profile?" the reporter asked, pulling out a manila file and a narrow reporter's notebook.

"I used to be a TV reporter," Temple said, knowing "public relations" people were suspect to print journalists.

"Me, too." Louise smiled wryly. "Obviously *long* before your day. I got a bit ripe for on-camera, so I moved into print media just before newspapers started sinking into the Great Recession."

"Bad timing," Temple said sympathetically.

"It's been grim, but I have this job now, and here you are to help me do it. What's your tip?"

Temple knew you had to give to get, in all areas of life and work. "A weird message showed up on Miss Fuentes's corpse in the morgue. It never got reported."

"Really?" Louise was staring down through her reading glasses, pencil poised for a note.

Temple smiled, so glad to see that long-honored notebook and pencil instead of a tablet computer. Since she loved vintage everything, beyond mere clothes, she lamented that everybody was stuck in the same computerized mass-market mode these days. Not that she'd want to break her fingernails on stiff manual typewriter keys.

"You laugh at my 'stone tablet and chisel.' " Louise noted. "You get to my age, you'll see your brain works best on what it learned young. I need that hand motion to get my little gray cells churning in think-and-remember mode."

Remember mode. Maybe handwriting would help Max. . . . He could transcribe his adventures from the time he came out of his coma in the Swiss clinic. She'd suggest that ASAP. And she'd be first in line to read them.

"You're smiling," Louise said. "Is my method so laughable?"

"No, not at all. I'm smiling because I like that idea. I'm not laughing."

"So how does a PR gal know this inside morgue information?"

"It's *because* I'm in PR. There have been . . . deaths on my watch at events I'm responsible for. Think about it. Almost forty million people a year hit Vegas, or did before the economic downturn. Many of them attend conventions where you can have twenty to eighty thousand people milling around. What are the odds of . . . unexpected death, given the heat, the excitement, the long hours, the fevered hype, and after-hours overindulgence in food, gambling —"

"And sex," Louise added. "So you see your job as supervising this giant aquarium of predators and prey."

"That's a bit colorful. Let's say I run into the occasional great white. Mention my name to Coroner Bahr. *B-a-h-r.* No relation."

"Makes me reevaluate the nickname 'flack' we journalists give those in your profession." Louise smiled at Temple like a colleague. "So Grizzly Bahr is on your speed-dial too? He'll just swear me to secrecy on this postmortem message. It's the only way the cops have a prayer of solving the Fuentes murder."

"Maybe there are other unsolved, and related, Vegas crimes you could look into."

"Maybe you could suggest some." Louise Dietz's pencil was poised.

"First, I could use more information on Gloria Fuentes's personal history."

"Deal," Louise said. "Not much there. She'd retired from being a magician's assistant a few years earlier when her longtime boss took his last bow onstage." Louise flipped through her notebook. "The guy worked as 'Gandolph the Great.' I can't find what became of him."

Temple glossed past that. "Do you think Gloria wanted to retire or . . . ?"

"Yes. Like me," Louise said, "she was probably considered too old for a 'visible' job. And she didn't just need her face on camera, she needed her whole bod in condition for fishnet hose and Playboy Bunny thong leotard. She'd gotten away with the

Vanna White look for the old-timers' shows."

Louise tossed a promotional eight-by-ten-inch color photo on her desk from a drawer folder.

"Gandolph worked in white tie and tails!"

"What did you expect of a traditional magician?"

"I don't know. Given his wizardly name, maybe a velvet robe with long, flowing sleeves. Gloria was lovely. And her floor-length gown is strapless."

"Leggy is where it's at in Vegas today. You know that."

"Yeah. Where'd you get this photo? I know a fan of Gandolph's act who'd love a copy if I could scan it."

"Really?"

"A sick friend," Temple said.

"I found this in a Vegas antique shop, actually, so you have to promise to return it unclutched."

"I will. You're right. This paper ephemera could be worth something someday."

"Anything for my pensionless old age. Or do I mean penniless?"

"You're not that old."

"No, but I'm on my own." Louise glanced ruefully at Gloria's photograph. "Like she was. Gloria had a lost personal history and a lost career behind her. She ended up working as a cashier at one of the Circus Circus restaurants."

"That's a big family venue. The restaurant must have been lively, with lots of kids coming and going."

"Lots of families reminding her that she didn't have any." Louise sighed. "I try not to identity with these cold case victims, but sometimes it's hard not to. You married?"

"Not yet, but it's a near thing." Temple lifted her left hand from her lap to flash significant bling.

"*Ooh.* He sure likes a-you. You're young. No, don't argue. If you have something going, hang on to it, kiddo."

"I plan to." Temple smiled. "So . . . what was with the church parking lot attack? Was the killer a repeat act?"

"Not that anyone found out. Gloria was active in her church, St. Jude's. I interviewed the old priest. They all seem to be very old these days. The young ones left."

"I suppose so," Temple said, trying not to look guilty.

"He indicated that she might have worked for a short while for another of those top hat and cloak magicians. I couldn't trace him. Parks? Anyway, Father Delahunt said she was very faithful, very 'old school,' he called it, and he was older than the Mojave Desert. "Daily early Mass, novenas, stations of the cross, confession. He said it was a wicked world if so much piety hadn't preserved her from the death that was visited upon her."

"Piety." Matt went to Mass, she knew, and prayed, although not with her, maybe *for* her, fallen-away UU that she was. Temple was feeling guiltier and guiltier.

"Father Delahunt said something strange," Louise went on, leaning inward for emphasis. "He said Gloria was overscrupulous and vulnerable to the 'other side' of religion. What do you suppose he meant by that?"

"I have no idea, but that's an interesting comment. It might tie in to the 'she left' on the body in the morgue."

Temple didn't mention she wondered if the Synth, or even that ever-lurking font of all evil, Kathleen O'Connor, was behind Gloria's murder. Gloria had "left" a magic career because age had forced her to. Maybe that was the wrong aspect of her life to focus on. Had Gloria also "left" the Church, just before she was killed or in a more permanent way. Like Matt had "left" the priesthood. So maybe she was a victim of Kitty the Cutter's vendetta against Catholics.

But Kitty should have applauded Gloria leaving the Church.

In fact, Temple had known, and could not share, that Gloria died right about the time a woman's dead body was found by Lieutenant C. R. Molina's old Volvo car in the Blue Dahlia parking lot. Molina had come out late after the usual impromptu gig as jazz singer Carmen and found the body, along with the SHE LEFT message fingered onto the dust on her vehicle's side.

The victim in the Blue Dahlia lot had turned out to be . . . an ex-nun.

Wow. Times were harsh for ex-religious and ex-magicians, and Temple had a big stake in both those categories.

"So what can you do for me?" Louise was asking as if they were in an echo chamber. "Temple? Are you still with me?"

"Yeah. Sure. Okay. Have you heard of a University of Nevada at Las Vegas professor named Jefferson Mangel who was killed on campus last March?"

"No." Louise's pencil was making cryptic marks only she could read. Temple wondered if they spelled "Ophiuchus." "Tell me more."

"He was murdered on campus in a classroom converted into an exhibition of magic show placards from pre-Houdini days to

400

Siegfried and Roy and the Mystifying Max."

Temple watched for Louise's reaction to the last magician's name, but she was only dutifully scrawling it down, as Temple would have.

"A professor." Louise screwed her lips into a moue and nodded. "That's a change of profession for Las Vegas. I'll look into it."

"Meanwhile, I can scan and return your photo of Gloria and Gandolph?"

"Sure. You think it would help solve the case?"

"I think it might make my sick friend happy." Or not. She had no idea what would break through Max's memory loss, or what would set him back.

Temple rose and tucked the photo carefully into a hard-sided folder in her tote bag. "Thanks, Louise. You've been a great help."

"Ditto." Louise stood to shake hands with her.

Temple trotted out to the clickety-chuckle of computer keyboards, hoping they weren't laughing at her for pursuing such a long shot.

Chapter 42
Back to School

Max strolled through the shady thronging university campus. It was almost as incredibly lush and green as Ireland. Acacia, sycamore, and oak trees thrived among the cacti and majestic desert willows. Discreet signs advised that the landscaping was desert-appropriate and water-saving. Max tried to let natural beauty and memory wash wavelike over him under the blazing blue sky, though he doubted he'd had many reasons to visit the site when he'd lived here earlier.

Students rolled past him in waves, energetic and vital, chirping like grasshoppers. They made him smile. Why did he feel so old?

"Mr. Randolph," a female voice hailed him, stunned him.

It was throaty and mature.

He turned. She was blond, she was confidently striding toward him, and she was the only woman he remembered ever sleeping with.

"Miss Schneider." Revienne. Her lovely first name, the word in French for "return." And here she was again, a beautiful but bad penny turning up?

Her smile remained dazzling yet mysterious. "So whom do I discover on this amazing campus in the entertainment capital of the world but my very recent . . . shall we say, exchange student from abroad?"

He stared at her, suspicious yet enthralled.

"And you're walking well. Very well," she added encouragingly. Like a teacher.

Normally, people would say, "You're looking well." No. This was a renowned psychiatrist, and a clever one. With one phrase she revived every moment of their recent escape/escapade through Switzerland. *You're walking well.*

"Thanks," he said. "Care to stroll, then?"

She hoisted a gold-metallic leather bag large enough to hold papers to her shoulder. A Prada silk scarf was loosely knotted around one strap. The gesture released a whisper of perfume into the dry desert air.

"This entire campus is designated as an arboretum," she commented, adopting the role of tour guide. "Isn't it lovely? I have no pressing engagements so I took a walk."

"That's lovely too."

"What about you? What are you doing here, Mr. Randolph?"

"Not skiing in St. Moritz," he said, reviving the fiction that he'd been injured in a skiing accident and had naturally ended up at a Swiss clinic. The four-week coma had not been so natural. And he'd let her think Garry's surname was his. That was how he had been registered at the clinic.

"And your memory, it is returning?" she asked.

"In bits and pieces. Enough to make things . . . interesting."

They ambled together, staid adults among hurrying students on foot and riding bikes.

"What an astounding coincidence," she said in her perfect but charmingly inflected accent, an icing of German, a tantalizing trace of French, to match her genes.

"Astounding," he agreed. Affably.

"I had no idea you had links to this area, this city."

"I didn't either."

"How are you really doing?"

The question was hardly casual. "Fine, as you see. And you? What brings you here?"

"Business, although an old school friend lives here and we enjoyed a reunion visit. I'd committed to assisting a former mentor from Lyon in a study of his, and am enjoying a visiting professorship on this beautiful campus."

"In what subject, may I ask?"

"You may *ask* anything." Her smile was more *Da Vinci Code* than *Mona Lisa*. "Psychology, of course. Herr Doktor Hugo Gruetzmeyer has a guest professorship here." She stopped walking, not because he needed to. "Why are *you* here?"

Of course, he was currently pondering the existential meaning of that common query, but he couldn't afford to seem needy with her, especially of information.

"An excellent place to recuperate. Lots of walking required."

"On campus, or on the Strip?"

"Both," he said.

"You seem . . . more stressed than when you left Zurich."

"American life. We're more stressed by nature than Europeans. The 'save the world' complex,' I suppose you'd call it."

She looked around so he had a chance to sum her up on his supposed turf. Cool, controlled, blond. The Hitchcock thriller movie femme fatale who seemed unapproachable, but who'd unravel at first contact with a stressed Hitchcock everyman who knew too much, or not enough.

She dressed, he realized in this American setting, like so many of the politically ultraconservative women pundits, high heels, short skirts, long blond hair. Barbie for the Tea Party set. This short-skirted suit was ivory linen over a familiar olive green silk camisole.

"You're wearing part of the ensemble I bought you in Zurich," Max noted, sounding pleased.

"Yes, thank you. You noticed."

One thing *not* politically useful he'd learned in Zurich was that Revienne Schneider wore scraps of silk and lace, not bras. Very French.

"But," she continued, "I found a fabulous new perfume at the Bellagio shops. Like it?" She brushed cheeks, leaving a comet trail of hair caressing his skin in her wake and a scent like walking into a wall of exquisite perfume flowers blooming in the south of France. This was a blend of jasmine and mimosa.

"I'd have to be a block of stone not to," he answered.

He and Garry had endlessly discussed on their trek from Zurich to Belfast whether Revienne Schneider, his assigned shrink at the Alpine clinic, was friend or foe. Max still didn't know. He did know Garry's reaction to Max sleeping with Revienne while they were on the run. It unreeled in his brain like a film clip.

"You have no idea who Ms. Schneider really is or what her agenda was, or still might be. You were foolish, Max. That kind of sexual bravura got you and Sean tangled up with the IRA all those years ago when you were green and seventeen. You don't need to act impulsively anymore."

"Why are you on campus?" Revienne asked him, now confronting the apparent coincidence. "It's insane we should run into one another a world away, like this."

"Kismet, maybe?" He chose flirting over frankness.

She wet her already glossed lips. "I never expected to see you again."

"Me neither."

"That's an odd expression."

"Colloquial English, although you do that well, as you do everything well. I meant I didn't expect to see you again either. What are we going to do about it?"

"You could enroll in my class."

"Yes? What is it?"

"Identity and the Troubled Soul in the Modern Zeitgeist."

"Sounds . . . mesmerizing. My legs don't care to sit for long stretches in Spartan classroom accommodations, though."

"A nice cushy leather banquette for dinner then," she said.

"Delicious."

"When?" she asked.

"This is Thursday. Saturday? Unless you're otherwise engaged."

"Not. And you?" she asked.

He did have a rather important engagement Friday night, but not Saturday. "Not."

"Where shall I meet you?" she asked.

"I can't pick you up?" He was surprised.

"You already have," she said.

He shrugged. "The Eiffel Tower restaurant at the Paris Hotel."

"What a very American place."

"I am American."

"And I am not."

"Vive la différence."

"It's rather dangerous to take a Paris resident to an ersatz version of the city," she pointed out.

"You already know I like danger. The view of the Bellagio fountains is particularly spectacular, and American."

"The Bellagio." She laughed merrily, something he'd never heard on their arduous escape from the Swiss clinic that perhaps was intended to imprison him.

"Yes," he said. "Americans spring from all

nationalities, and you can sample the best of each here in Las Vegas. I know Continental dining is late, but the earliest seating works best at the Paris. You can watch the sun set on the Strip from the corner table overlooking the fountains."

"Very romantic, Mr. Randolph." She was flirting back, but then an undercover agent would.

"I'm sure it'll be a . . . memorable occasion. I'll meet you at the private elevator in the Paris lobby at . . . six, say?"

She agreed and moved on through the hot, dappled shade created by the many trees. He watched her like a lovesick swain until she was out of sight, then quickly ducked into the nearest building to study the rosters of classes and instructors and the campus map on his cell phone. Amazing, what was on the Internet these days.

Revienne had just left that dreary seminar on existential angst. If he hurried, he could catch her partner in academic crime at his office, finishing up student appointments.

Max was "walking well." And his vague excuse for being in Las Vegas and on this campus, walk therapy, was proving genuine. Max bolted up the stairs to the third-floor office, not knowing if the class called Motivation and Emotion could explain his momentary burst of energy. Obviously, Revienne's incredibly *un*coincidental presence in Las Vegas either meant he was on the brink of a bracing duel of wits, or a love affair. Why not? He was fancy-free.

And so was Professor Gruetzmeyer free, at least after a lanky kid with a backpack slouched out of the professor's office door and down the hall.

Max knocked on the ajar doorframe.

"You're very late," the man's voice boomed from within.

When Max appeared around the door, he looked abashed to see a stranger. Excellent. It put the guy off balance.

"Professor Gruetzmeyer. How lucky to have found you in. I was on campus merely to explore the layout and ring up for an appointment."

"At least you look ahead, young man."

Since Professor Gruetzmeyer was only about fifteen years older than Max, he must be used to addressing younger students. He was a fit and youthful fifty, curly haired and missing the Freudian beard and mustache. He wore a dress shirt rolled up at the elbows and reading glasses perched on his strong nose, underlining his green eyes. Impressionable twenty-somethings might crush on him but he didn't seem Revienne's type.

"You're late for enrolling in the summer program," he was telling Max. "Are you returning for credits toward a degree?"

"Not at all, Professor. I'm a writer." The moment he said it, Max knew in some deep well of experience that this was true. Or was it Gandolph who was the writer? "My name is Matt Butler." Always pick a false first name that's close enough to yours. You won't jump if you hear someone call you by it. However, what had popped out was some Freudian port in a storm. *Matt?*

"Fiction you write?" Gruetzmeyer had a slight German accent and he'd used the Yoda-like word reversal of foreign-born English speakers.

"Nonfiction. Do you mind if I come in for a few minutes? I'm not sure you're the resource I need."

"Step in. Sit down. How can I help you?"

Max smiled his thanks and obeyed. Psychology was a "helping profession." Suggest that someone of that temperament *couldn't* be of help and they'd be eager to prove the opposite. Max didn't have a degree (that he remembered) in anything, but his instincts hadn't gone missing with his shorter-term memory.

He sat in the chair opposite an impressively laden but neat desk. "I am writing," he explained, "a book on the mystique of what some people consider a profession, others an art form, and still others an elegant con game."

"Tasty." The professor settled back. "Far more interesting than these earnest, labored class papers. Why come to me?"

"Because I've discovered that my prime source is, to put it right out there, dead."

He pondered that. "Did I know him? Or her?"

"I'm hoping so, because, from what I know of him, I'd think you would have been compatible colleagues."

"*Umm.* Someone who used to teach here then?"

Max nodded. "I'm taking a flier on this. Pure instinct and hope." He knew a psychologist or psychiatrist would love the combination of "motive and emotion."

"Who is it?"

"Professor Jefferson Mangel."

"Oh. Jeff. My God, yes. I knew him. A tragic loss. Then it's not his field, philosophy, but his hobby, the philosophy of magic, you're writing about?"

Max nodded.

"That wasn't Jeff's academic discipline, but it was his passion. He felt it should be taken on a psychological level. Yes, I do . . .

412

did know Jeff quite well and his theories on the subject. In fact —" He leaned forward to click on a menu on his open laptop. "— Jeff probably has some papers in the university archives on the subject."

"Not accessible to non-academics, I imagine."

"I'd be happy to check them out for you, put you on a course of study on the subject of how Jeff's mind worked. He was quite the, uh, magic trick detective, you know. I wouldn't be surprised if he advised that fellow who does a Strip hotel show based on revealing the classic illusions' underpinnings. The Caped Confabulator, or something."

Max smiled. Performers on the Strip were world-famous. It was humbling and encouraging that some Las Vegas residents had such a casual knowledge of the industry that drove the city, and Nevada.

"Professor Mangel, I understand, had a mystical view of the subject."

"Yes, yes. He was the true appreciative amateur."

"Wasn't his death very ironic?"

"More than ironic. Sinister. Murdered on campus. You can imagine that wasn't something anyone official anywhere wanted to dwell on."

"You think the murder was . . . magical?"

"Of course not. I said sinister. The poor man was stabbed to death among an exhibition of his collection of magic show posters old and new. He was found lying in a grotesque position on the floor, like in that insanely popular thriller novel of a few years ago about the Vatican and Mary Magdalen."

The Da Vinci Code," Max prompted from some reviving memory synapses. "You think there's a connection?"

"No. Of course not. Jeff didn't have an enemy in the world. He was single, so there were no, ah, what you call hanky-panky motives."

"A true mystery," Max agreed. "Is anything left of the professor's office or papers on campus?"

"Nothing I know of. That was months ago. He willed his estate to the university, so the small gallery has been named in his honor and his personal magical artifacts added to the poster display, which were a very small percentage of his collection. Jeff was ahead of his time in seeing that history of magic in Las Vegas deserved as much an academic mention as the history of the mob."

The word "mention" was not lost on Max. "So I can visit the . . . shrine?"

"Next building, floor three. We have abbreviated hours, since a guard must be on site, ten A.M. to three P.M."

"I can just make it." Max half rose before pausing to sit back down. "Wasn't Professor Mangel young to have made a will?"

"You can do it online now. Jeff was forty-eight, far too young to die." Gruetzmeyer shook his shaggy head. "I made mine after the calamitous fact of his death."

"He sounds exceptionally expert on the magic and the mantic arts. Did he advise any other magicians?"

"He had a couple of local pals. Let me see." Gruetzmeyer squinted his eyes tight on his own command, letting relinquished memories resurface.

Max understood that technique well. He'd done it at home with a glass of Irish whiskey. Some men drink to forget, they said. He drank to loosen up his subconscious, to remember.

The prof's striking green eyes popped open, brightening as they saw the light. "One was an older fellow. Larry Randolph, or some such."

Max nodded, holding himself very still.

"Then there was a practicing magician, but at small clubs around Vegas, not a big shot. Still performed in full white tie, tails and top hat. I don't think he pulled rabbits out of the top hat, though. His name was odd . . . 'Topper'?"

"Topper?" Max asked. "That could refer to the top hat."

"And Còsimo, like Còsimo di Mèdici, the Renaissance prince."

"Cosmo." Max muttered the word that leaped into his arbitrary brain before tying 'Cosmo Topper' to a character in an old TV show.

"No. Còsimo. That name is known in Europe. Còsimo and . . . something to do with fire."

"Cosimo Sparks?"

"That's it!"

"And you just recalled it now?" Max asked.

"Yes, thanks to your inquiries. Why, should it be familiar?"

"No. He was pretty much retired, as far as I can find out."

Max was sure some mention of the man's recent death had been in the newspaper or on TV, but Gruetzmeyer seemed the kind of old-fashioned intellectual who relied on books, not electronic media. Max recalled Temple bemoaning the ill luck of having media on hand to film the dead body as it was being discovered — her bright idea gone wrong — since she wasn't expecting a corpse to show up for her ceremonial opening of an old underground safe.

And Cosimo Sparks, also stabbed like Jefferson Mangel, had also been found with his red-satin-lined cloak arranged in a tortured shape.

He decided not to ask Professor Gruetzmeyer if he'd heard of Ophiuchus. The big question was whether Revienne had.

CHAPTER 43
ALIEN EYES

Poor Jeff Mangel. His honorary gallery was in an eight-foot-high space whose ceiling Max could dust with his upstretched hand, a bland former classroom sporting sound-deadening ceiling tiles spotted with tiny black holes.

The floor was covered by equally uninspiring vinyl tile in a pastel, smashed-worms-on-sidewalk pattern.

Flashback.

Max had gone to high school in exactly the same bland spaces. If he hadn't made himself a stranger to his family in his teens, as Gandolph told him, he would know where to go to confirm these unsettling slide shows in his brain. Wisconsin, Gandolph said. Max didn't feel like a Wisconsin sort of person . . . fresh air, bracing winters. More like an escapee from a Florida swamp filled with gators and snapping turtles and black mambas on the brain — oh, my.

He strolled around the perimeter to study the three-dimensional items under Plexiglas boxes.

Decks of gorgeously illustrated antique tarot cards; wood and metal coin boxes, the Okito, Boston and slot varieties; wands of all types . . .

He stopped and moved back to the coin boxes. One was made of beautifully grained cocobolo wood, as wands often were. Not a seam showed in its curved dimensions, but a ring of ivory inset on the top was carved in the shape of a worm Ouroboros, the snake biting its tail and a symbol of eternity that matched the ring Kathleen O'Connor had forced Matt Devine to wear for a time.

The image was commonly known to people with a mystical bent. This could be meaningless, but it had belonged to Jefferson Mangel, who perhaps had been a man who knew too much.

The Plexiglas cover wasn't locked. It had an "invisible" sliding seam on one side. Max had the cocobolo wood box in his hands in an instant, and the other four coin boxes in that section respaced to hide its absence. He could return the piece as easily.

The wood warmed in his hands. His fingertips felt no opening, but there had to be one. Time to play with it later. It slipped into his pants pocket.

Could there be something interesting in the ranks of posters displayed carpet-sample fashion? Max flipped through the giant aluminum frames like pages in a book, viewing show placards that pictured magicians from the Frenchman Robert-Houdin, to the Austrian he'd inspired, Houdini, to Blackstone to David Copperfield and to . . . the Mystifying Max. He started slightly as he came face-to-face with himself.

All magicians, except the Cloaked Conjuror, aspired to that Bela Lugosi as Dracula hypnotic stare, but Max was surprised in ambush by the dramatically intent expression. His green-eyed black-panther stare would do Midnight Louie proud.

Flashback.

He is standing, seeing his blue eyes in the mirror and then, blink, the green contact lenses glide into place on his vitreous humour, the glistening fluid of his eyes. He becomes the Mystifying Max . . . and also a few degrees closer to a disguise that will keep Max Kinsella a wholly separate entity, at least in international intrigue circles.

His own gall surprises him. By doing a show in Las Vegas in any guise he'd been taking a hell of a risk.

Why had he done the Vegas bit? Garry had

420

retired here, of course. He must have gotten an offer he couldn't refuse from the Goliath. Only for a year, but it must have been renewable. And . . . as his memory clicked into operation, the eyes on his poster shifted from feline green to a tantalizing blue gray, not quite either. Temple Barr's eyes.

Max shut his eyelids as memory replayed himself talking, selling, cajoling. She'd come here to Vegas because of his upcoming gig. Because of him. Leaving her home city, her career. That was a major commitment. Had he ever experienced anything but specific traumas of the distant past? Was he as brave as Temple Barr? Or just obsessed?

Max paged past his own frozen image. The Mystifying Max was history. Even if he remembered all his old stage moves and illusions, his compromised physique would probably be unable to duplicate them.

The next poster had him staring into Harry Houdini's truly mesmerizing vividly black gaze. That man had enough visceral charisma and drive to power a planet. The storied "escapologist" was pictured nearly naked, hunched over like an ape-man, metal cuffs and chains hanging from every muscle and sinew. He'd accomplished incredible feats of working in freezing water to free himself, of hanging upside down like a bat.

The illusions may all have stemmed from the same secret magical routines of his predecessors, but the marketing chutzpah and electrifying stage presence were individual.

Max searched himself and found no remembered driving motive. Revenge for Gandolph's death? That tragic recent incident in Belfast had been a last impotent cannon shot in a cause long left behind by a more tortured contemporary history. It wouldn't have happened if Garry hadn't been so loyal in tracking down Max's obsession with a past he didn't even have the good grace to remember.

Maybe it was good to have no one to hate, but it was more than bad to have no one to love.

Max flipped back to his false-eyed image. He did not know the man.

CHAPTER 44
MIDNIGHT AT THE OASIS

"You may wonder," Miss Midnight Louise says, sashaying back and forth in front of the Dumpster behind the police substation, "why I have called you all together this afternoon."

There is indeed a convocation of cats crowded around the closed Dumpster, domestic shorthairs and longhairs, big, small, chubby, lean, striped, spotted, calicos, tabbies, tortoiseshells, black-and-white tuxedos, solid whites, and, naturally, the royal color, solid black.

Of course, cats do not come with birth certificates unless they are purebreds, so you could say three generations of the Midnight clan are present, if you believe Miss Midnight Louise's claim that I am her long-lost daddy.

"Why indeed has your caterwauling awakened us?" Ma Barker grumbles under her Happy Meal breath as her forepaws box the sleep from her eyes. "This is the hottest part of the day and I need my afternoon beauty sleep."

I try not to choke audibly on that last statement. Ma Barker, as leader of the clan of Las Vegas cats called a clowder, bears many honorable scars from fierce territorial battles, but she is no beauty and proud of it.

She and I have the family eyes, hers more at half-mast, but both green. Miss Louise, however, sports eyes of old gold, and her hair is not thick and full for battle in the wrestling ring, but long and fluffy. If she is a descendant of mine, I believe one of my showgirl flings is responsible.

Miss Midnight Louise is, however, quite a tenacious little dame, like my Miss Temple, and there is no underestimating her.

"Listen up," she is saying now, passing among the troops with razor-sharp nails cocked as she gives some of the nodding-off nap crowd *NCIS* back-of-the neck slaps.

"I have been on solo stakeout," she continues, giving me the cold gold stare she wields so well, so you feel like you have been whipped with a guilt stick. "I have covered not only a major undercover mover in Las Vegas, Mr. Max Kinsella, whom some of those among us do not feel is a worthy subject of interest —"

"I get it, Louise," I howl. "Forget all this pointing paws stuff. I did underestimate what was going on when Mr. Max disappeared at the Neon Nightmare a couple months ago, but he is back and getting his black on, and that is old news now."

She leaps to confront me with a bound, growling in my face. "He is back and about to make major fresh news." Louise turns to rouse her minions. "And this emergency intervention involves another location I have been surveying on my own, the Oasis Hotel and its Lusty Ladies and Laddies sea battle attraction."

A hiss stirs the assembly. Louise has made a tactical error. We of the feline family do not, as a rule, like water.

I spot my opening and seize it, stepping in front of her. "Excuse me. The junior partner of the firm has done some fine legwork — and you gentlemen will all agree she has the legs for it. . . ." I am not surprised to raise a hiss from among the clowder females. "Just pulling your legs, ladies, to get your attention.

"Obviously," I go on, "we need a special ops team on this matter Miss Louise has brought to our attention. Midnight Investigations, Inc., offers services in all areas of crime prevention and detection, but we are a two, er, individual operation. Occasionally, we need to expand our arena of operations into a major public presence.

"So." I look around at every yellow, green, yellow green, and even blue eye. "I am calling the Cat Pack back into action."

The Cat Pack is the elite fighting cadre I put together for protecting my Miss Temple in matters involving major weapons, like a loaded handgun . . . in her purse. Not good. We all wear ninja black.

Ma Barker lurches in front of me. "Front and center, you volunteers," she orders, her slightly skewed gaze raking every black-haired dude or doll in the clan.

"What about Three O'Clock at Gangsters?" Ma grumbles to me under her breath. "We need a geezer?"

Since she is probably older than my esteemed sire, Three O'Clock Louie, gourmand and restaurant mascot, that was a low blow.

"No time to fetch him." Miss Louise blows past me to address the clan. One swipe of the fluffy train on that youngster's skirt puts enough fine hairs and dander into my eyes and nose to shut down sight and speech for half a minute.

"We could use a special team of the tuxedos," she adds.

A smaller but equally triumphal roar goes up. I have to admit these guys and gals look pretty sharp with their spanking white bibs and faces, white gloves and sox and formal black

426

topcoats everywhere else.

Sadly, those snappy white areas also make it easier for predators to spy them in the dark. You cannot beat nose-to-tail black for camouflage.

Once I can sneeze out her loose hairs, I go abreast of Louise and whisper in her little perked ear. "Those tuxedos are a mixed bag when it comes to nocturnal operations," I warn her. "Ma Barker will shorten our tails in tandem if we lose any of her gang."

"Relax, Daddy-O. I have this upcoming clash of Titans thoroughly scoped out. All we have to do is throw a big monkey wrench in the unfolding events, and our guys at the Oasis will come out up on top."

"We do not have any guys at the Oasis."

By now the grateful tuxedos are making like a Broadway chorus line in front of Louise, they are so delighted to be asked to dance at our party.

Miss Midnight Louise, I am thinking, is biting off more than I can chew.

CHAPTER 45
MILLION-DOLLAR COLLAR

"It's either you or Molina," the semi-familiar voice on Temple's smartphone intoned with resignation when she answered. "I much prefer you, Zoe Chloe."

"Um . . . is this Rafi Nadir?"

"My job's at stake. My access to my daughter's at stake. The Amy Winehouse of Las Vegas Boulevard is MIA. I need an insty, gutsy MC by eight tonight to replace the celebrity hostess that nobody knows. I figured you could do the job in a pinch."

"Who gets pinched?"

"Hopefully no one. It's for the prize drawing on the million-dollar see-through treasure chest at the Oasis. You *have* heard of that?"

"Yeah, but I don't want to resurrect Zoe Chloe. You just need someone to announce?"

"Like that creep Buchanan did on the body-in-the-safe event. You were there. You could probably do his job, right?"

"Yes. Is this dangerous?"

"I will personally keep a bead on your ass."

"That is not encouraging."

Rafi chuckled. "I have a feeling you are just what the situation needs. In case things get crazy."

Temple had a feeling too, a feeling that Rafi wasn't telling her everything he knew, or suspected. "The hotel honestly, truly had a semi-celebrity cancel?"

"Yeah. This ditzy dame named —"

Temple had a metaphysical moment. "— Savannah Ashleigh."

"Exactly right."

"And I just have to —"

"Hold a mic. Welcome suckers . . . I mean, eligible gaming card holders in the audience. Announce the winning card number after the executive manager spins the barrel and draws a winner. Then let the winner gush and the executive preen."

Temple ran through her short-notice wardrobe possibilities for something that went with a million dollars. Thanks to Bahama Mama resale, it was a go.

So she told Rafi.

The gig would keep her mind off Matt, so suddenly out of town on mysterious business. Temple could handle an audience, but nowadays she was used to being an anonymous PR person standing on the sidelines like a referee, yelling out encouragement and cringing at errors.

This was not "her" event. Yet here she was positioned in a spotlight in front of the Oasis Hotel's security force, arranged in an impressive semicircle around the glittering prize in front of the two-story-high elephant statues to either side.

Rafi had even arranged that she'd stand in *front* of the live elephant imported for the event, not at the back, where an anonymous jumpsuited man with a bucket and shovel stood.

That down-home touch was appropriate. Some large elephant doo-doo was going down in this event. Even as she stood there in her glitzy go-to-meeting network executives suit, Temple recognized that the same zodiac spotlight pattern as the Neon Nightmare's was programmed into the nightly highlighting of the prize.

The effect here was subtle, but it had stopped her in her tracks and her gold leather gladiator shoes. Luckily, not until she was in place alongside the treasure chest.

She watched the familiar image of a "man

versus serpent" smackdown flash over the cash-stuffed plastic trunk along with images of a lion, a ram, an archer, a scorpion, and a pair of fish that reminded her of Midnight Louie's precious koi.

Ophiuchus. That dastardly word gripped her brain like the grabby sign of the crab, Cancer.

"What's with the zodiac light wheel?" she'd asked Rafi, who looked seriously official tonight in his Oasis house cop uniform.

"It's all mumbo jumbo and hype," he'd answered. "The Cloaked Conjuror is making a secret, special appearance managing this, uh, 'dramatic finale' to the 'Oasis Apotheosis.' What the heck does 'apotheosis' mean anyway?"

"Granted. I'd never stick a five-syllable word on a big prize promotion, but 'Oasis' is a tough name to work with. 'Apotheosis' means the best, the model of supreme coolness, say. Whatever. 'Oasis Apotheosis" sounds like something mysterious."

"Yeah. Like an exotic disease."

"What lured the Cloaked Conjuror from his New Millennium fortress?" Temple wondered. "The Oasis is part of the same consortium of hotel-casinos, but, with all due respect, the security here must be less dictator-like than at his home hotel."

"I agree." Rafi's eyes kept darting over the crowd. "I think he's crazy to do it too. Maybe top management twisted his arm. Still, flaunting all that cash in a see-through steamer trunk out front sure drew a crowd this past week. I've been earning a lot of overtime."

Rafi squinted into the gathered crowds, which were hard to see against the eye-dazzling assortment of lights from the hotel opposite. "Our audience here is mainly card-carrying consortium members, but riffraff too," he added.

She emulated his squint. "I see what you mean. Some of the Strip street performers are using the *aah* factor of all that naked money to mingle with the onlookers and pitch them. Guess the Oasis has an irresistible event going on here, despite the weird name."

" 'Mingle,' " Rafi echoed her with a sour twist to his tone. "Probably pickpockets, every last one."

"You don't get to savor a drop of human kindness in your job, do you? The Strip never had itinerant street acts before the Great Recession. Nevada has been hit the hardest of any state."

"And I have a good new job, Little Miss

Sunshine, I know. But part of that job is anticipating trouble. I don't like this give-away drawing out here in the open, at night, one bit."

"Not to mention the elephant." Temple turned to eye the huge ankle cuff and chain that kept the immense creature tied down. "I don't approve of captivity."

"What you and I don't approve of is not in the mix here. Just stay put where I placed you, although that may be too much to ask of your inner Zoe Chloe Ozone."

Temple saluted sharply. "She's on leave. Yes, sir. I'll do my best."

Rafi moved back to inspect his troops, the two lines of ten guards at attention who served as set dressing for the million-dollar prize.

Temple kept focused on the circle of sidewalk that had been cleared for the drawing ceremony, watching the animals and symbols of the zodiac flash across it. If you weren't aware of the theme, you could stand in the crowd all night and not notice the zodiac-sign parade, especially the entwined strongman and giant snake that signaled Ophiuchus.

Why did Rafi want her to be present? Did he know about the Synth? That they'd already lost whatever had been hidden in the underground walk-in safe between the Crystal Phoenix and Gangsters hotels, and the Neon Nightmare nightclub?

Whatever Rafi's motive was for inviting her, Temple was betting these seasoned conspirators wouldn't let another opportunity to score a bundle, for whatever reason, evade them.

Chapter 46
Monkey-Suit Business

While Temple speculated about what was really going on, the recorded music, which had been on the cheesy tick-tock game show countdown side suddenly revved up with brass and winds as the main event neared.

The elephant behind her trumpeted — Temple shivered at the blaring teeth-rattling screech, being a mere ten feet from the creature. Though the heat had lifted as the sun went down, she smelled some Essence de Barn, hay and mashed cow paddies. She turned to see the trainer tap what passed for the elephant's knee, which was at her waist level. The impressive bulk of the beast lifted in what would have been a rear to a horse.

Temple gazed at the rising gray wall of wrinkled hide, speechless in her front-row seat. The elephant's open ankle cuff, about four feet in diameter, lay sprung like a trap beneath its momentarily balancing bulk.

Why did she think she had any business being here?

And then an airborne shadow came shooting from the right as the elephant turned and pulled back its massive ears. Ye gods! Talk about angels dancing on the head of a pin. Temple blinked as a resurrected Cosimo Sparks stood in a spotlight, dressed in top hat, white tie, and tails, the satin lining of his cloak flashing bloodred in the spotlights as he danced on the head of an elephant.

But Cosimo Sparks was dead.

Temple sensed everyone around her holding his or her breath. The effect was staggering, but was it a true surprise to some of the gathering, a resurrected Cosimo Sparks appearing to his Synth buddies and, perhaps, his not-yet-umasked Synth slayer?

Or was the Mystifying Max doing this elephant walk? Whoever, the figure moved like a puppet on a string, barely touching elephant head or back as it lowered and lifted. Max had been "retired" for more than a year from a major Vegas venue. In Vegas time that was an eternity. If you weren't the object of buzz, you simply "weren't" in Vegas.

So either way, a resurrected Sparks or

Max in disguise, this was a dead man dancing.

The effect had everyone, including the elephant, looking up.

Another figure shot into the lights and the rotating shadows of the zodiac on a batlike gliding descent. This massive, dark-clothed figure landed as lightly as a moth on the sidewalk beside the treasure chest as the crowd gasped.

Oh, my. Was this shaping up to be some sort of a superhero smackdown? Temple felt someone move protectively close to her back and glanced over her shoulder. Rafi.

The Cloaked Conjuror shook out his heavy cape like Batman, lifting his glittering tiger-striped face to the moon. Temple imagined a sidewalk production of *Cats* and expected CC to burst out singing "Memories" at any moment.

Temple's time as a repertory theater PR person clicked to the forefront on her dial of past and present media jobs. Everything so far was totally scripted, meticulously scripted.

She glanced at the elephant-dancing swell in top hat and tails. It was hard to see clearly against the intense lights haloing the hotel façade, but he was indeed too tall to be Cosimo.

The Cloaked Conjuror strode back and forth in front of the massive treasure chest crammed with a visible fortune in hundred-dollar bills. Was he too slim for CC? Could it be one of his stunt doubles, like Barry, the poor guy who had plunged to his death at TitaniCon at the New Millennium?

Wait. Max *could* be atop the elephant! Or . . . he could be "styling" the Cloaked Conjuror with the jackpot on the ground. He certainly wasn't confiding his moves to her as he'd used to. Ex-significant others got scarce on the reporting-in roster fast.

Temple inhaled. Hard. Something big was going down here. Scanning the crowd, she spotted an almost seething organic motion rippling through it, as if a giant . . . snake were threading through the onlookers' ankles, entangling their ankles.

Meanwhile, more than cell phones were waving on uplifted arms everywhere.

Here, there, everywhere . . . the flat disks of top hats were snapping into 3-D prominence as they did on Broadway stages or in magic shows. Five, six, eight, nine. Temple was impressed.

Max's act had used one of those collapsible toppers and they cost about three hundred apiece. This smacked of money and planning. On the other hand, Vegas thronged with high-and low-end costume rental outfits.

But wait! This is Vegas and there was more.

Here, there, everywhere, Darth Vader masks and cloaks were springing up like melting Wicked Witches of the West run backwards on the film reel. Three, five . . . no, eight. Holy breather apparatus! Darths were everywhere. But both the masks and black cloaks were pretty standard too.

Could some of the crowd, the street performers, all be part of a bizarre plot, probably a social-media-generated group flash mash-up? That would create enough confusion to hide a heist.

Fiendishly clever. Could tons of ordinary folks have been "e-vited" over social networks to show up in one of three costumes . . . Tap Dance Man, Darth Vader, or Security Guy? In a crowd this unsettled and also populated by gangs of identical fakes, the real money was vulnerable.

"Back, you minions," the Cloaked Conjuror's voice ordered, boosted by the major mic amplification of his headgear. The figure in front of the frail-looking Plexiglas chest gestured with one sweeping arm and gauntleted palm, like a traffic cop.

Except he wasn't one. Nobody here was

on the premises to stop anything, only accelerate the mob excitement and . . .

"You fools," CC intoned with much overacting. "I, the Cloaked Conjuror, will claim this prize. Watch and weep."

He strode past the treasure chest, snapping his cloak higher than a matador challenging a bull. By the time he let the cloak fall back to his side, the bill-stuffed chest had vanished. Only the entrance doors to the Oasis showed, and no one hustled in and out, as usual, because the two lines of Oasis security guards prevented anyone from surging out, or in.

The crowd gasped. Temple had never heard such a conjoined mass sigh.

Another amplified voice spoke during the lull. "Good, but not good enough."

The tails of the elephant-dancing man flapped like bat wings in the silence as he skated to the ground on an invisible spider-string. The costume was all Fred Astaire except for the Zorro-like black eye mask.

He faced the Cloaked Conjuror and flourished his red-satin-lined cape.

As he forced CC to retreat, he passed, obscured, and moved beyond the empty entrance. When he turned and again flourished the scarlet panache of his cape lining, the treasure chest reappeared, spotlights flashing off its clear plastic surface and the crushed greenbacks filling the almost invisible dimensions.

Temple's brain was whirling. She knew one of the dueling magicians was going to execute a final pass past the prize, the magical third time. Then the money would vanish and be gone for good. Most dramas had three acts, like fairy tales had three brothers.

There had to be an elaborate setup behind this illusion that jerked the crowd's perceptions back and forth like a saw blade cutting through a magician's case containing the endangered lady.

While she was thinking, something like a forefinger of King Kong — or a huge attacking serpent . . . the Ophiuchus serpent — whipped around her waist and lifted her up, up, and away, above the treasure chest, above the crowd, and into the glare of the lights and the rhythmic zodiac sign shadows, now recognizably only Ophiuchus . . . and *she* was the struggling human figure in the muscular, strangling serpent's grasp.

She was the distracting magician's assistant.

Her hands tried to grasp the snake's coil, but it was too massive to curl around. Oh. This was an elephant trunk, and the pressure it exerted was amazingly delicate for such a thick and rough-skinned appendage.

Temple kept her hands on the living noose that had circled her. The motion as she was lifted over the beast's high shoulder made her stomach dip. Before she could say "Dumbo," she was perched on its surprisingly hairy back in front of the palanquin. She grabbed on to its draped, gilt silk cloth . . . a flimsy "rope" as prone to tearing as a belly dancer's skirt. Far too far beneath, the animal tender was shouting commands even she couldn't hear. The elephant flapped back an ear to heed him, apparently in vain. If the corn was as high as an elephant's eye, as the song went, she was halfway up Jack's beanstalk.

The elephant man suddenly screamed loud enough to attract the beast's attention. Something black had climbed the elephant's dangling headdress decorations and was now midway through a leap to . . . the elephant's left scimitar of ivory tusk.

The elephant swayed its trunk, but Midnight Louie spun to hang under the tusk like a tree sloth. The behemoth uneasily shifted its weight from foot to foot. Above, Temple swung to and fro, a mere decorative tassel. Louie sprang upward to claw-cling to the harness on the elephant's forehead and then to the top of the head, where he leaned down to yowl in an ear.

Midnight Louie was demanding a one-on-one.

The huge appendage flapped back. One edge slapped Temple in the dangling calf. It felt like being whapped by a canvas sail.

The triumphant tap-dancing guy on the ground bounced once and achieved a spot on the elephant's shoulder blades. He bent to seize Temple around the waist — good thing she had a twenty-two-inch one — and bounced down to deposit her on the elephant tusk opposite the one Midnight Louie had used as a stepping stone before alighting beside the chest again.

Showtime! The elephant's trunk swayed from side to side. It was used to passengers and was getting into its performing groove. In a moment, it carefully went down on one knee, then two. Rafi was waiting there to swing Temple back to ground zero.

She looked up the elephant's kneeling form, anxious about Louie. Not to worry. He'd used his claws to climb farther and was sitting smack-dab center of the palanquin like a rajah, surveying the action below.

And what action!

The Vaders' dark forms were falling to the ground under a wave of black cats that swarmed their cloaks, unseen by the tourist crowds, who nevertheless had been conditioned by countless *Star Wars* movies to join in and keep any downed Vader in black . . . down.

Meanwhile, the masked white tie and tails guys were tap-dancing forward in formation as the dueling magicians pantomimed lifting the treasure chest with their sweeping cloak action.

The chest elevated four feet off the ground, nothing beneath it but air, as the eight formally attired men separated into pallbearer formation. The crowd parted as they escorted the floating money chest down the entry lane into a waiting 1930s black hearse.

In an instant the rear doors slammed shut and the top-hatted white-tie guys vanished behind the vintage vehicle's four doors, which also slammed shut as the hearse glided away.

Temple was as agape as everyone in the crowd, including the elephant handler.

Someone tapped her on the shoulder. She turned.

Rafi.

He pointed to a pale middle-aged man in an expensive dark suit turning a crank on a

Plexiglas rolling chamber filled with slips of paper.

Invited, she drew one. Rafi handed her a portable mic.

"Ladies and gentlemen," she intoned, "the winner is . . . Mr. Joseph Merrick."

The man in the suit had his impossibly anticlimactic moment in the spotlight. "Please come forward, Mr. Merrick, and we'll complete the process in the casino offices."

He seemed unconcerned about the disappearance of the prize money, and Temple knew why. The audience had accepted every moment as the usual Las Vegas overblown live theater. Joe and supporters rushed toward her. Beyond them, Rafi and security crew pulled downed Darth Vaders into custody. Onlookers melted away.

Besides having corralled a protesting group of black-cloaked street performers, Rafi's security guys were left holding three empty masks and cloaks.

Temple stepped up to him. "I guess you're not too worried about where the money went."

"Looked like to the bank."

"If you bank at Fontana Brothers, Inc., Rafi, you didn't set this all up on your own. You needed maximum diversion from two major magicians, three amazingly diverse mammal groups, and one prominent Las Vegas family, as well as one poor lone working girl. I claim credit for Louie and providing comic relief, but you and the moonlighting magicians engineered it."

Rafi's smile was as big as a million dollars. "And no official police action involved. With a little help from my friends, this gets me the security chief job here, and a step forward in my crusade to reclaim my kid from the big, bad Molina."

"Why did anybody need me? I was arm-candy for an elephant and did a three-sentence announcing gig."

"Well," Rafi said, "you had about —" He thought. "— about forty protective eyes on you, so it seemed a slam dunk."

"Even the elephant's trunk episode?"

"Sultana performs nightly with a petite woman."

"So that's two mammal groups down. What about the third?"

"We've all heard that 'Everywhere that Mary went, the lamb was sure to go.' I figured that might apply to domesticated wildcats. We needed them to soften up the Vaders, and someone assured me that they'd done the job before."

"Someone?"

Rafi shrugged. "The Cloaked Conjuror keeps an artificially amplified ear to the ground."

CHAPTER 47
AFTER-HOURS NIGHTMARE

"I could use a good PR woman," the voice on Temple's phone said.

"For what assignment?"

"Closure."

"Not in my job description."

"You'll like it. Trust me."

"I always did. But Max, it's almost one o'clock in the morning and we're supposed to be recovering from a . . . strenuous public appearance. We might still be a little shaky, your legs and mind, my sanity and cat."

"The closure is for the Synth."

"Oh. That does sound tempting. Now?"

"Yes. At the Neon Nightmare."

"Aren't they still open now?"

"They'd shut down to the public a couple days ago for 'reconstruction.' After the debacle at the Oasis, who knows when they'll reopen. I do think a small closing ceremony is required."

"Closed down? So what do you need me

there for?"

"Personal satisfaction."

"Mine, or yours?"

"Both, hopefully."

"I'm not supposed to be getting that out and about."

"It's metaphorical, of course."

"Of course. Okay. I'll bring Midnight Louie as a chaperone."

"Fine by me. Maybe not by the Synth."

"Even better."

"You'll be home again before Mr. Midnight signs off the air."

Max himself had signed off on that note.

Temple looked down at Midnight Louie, who'd come to sit by her feet and, she swore, eavesdrop by some mysterious placement of his ears as antennas.

"Mysteriouser and mysteriouser," she muttered. "Dare we trust a man who'd let us ride an elephant as mere distractions? What does he want us to distract from now?"

Louie yawned. It was late.

"Also, what does one wear to a closuring?" she asked rhetorically.

Then she padded barefoot to her bedroom closet to come up with something quick and clean and nautical, navy wide-leg capris and a red-striped knit top and rope-decorated wedgies. This certainly wasn't club wear, but Neon Nightmare didn't sound like it was doing too much rocking right now.

Louie was definitely in one of his climbing moods.

She locked her door and took the elevator down, but he met her by the Miata in the parking lot, having used the lone palm tree trunk as an exit. A suspicious number of light-reflecting iridescent green eyes lurked among the oleanders.

Temple took the Miata's top down for the short drive to Neon Nightmare, and Louie lofted over the low car's side into the passenger seat.

She checked her watch. Matt's return flight time forced him to go straight to his midnight-to-2:00 A.M. show, and he'd be home a half hour later. Temple wanted to be there to explain her Circus Circus moments at the Oasis. He'd been distracted by his mother's sticky romantic problems, poor guy. In fact, the whirlwind Chicago trip must have been pretty stressful. It would be great to get back to easy-as-pie normal, especially after a wearing heist-busting.

Speaking of which, what was Max up to? She wouldn't be meeting him like this if she wasn't sure it was old business, including circumstances she'd been deeply involved in. Max without a memory displayed no sexual interest in her at all.

That was a bit insulting, but mostly a huge relief. She looked over at Louie, who sat up in the seat like a person and looked around with great interest, like a dog. If you wanted to see "insulted," it would be Louie if he knew her thoughts at the moment. He regarded people, and certainly dogs, as inferior species. Sometimes she thought he had a point.

"Now," she told him later when she put the Miata into Park in the almost deserted Neon Nightmare parking lot, "this is another weird place full of weird lights and people." As far as she knew, the Neon Nightmare was new to Louie. Midnight Louise had led the Cat Pack raid on the Synth the first time she saw them in action, right here. And they'd taken down only two Vaders that time.

Temple eyed the black glass pyramid's exterior. The neon rearing horse still reigned atop the peak. She guessed the interior was the same overlit, sound-system-drenched bar and dance club as ever.

It pleased Temple as she approached the neon-arched entry that she and black cats had been the recurring bane of the Synth magicians who'd owned and run this building, and whose plans to plunder Las Vegas had been foiled so spectacularly at the Oasis, thanks to Max and the Cloaked Conjuror.

Temple yanked on one of the front door's huge handles. She'd recently brought a firearm into this place, it had seemed so dangerous. Could she really walk into this possible trap? Could she still trust Max, maimed as he had been?

As she hesitated, Midnight Louie stretched his yard-long frame up the massive door. He wanted in. She leaned all her weight on the bronze door to crack it, then did it again. As it opened with no protesting noises, they left the warm Las Vegas night to slip into the cool, stale silence of the dark interior.

Temple's shoes had ridged rubber soles. Louie's feet had soft pads. They made no noise as they moved into the massive central dance and drinking area.

Neon still silhouetted the bar area, the spinning disco lights still cast the thirteen signs of the Synth zodiac on the floor and . . . people still sat at the bar, drinking.

Temple edged nearer, unnoticed. Two women, one fat, one lean. One man, medium. No, the chubby woman was the medium, as Temple recalled. These were the three people Temple had seen threatened by the two Darth Vader invaders in the rooms concealed behind the nightclub's mirrored black walls.

They'd spotted her for only one lightning-flash moment, but they'd sure seen the Las Vegas Cat Pack take down their enemies, the Vaders. They'd resurrected those sinister figures for the Oasis caper, but Temple was sure the earlier Vaders didn't participate. They had carried serious weapons.

Right now, what was left of the Synth wasn't expecting to see anyone or anything. All hunched morosely over the cocktail of choice, the liquor bottles sitting on the glossy black bartop ready for several refills.

"The street troops did a fine job," the solo man said mournfully. "Their timing was perfect."

"So was the 'timing' of our enemies," the slender woman in a green satin gown answered, pointed elbows on the bar, a wide-mouthed martini glass cradled in her hands.

"*Two* sets of them," the heavyset woman said in a ponderous voice. Temple couldn't see past her voluminous caftan to what witches' brew she drank. "Who invited the tap-dancing fools to our sidewalk snatch party?"

"The Darth Vaders came here uninvited,"

the man reminded her. "We were helpless then too."

Temple was back-stepping on tiptoe. Max wouldn't have wanted her to be here alone with these Synth members. Why the heck had he called her here? At least Louie . . .

She looked down. Louie was gone. He'd probably ambled somewhere else in the empty nightclub, soundless and stealthy.

Well, darn.

Rethink that.

Well, *damn.*

Here she was alone with a trio of depressed magical mobsters who'd tried to heist a Strip casino only hours ago. She made out the shape of an upholstered banquette behind her and sank down on it, trying to become invisible.

"This place is kaput," the man said. "We can't pay the mortgage, just like Mr. and Mrs. America."

The plump woman spoke next. "Going for that prize money was a long shot, Hal, but Cosimo's death is what really did us in. He knew where all the money we'd been promised was hidden. Do you think he gave it up to whoever killed him?"

"It was never our money," the man told her. "We were in it for the glory of doing a mass illusion like tonight. Face it. We knew we were being set up as a distraction for another major heist by whatever crime elements amassed the supposed hidden fortune we were guarding, but look at the razzle-dazzle we stage-managed with the crowd tonight. Our street performers' transformation, the distraction, the scale, we almost waltzed that transparent treasure chest right out of there until that mob of tap-dancers co-opted our action."

" 'Close' is worthless," the Thin Woman said. "We were outmaneuvered by the Cloaked Conjuror and his freaking Fred Astaire accomplice. How did they know to do the white tie and tails bit? That was our gimmick!"

Hal was still mourning. "I don't know. It's just lucky we set up a flash mob of civilians to wear the same Vader heads and cloaks as the two thugs who accosted us in our own clubrooms only nights ago, or we'd never have been able to escape. How could CC know about our plans? We just put them together on the fly with . . ."

"Guess who's missing right now? Max Kinsella," the Thin Woman pointed out. "We stole the formal-wear heisters idea from his act, but he conjured a whole new illusion for us."

"So we were betrayed. What's new," Hal

asked. "We should slit our wrists? You're a medium, Czarina Catharina," he added bitterly. "What do you see in our future?"

The woman spun around on her barstool. The lighting from above made her face into a cratered dark side of the moon, excessive weight, age, and defeat evident in every highlight and shadow.

Temple glimpsed a giant bubble glass behind her, almost empty, with booze the color of C. R. Molina's electric blue eyes at the bottom. Had Czarina been drinking that much Blue Curaçao straight? Temple checked the bottle on the bar. Yes. Oh, the calories!

"I see dead people, Hal," Czarina intoned.

"Oh, shut up." The Thin Woman straightened her sharp shoulders and half spun to address Czarina. "Nobody died today. Just dreams died today. The Cloaked Conjuror is a bigger sensation than ever, the big, fat, rich, anonymous bully. He's okay, but we shed our Vader skins to escape and are okay too."

"Maybe not, Ramona." Hal spun to face into the deserted room, elbows pushed back to lean on the bar.

Oh, great. Temple was once again an unseen eavesdropper on the Synth at work and play, or, actually, idle and in despair.

She was a *witness.* They'd recognize her from the last time she'd shown up at their headquarters, would know she wasn't just a "lost customer." She wished she'd been foolish enough to carry a gun here again.

Would Max really invite her to this Synth pity party and not show up? Just how muddled *was* his memory?

She considered bending out of sight below the table, planning to crawl out in the darkness, a tactic both humiliating and scary.

A clinking sound stirred the banks of shelved liquor bottles behind the bar. The trio snapped their heads to the rear, spinning back around to face the mirror behind the wall of booze that reflected shards of their unhappy faces.

Temple froze in place. Any motion now would attract them.

"Poltergeists," Czarina intoned.

"The building settling," Hal said. "Why shouldn't it fall apart too? You just said 'nobody died' today, Ramona. What about yesterday? Just few days ago."

"Cosimo, sure," she answered. "Maybe one of the Vaders did it."

"Or one of us," Hal said.

"What? Are you crazy?" Czarina jerked half around to look him in the eye past the intervening presence of Ramona.

Hal shrugged and turned away. "A couple of our would-be recruits didn't make it either."

"Who?" Czarina demanded.

Temple noticed Ramona's long nails caressing the sides of her martini glass.

"Gandolph," Hal said.

The word almost made Temple's heart stop. She had to hear this.

Then she thought, *Which death is he talking about? Gandolph's fake death or the recent real one? Max. You wouldn't take this almost-confession lying down. Where are you?*

"Gandolph? He's been out of the picture for . . . months and months." Czarina stretched for the tall blue bottle and poured more liquid sapphire into her glass.

Ramona smiled as she turned around to hold her martini glass at her breastbone. "He died at that Halloween séance to channel Harry Houdini. He died disguised as a fat old female medium, the rumor went," she said maliciously. "Was he gay, or just crazy?"

"He was a longtime friend of Cosimo's." Hal lifted his highball glass in a solo unspoken toast. "Old-school magicians like those two will never come again. I thought at the time maybe you had killed him, Czarina."

458

"Me?"

"He'd outed you as a fake medium only months before. He may have lifted your likeness for the Houdini gig. That's a lot of hurt for your professional reputation, not to mention personal ridicule, Czarina. And now someone's killed Cosimo too."

"Hmm." Ramona lifted her glass like a chalice and sipped before speaking. "I'd always wondered if it was *you,* Hal."

"That séance death? Surely not Cosimo's."

Ramona shrugged, which did great things for her décolletage, especially in the dramatic overhead lights. "Both, maybe."

"So." Czarina was starting to sound soused. "Hal thought I killed Gandolph and you thought he killed Gandolph *and* Cosimo. Who do you think I thought *you* killed?"

"Are there any more deaths to go around, Czarina?"

"You bet, Ramona. You almost won the Cloaked Conjuror's assistant to our cause. What a coup that would have been. Then Barry tragically 'fell' from the stage catwalk during that TitaniCon science fiction convention."

"I don't do straight-up ladders for three stories with these shoes, Czarina." Ramona kicked up her slinky hem to showcase a high-arched foot wearing a killer spike heel. "Now, if he'd been *stabbed* to death . . . It was an accident. No police were on it."

"Then what about those would-be recruits Hal was mentioning, Czarina?"

"I happen to know, Ramona," Hal put in, "from Cosimo's own lips, that you tried to seduce that university professor to our side and he wouldn't seduce. How much about us did you tell him? Because he ended up dead in his classroom."

"That was an exhibition area," Ramona said, her face and body stiff with control. "Jeff was an . . . engaging man, more interested in my mind than my body, true, but I seldom encounter men like that."

"You don't give them a chance to skip over the obvious, rather," Hal said.

"I . . . was sorry he died." Ramona took another oh-so-controlled sip of her straight-up martini. "He had a genuine love for magic and those who made it their lives. He studied the mystification, the surprise, the delight of the audience. He had theories from old, old books. I'd never realized the history . . . He made me feel like a kid again, wanting to believe, to *be* believed."

Temple, the lone unacknowledged audience member in the dark, believed her.

460

"Someone jealous of your intellectual infatuation with your professor killed him," Czarina decided. "Hal? Did you contribute to Professor Mangel's 'study'?"

He nodded. "You too, I imagine. We're all suspects." He frowned. "I suppose you thought I killed Gandolph's female assistant as well. That I was attempting to seduce her to our cause and failed."

"Gloria?" Ramona was surprised. "She was a done deal. She was eager to join us. She disapproved of Gandolph's retirement quest of exposing mediums as fakes. She nattered on about people needing faith, needing spiritual guidance from the spirit world. I might have killed her myself to shut her up."

"But people *do* need that!" Czarina turned passionate. "It's not just a scam. We mediums are . . . deep-sea divers. We're trying to take our clients to a deeper level of their memories and emotions so they can *see* those they love are always with them in some way. Everybody mocks now. Everyone's a cynic. Everyone gets to see the man behind the curtain. That's why I hate the Cloaked Conjuror. He's wrenched the magic out of our lives."

"But you wouldn't kill him?" Hal asked.

"Knowing what I do of the spirit world?

Creating such a black hole of injustice in the universe as murder? I want my powers to heal, not destroy. I want recognition, yes, but not revenge. That's so poisoning."

"Hmm," Hal said. "So our heartless seductress became an acolyte of a mild-mannered professor and our ridiculed medium would never besmirch her afterlife with a destructive act and, frankly, ladies, I'm too old and honest with myself to care to kill anyone. So who did the crimes?"

Temple recognized her inevitable cue. A dramatic pause she had to fill. Now she really knew more than they did.

"Have you all ever considered . . . Cosimo Sparks?" she asked.

"Who's out there? Who is it?"

Three hands saluted the owners' eyebrows as they glared past the moving lights into the darkness to find her. Ramona let the hand shading her eyes tilt down to cover them. Hal and put his hands at the sides of his face. Czarina gasped and clapped a hand to her mouth to stifle a cry. They resembled the See No Evil, Hear No Evil, Speak No Evil monkeys gone catatonic.

Temple stood.

As everyone stared speechlessly during a long, flabbergasted pause, something thumped onto the bar top. One Midnight

Louie, taking a stroll through the Stoli and Beefeater and Blue Curaçao bottles.

A second unmistakable thump. Another black cat landed atop the barstool next to Czarina.

Thump. A black cat beside Hal bracketed the trio.

"Don't freak," Ramona told her confreres. "It's just those rabid cats that invaded our clubrooms when the two clowns in Darth Vader masks threatened us. These kitties clawed those invaders to shreds. And the woman lurking in the dark over there is Restroom Girl."

Czarina lifted glasses on a beaded chain invisible against her patterned caftan to her shocked face. "Yes, it is. She claimed she'd gotten lost on the way to the restrooms."

Hal pushed off the barstool and limped forward two steps. "What do you mean have we ever considered Cosimo Sparks? He was our natural leader, totally committed to making a statement. He knew we were . . . caretakers of those mysterious parties' hidden loot. He wouldn't have betrayed them, because when they got ready to do their biggest Vegas heist in history, we'd bring off the biggest magical illusion in Vegas history too. In person. Not like David Copperfield making the Statue of Liberty vanish on TV, but right in front of people. That's magic the old-fashioned way."

"Look," Temple said. "You all thought each other might have done it. You all deny it rather convincingly. That leaves . . . Cosimo Sparks as the murderer. These dead people were all 'recruits' for your secret Synth-esis of magic and mysticism. All except Gandolph. He wouldn't 'recruit.' They all knew too much once they refused to join."

"Gloria Fuentes was with us," Hal said.

"She was also highly religious and her confessor thought she suffered from too many scruples as well as superstitions," Temple revealed. "Her scruples may have won out in the end. She might have backed out. Such people tend to have loose lips. And Professor Mangel . . . his enthusiasm for magic would have stopped at anything dicey. He had credibility. If he became alarmed at your backing a dangerous heist that could hurt people, he'd out you live on Channel Five, believe it."

"I wasn't so obvious about what the Synth actually was with him." Ramona's curled lip distorted her beautiful face. "I know how to be subtle. Jeff would not have been a threat, whether he went along with me . . . us. Or not."

464

"Could Cosimo afford to believe that?" Temple asked.

Ramona frowned. Her prideful expression crumbled. "I did complain to Cosimo about Jeff being 'too Goody Two-shoes' for us. Oh, God. If Cosimo killed him because of what I said —"

Hal was adamant. "Cosimo died protecting whatever had been stored in that empty safe!"

"Maybe so," Temple said, "but he may have done it for his own fanatical purposes."

She paused, then quoted an unforgettable line from some Synth-related papers Max had found hidden long ago at Garry's house and she had reviewed lately. " 'The aberrant brother shall be declared anathema. The price upon his head shall be death.' "

The three jerked backwards as if snake-bit.

"How'd you get that?" Hal demanded. "That's from the sacred illuminated Book of the Synth, from the induction ceremonies. Only sworn members see the liturgy, and only once."

"That does read like a license to kill," she said, "and some sects consider all nonmembers are born to damnation, so offing a few who were a threat wouldn't be a big leap."

"The Synth had its ancient, revered ceremonies," Czarina said, "but it was a philosophy, not a religion. Nobody took that 'aberrant brother' and 'price upon his head' seriously."

"Maybe Cosimo did," Temple said, "and then he ran up against some desperadoes who had no compunction against killing to get what they needed for their own 'sacred' cause. And if those secret 'backers' of the heist-concealing illusion were putting the pincers on you to produce the money they'd stashed in Las Vegas, think what pressure they might have been putting on Cosimo. The coroner found multiple marks from the knife-point before the killing stab was struck. I'm guessing Cosimo, if he'd been willing to kill for his grand plan, would be willing to keep mum and die for it too."

"You can't prove this," Ramona charged.

"No. But you're all in jeopardy if my theory is true, from the law as accessories and from our mutual acquaintances we call the Vaders."

"You are just a Restroom Girl." Ramona advanced on Temple, each step a hammer strike on the hard black Lucite floor. "What makes you think you can stroll into our nightclub, onto our property, and make accusations with what they call impunity?"

"The killer cats?"

By then the number of black cats sitting tall on barstools and the bar had tripled.

The trio turned around to take in that eerie sight. Czarina and Hal froze into position.

The silence was complete again, and eerie, and sad.

An interruption in the rhythmic passage of the rotating zodiac made the drinkers look up. Temple and Louie too.

A tiny flash of white at the interior pyramid's apex seemed to be growing closer. It grew larger, and then you understood that it was *lowering* and growing closer. The trio at the bar seemed mesmerized.

Closer, and closer . . . a figure in white tie and tails, descending on an invisible black thread like a spider, silent and stealthy but relentless.

Temple eyed the three at the bar, prey for the descending black widower. They'd already drunk themselves into near-paralysis.

"Cosimo . . ." Hal stood, clutching at his bow tie, a melodramatic gesture that would have looked silly had he not been scared stiff. "He's alive."

"No. His ghost." Czarina was staring upward as if transported. "Speak to us, spirit."

"The only spirits here are in your glasses." Ramona stood and glared into the lights, hands on hips, defying the oncoming figure. "Enter our nemesis. Max Kinsella. He engineered our floating table trick with the street performers and then turned around and engineered the aerial high jinks and off-and-on chest-vanishing illusion with the Cloaked Conjuror and all his high-tech equipment."

Something came flying down out of the dark.

A black top hat.

An object as white and weightless as dove plummeted down next, and then another just like it.

A third such fluttering drifted down in the silence as the figure lowered in the same supernaturally smooth fashion. Looking up, into the lights, made him a man of mystery still, even for Temple.

She could see a silver wand tumbling down end over end, and then . . . it vanished.

On the nightclub's black Plexiglas floor lay a shiny black top hat, two empty white gloves, and a white bow tie.

Above, was nothing. No motion, no descending body. Nothing.

CHAPTER 48
BRINGING DOWN THE HOUSE

As dramatic exits go, that was a pip.

Especially since there was no entrance to start with.

I have got to give Mr. Max Kinsella credit for a true magical presence. First you see him; then you do not. Some people could call him irresponsible. Some people could call me just a cat. You can never go by "some people."

Meanwhile, I am more than somewhat pleased that I instructed the Cat Pack to assemble here at Neon Nightmare after the Oasis adventure, just in case Synth shepherding was needed. I released the tuxedo unit to go back to the police substation for a well-earned fast-food feast at the hands of Las Vegas's finest.

So Mr. Max is the only formally dressed presence here. I hope he spotted my reduced posse and me, and appreciated our letting him hog the stage. Again.

Meanwhile I set an example for our next

moves by sidling over to the almost empty bottle of Blue Curaçao and giving it a gentle swipe.

It crashes onto its side, leaving a macabre tail of blue blood leaking out of its lip.

Miss Czarina Catherina screeches and jumps even farther away from the bar, just as Inkadoo and Blacula jump up on each shoulder of Mr. Hal Herald. His Adam's apple sets his bow tie jiving as he swallows hard and recalls how the Cat Pack shredded the Darth Vaders' much heavier cloaks during the showdown in the Synth clubrooms.

With my Miss Temple armed, for the first time in her life, the Pack was there to see to it that no concealed carrying laws were visibly broken. Now we are here to see that certain shady characters scatter posthaste, so Miss Temple can leave safely under our escort.

Mr. Hal's shuddering session has encouraged Inkadoo and Blacula to jump to barstools to watch the back of his departing heels. Miss Czarina is wailing and calling on Bast to help her, so I merely escort her out the length of the bar and meow a polite good night.

Ramona is a hard case. She is eyeing Miss Temple with an aim to exercise a bit of territorial imperative. I well recognize the signs in any species.

It is then that Miss Midnight Louise chirps

from her spot near Miss Ramona's barstool, stretches with her posterior and big plumy tail up in the air, opens her dainty jaws wide, and extends one elegant black-velvet foreleg to the side of Miss Ramona's green satin gown and draws one claw down it from shoulder to décolletage.

Miss Ramona gets the message and scrams with an echo of very fast high heels.

My Miss Temple has watched all this with interest but without comment. She looks up into the empty peak of the almost empty night-club.

I stalk over and rub around her ankles, in and out like the famous Hollywood hamburger joint handles customers, to say that I will wait outside.

A couple head-jerks from me, and the Pack leaves various stations on the bar, stepping carefully around the sticky trickle of Blue Curaçao. I must say Miss Midnight Louise sashays out at her own speed and druthers, pausing like a statue of Bast to look up as intently as Miss Temple.

CHAPTER 49
MAX'S LAST ACT

Just as mysteriously as Louie could suddenly be there in less than the blink of an eye, Temple's intent stare caught a bit of white still at the peak of the building.

The zodiac signs still washed over the floor like a ghostly cleaning crew.

And the dove hovering in the artificial night sky slipped closer and closer until it was a white shirtfront and the face above it.

Temple bent to pick up the gloves, the wand, and the top hat.

"How can you do this?" Temple asked Max as he touched ground.

"Do what?"

"Risk an aerial stunt in this place, with this equipment?"

"Magicians have to do the impossible." He looked up. "The equipment Garry and I installed is sound, and was tampered with only after I'd inspected it and started down."

"Then the would-be killer was comfortable with heights and that kind of equipment."

Max nodded. "But you can see from the earlier events tonight how many unemployed aerial workers are available around Vegas now. Speaking of risk and the impossible, I knew you could do it."

"Do what?" she said in her turn.

"Get that instinctive yet clockwork mind of yours ticking on the real dynamics of the Synth."

"My theories would never get an arrest warrant or play in court."

"Maybe not. Maybe not yet."

"Is the Synth defanged now?" Temple asked Max.

"Pretty much. I can always yank out an extra tooth if they get forgetful."

She looked up into the vast dark disappearing into a peak, the disco lights now crackling in the night, heat lightning, and bathing their faces and bodies with a dizzying round of zodiac signs. Hers Gemini. His Aries. Theirs . . . always, Ophiuchus.

"I will never forget — and coming from a recovering amnesiac like me, that's something," Max said. "I will never forget you saying 'Max, come home.' "

Temple knew what she had to say then,

but she didn't know what to say now. So she let Max speak.

"When I did come 'home,' and I saw you, your situation, I thought 'This woman must be crazy.' "

Temple shrugged. That's what you do when you can't quite speak.

"I call this stranger that my best friend, my mentor, said I loved and I can't even remember, and she says, 'Come home.' "

Still silent, forced to keep silent. He didn't seem to notice.

"My biggest regret about still being alive —"

Temple tried to cut off that horrible way to put it. . . .

His hand lifted, the magician hypnotizing an audience into silence.

"— is that I still don't remember. And I promise, if I ever do, I will never, ever let you or anyone else know that I do."

Max grasped her shoulders and, slowly, kissed her on the forehead. "I'll wait outside to follow your car home. Just in case."

He left.

CHAPTER 50
A VERY VEGAS AFFAIR

Temple was having a nice, private nineteenth-century "swoon" on her living room sofa the morning after overseeing the total disintegration of the Synth and proposing a solution to three murders that would likely remain in cold case files for eternity.

What was frying her brain were the unpleasant facts. For every loose end and murder she might have tied up at Neon Nightmare last night, several messy threads remained. Not the least was the murder of the suspected multiple-killer himself, Cosimo Sparks.

If world-class architect Santiago had done it, as seemed possible, why would he risk killing such a deluded and low-level crook? And if the three head Synth members had appropriated the Darth Vader look for their panicked heist schemes, who were the *real* Vaders, the pair that had raided the club headquarters carrying serious weapons?

And where was the Jersey Joe Jackson loot, which had expanded from rare silver dollars from the Vegas early days to bearer bonds and weapons of mass seriousness?

Not to mention a series of unsolved "falling" deaths all over town.

Too much information for even an action heroine to process. She definitely needed downtime.

In fact, she was lacking only a mint julep and a pool boy (of her acquaintance, of course), when Midnight Louie leaped before looking and made a four-point, twenty-pound landing on her midriff.

"*Oooph,* you big oaf! That hurt. Can't a girl have a time-out to soothe her nerves around this place?"

Apparently not. Louie added insult to actual injury by using her as a springboard to the newspaper-strewn coffee table. Louie proceeded to dig frantically on the papers he'd been peacefully dozing upon barely a minute before.

Temple had to feed her leisurely daily print addiction; besides, nothing washed glass to sparkling perfection better than ammonia and ink-stained newsprint. Cats shared Temple's fancy for outmoded communication forms, and Louie especially.

Now his big paws were hurtling whole

news sections off all four sides of the big low table.

"*Lou-ie.* I'll have to get up, bend over, and pick up your mess. I'm not in the mood for physical exertion. *You* should understand that better than anybody. Use a litter box!"

When another Louie swipe revealed her cell phone screen lying one razor-claw away from disfigurement, she leaped upright and grabbed it from harm's way.

It purred its thanks in her hand.

No wonder the cat had disrupted the newspapers. Louie'd been sleeping on her hidden smartphone, and it was set on vibrate, not sound. She bet that had been one big buzz in the behind.

She put the phone to her ear and heard Matt saying, "Temple. At last I've reached you! I'm back in town; something monumental has happened."

"*Matt?* What?"

"I'm on my way to our place. *Your* place. At the Circle Ritz. I've been running around town at my wits end. I'm almost there."

"What's the emergency?" she asked. "Has something bad happened?"

"No! Yes. Something beyond inconvenient. They're arriving this evening on my heels. Where the heck am I going to stow them? What will I do with them? Who can I get on such notice besides an Elvis imitator? Help."

"Holy Hysteria! Are aliens landing?'

"Might as well be. I'm in the parking lot. Unlock your door and pour something ninety proof." He disconnected without a parting word.

This was so not like Matt. This sounded like Matt on speed.

"Thank you, Louie, you faithful alarm-kitty, you!" Temple jumped up, then bent down to grab up scattered newspapers. She also gave Louie a huge wet smooch on the head, which meant he'd be kept busy grooming the assaulted fur until Matt arrived. *Poison people lips!*

Temple checked her kitchen cupboards and found the only truly potent liquor: some iffy tequila left over from a margarita-making kick that had lasted about as long as Las Vegas had been marketed as a family-friendly venue . . . one year. See all the top-less pools opened since then in the City That Has No Shame.

Temple was aghast the Fall of the Synth had temporarily broken her 24/7 connection with Matt *and* she hadn't noticed he not only hadn't called from Chicago but also didn't check in with her after his show. Apparently something all-involving had kept him too off balance and busy to notice.

She stirred up some Crystal Light, her all-purpose mixer, and filled two lovely footed crystal glasses. Temple was a great believer that proper presentation covered a multitude of flaws, including her cooking. She added a three-count of the Tequila with No Name, making a silent toast to Clint Eastwood, spit-groomed her eyebrows, fluffed her hair, smoothed her mini-muumuu and hovered by the door to await and comfort her uncharacteristically stressed fiancé.

Matt was dead right. Temple could handle crises in a Chicago minute.

He burst through the unlocked door seconds later, shut it, sighed, and said, "You won't believe this."

"I believe that you cannot tell a lie. Here."

He took the glass she offered, sipped, and then gulped. Sighed again, said, "You rock."

"Come into my parlor and tell me what you need."

He followed her into the living area, observing Louie sprawling across the couch. "What do I need? Him off the conversation area?"

Louie leaped up and huffed away, tail at a right angle to his back, the feline middle finger salute.

"Sorry," Matt told the departing cat, sitting beside Temple on the empty sofa as they parked their glasses on newsprint "coasters." "It's a family matter."

"So what's the matter with your family now?"

Matt lifted his glass from the coffee table turned cocktail table and toasted her. "Nothing. Now." He brushed a couple wayward curls off her shoulder and behind her ear and set down the glass again. "I need a wedding consultant."

"How soon?"

"Yesterday."

"This is sudden."

"Yes, it is. I got the call last night, too late to call you."

" 'The call'? That sounds serious."

"We *are* sitting down. Mom and Philip Winslow are flying in this evening to get married in Vegas."

"Matt, that's awesome! They're thumbing their noses at both families? It's like Romeo and Juliet."

"In midlife. I'm supposed to 'fix' it. They cherish some long-gone image of Las Vegas as thronging with cheap drive-up, insty wedding chapels. They don't have a clue about legal steps and civil ceremonies versus religious ones. Of course, a civil wedding in Las Vegas isn't recognized in the Catholic Church. They're acting like a crazy pair of eloping kids."

"Romeo and Juliet rebooted, without the poison-suicide outcome, as we're here to ensure. Okay. Number one. Where to put them tonight? Easy. The Crystal Phoenix. I have insty connections there."

"Um . . . bridal suite, separate rooms?"

"Connecting suites." Temple made a pussycat face. "They can either go country or pop."

"I have nothing to say about this except Mom deserves to do whatever she needs. I don't want to be associated with the, uh, sleeping arrangements."

"We won't have to be. I'll tip off Nicky and Van. They'll greet them as VIPs and subtly scope out their intentions and fulfill them."

"Really?"

"Discretion is their job, Matt. Now. Your mother and Philip seem to be in a hurry."

"I guess they want this fait accompli, both of their families out of it until they return and present a 'done deal.' "

"Smart. We might take a page out of their book."

"But . . . don't you want the Kate Middleton gown and aisle walk?"

"Of course. In my dreams. Dreams are not where real life abides. What works,

works for me. Back to your old folks at home."

"Not at home. They'll soon be right here, on our turf."

"Exactly. Electra would *love* to work up a quickie wedding that will knock everybody's socks off, and maybe their shoes too. It's all drive-by business for her nowadays and her cozy, clever little chapel with the soft-sculpture congregation is gathering dust. Not to mention that darling spinet organ she has there. You could play for the wedding, since you can't officiate."

"Officiating is the problem. Electra's just a justice of the peace. The marriage would be recognized civilly, but without a priest . . . it's just silly for people from two Catholic families to do a Vegas wedding. No priest can officiate outside a church. I don't get what they're trying to prove."

"Maybe that they're two independent people, not an extension of family druthers and pressure. Maybe they just want to make their commitment fun and impromptu before making it official and solemn back home," Temple finished. "Quit sweating the small stuff."

"Temple, marriage is a serious step, a sacrament in my church —"

"Take it from a fallen-away UU. These two

adults have been through the mill and know what they want . . . and that's *no* family interference, including yours. Although I think your approval and participation would mean a lot to your mother."

Matt sat back and almost squished Louie, who'd again lofted up during their discussion.

Louie yelped and gave Matt a claws-in bat on the arm to emphasize Temple's points before jumping down and stalking away again.

Matt leaned back into the soft cushion. "You're right. I'm freaking. I'm trying to force my concerns on people who've been through enough already. I'm really relieved, Temple. My biological parents are much better off apart. So. What can we do to show Mom and Philip a wild and crazy Las Vegas time?"

"That's better." Temple smiled and cuddled into his opening arms. The consultation had become a billing and cooing session, as if they were discussing their own wedding arrangements.

"I don't know," she said, "what I'd do if *my* parents were single and embarking on matrimony on my watch. I'd probably freak too. What *you* will do is calm down and collect the happy couple from the airport. PR

483

whiz here will handle the rest."

"You're thinking of having it here at the Lovers' Knot Chapel?" he asked.

"Perfect. They'll have that impulsive Vegas feeling, but well in hand. We *are* talking about folks in their fifties."

"Who are acting like impulsive kids."

"When you think about it, they're being super smart. They don't need all the family drama and angst. They need to show up back home, decision made, deed done, and get on with their lives."

"My family was actually upset when Mom called off the marriage," Matt pointed out, "but the 'deed' isn't done if it's not performed at a Catholic church."

"The families will grouse that it wasn't held at St. Stan's Cathedral, but older people don't care for all that pomp and circumstance anyway. A lot of people don't nowadays, given the economy. There's a reason so many people get married in Las Vegas. Isn't there some way they can get the Church to bless their union?"

Matt thought hard for a few moments. "Yes, actually. They could arrange a private marriage with the parish priest afterwards. They'll have had the honeymoon first, but I was marrying couples who'd lived together and got separate residences three months before the ceremony back when I was still officiating." Matt got a funny look on his face. "Do you suppose this . . . tomorrow night, would be their first, uh, time? You know. Together."

"You are blushing. Probably. From what you've told me, they're both devout rules followers. This whole trip is only because your Mom really wants *you* there."

"Why? To okay her . . . living in sin for a few days?"

"No! To okay her making a good choice for her life going forward . . . and maybe . . . to okay *your* 'living in sin.' What is that about, Matt, really? Where's the sin if labeling people makes a hell of her life and yours? I say the shame is in the labeling."

Matt was silent for a moment. "Okay. What do we need?"

"While you're picking and dropping tonight, I'll alert Van von Rhine at the Phoenix and get Electra on the case here. The only thing that would thrill Electra more would be marrying you and me. First thing in the morning, eight A.M. sharp, we whisk them to the LV Marriage Bureau. They show ID, sign the paperwork, pay a sixty-dollar fee, and they are ready to commit matrimony."

"You've got this routine down." Matt raised an eyebrow, then ended organizational matters for the time being with a definitely living-in-sin kiss. "How long have you had designs on me?"

He was kidding, but Temple felt her cheeks warm. "Longer than even I knew."

Well, that called for another pause in the proceedings.

Temple explained herself. "It's part of my job to know how things work in this town. Also, we did talk about doing a civil marriage before a church wedding, once upon a time."

"Doesn't seem so long ago," Matt said. "Maybe we should do that now, make it a double ceremony."

Temple produced an expression of mock shock. "Now that your mother is skipping over the fences, *our* status worries you?"

"Your well-being worries me. If we were married, one way or another, I could forbid you getting involved in events that could kill you."

"Think again. I bet 'obey' is excised from the vows even in church weddings these days."

"You're correct," Matt said, "but I could keep you so busy and distracted that you'd never want to leave home again."

"You're absolutely right," Temple said finally, "but we don't have time for you to prove your point. Before you collect the bridal couple, let me make sure Electra can do the ceremony."

Her quick call and request were greeted by surprise and the usual efficiency.

"You want to arrange a wedding here? Tomorrow? This is so sudden, Temple, dear. No problem. 'Sudden' is a justice of the peace's expertise. I'll come right down to your place."

"Uh-oh," Temple said, signing off. "She thinks it's us."

"I suppose it *could* be us," Matt pointed out. Again.

"A double wedding is a sweet idea, but your mother should be the star of the show."

"There'll only be us and them and Electra attending. Not much 'show.' "

"That's why the Lovers' Knot is the perfect site. There's an entire soft-sculpture congregation present. And, unlike relatives, they keep their mouths shut."

"I don't know what Mom will think about having Elvis in the building."

Electra's finest soft sculpture was a jump-suited Elvis wearing blue suede shoes.

"We'll find out, won't we?" Temple jumped up to grab a narrow grocery list notepad from the kitchen. It was headlined by a dancing chorus line of spectacle-wearing carrots and Mr. and Mrs. Potato Heads. "Does your mother have a special dress? And she'll need flowers. A bouquet."

The doorbell rang, so Matt admitted Electra. Her signature muu-muu of the day was a snappy black-and-white print that coordinated with the very Lady Gaga black streaks in her permed halo of white hair.

"Did I hear you mention a bouquet, Temple?" Electra bustled into the living room and sat on the sofa spot Matt had deserted. "I'll provide the flowers. But why such a hurry, you two? This will have to be a very simple affair on such short notice. It's not like Temple is pregnant."

"It's my mother who's getting married," Matt said quickly, sitting on a side chair. "Her name is Mira Zabinski. She and her fiancé, Philip Winslow, are flying down from Chicago as we speak."

"Really? Well." Electra fluffed her hair. "I pride myself on immediate response. Vegas was built in the old days on blood-test-free quickie marriages, but the Lovers' Knot Wedding Chapel 'puts the classy in quickie.' They're not bringing down an entourage?"

Matt shook his head. "No. They want it low-key. Temple and I will be there. That's it."

"Sorry, my boy, that is not 'it.' I have flowers and music to arrange, on the house, of course."

"Matt could play the organ," Temple volunteered.

While Matt raised his eyebrows, Electra applauded. "Yes, I remember you noodling around on my Hammond electric in the chapel over a year ago. Quite respectably. What was that Bob Dylan tune you thought would make a great wedding processional?"

"You'd make a good memory-policewoman," Matt said, chagrinned.

He'd caught and interpreted Temple's raised eyebrows look, which wondered, *Were you mooning over little me way back then?*

He moved on, fast. "Yeah. It has a great processional vibe, and the lyrics are appropriate. That was 'Love Minus Zero over No Limit' . . . slash mark between 'Minus Zero' and 'No Limit.' "

"What does that title mean?" Temple wondered.

"Bob Dylan envisioned the words written as a mathematical fraction. 'Love Minus Zero,' then a line, and below that, 'No Limit.' It's a cryptic, non-schmaltzy way of saying unconditional love."

"I love it!" Temple responded unconditionally. "You're hired. Electra, can the bride's bouquet include something blue besides the usual pale tea roses? Her eyes are the most gorgeous clear light blue color."

"That's something blue," Electra said, checking off a mental list. "What about something borrowed?"

"I don't know," Temple said, "but I surely can come up with something unique to lend her. That leaves 'something old, something new.' "

"Matt's vintage Dylan song is something old," Electra suggested.

"Yes," Temple said, "but I can find something more material somewhere. And after the Marriage Bureau date early tomorrow morning, I'll treat Mira to a shopping spree on the Strip. If she didn't have a brideworthy dress at home, I'll find her the perfect one in Vegas."

"You women are loving this 'family emergency,' aren't you?" Matt asked.

"We are arrangers," Electra boasted, with an elbow nudge in Temple's direction. "Emergencies social and emotional our specialty."

Temple nodded. "Speaking of arrangements," she told Matt, "stop by here after you deposit the happy couple at the Crystal Phoenix."

"I won't have much time then before leaving for my *Midnight Hour* show. And that eight A.M. Marriage Bureau date will come early for a three A.M. lights out."

"I'll scoot along. Lots to do." Electra rose and skedaddled for the door. She clearly didn't want to overhear bedtime logistics discussed.

Temple didn't foresee much scandalous going on. She and Matt would be scrambling for the next twenty-four hours to bring off this impromptu wedding.

"This is crazy astounding," he said when they were alone again and cozy on the sofa except for Midnight Louie watching them avidly from the armrest. "Why are they doing this Vegas thing again?"

"Because there's only one person whose presence would make Mira's wedding extra memorable. You. She doesn't really want to share this moment with anybody else."

"Because . . ."

"Frankly? You're the son she was frantic to give legitimacy and instead she gave you, and herself, years of grief."

He looked unconvinced.

"Hey, Mr. Voice of Shrinkology." Temple put her hands on Matt's shoulders and leaned even closer to whisper in his ear. "It's hard to see your own family forest for the trees sometimes. This is what Mira wants, this is what she needs, to step away completely from family influences and do what's best for her. Trust me."

He nodded, pulling her into another long, deeply promising kiss that would have to hold them for at least a day. "I do," he said, mimicking the marriage vows. "We'll have to say that for real and all as soon as we decide what *we* want, free of family influences."

"Good thing we waited," Temple said, grinning. "I get to be *maid* of honor again. I'm just not ready to be a 'matron.' It sounds so Girls Gone Wild in jail."

CHAPTER 51
MAKEOVER OF HONOR

Eighteen hours later, after the Marriage Bureau business was followed by a celebratory brunch for four at the Paris hotel, Temple banished the prospective groom from seeing his bride until the 5 P.M. ceremony. The women left the men bonding over coffee while Temple led Mira into temptation . . . the Bally's-Paris Promenade.

Under an artificial cloud-airbrushed blue sky, quaint three-story storefronts promised Paris byways lined with excessively smart and expensive goods.

Mira was unsure about this expedition. "I brought along a perfectly good suit. Beige silk from Marshall Field's."

"Piffle," Temple said. "Beige silk suits are for luncheon benefits. This is your wedding, girl! We are looking for splash. We are shopping for smashing!"

"At my age —"

"You certainly don't want to go for sedate.

We need something sophisticated." She stopped and examined Mira. "Something feminine. What jewelry are you wearing?"

"Just . . . earrings. The blue topaz ones Matt bought me. I thought they could be something semi-old and something blue."

Temple smiled approval. "Now we get 'new.' "

"I really can't afford —"

"Nonsense. This is on Matt and me. Well, mostly Matt. I'm the poor creative one."

"Temple —"

"Tut-tut, 'Temple,' good-bye." She linked arms with Mira and steered her to the goal; a nearby shop front.

" 'Nina Ricci,' " Mira read aloud the elegant letters above the entrance. "Isn't that perfume?"

"You're thinking of L'Air du Temps, the perfume in the Lalique glass bottle with two doves atop it. So symbolic for weddings. This brand is way more than perfume now. Every designer has expanded into across-the-board merchandise."

Temple swept Mira inside before she could offer more objections. Clothes ringed the perimeter of the spare space that featured gift-worthy accessories and lingerie in the center. Only a few choice pieces of clothing hung in each display bay. Size and price were extremely invisible. Many of the clothes were neutral in tone, otherwise known as the currently fashionable "nude."

Mira was confused. "But isn't that color there, sort of, in a very extravagant way . . . just beige?"

"Shhh," Temple whispered. "Are you saying the empress wears mere beige? What we have here is designer 'blush' silk chiffon. It does wonders for the complexion."

"And ruffles . . . so immature."

"Loose, flattened folds."

By then they'd attracted a sales assistant, tall, thin, and balancing like a Cirque du Soleil acrobat on extreme platform heels almost higher than her skirt was long.

Temple indicated the bay full of dressy summer numbers just shy of being formal. "Something for an informal wedding."

The sales clerk's kohl-rimmed eyes darted from the clothes to Temple and Mira, then settled on the right candidate. "My name is Briana. What size, madam?"

"Ten." Mira couldn't help looking like she expected to be admonished for her answer.

"Excellent. We have several delightful options for you. Please follow me."

Armless upholstered white leather chairs awaited at the shop's rear. Briana vanished, and Mira leaned close to Temple to whisper,

"Don't I have to pick some things to try on?"

"Briana does that. She'll bring out pieces in your size and we decide from there what's in the running."

"What about the price?"

"We don't ask about such trivial matters until you've tried on some candidates and whittled down your choices. Frankly, if you've found 'the' dress, you'll get it no matter what."

"But I don't . . . I'm not, I didn't expect —" Mira looked around the shop. "She'll see I'm not wearing underwear like the things in here."

"Excellent. Something more she can sell you."

"I'd never wear these."

Temple shrugged. "A bride should have a mini-trousseau at least. Mira, isn't Philip a successful businessman from a well-to-do Chicago family?"

"Yes, but that had nothing to do with our . . . connection."

"I'm sure not, but do you really want to play the poor little match girl forever?"

Those mild blue eyes flashed a smidge of white-lightning anger. "I know I'm not of the same class. I don't have to try to be something I'm not."

"You've already done that, Mira. You've tried flying under the radar for a lot of years and it was a disaster. Now maybe you can, you know, spread your L'Air du Temps wings and soar a little. Matt would want you to. Your husband-to-be would want you to. You can go back to Chicago and knock all those snobby rich bitches off their platform heels."

"Temple!"

"Just saying. Pride can often go in drag as false modesty."

Tears made Mira's eyes sparkle like those signature blue topaz earrings. She looked away. Briana appeared and took a perky pose, two soft, luscious silk dresses hanging from either hand.

Mira looked back, her spine straightening. "The one on the right," she said. "Possibly."

Briana was actually going to have to "sell" this client.

Temple bit back a smile and sank back in her cushy chair with a sigh.

CHAPTER 52
HERE COMES THE BRIDE

For church weddings, Temple knew, the bride was usually with her girlfriends fussing over her apparel in one room, and the groom was with his cronies in another.

Here at the Circle Ritz, Mira prepared in Temple's condo and Philip changed into his wedding suit at Matt's place directly above.

Temple's fairy godmother duties were almost done. She changed into a saffron '80s dress with a full pleated chiffon skirt and puffed-sleeve fitted jacket. She'd been tempted to wear the Midnight Louie pumps, being they were black and white, but decided that pavé Austrian crystal shoes with black cats on the heels were too scene-stealing for a wedding.

She gave Mira a last, fond inspection. "Those beige silk slingbacks that go with your Chicago suit are perfect with the new outfit," Temple said.

The "something new" dress was divine, or

Devine. The bodice was pleated chiffon, the waist emphasize by a soft ruffle above it, and the skirt's slanted tiers of alternating lace and chiffon bands flared out below the knee to tea-gown length. The high neck ended at the back in a lavish bow with tails to the waist. And the lace jacket ended with marabou cuffs below the elbow, which would look smashing in the bouquet-at-waist position all brides made on their entry.

Temple knew the guys wouldn't have a clue about these high-design details. They'd just think Mira looked like a movie star.

She gazed at herself in the full-length mirror in the condo's second bedroom that served as Temple's home office. "This looks . . . nice." She sounded surprised.

"And so do you. Now, bend over from the waist."

Mira obeyed, completely on program. Temple ran her brush through Mira's Chicago-set hair from nape to tips.

"Straighten up and shake your head."

Mira checked out her fuller, looser hairstyle, which also showed off the blue topaz earrings better. "You're an amazing woman. Where do you learn these things?"

"Girly School. TV news makeup departments, at repertory theaters, in *Allure* magazine. I always had to scrounge to get my girl on, having all older brothers at home. Now, I collect my heels and we're ready to go downstairs and knock 'em dead."

Temple raced across the condo's living room to the master bedroom on the other side, Mira trailing her like a duckling.

Since the Stuart Weitzman Austrian-crystal pumps were off the menu, Temple had chosen a dainty pair of '80s-vintage silver satin pumps with ankle straps buttoned by gold crystals. Only one was standing upright in front of her ajar closet door.

"Darn! I do not want to go digging on my knees in the closet in this outfit." Temple searched the bedroom, finding no mate for the shoe. "I could have sworn they were both standing paired together like soldiers on parade. Louie?"

A meowed protest came from the floor beyond the far side of the California king-size and ended abruptly as Louie landed on the zebra-pattern coverlet. He sat to lift his hind leg and scratch at the band of vintage white silk bow tie around his neck.

"Meet your 'something borrowed,' " Temple told Mira. "Louie will be the ring bearer. Don't worry. It's his second wedding gig. I tie the ring to his collar like a tag."

500

"Is he all right?" Mira wondered. "He's recovered from his ordeal in Chicago?"

"Fit as a Stradivarius. He lost a couple of nail sheaths, that's all. Well!" Temple put her hands on her hips. "I'm just going to have to wear different shoes. Let's see. White is too gauche, black too somber . . . so it's the white-and-silver print Weitzman's with the bows on the back of the heel. They'll match your blouse bow."

"Whatever you say, Temple." Mira shook her fluffed-out hair. "You're such a dynamo, I don't even have time to think about being nervous about the ceremony."

"Then I'm doing my maid of honor job." Temple pulled out the new pair of shoes and donned them, glad to do a last survey from her usual height.

"Wait!" Mira ordered. "Look at the floor."

"You've spotted the missing shoe?" As Temple bent down, Mira stepped close and drew the hairbrush from Temple's nape to the curling ends of her hair.

"Now *you're* fluffed."

"Tricky lady."

"Oh. What pretty earrings you have too."

Temple touched the delicate webs of tiny rubies and diamonds. "Your son is a really good judge of earrings. And rings. So. Let's go down and cause dropped jaws."

"What about the cat?"

"Oh, he'll come along in his own way and his own time. He always does."

Temple winked at Louie and took Mira's arm. "Let's get married."

CHAPTER 53
EVENING IN PARIS

Max couldn't decide whether he was at work as an ace agent or not at work at all as a Los Lonely Guy when he abandoned the black Maxima from Garry's garage to the Paris Hotel parking attendant.

It was still daylight, yet entering the casino immersed him in the always-nocturnal landscape of velvety black punctuated by a couple galaxies' worth of supernovas.

No one stood in line for the single elevator to the Eiffel Tower restaurant at this unfashionably early hour. Tourists ran on a schedule hotel hours subtly established. About now, the women were still moving from baking in the hotel pool areas. The pools closed early to shoo the women back inside to dress for a long day's night on the town in the restaurants, shops, and casinos. The men were still killing time at the blackjack, baccarat, and craps tables.

Revienne was already primed for the

night. She perched on a stool beside a nearby bank of slot machines. Her blond hair was sleeked back into a bun the size of a doughnut hole that emphasized her swan-like neck and shoulders.

She wore a loose-knit sleeveless top woven with beige and iridescent yarns, braless, and a short white-silk pencil skirt, both highly seduction-worthy. He'd expected no less.

He came up behind her and produced a twenty-dollar bill for the slot machine before her hand could slip in another ten. "You're losing. Try my money."

She stood and slipped his bill into the toy purse set beside the slot machine, along with a casino card for the Paris consortium. "We can gamble later, dine now."

"You'd never know you were new to Vegas," he commented.

"I'd never have known you were here if you hadn't visited the campus," she answered, eyeing his newly shorn hair with the bit of gel nonsense at the top. "I hope that's not a result of brain surgery — ?"

"Heat exhaustion preventive."

"Then you're new to this so very hot climate."

"As you know, I'm a world traveler. Nowhere is entirely new."

He escorted her to the elevator that

whisked them up a mere eleven stories to the first stage of the half-scale replica of the Eiffel Tower. The hostess and the bar were straight ahead, so they were swiftly escorted to the prized corner table in the glass-walled restaurant, facing northwest into the mountains and directly across from the Bellagio's famous dancing fountains.

"You have 'pull,' " she noted discreetly after the waiter had seated her. He'd taken the corner seat so she could look past him at the floor show of the lighted fountains. . . . Also, his back was to the wall of glass so he could survey reflections of the restaurant and bar like a security camera.

"You'll see the sunset during this early seating," he told her. "I know most people prefer to be fashionably late. Especially the French."

"So you've been in Las Vegas before?"

"Don't know," he lied.

"As you had been in Zurich?"

"Zurich? No. That was a first."

"As with me." She glanced down to her glittering petite purse, slowly opened the jeweled clasp, and slipped out a slim gold compact to apply a nearly colorless gloss to her lips.

Whew, Max thought. Frenchwomen lived up to their seductive reputation, even when they were half-German.

"It's so dry here in this climate." She snapped the lip gloss compact shut.

Now that she'd invoked memories of their impulsive rendezvous in Europe, Max figured she found him sufficiently drugged, web-bundled, and ready for devouring. The question was whether she worked for the Real IRA or the old IRA, or some other interested international entity. Max wondered if it was necessary to play cat and mouse with her, but he supposed it would exercise his brain, if nothing else.

They ordered boutique martinis while scanning the menu.

"I hope, Miss Schneider, our necessary detours in Switzerland didn't interfere too much with your forthcoming academic obligations here in Las Vegas."

"No. Quite the contrary, Mr. Randolph. It was a very existential romp. Who am I? Who is he/she? Who is trying to kill us? Will we kiss or kill each other? Or both? Believe me, for a woman with a challenging but never lethal psychological practice, it was quite invigorating."

"Exactly my response." Max toasted her with his martini. "I'm not surprised that you're in international demand."

"Nor I, you."

"I didn't know the local university had such a prestigious psychology department," Max observed.

"Sadly, you must have only availed yourself of the gaudier features of Las Vegas on previous visits."

"Remedial classes are not on my schedule."

She shrugged. "We all can improve on past performance."

Clever. She was trying to egg him into topping himself. He recalled their previous engagement perfectly. Too bad. It had been intense, but he was pretty sure he'd been confused, haunted, and hurting more than he had ever allowed himself to be with a sane mind. More vulnerable, ugly word. She'd never believe it, but if he had it to do over again, he wouldn't.

"I mean your memory, of course," she said.

"Of course. I didn't realize your work would take you to the United States."

"Hugo, Herr Professor Gruetzmeyer, is a mentor of mine originally from — please don't laugh — Vienna, home of Herr Freud and my father. Also, I can fly to Los Angeles easily from here to work with teen anorexia there. California is very hard on women's self-esteem. Many female performers are on the 'cigarette and cocaine' diet, and of course, women young and old face the same issues."

He should have remembered, a common thought for him nowadays, that her older sister had committed suicide because of anorexia when Revienne was only twelve or thirteen. That she had shared that personal trauma with him, at a time when he was all trauma, all the time, might explain their strangers-in-the-night connection.

Without thinking, he said, "You're an extraordinary woman." Even if she was an enemy.

"Why do you say that?"

"I know it's hard to lose a sibling young."

"You never mentioned any family."

He shrugged. "We lost touch."

"Over that sibling death?"

"Yes."

"Who blamed whom?" she wondered.

He suddenly knew. "Everybody tried not to blame anybody and it went horribly wrong from there."

They were silent as waiters danced around them, refilling, removing, replacing. The act of eating would have been an almost weightless, timeless process, except that their conversation obliterated everything, even the fountains.

"My first boyfriend," she said, attending to whatever was on her plate, "was a radical Socialist."

He laughed at the radical change of subject.

"I know. It's ridiculous. So goes politics in France. I thought it was so . . . cool. We were in the student protests. I don't remember over what, just the marching and singing and dodging the police. I took him for a hero, but it was all about him being a big shot, as you say."

"So Frenchmen are really like the notorious DSK? Lord, that sounds like a rap star name. It's true they're into assault?"

" 'Into'?"

"An expression. Prone to."

She made a noise of dismissal. "They are selfish and think Frenchwomen should feed their egos. Unlike in the Muslim countries; women are beaten up in the press only if you speak out against their indignities. So the women shut up and starve themselves. Simplistic, but that's why I work with young women."

"Gratis."

"Gratis?"

He'd forgotten English was her third language. "You don't take pay for that work."

"Yes. Do you do anything gratis?"

"Just my whole life," he said, appalled to realize it was true. Everything was to make up for his cousin's Sean death. Just as everything evil Kathleen O'Connor had done was to make up for her mother's utter rejection by her time and society.

"You are an extraordinary man, Mr. Randolph."

The use of Garry's surname brought him back to reality.

What was he doing? Getting vulnerable again with the possible enemy. Or she might not be. No, *had* to be; just the fact of her being here proved it. No sense kidding himself.

Dessert was descending on them and he couldn't remember what they'd ordered. Relapse. So many more important things were coming back. Or maybe this moment was important.

Revienne was beautiful in the reflected light from the illuminated fountains dancing like aurora borealis across the Strip. Max turned around to view the fiery blue green water show in front of the spotlighted Bellagio palace façade, with Caesars Palace towering over it all. This was magic time, as he'd so carefully arranged it.

"The view over your shoulder is glorious,"

she said. "Quite as lovely as Paris at twilight, more so, because of the mountains, which I love. They are so lonely and strong. Impassive sometimes, it seems, but they are always shifting under the surface, changing in the light."

"My only official memories," he replied, "of the Alps, are not as enthusiastic."

She laughed as their coffee and liqueurs arrived. Baileys Irish Cream, as he'd always had with Garry.

Work on the road, lonely, ironic, never make personal connections.

"You know I've never trusted you," he heard himself say.

"You shouldn't. I know I've never before met a man as wary as I myself am."

"So. How many patients have you slept with? A rough estimate will do."

"It matters?"

"Male ego. You must have learned about that in school."

"Let me burnish yours, then. None. That is totally unethical and I would never, never do such a thing."

"What do you call *me*?"

"My dear Mr. Randolph, you were no longer my patient the moment you forced me to 'escape' with you from the Swiss clinic. Thanks to my unwilling association with you, my nails were broken, my shoes destroyed. I had to beg for food from farmers along the way and saw off leg casts, as well as tend a stubborn delusional stranger who was quite possibly insane but the gutsiest, cleverest person I have ever met. I was kidnapped by brutal men in a fast car, fought over on the most expensive street in Zurich, made love to in the most innovative positions of my life and wined, lunched, designer-attired, and dumped on the street outside the Zurich train station. I have never had such a wonderful time in my life."

"Why me?"

She actually thought that one over, then gave a very French shrug. "Questioning such things is counterproductive. I found it refreshing that your memory loss meant you had no romantic, what they say here, 'luggage.' "

"Baggage."

Not true. There was the unsinkable Temple Barr. Obviously, she and Matt Devine were forthright, delightful people. Obviously, they made a forthright, delightful couple. All tucked away for the night and life ever after.

The fact was, he and Revienne had confided in each other. They shared a devastating teenage sense of failure and loss. The question was, Did you do that with mere strangers because there was no risk, or because it was all risk in lives so carefully lived ever after?

Max's instincts were out to lunch. The adage about keeping your friends close and your enemies closer rang true, but he couldn't define his motives when it came to Revienne.

"In your position," she said, sipping from the demitasse of coffee and the tiny liqueur glass and sampling the plate of miniature sweets, including a white chocolate Eiffel Tower, "you are having a total eclipse of the mind and emotions. That's my professional opinion. Anything you might think or do now is extremely unreliable. You shouldn't trust yourself and you shouldn't trust me."

"An excellent diagnosis. When do you leave Las Vegas?"

He pulled her toy purse over to his side of the small table, opened it, and inspected its contents. The twenty-dollar bill he'd contributed, the lip gloss compact, a European brand he'd never known or couldn't remember. The case had no hidden sections. The gambling card and the room card.

"When my work is done," she said, unperturbed.

"Your classes in existential angst?"

"It's a more common problem than you'd think."

"Your 'baggage' is annoyingly innocent."

"Thank you." She reclaimed the compact and reglossed her lips as he put the credit card that read GARRY RANDOLPH with his green-eyed photo in the bill packet. Nothing he or Garry did had ever been innocent.

"Look," Revienne said, "our last chance to see the Bellagio fountains dancing."

He turned in his chair, watching the silent waltz of water and lights and music. The fountains were diminishing into sprinkler height as he escorted Revienne out of the restaurant.

She wanted to pause at her previous spot to put his twenty bucks in the slot machine.

He took the bill, studied the scene, then moved it and them to the end of another row. "This one."

A skeptical blond eyebrow almost distracted him from the white skirt stretched tight as she sat on the stool and slid the bill into the waiting slot.

The moving icons chirruped and blinged and binged. Coins plinked into the stainless steel apron under the computerized slot machine. Revienne scooped them with her white-tipped French manicured nails into the paper cup Max held. Again she pushed the button. And again.

In a few minutes she'd won a hundred and fifty dollars. And she laughed like a kid while doing it.

"That is magic," she said.

He shook his head modestly. "They position sucker slots to let someone win for a while and lure others to lose."

"It's all programmed?"

He nodded as she set her full cup on the shelf.

"It was fun, winning, but I don't need the money. It's not worth the fuss converting all these coins to cash." She rose. "Let someone else find it, and think they got lucky too."

Max laughed. And escorted her to the drive up.

"We can hear the fountains' music from here?" Revienne asked.

"With a short stroll."

"After dinner, a stroll is always good. Very Parisian."

Max led her near Las Vegas Boulevard. As they arrived, the fountains paused for a moment to take a deep breath and then gushed up like geysers to the accompaniment of symphonic music paced by the lights and water. Behind the dancing shafts of water the Bellagio façade was lit with its own symphony of light.

"You know," Revienne said, turning to view the spotlit Eiffel Tower behind them and the Paris's festive neon balloon, "this almost reminds me of Paris, out of the corner of my eye, anyway."

Max looked at the Vegas he remembered in bits and pieces, compared it to crisp images of bustling Zurich and the mist-blurred landscapes of sweet, savage Ireland and Belfast. This was new territory to his unraveled memory, and he stood isolated, having no remaining remembered intimate connection, except one.

The evening wind blew a wet mist from the fountains across the Strip. Revienne recoiled and then laughed, welcoming the cooling shower.

Max's hand had automatically gone between her shoulder blades for support and she relaxed into his shoulder.

The Bellagio fountains continued their assault on hot Las Vegas with waves of cool Irish mist.

"My clothes, hair, everything, will be wet, ruined," Revienne said, laughing. "It's wonderful!"

He remembered the hardships of their on-foot escape in the Alps.

She turned her face into his shoulder and lifted it, eyes closed to the tiny wet crystals of water dewing her eyelashes, lips, and all that everything that was getting wet.

He wondered if they would get to first names this time. She thought his was Michael, and Garry had told him it actually was, once upon a time.

"You want a return engagement?" Max asked. "Why?"

"Because this is somewhere very special and free, and your strength of will is phenomenal."

"I'd be much better now."

"Yes," she said, smiling even more. "That too."

CHAPTER 54
MEDDLING BELLES

"Tell me about the wedding," Miss Midnight Louise demands. "I understand you wore a sissy white bow tie."

Louise has buttonholed me while I dallied in the Circle Ritz parking lot, after the wedding party saw the happy couple off to their Crystal Phoenix digs.

I do not mean my business partner literally buttonholed me, but she did stick a tiny but sharp shiv in my black velvet shoulder that gives me pause.

Girls just like to hear about weddings, even if they are fixed.

"Who has ratted on me?" I ask.

"I heard your very own roommate *ooh*ing and *aah*ing to Miss Van Von Rhine in this very parking lot about how adorable you looked in white tie and black tail. They were giggling about you revisiting this role again soon."

Gag me with a can of politically correct, dolphin-safe tuna. I put in my vote for all species forgetting the folderol and eloping . . . me with Miss Topaz from the Oasis. Now that I am playing Gossip Guy, I will confess that I am so over lion-cut shaved Persians.

"Well." Miss Louise nudges me. "I want a complete report, down to the wearing apparel, besides yours."

It is to yawn, but there is only one way I will be left to my own devices.

"The bride was totally drool-worthy. She wore a silky soft, tiered lace-and-ruffle dress that flared below the knee into a mermaid skirt. It was a pale peach mauve color like really diluted blood.

"The bodice featured an oversized soft chiffon bow in back, with the tails reaching all the way to her hips. A pity it will hang in her Chicago closet from now on."

Louise is as close to swooning as I have ever seen her. *"Ummm,"* she purrs. "Totally climbable and clawable. A ten on the Shred Scale. What about your roommate?"

"Even better. As maid of honor she wore pale saffron —"

"Saffron?"

"We fashonistos don't say 'yellow.' It was a saffron full-pleated skirt, '50s length."

"Oooh, the hem at calf-level, so accessible *and* a potential carousel of swing."

"Unfortunately, there was no dancing afterwards. The Misses Van Von Rhine and Kit Carlson —"

"*They* were there?"

"Along with their spice, which is the plural of spouse, as mice is of mouse, Nicky and Aldo Fontana. Nicky was best man, and Matt led his mother down the aisle to some organ music he'd recorded earlier."

"The standard Mendelssohn wedding march?"

"The very unstandard Bob Dylan. That music did work well. It was slow enough I got an excellent ankle-level perusal of footwear."

Louise nods judiciously.

"Unfortunately, from groom to best man to the eight Fontana brothers in attendance, the uniform was shiny black patent loafers."

"Hard candy," Louise agrees. "As chewable as stale licorice twists."

"Not worth raiding the closet for," I concur. "Speaking of which, my Miss Temple had chosen a toothsome gold silk sandal with an Austrian crystal ankle button —"

"Glittering baby balls! So Las Vegas. Much fun, if you can detach them from the strap."

"Miss Temple could not find both of them just before the wedding. I was falsely accused of making off with it."

"You missed copping such a prize?"

"My role of the day was 'little gentleman.' "

"And you wore the white-tie collar to prove it. I hope that is preserved on film and photo. Why did you not grab such a classic toy?"

"I was busy in the wedding chapel making sure that all the soft sculptures were sitting up pretty."

"You were napping!"

"I had a very active time in Chicago, Louise. Philip Winslow wore a black tux, but all the dudes wore faint diamond-pattern tuxes in shades of gray and silver and gold, with black satin lapels to match the side stripes in their trousers and white-on-white paisley ties. Regular ties. I was the only one in a bow tie. Apparently the Fontana brothers' Gangsters franchise can supply party garb as the well as the limos to wear it in. They all were pretty duded up, considering this was a hurry-up affair."

"Not from what I heard in your Chicago reports. Miss Matt Mama took some long and winding roads to snagging a decent mate."

"I meant the wedding was a hasty event, not the events leading up to it. You will remember, Louise, that had I not investigated Miss Matt Mama's premises and sacrificed myself as handy kidnap victim to two Chicago Outfit thugs, our detecting friends would never have uncovered the Effinger connection. Makes you wonder about fate and redemption and true love."

"Makes me wonder about your mental stability.

"I know you favor Mr. Max, but I will tell you Mr. Matt looked so good in his silver suit, Miss Temple seemed likely to make them the next couple in front of Miss Electra Lark in her black justice of the peace robes. They were a symphony in gold and silver."

"And you were a tuxedo cat for a day."

"For a couple of hours. I performed impeccably, by the way, when Mr. Matt bent down to unhook the wedding ring from my white tie and collar. I held still."

"So, what was the ring like?"

"I heard Miss Kit Carlson describe it to Miss Van Von Rhine as a 'fancy blue diamond solitaire surrounded by diamonds with a matching diamond wedding band.' As per the usual wedding, the gemstone was outshone by the glitter in the eyes of the female guests."

"Anymore pant-worthy details?"

"For the ceremony, which was short and sweet, all the unattached Fontana brothers sat in the pews next to Miss Electra's soft sculpture congregation. It was interesting to see them paired with the likes of Gloria Steinem, Judge Judy, and Bette Midler.

"I, of course, cuddled up with the King, because I really did wear a ring around my neck, and I was 'his, by heck.' And that's all she wrote."

CHAPTER 55
TWISTED TIGHT

It was over.

Matt moved aimlessly through his apartment at the Circle Ritz, not that it was a very big space. Mom married. The wedding banquet at the Crystal Phoenix had been festive . . . and underwritten by Nicky and Van. Temple had been amazing, as usual.

They'd kissed the happy couple good-bye and come home to change finery and chill out. Matt relished this time alone. He'd come to Sin City hunting the ghost of his mother's almost willfully unhappy marriage and, now, thirty years later, had watched that misery dissolve into a midlife renewal with a good man.

He himself had been remade by coming to terms with the past.

Matt loosened his tie, kicked off the fancy black patent leather loafers, sat on his red suede vintage couch. So many of the people he'd met here in Vegas had helped him make a deep personal transition. . . . The staff at the ConTact phone help line where he'd first worked. Janice Flanders, the police sketch artist. Danny Dove, choreographer and friend extraordinaire. Letitia Brown at WCOO. Carmen Molina, always tough and resilient. Even the Mystifying Max Kinsella.

And Temple. He could never do for his mother what she had done, taken Mira in hand and out of her self-imposed isolation. Temple was always the warm, steady heartbeat of everyone around her. Especially him. His love for her was an inner island of calm . . . easily ruffled by waves of shore-shaking excitement.

Now would be time for Temple and himself, solely and exclusively, and their own wedding plans could commence without any baggage from his past. At last.

As he sat there, enjoying the silence, the thoughts of the future, he noticed a nagging background sound. Something tap, tap, tapping somewhere.

Matt shut his eyes. Breathed deep. Relaxed.

Still that annoying rapping, like Poe's darn raven.

He stood up. Listened. Was it a water pipe? They could make that noise in an old building like the Circle Ritz.

He made the brief rounds, but the kitchen and bathroom taps were twisted tight.

Back in the main living area, he sighed. No clocks that ticked. Maybe something on the patio. He rarely went there, had never furnished or used it. He wasn't used to providing for himself. He'd called rectories home for too long, had been spoiled by the parish housekeepers for too long. He'd have to watch that self-centered domestic side of himself when he and Temple were married.

He wandered to the dark row of French doors. Danny had insisted on installing shadow-box blinds over them for "privacy."

Matt flipped the lock and opened one door. The pecking sound was louder.

Not a bird. A bird would fly away at this human approach.

Was it a lizard or insect of some sort making a maddening mating call to some rhythmic internal clock ticking?

No. The sound came from above. Something was spinning, something attached to the roof overhang above one French door.

A . . . mobile? A wind chime?

Certainly a shadow against the darker shadow of night.

Matt moved into the glow of the tall parking lot lights to reach up, touch, stop the spinning object.

A shoe.

A light, glinting shoe strung up like a wind chime. A petite silver satin pump with a glitter of gold crystals buttoning the ankle straps.

Temple's shoe. He'd remembered her fussing about not finding a mate to the "real" shoes she'd chosen.

That had gone missing before the wedding.

That someone had gotten into Temple's unit to *make it* go missing and had kept to call her very own and had broken into his place, again, to display it here like a prize, like a serial killer's ritual object.

The hairs on the back of Matt's neck rose. A chill of murderous rage crawled up the back of his head. He knew the threat was deadly, and he knew who, but he didn't know where.

Luckily, he knew just how to change that last condition. Right now.

CHAPTER 56
REMATCH

Molina jumped when the doorbell rang. She never jumped. She'd schooled herself to never show surprise.

This wasn't a surprise. It was something . . . worse. Even though she'd expected this caller, she'd never expected opening her door to this man for this purpose.

When she unlocked and cracked open the big wooden front door, he was turned away, back to her, studying the street. In the glow from the porch light above the door — a warm, old-fashioned incandescent bulb because she saw too many mean streets under harsh fluorescent lighting in her job — his hair looked Black Irish dark.

What the heck was he doing here? She had to ask herself that for the fortieth time. She liked blond men, even dirty blond like Dirty Larry, the ex-narco undercover guy. Ideally golden in all respects, like Matt Devine.

So *who* had she gotten involved with?

Molina had never wanted to look too closely at the answer to that question. She stared, barring the doorway, until he turned to face her.

"Come in, Rafi," she said, stepping back.

"Make sure you ask the right one in," he said, eerily paraphrasing one of Mariah's stupid fave bloody vampire film titles.

"You've been studying Mariah's Facebook page."

"And Google-plus too." Rafi grinned, stepped over the threshold, paused. "You sure, Carmen? I'm your worst nightmare."

She pulled back, grimaced. "Don't flatter yourself. You're just a teensy little bad dream."

"Diminutives don't thrill guys. Just a tip on something you may have forgotten after all these years."

She fought back an embarrassed flush. She hadn't meant to — No going back on stupid comments.

"Where's Mariah?" he asked as he followed her into the living room, knowing the way now.

"Where she always is. In her bedroom texting, Googling, Internet-cruising, Face-booking."

"Singing?" Rafi asked.

Molina turned to let him see the face of

her frustration. "That too."

"Sit down," he said. "Can I get you a beer?"

She stared at him. "My house. I'm the hostess."

Rafi pointed his left hand toward his right shoulder. "The fridge is visible right there. I know how to do twist-tops, or find a kitchen church key. Why don't you sit down, Carmen, breathe deep, and realize I'm here to help. And bring you a cold beer."

She cleared her throat. Actually, that would help. And her acute law-enforcement summing-up eye had noticed he'd look a lot buffer than Dirty Larry, but safely middle-aged so Mariah couldn't crush on him, unlike Matt Devine.

God, what am I thinking?

She buried her face in one hand, both rueful and annoyed and about ready to say, *No go, get outta here, Nadir,* the way she'd dismiss a snitch.

A dewy-cold bottle appeared in her free hand. The sofa in need of replacing shifted as Rafi sat down beside her. "This is about Mariah," he said. "She's at the age when her dreams, her path, even her mistakes are forming. Let's not mire her in ours."

"Dreams, or mistakes?"

"Either one."

"Why do you care?"

"Why wouldn't I?" Rafi said. "Did you ever ask yourself that?"

Molina put the cold wet side of the beer bottle against her temple. "No."

"Why didn't I see what a crazy, judgmental witch you were?"

That roused her, wanting to defend herself, but he went on too quickly.

"Why didn't you see what a controlling, manipulative bastard I was. You wanted to be a police detective, didn't you?"

"We weren't like that," she said, finally sitting up and setting the beer bottle on the sofa table.

"No kidding."

Her deep, frustrated exhalation stirred the hair still hanging forward over her face. "I panicked." She eyed him through the defense of her veiling hair. "I hadn't planned on getting pregnant."

"Like I had?"

"I couldn't understand. We'd always been careful. I thought. There was a pinhole in my diaphragm."

"Oh. Evidence of tampering. You want to go to the prosecutor with that today?"

"Circumstantial," she admitted. "But I'd been so careful —"

"Yeah, I get it. You were the 'little mama'

531

to your however many stepbrothers and sisters after your mom remarried when you were a toddler. Enough already on the kids. I get that. And I didn't want to be tied down either. You do remember that about me?"

"We were being pitted against each other at work. Would the system reward the minority guy or the pushy woman?"

"We had a lot in common. We shouldn't have let them use it against us."

"I panicked. Having a kid made me even more vulnerable on the job, not to mention my druthers."

"Did you consider doing what you accused me of not wanting, ending the pregnancy?"

"None of your business."

"Carmen, listen to yourself."

"Yes. Okay? I couldn't do that, anyway. I wasn't looking for anything like that. I was probably a hormonal mess by the time I realized what was happening."

"So you ran. Did you ever think what that might do to me?"

She shook her head. "Try being pregnant. It's all about you and the baby. I'd decided you'd won the rookie contest and wanted me at home and pregnant, like my stepdad wanted my mom to be, even if it took my child labor to keep the family fairy tale going."

Rafi didn't say anything more, just pulled out his smartphone. Molina was thinking if she saw another one of those today, she would scream.

"Okay, we're caught up on our past. What about Mariah's future?" he asked.

"You can't seriously be saying it's anything more than school and good grades and some career direction in choosing a college."

"Would that scenario excite *you*?"

"No, but I had to leave home and put myself through a criminal justice degree on my own. I had no support. Nada. I can afford to provide Mariah with what she needs. If you want to informally help underwrite that and won't be interfering, I'm okay with it."

Rafi just laughed. "This is sounding like a two-party deal in Congress these days. You get all the authority and time with our daughter, I get to provide underwriting."

"What do you want, outings with her at the Circus Circus Adventuredome? All you can eat brunches off the Strip? Twice a month, say."

"Carmen, Carmen, Carmen." He watched her flinch at every repeat of the name only her intimates dared use, like Detective Morrie Alch on a good day, smiling almost tenderly at her obvious unease. "That would have been fine a few years ago, when Mariah was a kid. Now? No. Mariah is a young adult and she'd run away screaming from those lame, useless outings, and you know it."

She did, but didn't admit it.

"Let me help her with her dreams, Carmen, like I did with you those many years ago."

"Singing? I never went anywhere with that," Molina said.

"You still could. I was pretty good as your agent-manager, and nowadays, everybody's their own record mogul."

She thought, desperately seeking wiggle room.

"You'd keep her away from sleazos like that Crawford Buchanan leech," he said.

She kept silent.

"And, the real sweetness of the deal is that you don't have to introduce me as her father, just as the guy from the teen TV reality show house. She almost won that talent show."

"If that obnoxious Zoe Chloe Ozone hadn't distracted everybody with such a ridiculous rap number."

Rafi smiled. "Come to think of it, Temple's persona had that Lady Gaga freak thing going before Lady Gaga became a household name. What do you say? I'd find Mariah a really good voice coach, help her make some credible YouTube showcases. Drain off some of that incredible energy that could get her into trouble on her own. And," he added, "she likes me."

Molina had seen that, and it worried her. "You won't expect paternal credit."

"She's not ready, you're not ready. I'm not ready."

"But . . . if *we* keep that from her, she'll be angry at both of us if it should . . . when it came out."

Rafi smiled to himself, as if thinking of something else, before meeting her pointed gaze head-on. "Yes, that takes the burden off you being the only liar in the house."

Bingo! He was right, dammit. "It was a necessary evasion."

"It was a Big Lie, Carmen, and I could make a Big Stink about it if I wanted to blow up your credibility with Mariah. But that would hurt her more than we could hurt each other. So. I'm not backing down on the bottom line that she knows me as her father. Someday. And maybe I'll earn a chance from her you never gave me."

"Below the belt, Nadir." Lieutenant Molina was back in there, punching.

"Deserved, Officer Molina."

Amazing. Rafi had offered her a built-in way of fending off Boyfriend Day and ceding his own high moral ground over her own pretty unforgivable fiction of a dead hero father.

And from the steadfast, noncommittal look he was giving her, he knew it.

"Deal?" he asked, extending a hand.

She met his gesture halfway. "Deal."

It never made it to a shake. They shared a mutual understanding for the first time in many years. Molina felt a burden liberate her chronically clenched shoulders, not ready to explore yet what had changed, and why they were holding hands.

"Guys!" a voice chided.

Hands dropped; heads turned.

"Hey, it's awfully quiet in here." Mariah stood in the hall archway, looking perfect 'tween queen with her new bobbed haircut and the leggings and short skirt, cell phone in her hand, frowning as she looked from one to the other. "Am I going to have to insist on a feet-on-the-floor-at-all-times policy around here?"

Rafi laughed his head off, recognizing that she quoted a parental edict for entertaining boyfriends, which Mariah didn't have quite yet. She was too busy trying to be a media star.

Mariah eyed them suspiciously.

"What are you doing out here?" Molina asked, more flustered than she ever wanted to be.

"I thought," Mariah said, tossing her Katie Holmes hair, "it's what you wanted. I'm supposed to quit 'hiding in my room.'"

"It's okay when there are people in the front room trying to hold an adult conversation without having it drowned out by Justin Bieber."

"Yeah. You're just sitting here. Don't think I don't know that something is going on. Embarrassing, dudes."

Mariah made a face and vanished back down the hall, her bedroom door shutting with a clap a second later.

Molina blinked at their quick dismissal by the resident media princess. "Daughters and mothers," she told Rafi. "This is a rough stage. She seems to accept you," she admitted.

"I accept *her*." Rafi smiled. "I'm not under the daily pressure with her you are. Say, that's nice."

Molina was confused by his apparent change of subject. "What?"

His forefinger made a circling motion near the protective wing of her hair. "Those thin, big hoop earrings you're wearing nowadays."

"I did have pierced ears, if you remember. From babyhood. It was a cultural thing."

"I remember, and you used to wear tiny turquoise stud earrings, your sole concession to femininity off the job."

"I . . . they'd closed down, the piercings, so I thought I'd try again. Not for wearing at work nowadays either, of course. That's . . . silly."

"No, not for at work. But not silly." His eyes squinted at her for too long to be comfortable. She was seeing the hunky young cop again. "If you do any more Carmen gigs," he said, "throw out the retro silk flower over your ear and go with high-end shoulder-duster earrings."

She shot him a glance. *If?* Why . . . why?

"They'd uplight those electric eyes." Her manager speaking again, after all these years.

Carmen didn't know what to say. Any answer would tick off Molina.

Rafi's lips made a slight moue. "Mariah sure missed out there when she inherited your dark voice and my dark eyes. On the other hand, we get to see yours."

Chapter 57
Invitation to a Duel

From an early evening wedding to a worknight. Matt usually came in a half hour early for his *Midnight Hour* talk show, which ran two hours, thanks to popular demand.

Hosting a live radio talk show five nights a week was a responsibility. He'd been used to relentless timetables when he was a parish priest, so he always allowed for small, unexpected delays. *Oooph,* those 6 A.M. Masses. Now he was a night owl.

And he'd much rather be at the Circle Ritz having another honeymoon night with Temple. She'd made his mother shine and he wanted to return the favor.

He filled two tall cardboard glasses with chilled Dr Pepper and headed from the station kitchen to the control room, where he lifted them to greet his boss, Letitia.

She was nearing the end of her nightly gig as "Ambrosia," the black-velvet voice of consolation and Top Fifty songs from recent decades fit to soothe the savage soul.

Ambrosia cooed soft encouragement to her latest caller and started Jim Croce's "Time in a Bottle" to put that stressed caller to bed.

"Matt," she mouthed through glass, waving him closer with a flounce of one long, knuckle-brushing orange chiffon sleeve. She dressed like Joan Rivers for the red carpet, if Joan had been black, thirty years younger, and weighed two hundred pounds more.

But hyper and abrasive were the opposite of Ambrosia's style, on or off mic.

"Toodle your globe-trotting tuckus over here for a hug."

He set down the soft drinks before obeying. In a moment, he was encompassed by a warm, spice-scented cloud of affection the color of a desert sunset.

Ambrosia had taught him that if you didn't feel good about yourself, you couldn't make other people feel good about themselves. Her listeners pictured a seductively sympathetic siren reclining on a chaise longue while extending a languid hand to press a button and surround them with healing song and, well, schmaltz.

Darned if they weren't right.

"So how was that 'toddling town'?" she asked about his trip home and indirectly about the job opportunity.

"Interesting," was all Matt was going to say. Moving to the network and Chicago was history now.

"You're early." Ambrosia checked the glitzy Home Shopping Network watch on her wrist. A long lacquered false fingernail colored dead-on orange to match her caftan tapped him on the hand.

"I have a special request tonight," he said.

"Anything for you . . . insane, illegal, whatever. Unless it's fattening."

"Calorie-free," he promised. "The one thing you won't like is I don't want any questions or second guesses."

"That's tough. Second-guessing is my favorite hobby. Okay. You're the guy on the way up. What is it?"

Commercials were still blaring. He'd developed her instinct for knowing how much time off the air they still had.

"I brought a golden oldie you can slip in that I want you to play at the end of your set as a segue into mine." He handed her the DVD.

She glanced at the label. "John McCormack? Not on my playlist."

"Great but long-dead Irish tenor. Just say it's 'I'll Take You Home Again, Kathleen,' from Mr. Midnight for 'she knows who she

541

is.' Then you finish your show with a second song, requested by Anonymous. 'I Know You're Out There Somewhere.' "

"Matt, honey, what a great idea! Vintage schmaltz. I betcha this DVD is some ancient Irish crooner with crackle in the vinyl recording and all. Is this for your mama in Chicago, you favorite son, you? You do realize every Kathleen, Kathy, Katy, Kat in the world will think she's Mr. Midnight Hour's 'she'?"

"Just play it. I'll worry about the reaction."

"*Hmm.* That Moody Blues oldie is so fine, like a moose call on a hunting trip, only to an old flame. 'I Know You're Out There Somewhere.' Everybody has somebody they think of that way. You too, honey?"

"Oh, yeah."

An hour and forty minutes later, Matt was winding up a call from a grandmother worried that her granddaughter had taken Lady Gaga for a role model, at least in her wardrobe.

"Kids all go through trying to look different from the crowd," he consoled her. "I doubt meat dresses will catch on. They're too expensive, require a freezer for a closet, and attract flies as well as paparazzi."

Leticia had left, chortling over Matt the

mama's boy and his old-fashioned "tribute" to his visit home to Mom.

If only.

Why was he doing this, trying to draw Kathleen O'Connor out? Couple obvious reasons: He felt guilty — always a personal failing with him — that he hadn't told his cohorts in private detection that he suspected Kitty the Cutter was stalking him again.

And, in his judgment, better she should tangle with him than with her long-sought love–hate object, Max Kinsella. He'd lately been unable to dodge the feeling that Kinsella was his resented, older, sexier, savvier brother. With his memory in meltdown, all the fabled Kinsella advantages boiled down to making him a sitting duck. And Matt did not need a dead martyr for a romantic rival.

He eyed the LED clock that counted down seconds as well as hours and minutes. Luke in the control room was signaling "end" with the hand karate chop gesture Elvis had loved to use in his stage shows.

Matt removed his padded headset and pushed the big wheeled chair back from the now-dead mic. Luke was making his final bows to the equipment boards, setting up programmed music for the rest of the night.

WCOO-AM wasn't the biggest little radio

station in the West, but it had two syndicated shows between Ambrosia and him. She'd been so supportive when his initially local hour show had gone to two hours and national. Matt smiled as he exited into the night air, the usual Las Vegas warm soup.

His silver Jaguar sat alone in the parking lot. That gift from the Chicago producers was an albatross. Maybe expensive wheels were okay if you went from costly city apartment to major office building, both with locked and guarded garages, but Matt's pattern was from modest and quirky little apartment building to remote radio station to the grocery store and gas station.

Unless he and Temple moved to Chicago and a life of parking valets.

He approached the Jag, already beeping it open. Then he remembered to check for tire slashing. A tour around the gleaming streamline body revealed . . . no tampering.

Gosh, Matt thought as he allowed the front seat leather to wrap around him, and the engine to clear its expensive throat, he couldn't even match Max Kinsella at attracting psychos. He'd always been a substitute for the real object of Kathleen's warped affections and now he felt as impelled to protect the newly vulnerable Max from Kitty the Cutter as to save Temple. . . .

Still, he scanned his surroundings, checking the rearview and side mirrors until the red blinking light atop the WCOO tower was zooming away behind him like a suddenly shy retreating UFO.

Matt saw nothing in the rearview mirror. At 2 A.M. this was a deserted stretch. The person who'd followed him several times by motorcycle months ago along here knew that.

Out of nowhere, the rearview mirror showed what Matt hoped was a car with a burned-out headlight. Spotting those had been the object of a classic car-traveling game called padiddle.

"Padiddle," Matt said to the road-level Cyclops. Nobody else was riding along to give him points for spotting it, and, frankly, newer cars didn't seem to burn out their perpetually "on" running lights. Only the old junkers.

Wait. Some crook in a junker could be interested in carjacking the Jag.

Matt sped up, but the light behind matched him. The radio station was situated in a semi-industrial area pretty dead at night. He'd noticed that more when he rode the Vampire motorcycle for a time.

Back when the phantom motorcycle had shadowed him.

Had that rider been pursuer, or protector? Those episodes had ended. Matt had never known whether he was haunted by the ghost of Elvis, who'd been "calling" in to his show at the time, or whether he was escorted by Max Kinsella. And, if so, whether Kinsella had been guarding Matt's skin or the prized Hesketh Vampire motorcycle's sheen.

And, of course, it could always have been Kathleen O'Connor.

Or . . . considering how Max Kinsella swore she'd died, in a motorcycle pursuit of his car, Miss Kitty's ghost. Both Max and he later swore they'd seen her dead, but they both had been wrong.

Or . . . a cop. His reverie had upped his speed well beyond the limit — easy to do without noticing when driving a car designed to slip through wind resistance like an eel — and he could have run afoul of a speed trap.

Any possibility he considered was a trap of some kind he wouldn't like.

So he pulled over under the nearest streetlight to stop. And wait.

CHAPTER 58
DOMESTICATED SPECIES

Aaah.

I do love it when an act of derring-do has made me the solo King of the king-size bed once again. I omit the white-tie wedding nonsense and finally recall our shared adventure at the Oasis.

Here we recline in the very wee hours, my Miss Temple and me. She has showered off any remaining Essence du Elephant and I have given up my gilt-brocade throne for a simple zebra-pattern throw.

I have arrayed myself along her side, permitting her easy access to stroking my noble brow, my masculine shoulders, my svelte sides and back. I do enjoy a good massage, and contemplate rolling over for an undercarriage petting, except I am opting for the dignified, superior, and mysterious role at the moment.

Miss Temple sighs. "Here we are, Louie, alone together by the phone again. What a long, big day, from Marriage Bureau to wedding banquet. No wonder Matt was a little distracted at dinner and headed off to WCOO early, but he should be on the way and calling to let me know now. I am beginning to get why he wants a daytime talk show.

"Louie, would you ever want to return to Chicago after those nasty thugs kidnapped you?"

You bet! That was the most fun I'd had before climbing Mount Elephant and tangling up the ankles and black bedsheets of the Synth's heist team at the Oasis Friday night.

As often happens, Miss Temple picks up my thoughts.

"On the other hand, I shouldn't be so eager to see Matt. Just how much does he need to know about my part in that busted Oasis heist 'production' and wake for the Synth at Neon Nightmare afterward? Matt might frown on my consorting with Max."

She sighs again. "Being a fiancée is not always simple."

Being a fiancée apparently is being a worry wart.

Being King of the Cat Pack is much easier. All have scattered to their usual hangouts, but only mine is so soft and comfy and comes with a built-in massager.

This time I sigh and close my eyes. I personally am enjoying a little alone time with my roomie. Mr. Matt can take his own sweet time about getting home.

CHAPTER 59
MOTORCYCLE MELODRAMA

Matt's heart rate at the moment was nothing he'd want to parade on a visit to his primary care physician.

The single headlight had stopped behind him. In the red glare of his brake lights — he'd kept the car in Drive, brake on — he could see the massive bulk of a heavy-duty cycle tilted on its kickstand.

The ride was in his left rear blind spot, but he heard the creak of leather through his slightly lowered driver's-seat window.

A black helmet with a smoked plastic visor made the approaching rider into an alien in his side-view mirror.

Matt waited, ready to burn the Jaguar out of there at zero to sixty in 4.4 seconds, as advertised.

The rider passed the window and self-boosted up onto the car's sleek front fender.

The bare-knuckled black leather half

gloves came off one by one and hit the car's hood.

Matt winced internally.

The helmet came off to sit atop them.

Matt watched the rider shake out her long black hair. Motorpsycho Medusa.

The hip-length leather jacket was unzipped to reveal the feminine version of a wife-beater undershirt, not in Marlon Brando white, but femme fatale black.

She crossed leather-clad legs, the lower booted foot swinging against the Jag's front wheel well.

Matt breathed an invisible sigh of relief to see no weapons drawn . . . yet. He zoomed the window full down.

"So," she said, leaning out over the hood to address him. "The frequent Chicago trips weren't just to cozy up to the audience of *The Amanda Show.* You have family there, and here, be it ever so humble." "Most people have family," he said, "unless, like in a melodrama, they're separated at birth."

His remark had hit the target dead-on. She slid fast off the fender, her boots hitting asphalt hard together. "*You* were separated at birth, from your so-called father."

The last word curled off her lips with loathing.

He understood why Jesus had banished

551

demons. Some people lived with them for so long, they became them. How did she know his family drama? A job for Super-Max.

Matt got out of the car to face her. It was hard to read expressions in the dark.

"You were a pariah," she charged. "From birth, as I was."

He kept an unemotional tone. "True, on the surface of things. Your childhood was living hell. I just had purgatory."

"I know who told you about me."

"I know who you really want to harass. Why bother with me?"

"You're easier."

"Maybe not."

"Being Mr. Big-time Radio Headshrinker has gone to your own head. You think you can get into my mind? I can get into those crawly little places in your soul you don't want to admit exist."

"I guess I'm as entitled to 'crawlspace' as you are." Matt thought of the two casinos where the security "crawlspace" had been invaded by death in the past couple years. That was a great metaphor for what was happening here.

"You don't want to kill anyone . . . at least not right away," he told her. "You like to play with your prey. This is Las Vegas. Let's make a bet."

"You, Mr. Careful, gamble?"

"Stay away from your other favorite targets and sign up for some personal counseling with me. I bet I can 'reach' your inner angel."

She laughed delightedly. "You're actually being sardonic, Mr. Ex-Priest. 'Inner angel.' Even you don't believe that."

He could sense her eyes searching his expression for underlying motives. He kept it noncommittal. She fed on extreme emotion.

"You'd see me secretly?" she asked. "Leave your precious fiancée in the dark?"

"You can certainly see me secretly any time you like," he pointed out.

She edged closer. "You think you can save my soul."

"I'd have to find it first."

"What arrogance! Souls don't exist, but guilt does. Do you want to know my bet?"

"Breathless about it." He was already seeing his refusal to overreact had drawn her into his bargain. He would have felt a little like Satan if she hadn't been playing the same role.

She pressed herself close, full frontal, her upraised hands at his sides. He controlled the urge to draw back or push away, but his fingers made claws, ready to repulse another razor-knife attack.

She whispered, "I'm betting I can unchain your inner devil. Your body will betray you before my lost soul will fail me."

Her hands clapped to his sides. He resisted the instinct to grab her wrists to hold off any unseen weapon. Her raised knee slid up the inside of his thigh. She habitually won by making love–hate, not war.

Matt was betting Kathleen's obsession to seduce would keep her from killing him . . . too soon anyway. This unholy bargain with a sociopath would test just how good he was, as a psychologist and a man.

TAILPIECE:
MIDNIGHT LOUIE
HAS MIXED FEELINGS

I cannot believe it. After my expedition to the Oasis Hotel and reunion with the winsome Topaz, it looks as if little me is finally going to get the girl! This is unprecedented for the usual hard-luck noir hero. Usually the girl gets him.

I am an unusual dude for one of my breed, although I will admit, when pressed . . . or petted . . . that I am an exceptional example of it.

Yet both of my poor Miss Temple's beaux are dallying with wicked women. What a rude turn of events. I must have words with my collaborator. She had not mentioned my promotion to Number One Male in this book.

I would have taken a thorough bath while Miss Temple was showering so I could appear in peak, glossy glory in the key bedroom scene of the Entire Book. At last my potential as an all-species sex symbol has been realized and allowed to shine forth.

I must admit I am . . . speechless.
Please do not mistake that for modesty.
I do not.

Very Best Fishes,

Midnight Louie, Esq.

If you'd like information about getting Midnight Louie's free *Scratching Post-Intelligencer* newsletter and/or buying his custom T-shirt and other cool things, contact Carole Nelson Douglas at P.O. Box 331555, Fort Worth, Texas 76163-1555 or the Web site at www.carolenelsondouglas .com. E-mail: cdouglas@catwriter.com.

TAILPIECE:
CAROLE NELSON DOUGLAS
ON OTHER MATTERS

Because some of the earlier Midnight Louie mysteries are dedicated to "the real and original Midnight Louie, nine lives are not enough," some readers have thought the inspiring stray cat was part of my personal family.

Not so. His rescue was detailed in the Tailpiece to the first Midnight Louie book, *Catnap.* The woman who rescued the koi-loving homeless black cat from a Palo Alto motel and shipped him to her Minnesota apartment found him friendly but unable to adapt to confined living arrangements.

She put a long and intriguingly expensive ad in the classifieds section (remember those?) of the newspaper I worked for as a reporter and feature writer, offering him to a good home for one dollar. (She'd spent a lot more than that on his airfare back.)

I'd always liked to follow offbeat "leads" and wrote an article on Louie's journey and the new home he found on a farm. After writing the first who/what/when/where sentence, I paused. Maybe I should let the cat tell his tale in his own words. Maybe the real and original Midnight Louie inspired me to do just that. Black cats do have that "mystical" aura.

Eleven years later, when I left my union-guaranteed-for-life newspaper job (remember those?) to write fiction freelance, that feline "voice" revisited me and demanded a cameo role in four Las Vegas–set short romances (with mystery). The editor happily bought the quartet, then cut much of the mystery and Louie out, without telling me.

I told you nine lives were not enough for this canny feline survivor. Midnight Louie did an athletic flip-flop, landing on his feet in a mystery series bearing his name that featured any ongoing human romance elements in their proper place, as subplot.

In 1996, the series publisher, Tor Books, sponsored a wonderful Midnight Louie Adopt-a-Cat tour that brought me and homeless cats to adoption/book-signing events in every region of the country. They started in my new home state, Texas, with multi-city events. And, new to the animal rescue scene, the publicists didn't know about no-kill shelters and "booked" me into the main city shelters.

I had six rescue cats and a rescue dog at home, but I saw so many, many beautiful kittens and cats, so many cats only a year old and kicked out, at stop after stop, it was heartbreaking.

When a small black cat in the open colony at Lubbock Animal Services looked up at me and "skritched," I bent to pick it up. Midnight Louie Jr. had me on hello. There's more to the story, but it wasn't until three weeks later my husband and I drove almost seven hundred miles round trip to fetch our seventh cat.

We stayed overnight at a nice motel and came back to the room after dinner. I have never seen a cat so aware that he'd found a home, and so happy, not anxious at all. He jumped on the bed when we retired and moved back and forth on our chests all night, purring and meowing until he was hoarse by morning and we were sleepless in Lubbock.

He wasn't very big, his coat was dull, and his tail had been broken in two places so he couldn't lift it higher than a croquet-hoop position.

Long black hair turned glossy, and his tail did lift again, the mysterious break hidden. A short mystery story, "Junior Partner in Crime," is my imagination of how he might have got in that condition following in Senior's fictional crime-fighting footsteps.

Since there is only one "real and original" and eternal Midnight Louie, he became, after a brief detour as "Midnight Louise" (sometimes it's hard to tell in busy shelters), the Midnight Louie Jr. seen with me in the dust jacket photograph.

After fifteen years, he was called to the Rainbow Bridge as I was finishing this book. He fought hard not to leave, and he did not go alone.

Xanadu, his longtime pal and the chow-husky cross pup I'd found on the street four months before meeting Louie Jr., had a massive seizure the very morning we were about to call the vet for Midnight Louie Jr.'s last appointment.

He may not have been "the real and original," but he was the best and the brightest in our lives for a long time and will never leave, not really.